THE PREQUEL:

IT HAPPENED HERE

A Novel By John Kingston

THE PREQUEL:

IT HAPPENED HERE

A Novel By John Kingston

AN ALTERNATIVE TRUE HISTORY

Copyright © John Kingston 2017

The author was responsible for the design of the three covers and SpiffingCovers.com produced the artwork.

The work has been printed in Arial fount script size 10.

First published in England by John Kingston Publishing Ltd.2017

VOLUME THREE OF THREE

ISBN: 978-0-9955703-2-0

9 780995 570320

STATEMENT

With the exception of Mr. Michael Randle, Mr. John Wrighton and Mr. Lawrence "Larry" Questad all characters appearing in this work are fictitious. Any resemblance fictitious characters bear to real persons, living or dead, is purely coincidental.

DEDICATIONS

I WISH TO THANK DOCTORS PHILIPPE RIBET , ROBERT GREENBAUM AND ESPECIALLY MR.STEPHEN EDMONDSON FOR GIVING ME A 'SECOND CHANCE' IN MAY 2007 AND THE OPPORTUNITY TO FINISH THIS WORK.

MY PERSONAL GRATITUDE TO MR. SHERIF HABASHI, DR. NEIL KITCHEN AND PROF. MICHAEL GLEESON FOR SAVING THE LIFE OF MY YOUNGER DAUGHTER, LAURA.

TO EVERYONE, AND ESPECIALLY MY DEAR FRIEND ROGER BALL, FOR THEIR HELP AND SUPPORT IN MY JOURNEY THROUGH LIFE.

INDEX

VOLUME THREE

THE PREQUEL: IT HAPPENED HERE

AN ALTERNATIVE TRUE HISTORY

VICTORY OF FAITH

ONE

FROM THE TRIAL OF RUDOLF SLANSKY (NOVEMBER 1952)

EXTRACT OF A STATEMENT MADE BY THE PUBLIC PROSECUTOR JOSEF URVALEK...

"In the end every gangster will get his just deserts, everyone will get his well-deserved punishment. The conspiring gang standing in the dock today is a nest of rats who were caught. They are hated and despised by all honest people of our country. Citizens, you who are in the position of people's judges, in the name of our nation, against whose freedom and happiness these conspirators were subverting, in the name of peace and against the dastardly conspiracy, I demand for all accused the death sentence.

THE AUTHORITARAN STATE

ITS MEANING AND FUNCTION:

CHAPTER-DEMOCRACY HAS FAILED:

"The empire has gone in all but name...

Our armed forces, now incapable of defending what world interests we still possess, are compelled to lean on the dominating arm of America, who now maintain an army of occupation in every British country, and without whose permission scarcely one British gun is allowed to fire...

To all these events not the flicker of an eyelid has been turned by those little men engaged in the pantomime of party politics. Engrossed in the rat- race for votes and seats in Parliament, mostly won by fraudulent promises, our "(D ? d –author's specific query) emocratic" leaders have shown themselves and their system no more capable in this age of governing a mad-house than a highly-developed modern state such as our own.

The system today is failing."

Albert Camus:

None of the evils which totalitarianism... claims to remedy is worse than totalitarianism itself.

Joel Ben Yitzhak:

Truth is comparable to Albert Einstein`s concept of space and time. It is flexible and depends on the observer.

There was a more simple and dramatic reason why the American ambassador was both unwilling and unable to immediately receive Manny Gold and why Gold had been tasked to prepare a lengthy and time consuming report, for the ambassador was both coordinating and supervising the flight of the British Royal family in American military aircraft from a number of U.S. air force bases and a submarine to the safety of Canada.

We can only conjecture and surmise if, how and when the Queen received news of Wilson's arrest and possibly, but unlikely, 'got wind' of the further arrests and executions ,however she, and most likely, her trusted advisors realised that her worst expectations had been proved correct and that there was no alternative but to flee the country before she and her family, including the Heir Apparent, were incarcerated.

We can only also assume that she, or her representatives, appealed directly to the leaders of the United States and Canada for help, for ultimately the arrival of the Royal family in Ottawa and Canadian territory was jointly and simultaneously announced in the two capital cities late on the Friday, once and significantly, when the last of the party, Prince Charles, had safely arrived in Newfoundland.

The announcement, made by the Canadian Prime Minister, Mr. Lester Pearson, confirmed in vague terms that the Royal party had made the journey to show their support and as representatives of the British people (observers who were aware, in broad terms, of events in Great Britain noted that the British government was *NOT* mentioned) following the recent national mining disaster that had claimed over two hundred lives.

The National Council later learned that the whole party, including a retinue of trusted staff, numbering fifty three people, all of whom, except Prince Charles, had been flown by, and from, sovereign American military airbases and that the Prince had escaped by submarine having, if reports can be believed (carried exclusively in a Swedish newspaper), argued with his saviours that he required his whole entourage to accompany him together with unspecified documents and artefacts. Perhaps, if anecdotal and third hand gossip is to be further believed, he was forcibly pushed inside the American submarine to secure his safety.

No doubt there were internal stresses and recriminations within the National Council once they discovered that the Queen and her family had fled the country, even though no plans had even been considered or laid for their participation in the New Order, however the most immediate consequence was a draconian and ruthless clamp down on travel outside of the United Kingdom.

The purpose of Wilson`s arrest was not primarily the consolidation of power but in order to finally and totally crush and discredit trust in the nation`s political and social systems and to expose its failure to protect the nation`s best interests.

Unlike the 'show' trials in pre war Stalinist Russia which were imitated in Eastern Europe after the Second World War, the treason trial of Harold Wilson was *ORIGINALLY* [author`s *SPECIFIC* emphasis] intended to be conducted to the highest professional standards and ethical behaviour however it was recognised that the exact nature of his treason could not be publically announced and that he had to be charged with at least a second, additional crime.

The trial, which would be held *in camera,* but recorded for posterity by camera, was scheduled to commence within days of his arrest but was delayed when a cornucopia of unexpected evidence was discovered in the empty Royal apartments in Buckingham Palace. Such was the Queen`s haste that a wealth of documentation had been abandoned without thought of its consequences.

The treasure trove was a library of personal diaries hand written by, and accumulated by the Queen, expressing her most private thoughts and more importantly her personal and very occasionally her intimate thoughts concerning her private meetings or audiences with her Prime Ministers beginning with Winston Churchill in nineteen fifty-two and ending with Harold Wilson in April nineteen sixty-five.

He would be confronted with Her Majesty`s statements, in her own handwriting, where incontrovertibly she wrote that (verbatim:

"I warned and counselled him not to acquiesce to Soviet pressure or promises and never to leave our nation naked and defenceless."

Prosecution of the charges would not need the brutality of the 'Conveyor Belt' or the cruel almost medieval methods of Nikolai Yezhov or Lavrenti Beria to secure an admission of guilt and consequent conviction, however subtle pressure would have to be applied to guarantee a confession, though in the future, because the laws and rights protecting the individual had been swept away, terror would permeate throughout the nation as fear of the midnight arrest and disappearances gripped every strata of society.

First came the purges and then the terror.

THE PROTOCOLS OF THE MEETINGS OF THE LEARNED ELDERS OF ZION

(EXTRACT FROM) PROTOCOL NUMBER FIVE:

"We shall create an intensified centralization of government in order to grip in or[sic]hands all the forces of the community. We shall regulate mechanically all the actions of the political life of our subjects by new laws."

(EXTRACT FROM) PROTOCOL NUMBER SIX:

"In every possible way we must develop the significance of our Super-Government by representing it as the Protector and Benefactor of all those who voluntarily submit to us."

The National Council, now the *de facto* sole body of power, was confronted with three urgent problems; the imminent shortage of essential foodstuffs (and the means to pay for what was being imported, to cover inadequate home production) and the overwhelming necessity to impose rationing, the trial and 'disposal' of Harold Wilson and subjugation of the nation. The three problems were inter-related.

It was unanimously agreed by the eleven remaining members of the National Council that replacement of the twenty-four Regional and deputy Regional Commissioners could be delayed in order that the most suitable candidates be chosen, but more importantly and with urgent necessity, all the political parties, other than the New Order, which would become the official party of the State, be proscribed and that the official statement, by the issue of a State of Emergency - Martial Law. Third Edition, be drafted and made public on July the fourteenth, which they later discovered, with wry irony, was the thirty second anniversary of the Nazi party being declared the only legal party in Germany.

John Tyndall was delegated to rekindle and literally, inflame and ferment a new spirit of national patriotism with a series of rallies and meetings at which he was also to appoint local leaders primarily for their blind obedient loyalty but also for their administrative abilities since the party was to be temporarily organised as a new *quasi* civil service and would oversee the inauguration of Gold's plans introducing nationwide the new identity card document.

News of Wilson's arrest, impeachment, trial, conviction and finally execution could be announced shortly before Tyndall's rallies began or when it was believed notice would have the maximum impact and whilst no specific details would be disclosed concerning the nation's military impotence it would be stated that his convictions for High Treason included an offence and a crime that for national security could not be disclosed but was a most heinous betrayal of the nation's security. He would also be convicted of two other offences, both punishable by death, details of which would be made public.

With the approval and authority of the National Council, Tyndall, with almost demonic fervour and the nature of a demagogue would incite and fan public anger bordering on hysteria against the now totally discredited political and social systems which the National Council would proscribe and simultaneously, cunningly the people were to be persuaded to blame the old order for the sacrifices that the country was to bear. One slogan that initially caught the public's imagination and succinctly caught the mood of the day was...

"We are all in it together."

Wilson had cowered in a secret military base whilst the nation's cities had been subjected to nuclear destruction wrought by Soviet bombers and had cowardly refused to go to Stockholm where it was left to the nation's American ally and friend to force the Soviet Union to halt its attacks, but the consequences of events since November nineteen sixty-three meant that the country's production of food, including especially wheat, had been dramatically reduced, and that despite supplies from Canada and the United States there would be a significant shortfall and that rationing was absolutely inevitable.

One of Wilson's crimes was that, and 'documentary evidence' and witnesses could be produced at his trial, throughout his Prime Ministerial period he had not, despite many requests from fellow ministers or civil servants, even attempted to address the problem (which, in fact, was true).

Tyndall would announce at his rallies that rationing would be fair, for the New Order represented an equitable society and that the weak would be protected ahead of the strong.

The repatriation of British prisoners of war virtually 'dried up' and ceased soon after the initial flow of those who had suffered the worst consequences of the chemical warfare attacks on the European mainland had returned. The prosecution case against Wilson supported again by 'documentary evidence' and witnesses clearly exposed both his negligence and total disregard for the fate of those that had fought to protect the security of their homeland and the unsuccessful defence of Britain's allies.

It was essential that whilst the prosecution case should succeed (and the nature of the circumstances guaranteed the outcome), Wilson should be clearly seen either to admit his guilt or that the weight of the evidence proved his crimes beyond doubt for the trial was to be recorded and Tyndall and Duggan cynically and corruptly agreed that the recording, and excerpts, could be edited and that even additional scenes be created, by the use of a 'double' and the technique of using dubbing was to be utilised to create additional confessions or statements.

The Stalinist method of using subtle pressure would also be used to ensure, if not Wilson's complete cooperation, his acquiescence to the desired outcome of the proceedings.

Preparation of the prosecution case was completed on Thursday June third and a suitable site, almost under the 'noses' of the National Council had been accidentally located in the nearby town of Barnet, specifically a Territorial Army building just off of the High Street and suitable film cameras, film, lighting equipment and above all trusted, non union technicians to operate the equipment had been secured from one of the film studios that was close to the Thatched Barn hotel in Borehamwood .

On the same day his defence counsel, a serving army officer in the former legal department, introduced himself and informed Wilson that he was to be taken to a local hospital for a complete medical check up and that ,as his legal representative, he was willing to accompany him. That evening, at about ten-fifteen, they were collected by an unmarked inconspicuous car driven by an anonymous civilian driver, and taken to a hospital also in Barnet which now is a new modern complex, offering (it is said) excellent facilities for wounded and recovering injured senior officers but the hospital and its facilities are now no longer open to the general public, having been taken over by the military.

They began working on him after he had slept, washed and eaten either a very late breakfast or early lunch, beginning a process that would enfeeble and beleaguer him.

It was purely an intellectual confrontation without even a hint of physical pressure. He would never see his family again and their future, even their very survival, would depend on his cooperation. Even his location and condition were now a state secret and any news would depend on him working with the prosecution to deliver a guilty verdict but more importantly any argument that he might construct or instruct his defence to submit had to justify, explain and admit his guilt.

The end justifies the means and as the boundaries of decency and humanity crumbled, so the methods to obtain confessions or cooperation to subsequent and later enemies and traitors not only became more brutal but also more perverted as the terror magnified and its all encompassing and virulent actions consumed every part of society.

Within twelve months one method was developed with great success and guaranteed both the total degradation of the accused individual and their boundless, nearly uncontrollable enthusiastic cooperation. There are a number of pig farms in the surrounding area and family members of an accused, even including children and babes in arms would be, without conscience, placed in a pig sty where they were forced to live alongside the animals who not knowing any better would defecate over their human co–inhabitants. It was a physical and mental torture and in degree beyond vile and repugnant that would destroy their health and resolve and would put such pressure on their accused family member who would normally acquiesce to any confession and cooperation to secure the freedom of their family.

Gold, assisted by a small group comprised of senior civil servants and businessmen, completed his plans by early June which were unanimously approved by the other ten members (other than one major procedure) who also, by mid June, had agreed upon the one new member to join the National Council. He was the new Commissioner of the Metropolitan Police, representing police forces nationwide. New, because the previous incumbent had been found to be in disagreement with the objectives of the New Order.

Additionally two representatives became 'non voting associate members' who were co-opted and entitled to be involved in the affairs of the National Council and in the event of a member being replaced, for any reason, then they *MIGHT* [Author's emphasis] be given priority.

One was the leader of the moderate mining union that had stood firm against Bill Martin and his bullying rapscallions and finally, representing the media and their choice and recommendation, the proprietor of the 'left of centre' mass circulation, *Sun* daily newspaper.

Slowly, but inexorably, the leadership would change by internal purges and shifting alliances and allegiances to represent a system intent primarily on the retention of power for its own sake, and the subjugation of the nation in pursuit of its primary objective.

Gold's task proved to be an exercise not exclusively restricted to the creation of a multi purpose combined identity card, internal passport and ration card together with an identical 'mirror' copy including a duplicate photograph for record purposes, but a system that would administer the applications, issue of documentation and record creation of some forty five million men, women and children. It was recognised, from the outset, that however meticulous the planning, that problems would inevitably occur but the titanic operation was to take place in a relatively short period (originally estimated to be twenty-one continuous uninterrupted days, working *SIXTEEN* hours a day, backed by the total resources of the state).

M.I.5, who were responsible for the nation's internal security, observed that once the system was in operation it would be far easier to trace people and even possibly their movements, for individuals, without reason, could be stopped for identification purposes, or to ascertain the purpose of their journey and destination, justified by the spurious reason that the authorities were in pursuit and hunting down terrorists or potential Fifth Columnists.

However there was one underlying problem that concerned Gold and was not solely the tidal wave of applications when it became public knowledge that rationing was to be introduced but, understanding human nature, the inevitable rush to obtain food and goods before rationing came into force.

The army would have to be brought in to control the tidal surge of applications and to guard the shops. Arrests could and would be made and intentionally made very public. The STATE OF EMERGENCY-MARTIAL LAW. SECOND EDITION, (Part One, item Sixteen would apply, though a Military Tribunal would undoubtedly convict to set an example because overwhelmingly they were concerned not with the law, guilt or the individual's rights, but maintenance of power and control).

Increasingly, over the next twelve months or so, as the New Order strengthened its grip, the Military Tribunals became feared, for their actions were correctly perceived and viewed as a body , not of justice, but of draconian control over the lives of the individual.

It was decided that during the interim period, the 'changeover', when people would exchange their existing identity cards for the new multi purpose document, that the old style card could be endorsed and serve as evidence to obtain food before it became rationed.

Rationing and the weekly calorific allowance would only be a temporary measure for the nation 'was in it together' and once national food production was sufficient then rationing would slowly be phased out.

The nation's life, more so in the cities and larger conurbations, effectively halted when the registration procedure began.

It was to be preceded by an earlier three week period to allow as many people as possible to have their photographs taken and therefore to spread the surge to obtain new identity cards.

Each registration area was to be controlled by a recently appointed (Area) Controller, a new creation and status within the New Order who, along with their fellow controllers had been through a relatively comprehensive secret training programme that had taken place in one of five regional centres and to remind the reader, they had primarily each been chosen for their loyalty to the party and secondly for their administrative abilities and where they were deficient they were permitted to nominate and utilise a local solicitor to assist in the management of the actual operation.

Central to the operation was the use of existing public records including the Electoral Registers and to a lesser extent local telephone directories and school registers, combined with the presence of local professionals, specifically priests, solicitors, doctors and dentists to identify the applicants who could only attend in person provided that they had completed the simple application form, had available their current identity card(s) and finally two identical passport style photographs.

It was to be an immense operation comparable in concept and depth to the Domesday Book which was produced to give an inventory of the nation's material wealth and assets whilst this operation was to count and record every person in the land.

Finally, to stop profiteering, the brief...

STATE OF EMERGENCY- MARTIAL LAW. THIRD EDITION

incorporated a special section applicable to photographic firms which included details of how they were to operate and what prices they were permitted to charge together with a further, innocuous section which was deviously inserted and could, and would, presage price and wages control .

Deliveries from the Kodak Company began arriving around the fifteenth of June.

Gold was charged with drafting the proclamation which would be published on Friday, July ninth, but the complexity of the operation meant that the announcement only specified the timetable together with a brief schedule of the procedure (always subject to a supplementary appendix) though specifically emphasising the authority of the Regional Commissioners, their deputies (even though there was currently a void which had to be filled) and the special application of the Second Edition of the State Of Emergency - Martial Law and, in what was later to be spoken of in frightened tones, The Courts of Protection which were effectively military tribunals.

The National Council had wisely rejected one procedure of the operation only:the massive deployment of troops whose very presence could cause fear and resentment. The nation's police forces, who had been promised and received, in Wilson's premiership, an unreasonable increase in their salaries would have to bear the brunt of crowd control and could, if necessary, be supplemented by members of the armed forces who could be suitably dressed (in police outfits). Finally, in a cynical and callous move, that was suggested by one of the two industrialists, it was overwhelmingly agreed, without objection, that with immediate effect, supplies of food and other goods to retail outlets be reduced, creating, *de facto*, artificial rationing and allowing the stocks of food and essentials, at the warehouses, to be built up.

Tyndall, in his speeches, could and would blame Wilson, for by July ninth Wilson had been executed and his ashes unceremoniously scattered, the records showing that they were the remains of an anonymous foreigner suffering from a rare case of leprosy and his body had to be incinerated for obvious hygiene reasons.

THREE

THE GREAT TERROR
STALIN`S PURGE OF THE THIRTIES:
BOOK TWO: THE YEZHOV YEARS:
THE PARTY CRUSHED:

Of Rosengolts ...

"When her husband was finally arrested, the routine N K V D search revealed, sewn into his hip pocket, a small piece of dried bread wrapped in a strip of cloth. Inside the bread was a piece of paper on which she had written out, as a charm against evil fortune, eight verses from the 68th and 91st Psalms, ancient cries of the helpless against their oppressors.

PSALM 68

א-ב לַמְנַצֵּחַ לְדָוִד מִזְמוֹר שִׁיר: יָקוּם אֱלֹהִים יָפוּצוּ אוֹיְבָיו וְיָנוּסוּ מְשַׂנְאָיו
ג מִפָּנָיו: כְּהִנְדֹּף עָשָׁן תִּנְדֹּף כְּהִמֵּס דּוֹנַג מִפְּנֵי־אֵשׁ יֹאבְדוּ רְשָׁעִים מִפְּנֵי
אֱלֹהִים:

[1] For the conductor, by David, a psalm, a song. [2] May God arise, let His enemies be scattered, and His foes will flee from before Him.

א־ב יֹשֵׁב בְּסֵתֶר עֶלְיוֹן בְּצֵל שַׁדַּי יִתְלוֹנָן: אֹמַר ַלַיהוה מַחְסִי וּמְצוּדָתִי אֱלֹהַי
ג־ד אֶבְטַח־בּוֹ: כִּי הוּא ַיַצִּילְךָ מִפַּח יָקוּשׁ מִדֶּבֶר הַוּוֹת: בְּאֶבְרָתוֹ ׀ יָסֶךְ לָךְ
ה וְתַחַת־כְּנָפָיו תֶּחְסֶה צִנָּה וְסֹחֵרָה אֲמִתּוֹ: לֹא־תִירָא מִפַּחַד לָיְלָה מֵחֵץ
ו־ז יָעוּף יוֹמָם: ַמִדֶּבֶר בָּאֹפֶל יַהֲלֹךְ מִקֶּטֶב יָשׁוּד צָהֳרָיִם: יִפֹּל מִצִּדְּךָ ׀ אֶלֶף
ח וּרְבָבָה מִימִינֶךָ אֵלֶיךָ לֹא יִגָּשׁ: ַרַק בְּעֵינֶיךָ תַבִּיט וְשִׁלֻּמַת רְשָׁעִים
ט־י תִרְאֶה: כִּי־אַתָּה יהוה מַחְסִי עֶלְיוֹן שַׂמְתָּ מְעוֹנֶךָ: לֹא־תְאֻנֶּה אֵלֶיךָ רָעָה
יא וְנֶגַע לֹא־יִקְרַב בְּאָהֳלֶךָ: כִּי מַלְאָכָיו יְצַוֶּה־לָּךְ לִשְׁמָרְךָ בְּכָל־דְּרָכֶיךָ:
יב־יג עַל־כַּפַּיִם יִשָּׂאוּנְךָ פֶּן־תִּגֹּף בָּאֶבֶן רַגְלֶךָ: עַל־שַׁחַל וָפֶתֶן תִּדְרֹךְ תִּרְמֹס
יד כְּפִיר וְתַנִּין: כִּי בִי ָחָשַׁק וַאֲפַלְּטֵהוּ אֲשַׂגְּבֵהוּ כִּי־יָדַע שְׁמִי ׀
טו ַיִקְרָאֵנִי ׀ וְאֶעֱנֵהוּ עִמּוֹ־אָנֹכִי בְצָרָה ֹאֲחַלְּצֵהוּ וַאֲכַבְּדֵהוּ: אֹרֶךְ ָיָמִים אַשְׂבִּיעֵהוּ
וְאַרְאֵהוּ בִּישׁוּעָתִי:

¹ **W**hoever sits in the refuge of the Most High, he shall dwell in the [protective] shade of the Almighty. ² I will say of HASHEM, "[He is] my refuge and my fortress, my God, I will trust in Him." ³ For He will deliver you from the ensnaring trap, from devastating pestilence. ⁴ With His pinion He will cover you, and beneath His wings you will be protected; His truth is shield and armor. ⁵ You shall not fear the terror of night; nor of the arrow that flies by day; ⁶ nor the pestilence that walks in gloom; nor the destroyer who lays waste at noon. ⁷ A thousand may fall victim at your side and a myriad at your right hand, but to you it shall not approach. ⁸ You will merely peer with your eyes and you will see the retribution of the wicked. ⁹ Because [you said], "You, HASHEM, are my refuge," you have made the Most High your abode. ¹⁰ No evil will befall you, nor will any plague come near your tent. ¹¹ He will charge His angels for you, to protect you in all your ways. ¹² On [their] palms they will carry you, lest you strike your foot against a stone. ¹³ Upon the lion and the viper you will tread; you will trample the young lion and the serpent. ¹⁴ For he has yearned for Me* and I will deliver him; I will elevate him because he knows My Name. ¹⁵ He will call upon Me and I will answer him, I am with him in distress; I will release him and I will bring him honor. ¹⁶ With long life will I satisfy him, and I will show him My salvation.

BOOK TWO: THE YEZHOV YEARS:

THE GREAT TRIAL:

"For all the threads were now pulled together...

In the dingy winter daylight and under the stale glare of the electric lamps, a wide variety of prisoners sat in the dock...

This time three members of Lenin's Politburo stood in (the) dock- Bukharin, Rykov and Krestinsky. With them were the legendary Rakovsky, leader of the Balkan and Ukrainian revolutionary movements, and the sinister figure of Yagoda, the Secret Police personified, looking right and left with a certain rat-like vitality. A group of the most senior officials of the Stalinist state who had for many years served it uncritically formed the bulk of the accused: Rosengolts, Ivanov, Chernov and Glinko - all People's Commissars until the previous year; Zelensky, Head of the Cooperatives; Sharangovich, First Secretary in Byelorussia...

Lastly, by a fearful innovation, there were three men far from public life, the Doctors Pletnev, Levin and Kazakov - the first two highly distinguished in their field and the oldest men in the dock (sixty-six and sixty-eight respectively).

The indictment was a comprehensive one-of espionage, wrecking, undermining Soviet military power, provoking a military attack on the USSR, plotting the dismemberment of the USSR and the overthrowing of the social system in favour of a return to capitalism...

A number of them had been spies of Germany, Britain, Japan and Poland since the early twenties...

A brand-new charge, against Bukharin alone of those in (the) dock, was of having plotted to seize power in 1918 and to murder Lenin and Stalin at the same time."

A persistent rumour, which continues to this day, is that the defendants were watched, unobserved, from an upper floor balcony by the Jew, Joel Ben Yitzhak.

It is now clear that the trial of Harold Wilson marks a watershed in the actions of the New Order for whilst the earlier mass executions had been accomplished without the murdered being granted the right of even a show trial , the trial of Harold Wilson had the superficial veneer and image that the procedures of due process were being rigorously followed so that when the trial, conviction and finally the execution were publically announced, it could be openly declared that the defendant had been tried under the rule of law which the general public believed would apply to every part of the community.

The greatest tragedy is that even now an actual faithful record of the trial is hidden in a mist of conjecture and the absence of an official court transcript, though whilst the trial was mostly held in camera, the final part relating to the defendant's alleged wilful and criminal neglect of the interests of British prisoners of war was witnessed by neutral journalists from both Switzerland and Sweden (and, most probably, diplomats from the United States, Canadian and Australian embassies) and extracts, suitably edited are incorporated in the following report. No primary statements of anyone who was present throughout the trial exists, other than a heavily redacted statement made by Gold to the American ambassador, and now only rumour, gossip and hearsay are the unsatisfactory bones upon which other writers base their reports.

As if one was in a hall of mirrors it is possible to obtain a partially distorted report of the events by the analysis of one source that had been specifically produced to inflame and mislead the nation.

It was necessary, as I have emphasised before, that not only was Wilson to be found guilty, but he would admit his guilt and therefore allow the new regime the grounds to bring in policies, beginning with rationing, to control the nation with its own tacit agreement.

It was not until some five years after the trial that a 'definitive' film of the complete trial was released by which time it was clearly totally corrupt and did not, in any way, truly report upon or represent any of the actual events. The first time that the nation had the opportunity to view an alleged recording was some six months after the trial when a very brief extract was shown on television almost as an advertising trailer for a slightly longer report which was also shown at every cinema as part of the news.

The cinema news report was preceded by a scrolled, printed statement, produced in the style of an introduction to a Hollywood epic, that James Harold Wilson had been convicted on three separate charges of high treason but the first charge (which, of course, related to the transfer of the 'V' bomber force to South Africa) was so grave and heinous and related to the very foundations of the nation's security that details could not, for national security, be disclosed. The brief film record, which for reasons to be shortly explained, then and still now, appears genuine for they are statements made by Wilson and his face and mouth, etched with frustration, desperation and resignation are clearly synchronised with his oral admissions.

"The political situation had become desperate. Whilst we still received support and encouragement from our old friends and allies in North America, the Soviet Union was becoming more and more aggressive and intransigent and we were unable to use thermonuclear weapons for their counter attack would have completely wiped the nation from off of the face of the earth. It was not possible to continue negotiations, through a third party, to secure the release of further contingents of British prisoners of war so *ON MY OWN INITIATIVE I HALTED ALL CONTACT* [sic-author`s specific emphasis]. The reduced production of basic essential foodstuffs, especially wheat, I blame on abnormal seasonal weather conditions and the consequences of radioactive fallout especially in East Anglia."

During the following five years, new versions of the trial appeared, each in increasing duration but every new version became more corrupt than the previous one and *IF* they could be compared, especially when the later productions blatantly used a 'double' (wearing Wilson`s original clothing) whose voice was clearly dubbed, his confessions became more and more incredible and clearly reflected the current political situation and like a barometer the rise and fall of members of the National Council.

On Sunday morning, June sixth, Wilson was interrupted during his regular morning stroll through the estate, by the unexpected arrival of his defence counsel, dressed in civilian clothing, who gave the impression of urgency for he was short of breath as if, and it was the case, that he had rushed to meet his client. His news was confirmation that the trial was imminent, indeed it was scheduled to begin within the next forty-eight hours, allowing the usurped former Prime Minister the opportunity to form the sensible assumption that the hearing would be heard the following morning or on the Tuesday.

Unofficially he had been informed that the trial was scheduled to be heard over two days and that the verdict would be given within a further seven days in order to give the three military officers, who would hear the case, an adequate opportunity to consider the evidence and reach a verdict.

It is not possible to look into a man`s mind or if it exists, a human being`s soul, however Wilson`s undoubted foreboding was unequivocally exposed early that afternoon when, unusually, with great courtesy, he was requested to visit the Commanding Officer`s office where he was asked to receive an important personal telephone call.

Perhaps it was to be the one that he desperately hoped to receive or the one that he was dreading receiving. He was alone, for the Commanding Officer had left the room together with Wilson's two guards.

It was to be both. He heard the unmistakable voice of a family member, but it was unnaturally subdued and he could also immediately sense that it was tinged with fear. They were well and adequately fed but they had not seen natural daylight since being placed in 'protective custody'. He felt powerless to protect his family. He reciprocated with vague details of his condition and despite the warning that he would never see them again, plaintively promised to...

"See them soon when they would be reunited and that he promised that they would never again be separated."

It was an irrational and emotional promise that was both impossible to fulfil and instantaneously broken when the real reason for the telephone call emerged.

"We will never see each other again and our only hope that we live is if you completely cooperate with your jailors. You must do as they say if you want us to live."

He knew then that all was lost but he hoped that they might keep their word and spare his family.

He went to bed normally just after ten p.m. expecting to be woken early the next morning but at one a.m. he was woken, brusquely told to shave and then dress, strangely also being told exactly which particular clothes to wear.

At about one forty that morning he was driven in the same Armstrong Siddeley Star Sapphire that had transported him from the aerodrome, sandwiched in a convoy of military vehicles, along an unlit rural road that meandered through the undulating countryside before shortly reaching the St. Albans Road which directly led them to the Territorial Army building and his predetermined destiny.

It is from this point onwards (till the end of the chapter and part of the next) that I have taken advantage of some literary licence, basing the following report on the first very brief public film of the trial, reports in neutral Swiss and Swedish newspapers and distilling the rumours, gossip and hearsay that were circulating in the weeks and months after the trial, crucially some of which were current even before an announcement of his conviction and execution was made.

The court had been built in a drill hall permitting the three military officers and a professional advisor to sit on a raised platform whilst the dock, which would house the defendant, was at a lower, ground level, psychologically placing Wilson on the defensive.

As he entered the room at precisely two-thirteen a.m. he was briefly blinded by the intensity and luminosity of a number of powerful arc lights that were strategically located throughout the hall permitting a number of film cameras to capture and take images of the main participants but especially of the defendant from various angles and proximities. For an instant he thought that he was the star of a surreal dream surrounded by costumed actors but then he recognised that this was no drama and he chillingly remembered his family's desperate plea.

He turned through three hundred and sixty degrees and noted seating for no more than about two dozen people and, though partially blinded by the lighting, unmistakably saw his dear friends and assistants Manny Gold and Gerald Kaufman who, no doubt, were there to support him.

His counsel, now dressed in military uniform, stood by his side, as the prosecuting counsel, also in military apparel announced, with cold, calculating callousness, that the defendant in the dock had been charged with three separate offences of High Treason and that the prosecution had irrefutable documentary evidence and witnesses to substantiate, beyond reasonable doubt, the culpability of the defendant (who realised that the charges had not been read out in court and that he had not had the opportunity to plead his innocence or guilt). He hurriedly scrawled a note which he passed to his counsel who turned and whispered to him that...

"The procedures of a Court of Protection were determined by the tribunal's three members in conjunction with the professional advisor who was sitting with them."

Manny Gold and Gerald Kaufman were the first witnesses to be called and their testimonies were both damning and independently delivered in such a manner that it was clear that both had deserted him and that their individual observations were jaundiced and biased. Each statement confirmed that unilaterally, without consulting his fellow Cabinet members, Wilson (for reasons that only he could explain) had ordered the nation's 'V' bomber force to be flown, with their weapons , on an epic journey to South Africa, therefore nullifying the nation's ability to defend itself and against the shocked disbelief and protestations of the heads of the armed services, a statement of fact that was hearsay and when his defence counsel challenged the remark he was informed that the tribunal members would take into account any information that they thought pertinent.

Shortly afterwards, in an expression of his frustration (and perhaps desperation),despite the presence of his increasingly supine and ineffective counsel, during a statement that was being made by a Buckingham Palace servant, Wilson called out to the three members of the tribunal (incidentally one each from the three armed services) and according to a rumour that surfaced perhaps only days after the trial must have ended and the verdict delivered, pugnaciously asked why the three witnesses had not been sworn in; the response from the Royal (sic) Air Force officer delivered with unusual speed was that the court and its officers had been legally convened and its terms of procedure were, and had been, correctly pursued and it was not for the defendant to not only question its competence but to harry and distress the witness.

"On that particular evening I do remember the defendant entering Her Majesty's ante room and it was my responsibility to refuse entry to anyone whilst the Queen held an audience, especially if it was with her Prime Minister. I can honestly say, having been responsible for this duty for some four or five years that I have never, before this time, ever heard either party's voice or a raised voice. But this time, this one time only, Her Majesty actually all but shouted at Mr Wilson. That 's the best way I can describe what I heard."

Then the prosecuting counsel, with feigned humility, approached the raised platform and requested that:

"I be permitted to produce the following document which I will momentarily identify but beforehand I would request that the defendant be instructed to read out to the court one particular section that I will point out to him."

Harold Wilson was handed a leather bound book of exquisite quality and superb condition and the prosecuting counsel was clearly seen to point to a particular part but his demand or request was inaudible to the court.

Harold Wilson delivered the short extract three times, each time directly to the bench, in a manner that was clear and audible though his voice trembled, however after the first two deliveries he was asked by the prosecuting counsel to repeat the extract ,no doubt because the contents were so damning...

"I warned and counselled him not to acquiesce to Soviet pressure or promises and never to leave our country naked and defenceless."

The prosecuting counsel, perhaps unsuccessfully concealing his anticipated imminent triumph, then requested the bench for permission to question the defendant, which was not challenged by the defence counsel who perhaps had been dumbfounded by the statement that had been read out to the court and would also soon be completely crushed by the facts that the pit bull terrier like questioning would expose. The questioning became bellicose, staccato and devastatingly incisive.

"Mr. Wilson do you understand the meaning and reasons for the statement that you have just read out? "

"Yes" (The reply was quietly spoken as if he thought that his response would not be heard).

"Do you recognise the elegant handwriting?"

There was a brief period of silence before Wilson replied.

"I cannot agree that the handwriting is elegant, it appears distressed, however I believe that the note was written by Her Majesty."

"You say that the handwriting appears distressed, why do you specifically use this highly emotional word?"

Wilson turned to his counsel, perhaps for help, but he was lost and the defence counsel averted his eyes possibly to induce sympathy from the tribunal. The defendant hesitated and then abruptly blurted out with the force of a boxer's knockout punch...

"She feared for the safety of the nation but she did not fully comprehend our situation and..."

He stopped, dropped his head, and murmured to himself, words that the tribunal and other members of the court could not discern.

The prosecuting counsel, disregarding the defendant's state, turned to the bench, held the book in his raised clenched fist and stated that:

"This book forms part of a collection rescued from Buckingham Palace and is the Queen's personal and private diary recording her most intimate thoughts, beginning with Winston Churchill, in nineteen fifty two and terminating with this maggot..."

He was stopped in his short tirade by an almost synchronised rebuke from the three member tribunal and, it must be added, an outburst of objection by the meek defence counsel, however the crucial point had been made and Wilson was lost. The defence counsel requested an adjournment for dawn was breaking outside and the tribunal members, having sought the advice of the professional advisor, announced that the hearing was to adjourned to ten p.m. that night.

Wilson was in too much of a daze to remember the twelve minute journey back to the Wrotham Park Estate or that the defence counsel helped him to undress but he slept well and at five p.m. awoke, then washed and dressed himself automatically in the same outfit, before eating but he gave the impression that he was a broken man.

Deprived of news in any form and subject, he was unaware that the Queen and members of the Royal family had fled the country on news of his arrest; he sat motionless, almost indistinguishable from a statue, his gaze directed towards infinity and was only brought back to reality when his counsel arrived at about nine p.m.

"Only about two hours ago I was given the following document by the prosecuting counsel, which I have read and made certain minor alterations which do not substantially materially alter the contents and is a confession. The rules of law and natural justice have been swept away and you are to be the first casualty (they, of course, were completely unaware of the fate of the Regional Commissioners and the others). I have secured a promise from the prosecuting counsel that your family will be fairly treated after all matters in connection with your trial have been completed but that is all that I have been able to secure.

FOUR

THE GREAT TERROR

STALIN`S PURGE OF THE THIRTIES:

BOOK TWO: THE YEZHOV YEARS:

THE GREAT TRIAL: BUKHARIN IN (THE) DOCK.

"And now, at last, the main subject of the trial was brought to questioning.

Bukharin had not been tortured... After three months of interrogation, and threats to his young wife and child, Bukharin agreed, in a long talk with Yezhov... to confess to all the charges, including that of having planned to assassinate Lenin.

But when, two days later, his confession, amended and corrected by Stalin personally, had been given to him to sign, he was so shocked that he withdrew his whole confession... He finally agreed to testify, but refused to say that he had planned Lenin`s death.

... Bukharin asked the court to allow him to present his case` freely` and to dwell on the ideological stand of the `bloc`... He then made his carefully phrased acceptance of guilt:

I plead guilty to being one of the outstanding leaders of this `bloc of Rights and Trotskyites`. Consequently, I plead guilty to what directly follows from this, the sum total of crimes committed by this counter-revolutionary organization, irrespective of whether or not I knew of, whether or not I took a direct part in, any particular act."

THE PROTOCOLS OF THE MEETINGS OF THE LEARNED ELDERS OF ZION:

(EXTRACT FROM)

PROTOCOL NUMBER FOUR:

"We appear on the scene as alleged saviours of the worker from this oppression when we propose to him to enter the ranks of our fighting forces - Socialists, Anarchists, Communists - to whom we always give support in accordance with an alleged brotherly rule (of the solidarity of all humanity) of our social masonry. The aristocracy, which enjoyed by law the labour of the workers, was interested in seeing that the workers were well fed, healthy and strong. We are interested in just the opposite- in the diminution, the killing out of the *GOYIM* (sic).

OUR POWER IS IN THE CHRONIC SHORTNESS OF FOOD AND PHYSICAL WEAKNESS OF THE WORKER [The author`s deliberate emphasis!].

(EXTRACTS FROM)

PROTOCOL NUMBER TWELVE:

"The word 'freedom', which can be interpreted in various ways, is defined by us as follows:-

Freedom is the right to do that which the law allows. This interpretation of the word will at the proper time be of service to us, because all freedom will thus be in or hands, since the laws will abolish or create only that which is desirable for us according to the aforesaid programme."

"We shall deal with the press in the following way:

What is the part played by the press today? It serves to excite and inflame those passions which are needed for our purpose or else it serves selfish ends of parties. It is often vapid, unjust, mendacious, and the majority of the public have not the slightest idea what ends the press really serves. We shall saddle and bridle it with a tight curb:...

For any attempt to attack us, if such still be possible, we shall inflict fines without mercy... No one shall with impunity lay a finger on the aureole of our government infallibility... Not a single announcement will reach the public without our control... Let us turn again to the future of the printing press. Every one desirous of being a publisher, librarian, or printer, will be obliged to provide himself with the diploma instituted therefore (sic), which, in case of any fault, will be immediately impounded. With such measures the instrument of thought will become an educative means in the hands of our government.

Literature and journalism are two of the most important educative forces, and therefore our government will become proprietor of the majority of the journals. This will neutralize the injurious influence of the privately owned press and will put us in possession of the tremendous influence upon the public mind... If we give permit for ten journals, we shall ourselves found thirty, and so on the same proportion. This, however, must in nowise be suspected by the public. For which reason all journals published by us will be of the most opposite, in appearance, tendencies and opinions, thereby creating confidence in us...

...We shall set up our own, to all appearances, opposition, which, in at least in one of its organs, will present what looks like the very antipodes to us. Our real opponents at heart will accept this simulated opposition as their own and will show us their cards."

MY STRUGGLE

PART TWO - CHAPTER FOUR:

PERSONALITY AND THE CONCEPTION OF THE NATIONAL STATE:

"...I may remind my readers that the parliamentary principle of decision by majorities has not always governed the human race; on the contrary, it only appears during quite short periods of history, and those are always periods of decadence in nations and States."

Author's comment: I hope that I have made my point.

What is now perceived as the beginnings of the totalitarian state have their foundations in the events of the next two to three months, the successful result and culmination of acts derived from a single minded purpose and a clear, well defined strategy.

Dwarfing all others was the introduction of food rationing, preceded by the clamour and social unrest caused by the phased withdrawal of food and goods from the shops and markets, partially, and deliberately , stoked by the rhetoric of John Tyndall.

An analysis, or overview of the events, and the people directly, or indirectly involved, will perhaps explain how the British people not only acquiesced, but openly demanded the nation's leaders to implement what was intended, which ultimately became a weapon that was used to control, physically weaken and subdue the nation.

The trial of Harold Wilson was effectively held 'in camera' and whilst, towards the end, it was held 'in open court' in the presence of a restricted audience of approved foreign journalists and diplomats, the general public was unaware of the trial or even of Wilson's arrest and impeachment.

The second session saw a broken man in the dock. There was no pretence or need for further cross examination, indeed the circumstances of the unfolding events permitted those who were to eventually create the perverted record of the trial, adequate opportunity to weave their own version of events around the original recording which eventually would cease to form any part of the final version.

When Wilson opened his statement, his old, confident, even paternal authority was shattered and his oration was perhaps a final desperate plea for understanding but they were, at least, his own words and thoughts, giving his definitive, although biased observation, on the events that had literally overwhelmed the government:

"The political situation had become desperate. Whilst we still received support and encouragement from our old friends and allies in North America, the Soviet Union was becoming more and more aggressive and intransigent and we were unable to use thermonuclear weapons for their counter attack would have completely wiped the nation from off of the face of the earth. It was not possible to continue negotiations, through a third party, to secure the release of further contingents of British prisoners of war so *ON MY OWN INITIATIVE I HALTED ALL CONTACT* [sic – author's specific emphasis]. The reduced production of essential foodstuffs, especially wheat, I blame on abnormal seasonal weather conditions and the consequences of radioactive fallout especially in East Anglia."

He then read, without conviction, but tinged with melancholy, the slightly amended confession that had been prepared by his nemeses and which would seal his fate, not knowing that each of the tribunal members were currently of the independent opinion to find him 'not guilty' on the charge that he had wilfully neglected the interests of the remaining British prisoners of war.

Undoubtedly his prime, and perhaps only consideration, was the wellbeing of his family, however the delivery of 'his' confession was nearly robotic and almost mechanical and twice he stumbled when he reached his counsel's amendments, which he read out in full creating a statement that was ambiguous and illogical.

Briefly, he admitted that he had been derelict in his duty and that he should have sought the advice of his cabinet and the armed services, but he truly believed that the leaders of the Soviet Union, potentially fearful of the awesome power of the United States, would keep their word and respect the integrity of Great Britain, and that his actions would be appreciated by the many anti–war groups including the Campaign for Nuclear Disarmament (C.N.D.) who for some years had received his tacit, but unspoken support. It was now clear that he had been misled and should have heeded the sound advice of the Queen.

Such was the deteriorating political situation, which virtually consumed his full attention, that he had not pursued, despite the many references to the increasing problem made by his cabinet and senior civil servants, action to stockpile and consolidate the dwindling stock of food supplies, relying on the continued, ongoing imports from North America. Neither had he even considered taking action to curb and halt the commodity speculators who were the only group to profit from the calamity that was now about to unfurl.

He referred to the energy and time that had been expended creating the new identity and ration card system - which had an inherent flaw which was the absence of a personal photograph - designed not only for its superficial purposes but as a bulwark against infiltration by the nation's enemies and also to identify internal subversives representing extreme groups on the fringes and outside of the democratic process which the prepared statement did not name or define.

His final words and a complete admission of guilt was his heartfelt regret that he had not pursued every avenue available to secure the repatriation of the many British prisoners of war who were languishing in unknown camps which perhaps were scattered in the most inhospitable areas of the Soviet Union, possibly in the Gulag camps of the Arctic region.

In a final statement of contrition he confirmed that he should have acted in conjunction with his American allies who had secured the release of all of their forces, together with their families, and civilians who had been caught up in the disastrous and unsuccessful defence of their now enslaved former allies.

His horizon was now limited to the sole desire to be reunited with his family or if that was not possible to be content in the knowledge that they were, or would be safe, the goal which fuelled his existence.

On Thursday June tenth, whilst shuffling around the grounds of Wrotham Park Estate he was interrupted by his counsel who was ominously wearing full military dress and informed that the tribunal was imminently reconvening and that they would both have to appear before the three military officers within the hour and the urgency meant that there was insufficient time for him to dress in clothes that would show respect for the court.

Whilst he was prepared for the intensity of the strong artificial lighting in the otherwise desolate and bare hall, his reception, as the caravan of military escorts sandwiching them in the middle turned into the centre, completely unbalanced and disoriented him, for his vehicle was assailed on every front by a mob of baying civilians (an assembled group of actors and extreme New Order members) shouting expletives and throwing eggs. All he could hear above the obscenities was the chant of 'traitor' and he did not notice the film cameras that were recording the *melee* from different angles.

As he walked into, and along the makeshift court towards the now intimidating dock, he recognised some of those seated in the area reserved for the general public as members of the National Council including Manny Gold (who turned away from him) and the man whom he had personally dismissed, Hugh Stephenson, not comprehending that now they aspired to, and had greater responsibilities and ambitions to achieve, but then he saw the dock and realised that his fate was about to be sealed.

He felt faint, the heat of the arc lights made him also feel nauseous and the presence of the three military officers looking down on him irresistibly intimidated him. For a few moments he was unable to rely on any of his five senses. Minutes later as he was led from the court his counsel patiently explained to him that he had been found guilty on each of the three charges and that the sentence would be carried out within twelve hours, however he had again spoken to the prosecuting counsel who was most emphatic that the promise of the National Council would be carried out and his family would be looked after.

As was now usual, he sat alone in the dining room at Wrotham Park, having enjoyed an excellent hors d'oeuvre of thinly sliced smoked salmon and awaited, as the clock relentlessly moved on, the entree of Scottish Beef, well hung and cooked medium rare. Perhaps he salivated as he heard the waiter enter the room but in anticipation of his final supper he did not look round, which perhaps was best in the circumstances, for had he done so then he would have been gripped by shock and fear. They grabbed his shoulders and neck firmly and he was shot through the back of head three times.

Two death certificates were issued, incidentally in two different areas, one for a phantom patient who had died of virulent multibacillary leprosy in an isolation hospital some twenty-five minutes away (Coppetts Wood) and a second, confirming that he had been lawfully executed by a firing squad. His clothing was carefully removed and later cleaned for future use, whilst the still warm body and the hospital death certificate were transported to the crematorium in New Southgate, immediately cremated, and the ashes were then scattered in the street (Brunswick Park Road) without ceremony and certainly without any respect or dignity.

The final irony and tragedy would be that he did join his beloved family, for they had all been murdered earlier the same day whilst asleep and before he had been rushed to the court. A pillow was placed over their sleeping faces and the same pistol that was to kill him was fired through the pillow thus reducing the spurt of blood. As for the bodies and the location of their burial I am afraid that there is no information available or knowledge whether a Christian burial ceremony was performed.

Manny Gold left the court without an iota of guilt for he had now been totally corrupted by many small, but cumulative acts over the years and any scintilla of conscience now ceased to exist. He could only look to the future and the impending introduction of the new joint identity, internal passport and ration card. The original form and documentation would be updated and nominally altered over the ensuing years but fundamentally would retain its, his, original concept. The first section would incorporate the basic identification information:

> The bearer's full name and in the case of a married woman, her maiden name.

> The bearer's signature, witnessed by the issuing official.

> Any previous names or aliases.

The current residential address (which would determine in which area or adjacent areas the bearer was permitted to travel without special permission).

Date (and place) of birth and the place where the birth was registered (if known).

Any (visible) physical defects *INCLUDING* [author`s emphasis] whether, for a man, he had been circumcised.

There then followed a series of numbers and letters which, for those who knew their interpretation, confirmed, amongst other facts, from which centre the document had been obtained and the person who had authorised the issue of the document, the date of birth, sex and area code (the numbers 01-12, corresponding to each area of the twelve Regional Commissioners and then further number sequences to identify area sub- divisions). The section which incorporated the ration card was preceded by the bearer`s photograph, stapled and stamped, which had previously been verified by one of the panel of professionals who were permanently on duty, though on a rota. There then followed a brief section divided into sub groups, covering pregnant mothers or those with a child under the age of twelve months, heavy manual workers or undefined workers who were exempt from rationing or subject to a special diet. Finally there was a section, in small boxes, numbered from one to one hundred and four covering the first two years of rationing and which would be verified by an official stamp used each week by the provider of the rationed food and goods.

The document ended with a statement of conditions, some draconian in their warnings, including:

The document had to be carried at all times and was to be shown to any person duly entitled to request sight of the document.

It was an offence to obtain the document by deception or to alter the document by any means.

It was an offence to travel outside of the area or areas permitted by the document without prior written permission.

Obtain items that were rationed other than through the official system and the use of the document.

Assist another person or persons to obtain any benefit that could be only be provided by the use of an officially issued document.

Medical services could only be provided on *PRIOR* (sic) production of the document.

On the death or imprisonment of the bearer the document had to be immediately returned to the nearest police station or local registration bureau.

The document did *NOT* specify the nature or extent of the consequences following a breach of the card's conditions.

Two vast, existing centres were to be commandeered and exclusively dedicated to the storage and maintenance of every application form and validated duplicate identity photograph; in the 'Southern' region, records would be stored in the Cheltenham, Gloucestershire centre and in the region covering the North and Scotland, at Menwith Hill, near Harrogate, whilst a relatively new police centre in Aerodrome Road, Colindale, North London had been identified and would be the central operations and surveillance command centre (known as G.C.H.Q., General Control Headquarters).

Twenty-four appointments were made from the three branches of the armed forces to replace the twelve Regional Commissioners and their deputies ,all totally loyal to the National Council but above all to their values and ideals. Beneath them, in a pyramid of power, the twelve areas would be subdivided into ten areas(a new 'second 'layer), each under the control of an Area Commissioner and beneath that, a new 'third' layer, again sub divided into ten local areas each headed by a Local Commissioner.

Originally it had been decided that the 'layer' immediately beneath the Regional Commissioner (and his deputy) would be appointed by, as previously agreed, John Tyndall, during his forthcoming series of national rallies but since he was now scheduled to make only seven speeches in seven different cities, it was finally agreed that the responsibility in the remaining five areas be delegated to the local Regional Commissioner, however to avoid any intentional or unintentional favouritism, or even nepotism, as a formality the appointments would be verified and approved by two of their counterparts.

The new second layer of Area Commissioners, chosen for their absolute loyalty to the New Order and their administrative abilities, would immediately be sent for training at one of the five centres where the original deputy Regional Commissioners had been inducted, in preparation for the introduction of the joint card . The third level, the Local Commissioners, would , under supervision, perform the actual operation of registration assisted by 'volunteers' all of whom were loyal and active members of the party. Ultimately this hierarchy would supersede and then replace the previously long established organisations of local government officers and the civil service.

Thus, within a short period, control of the nation and its administration was to be handled solely by the party organisation which would not be accountable to the community but to the party itself, embodied in the twelve Regional Commissioners. Power cascaded down from the twelve Regional Commissioners, becoming ever more diluted, finally being administered by the 'voluntary army 'of loyal, obedient supporters of the party who would be charged to operate the day to day running of the nation under strict supervision.

Later, and certainly within two years, when the absolute totalitarianism of the edifice became apparent, control of the party became more rigid for not only was total loyalty a prerequisite, but also that unwavering obedience to the party was to be absolute, together with total, unquestioning obedience and acceptance of any of the party`s acts or demands. Disloyalty or dissent in any form or degree, was not tolerated and was to be an offence under an amendment incorporated in the...

STATE OF EMERGENCY- MARTIAL LAW.
FIFTH EDITION

Law and order, together with the security of the State were originally the responsibility of the area police forces and of M.I.5 and 6, who respectively were responsible for domestic and foreign security and intelligence. The three members of the National Council representing M.I.5 and 6 and the national police forces were predictably unwilling to loosen hold of their fiefdoms and power, each convincingly arguing their valid cases and it was apparent that even allowing and permitting the other Council members to evaluate and then vote on the merits and demerits, might not resolve the *impasse* or reach the most effective result. Finally it was agreed that a single body be created, operated equally by the same three Council members who would ultimately be responsible to the National Council and its members, to be known as the Bureau of National Security and Intelligence (BoNSaI).

Matters of law and order would fall within the jurisdiction of the former civilian police who would soon become a lightly, but permanently armed *quasi* paramilitary force, whilst between them and the departments responsible for internal and foreign intelligence matters would be a new, mobile, permanent force composed of current or former military staff, with access to, and knowledge of the use of most military equipment to be used to control, quell any major civil disobedience or when they were first employed ,initially to *SMASH* [Please note both the author's emphasis *AND* the initial primary use of the force] the Trade Union movement and the maverick Bill Martin.

The archaic concepts of 'law and order', civil disputes and criminal offences were swept aside. Thus for civil conflicts, the County and High Courts were deemed obsolete and whilst major criminal offences would be covered by the provisions of the Second Edition, the new Fifth Edition would cover less serious offences (such as theft). The new quasi paramilitary force which, on a local level, was the nearest body comparable to the now superseded regional police forces would disturbingly act as both judge and – opening them to inevitable corruption - jury, usually dispensing justice by the crude, but highly effective, method of fining parties involved initially one week's ration allowance and in more serious cases, even up to four weeks allowance. Soon there would be methods available to deal with more persistent or dangerous offenders.

Following the issue of the STATE OF EMERGENCY- MARTIAL LAW. FIFTH EDITION (on August first nineteen sixty-five), was the threat and option of arbitrary imprisonment in one of the new 're-education' camps that were being set up in the desolate, isolated and windswept wilds of the Scottish Highlands, the Yorkshire Moors and in the most inhospitable parts of Dartmoor.

FIVE

John Tyndall was in Glasgow, about to begin the first leg of his seven leg speaking tour, when he was informed by telephone of Wilson's fate and he immediately decided to contact Sir Oswald Mosley, and at the same time resolve, once and for all, the future of his rival Colin Jordan, for he felt certain that Mosley would arrange for the presence of his other *protégée*, whether or not he had been formally requested not to bring him along. A meeting was hastily arranged for shortly after his final speaking engagement in Southampton.

"A private room, well of course, immediately."

The River Room at the Savoy was now only just suitable and he chose the benefit of a private dining salon not only to confirm proof of his status but more importantly because he did not want to be observed, in public, with Jordan, who not unexpectedly arrived with Sir Oswald.

Details of the superb menu are unimportant, however they concluded the meal with a specially prepared bread and butter pudding studded with raisins and immersed in double cream.

By nineteen seventy-three, the wheel of fortune would have turned and Tyndall would no longer be in the ascendancy, indeed his fate had been sealed some time before, whilst Jordan and Mosley would look back on this fortunate meeting with cynical pleasure and satisfaction.

Tyndall was genuinely concerned with his mentor's current situation and above all, his health. His guests were not surprised to learn that compulsory registration and rationing were imminent but surprised that the new documentation would include an Internal Passport at which moment Jordan, perhaps foolishly, enquired if the document would be stamped with a prominent J - for a certain group in the community - but was promptly admonished by Sir Oswald Mosley, who chastised him by informing him that:

"Those days and times were over though the black men (he used a more vicious word beginning with the letter n) were the new danger."

However both men smiled, as though the promised land was still achievable, when Tyndall confirmed that the new documentation would include under 'any physical defects' details of any male's circumcision.

He would arrange that Sir Oswald, his wife and family, be provided with documentation that did not restrict their ration allowance or their movements, finally confirming that they would not have to follow the exhausting and time consuming procedure to queue for their papers.

He would arrange that Colin Jordan be appointed as a Local Commissioner under his ultimate authority and that he was at liberty to employ his gang of thugs (sic) provided that they all promptly joined the New Order and...

"Behaved themselves, for he would arrange for their acts to be monitored as it was still not yet prudent or possible for them to assert their real intentions.

SIX

THE PROTOCOLS OF THE MEETINGS OF THE LEARNED ELDERS OF ZION

(EXTRACT FROM)

PROTOCOL NUMBER FIVE:

"Moreover, the art of directing masses and individuals by means of cleverly manipulated theory and verbiage, by regulations of life in common and all sorts of other quirks, in all which the goyim understand nothing, belongs likewise to the specialists of our administrative brain."

(EXTRACT FROM)

PROTOCOL NUMBER THIRTEEN:

"The need for daily bread forces the goyim to keep silence (sic) and be our humble servants. Agents taken on to our press from among the goyim will at our orders discuss anything which it is inconvenient for us to issue directly in official documents, and we meanwhile, quietly amid the din of the discussion so raised, shall simply take and carry through such measures as we wish and then offer them to the public as an accomplished fact."

(EXTRACT FROM)

PROTOCOL NUMBER FIFTEEN:

"Our government will have the appearance of a patriarchial (sic) paternal guardianship on the part of our ruler."

MY STRUGGLE

PART TWO - CHAPTER FOUR:

PERSONALITY AND THE CONCEPTION OF THE NATIONAL STATE:

"The national State must work untiringly to set all government, especially the highest, that is the political leadership, free from the principle of control by majorities - i.e., the multitude - so as to secure the undisputed authority of the individual in its stead."

THE AUTHORITARIAN STATE

ITS MEANING AND FUNCTION:

CHAPTER -THE AUTHORITARIAN STATE:

"In place of the modern Jew – inspired illusion of 'freedom' we substitute the honest reality of freedom, i.e. *FREEDOM FOR THOSE FIT TO USE IT AND A CURB ON THOSE WHO ARE NOT* [author's emphasis]. Such a principle forms the basis of the authoritarian state, which we seek to build in Britain.

Most people believe in government...

Our conception of the state is based very simply upon this principle...

Very briefly such precautions can be outlined as follows:-

(1). In the sphere of political life it will be necessary to secure the operation of the nation as an efficient and smoothly-functioning unit... This is only possible if national policy stems from a *POLITICAL ELITE* [author's emphasis].u (sic) nited in aim, and responsible in the final analysis to the Prime Minister, who must have complete power of decision in all matters."

And it was, in the final sentence of the above extract from John Tyndall's 'pamphlet', printed and published by the National Socialist Movement in April 1962 (price one shilling and sixpence) that the seeds of his downfall, combined with the rise of Sir Oswald Mosley and, independently, of Colin Jordan were sown, but that would be some five or so years hence. In the meantime, his star not only rapidly rose, both symbolically in the heavens, but increasingly shone brighter, during which time the terror and the purges, along with the vindictive use and constraint of food rationing would begin and rage like an uncontrollable plague that would cow and bludgeon the nation into placid submission.

John Tyndall, backed by the resources of the State and, more importantly, the approval and wishes of the National Council, readied himself for seven important speeches that were designed to inflame both his audiences and the country, with the intention of imposing rationing to satisfy the demand of the people for a fair distribution of the country's dwindling resources and reserves. Concurrently he had also been charged with the task of approving the appointment of seventy Area Commissioners but he would have available experienced senior civil servants who would, in reality, perform the task which would require his imprimatur and sanction. It would be, for him, a formal exercise in approving others' suggestions ,however he chose, without logical or valid reasons to decline some of the recommendations, if only to prove his status.

His national tour was scheduled to begin in Glasgow, then zig zag south via Newcastle, then subsequently Manchester, Liverpool, Birmingham, Bristol and finally Southampton and it was planned that in Liverpool he would dramatically announce to his audience and the nation, who would be listening on the radio, the treachery of the former Prime Minister and his fate, blaming him personally for the catastrophic state of the nation's food reserves and the availability, or lack ,of food and goods in the shops (of course deliberately ignoring the fact that the National Council had been withholding food supplies which were being stored in, using a Biblical term, overflowing granaries). There were no set speeches other than the carefully worded statement to be made in Liverpool and he was (again) prepared for his task by a team of acting coaches who very successfully enabled him to deliver his key messages with apparent honesty and sincere integrity ,whilst another group, of advertising copywriters, who were specialists in the field of consumer sales, had prepared a series of set key words, phrases, arguments and exhortations which he became adept at using in various combinations.

The media, that is the reduced number of national newspapers, radio and television, now under the strict control of the National Council, gave Tyndall extensive coverage, whilst the so called 'independent' commentators were always positive in their analysis of his statements and indeed of the suggested joint sacrifices that the people and the Party would have to make. All this was in response to a backdrop of ever increasing food shortages, public anger spilling over into impromptu protests and even demonstrations provoked by agent provocateurs with the intention of creating a national groundswell which would demand the introduction of a fair rationing system. Thus in the speeches before the dramatic announcement in Liverpool, emphasis was placed on the leadership's intention of confronting the growing crisis by taking action to protect the 'National Interest'.

The final rally, which was held in Southampton before a crowd of some thirty-five thousand people, on Sunday June twenty-seventh, allowed Manny Gold and his small group of assistants adequate time to finalise and complete their preparations for, first, the issue nationwide of the new joint card and then soon afterwards, the introduction of rationing.

It was recognised that however much every foreseeable contingency had been taken into account, and the actual procedures rehearsed, there would be administrative problems, delays and errors, however special plans were put in place to transfer the blame to various scapegoats thus create a 'soup' in which the terror would ferment and begin.

The new policy of revisionism has already been mentioned and in reality meant that the achievements and the career of John Tyndall, after his fall, would be wiped clean from the slate of history. The rewriting of history allowed press coverage of his whole career and of his seven rallies to be expunged and were rewritten to comply with the current view of history, thus...

Even a recording of the crucial broadcast (from the ground of Liverpool F.C., in front of a crowd estimated to be in excess of fifty thousand people) was presumably destroyed and the author has had to rely on press reports in United States newspapers and from the leading Swiss newspaper, L`Impartial published daily in the Canton of Neuchatel and read by the British embassy in the capital, Berne, to summarise what was his definitive speech.

He was, this time, unable to arrive in what he had become to accept as his now normal method of conveyance, the helicopter, which had previously both strikingly caused awe and excitement in his audiences and which had delivered the unsuspecting Harold Wilson to his fate.

His carefully rehearsed and meticulously prepared speech was preceded by the National Anthem which was again played after his speech was concluded, an act of blatant hypocrisy since he was aware of, and a party to, the state secret that the Queen and members of the Royal family had fled to Canada. Indeed, whilst no mention is made in the following summary of his speech, the Swiss newspaper clearly confirms that Tyndall emphasised his loyalty both to the Crown and the concept of national duty. His personality and oratory were certainly not charismatic but the National Council had recognised in him a figurehead whose resonance with the nation could promote their aims and plans.

"As you may know I have recently spoken to vast crowds in Glasgow, Newcastle and Manchester on the twin themes of our nation`s destiny and future. I, and all the other members of the National Council, are not unaware of the situation that you are now encountering in the streets and shops as you go about your daily lives. Food supplies are becoming scarcer and scarcer though fortunately there still seems to be an abundance of bread, milk and bacon still available throughout the country. I have been regularly kept informed by my assistants of the deteriorating situation and have myself experienced the shortages (pause). We are all in this together and that means that when rationing is brought in, as it must be, that it will be fair; members of the National Council will not receive preferential treatment because of their position, why should we? If our new society stands for anything, it will mean that the pregnant or new mother will be protected along with the weak and those who have previously contributed to the country`s best interests but are no longer fit or well enough to promote their own cause. It is a sacrifice that we, not you, will have to make and endure for it is up to everyone here today to be in the vanguard of fairness and compassion. (Tyndall stopped as a wall of clapping and cheers engulfed the football stadium and in order to deliver a Churchillian slogan).

Let us go forward together.

Who is to blame for the shortages that ravage this country? It is not the farmers who diligently plough the fields and herd the cattle. It is not our kith and kin and old allies in Australia, New Zealand and North America from whom we buy, at generous concessionary prices, the staples of life to supplement home produced essentials. It is those politicians and leaders that have insidiously undermined, corrupted and deliberately betrayed you and me (press reports confirmed that an ominous silence enveloped the football stadium, as if an away team had snatched a winning goal in the final moments and dying embers of a match).

We have a duty to each other to stand resolute and firm in the face of adversity. A duty to recognise that others have and are still sacrificing their lives for your tomorrow.

A disastrous war was fought on the European mainland by your husbands, sons, brothers, friends and neighbours to defend our freedom but may I remind you that our pygmy politicians did not think fit to adequately arm them, squandering vast sums of the country`s wealth on policies that had no apparent benefit other than possibly the enrichment of friends and avaricious businessmen. And what was, what is now the outcome of their plans? Let me remind you that today, now your husbands, sons, brothers, friends and neighbours are languishing in prisoner of war camps somewhere in Eastern Europe or worse in one of the bestial camps in the Soviet Union which are the legacy of Stalin and his gang of thugs (pause).

What action, what attempts were made by the politicians that betrayed us to repatriate our brave forces? True a very, very few did return but they were rescued by our allies, the United States, and represented a tragic example of Soviet callousness and brutality. The truth is that the government did nothing, effectively washing their blood stained hands of any responsibility. But I have news for you and the nation, who I understand are listening to this rally and stand beside you as if they were here themselves in person, indeed the nation stands here united in its determination to forge a new better Britain (again a pause, but this time much longer).

I received news less than an hour ago, so dramatic that when I first heard the substance I could not believe how heinous were the crimes of its perpetrator. May I be allowed to stand down for a few minutes in order to prepare myself and inform you all of this astonishing development? (he quickly left the podium surrounded by staff, almost theatrically being assisted as if the events had overwhelmed him both physically and mentally, though the real truth was to permit a mood of anxious excitement to breed whilst allowing them to conjecture on the substance of the impending news. He returned to the podium some ten minutes later to a still and hushed audience).

Harold Wilson has committed suicide along with his family. He has cheated the hangman`s noose for he had been arrested, impeached and charged with three offences of High Treason, to all of which he pleaded guilty, but worse was the fact that he did not accept any moral responsibility. Before he was sentenced ,and the only punishment of a military tribunal for High Treason is death, this coward took first his family's lives, and then his own.

The first of his three crimes was so dangerous to the security of the State that I am not permitted to divulge its exact nature, however he was both reckless and negligent in the defence of the Realm. Of the other two charges, he admitted that he had not pursued, by every means possible, attempts to repatriate any of our forces, your boys, from their incarceration, effectively leaving them to an uncertain but likely unpleasant end. His duty to you all has been just as irresponsible! He actually admitted, despite requests from the small band of Ministers that surrounded him like fawning, sycophantic weasels and his senior civil servants and advisors, that he had been completely overwhelmed by the political situation and had not authorised contingency plans to provide for long term food supplies. When you now look into an empty shop window or a bare cupboard, remember my words!

The decisive hour is close at hand, the forging of a bond between the people and those that lead them, but who serve them, prelude to a new day and era bathed in the sunlight of freedom, equality and fairness. When you leave this gathering remember that the road ahead will be difficult, but together we will build a fairer and better society for all."

SEVEN

THE AUTHORITARIAN STATE

ITS MEANING AND FUNCTION:

CHAPTER-THE AUTHORITARIAN STATE:

"Freedom for those who work, for those who create, for those who conscientiously remember their duties of citizenship; such freedom we would never wish to destroy. What we will not tolerate in the state of tomorrow is the loafer, the spiv, or the degenerate. In short, what we intend to build is a national community in which that natural Nordic birthright of freedom is not something to be taken for granted by the dregs of society, but something earned by labour, loyalty and service."

The national mood, inflamed by the speeches and news announced by John Tyndall and exacerbated by the subsequent promotion of his pronouncements by the national press, television and radio, combined with the ever diminishing availability of goods and food in the shops, together with price increases where supplies were available, and finally the rise of the 'Black Market' created a breeding ground for anger, not against the New Order, but against the *'Ancien Regime'* that had clearly, in the eyes of the people, caused this chaos.

It was little less than three weeks later that the first of the three new editions of the State Of Emergency - Martial Law was published on July the fourteenth, closely followed on the sixteenth by the fourth edition and then, on August first, by the fifth edition.

The wise and perceptive could now see the demise of democracy and the unstoppable rise of totalitarianism. But for the 'man in the street, 'the backbone of the nation' he was unconcerned with such trivia; decisive action was being taken by men who held the national interest ahead of their own aspirations, so eloquently expressed by John Tyndall and confirmed by the press, television and radio.

Nationwide, commercial photographers were soon inundated by the expected tidal wave of demand for duplicate passport style photographs. Supplies of suitable paper and chemicals were abundantly available and they, their staff, and very soon afterwards the temporary staff employed to meet the massive surge in demand, realised that the operation had been, or must have been, carefully planned over some time. As in all cases demand was also satisfied by the initiative of capitalism as competent photographers offered their services to those who were prepared to pay for priority attention or those who were deceived by the dishonest claims of criminals.

The initial chaos subsided when people realised that there would be a period of grace before the process of registration began when all areas (other than for the commercial photographers) of industrial production, trade and commerce were interrupted, but the ruling elite were concerned only to finally have in place the identification and registration of the whole nation and total control and distribution of the food supply.

Registration was alphabetically based, still in itself a massive operation, but it brought a measure of order that avoided the chaos of a 'first come, first served' avalanche, though there is anecdotal evidence, which of course was denied, that many centres ran out of glue and staples with which to attach the photograph to the identity card and likewise the copy to the record sheet, but with the British ability to 'muddle through' supplies were harvested from businesses and wholesale suppliers.

At the end of four exhausting, long working weeks the mammoth task had all but been completed, however...

It was rumoured that literally thousands, if not tens of thousands of mail bags, each meticulously labelled with their region, sub area and finally the local area had been deposited at two secret centres (in Cheltenham and Menwith Hill) for sorting, filing and registration and that significantly, staff were unable to cope with the volume at either location. No definitive confirmation of the allegation, however spurious or factual, can be verified but within some six months, or by early nineteen sixty-six, it was claimed that the centre in Colindale, North London (G.C.H.Q.) was in full operation and that applications for records to the two centres in Cheltenham and Harrogate were being answered in full within one working day and for priority cases within two hours. The reader should have observed that the location of Harrogate was now used, though all enquiries for the Northern and Scottish regions included the address at Menwith Hill. All evidence points to the administration being transferred to Harrogate, en masse, and the location of Menwith Hill being taken over by the United States government for their own purposes.

Readers may also ask why such an important, pivotal event, was recorded in little more than a paragraph, when deviously, the rights of the British people were being taken from them? Primarily, because the whole operation was, in hindsight, consummately planned and organised and the actual operation at 'the coal face' seems to have been smoothly transacted by the many staff (who were all idealistic, voluntary members of the New Order) that were brought to bear by the Local, Area and Regional Commissioners. Indeed an independent report by a journalist from the Swiss Daily, L'Impartial, who visited a number of registration centres in different areas over a period of ten days or so (admittedly accompanied by Area Commissioners from the three Regions that he visited) was clearly impressed by the efficiency of the staff but above all the stoicism and patience of the local residents as they waited, drawing, in the newspaper articles, comparisons with the British fortitude during the Blitz in nineteen forty and forty-one and their quiet confidence in, what was then, an uncertain future. Furthermore news reports 'filed' from London by individual American journalists confirmed their Swiss associate's reports.

But the continuous, ongoing story that was not reported, was the arrests made by the authorities - you, the reader, should note that the men and some women officers involved, were no longer described as police officers but as regional security officers - essentially to maintain the efficient operation of the registration programme.

It was self evident that their behaviour and procedures had been carefully planned for in every case, without exception, nationwide, the offending person was courteously warned that their misbehaviour was causing offence both to other people waiting to be given their new combined identity card and also to the staff. Those that subsequently disobeyed the request were publicly arrested, despite pleas from family members, and...

EIGHT

STALIN'S PURGE OF THE THIRTIES:
BOOK TWO: THE YEZHOV YEARS:
IN THE LABOUR CAMPS:
FOOD AND DEATH.

"In the camps, the commandants operated the norm system vis-a-vis the prisoners. As a general principle there were various 'cauldrons', or food allotments.

The principle is simple enough. Precise figures varied considerably, but the following shows a typical proportion. In the Kolyma camps, for men doing *TWELVE TO SIXTEEN HOURS*" [author's emphasis] heavy physical labour a day, eight months of it in very low temperatures, the daily ration, of very poor bread, is given as follows by a former prisoner now in the West:

for more than 100per cent

of the norm	up to 930 grammes (32 oz.)
for 100 per cent	815 grammes (28.5oz.)
for 70-99 per cent	715 grammes (25 oz.)

for 50-69 per cent	500 grammes (17.5 oz.)
disciplinary ration	300 grammes (10.5 oz.)
plus soup,	3.5 oz. of salt fish and just over 2 oz. of groats.

A Polish account, of 1940-41, gives

500 grammes for 50 per cent norm and 300 for less.

Another reported ration scheme, in one of the northern camps in the winter of 1941-42:

for the full norm	700 grammes of bread, plus soup and buckwheat

for those not obtaining the norm

400 grammes of bread plus soup

Most Arctic arrangements were probably close to these two. The ration outside the Arctic proper was rather lower; typically:

over 100 per cent	750-1000 grammes
100 per cent	600-650 grammes
50-100 per cent	400-475 grammes
penal	
(under 50 per cent)	300-400 grammes

We can make certain comparisons. In the Ukrainian cities in the famine period of the thirties, the bread ration was 800 grammes for industrial workers, 600 for manual workers, 400 for office employees. In the siege of Leningrad, in 1941-42, about one third to one half of the population remaining in the city died of hunger, mostly during the first winter. The rations in the worst period were:

October 1941　The basic ration was down to 400 grammes of bread a day for workers and 200 grammes for dependants.

Late November 1941

> 250 grammes for workers,125 grammes for dependants.

Late December 1941

> Up to350 grammes for workers and 200 grammes for dependants.

At Leningrad there were small additional rations of meat and sugar; lumber workers got a supplementary ration above the norm."

THE AUTHORITARIAN STATE

ITS MEANING AND FUNCTION:

CHAPTER: COMMON OBJECTIONS TO AUTHORITARIANISM:

"Having outlined the basis of the authoritarian state, we should give a brief hearing to those oft-repeated attacks that are made on it. The main ones are as follows:-

OBJECTION: You wish to stifle all opposition.

ANSWER: This is not true as regards any opposition that is based upon a sincere attempt to advocate changes of policy beneficial to the nation. Any man, or group of men, who believe that a certain department of government is not being directed in the best way should, and will, have every opportunity to make their views known. If they have a constructive alternative, then it can be looked into and its merits assessed. This is opposition of a useful type. On the other hand we have to consider a totally different form of opposition; that which is deliberately calculated to undermine the well being and safety of the state, i.e. subversive opposition - of which Communism, in all its shades, offers the prime example. Communism, along with any other activity of a treasonable nature, will be outlawed with the same uncompromising ruthlessness as it would itself deal with us Nationalists were it to gain power in Britain."

The New Order inherited a highly developed and widespread secret plan to control the civilian population in the event of an impending crisis, including facilities to intern 'subversives' in special internment areas which were usually former army camps amongst which were Rollestone on Salisbury Plain, Beckingham in Nottinghamshire, Bicester near Oxford and Bordon in Hampshire, however new plans to develop centres in the Scottish Highlands, the Yorkshire Moors and on Dartmoor superseded existing arrangements because the intended regime was to be harsh, penal, far more ruthless than the general public would expect and was designed to cow both the internees and the population to the consequences of public disorder or dissent.

Thus those who had caused disturbances at the registration centres were to be the first to suffer the force of the terror and their treatment was to be a warning to them and the community as a whole. The 'tariff' was simple and immutable. For the first offence - thirty days incarceration, the second - six months and the third- three years; there was no hope or the promise of early release for 'good behaviour' or illness, for time lost recovering from an accident or illness was added at the end of the sentence.

For disciplinary offences, the food ration was normally halved and the person was sent to solitary confinement in deliberately unheated rooms and on release they had to serve the balance of their sentence. On completion of the sentences, detainees were encouraged to speak openly of their experiences as a warning to the community.

The inmates' diets were carefully controlled and at one end of the spectrum defined the authorities' intention to demonstrate that the internees were being punished (and re-educated) and at the other end, to maintain their heath or ability to fulfil the physical demands that were required of them, for their incarceration created a vast pool of labour.

Rations varied from camp to camp and even within the same camp and whilst there were no regulations that specified any upper or lower limit, for members of a 'work gang' that reached their quota (which over a period of years increased) a typical daily allowance would be:-

   16 ozs. of bread (allegedly adulterated with sawdust)

   one pint of semi- skimmed milk OR,

   one ladle of soup comprised of boiled potatoes, carrots and
   cabbage

   one apple

one rasher of bacon (when available or on special political anniversaries).

For the members of a 'work gang' not reaching their set quota, the food allowance was reduced, at the whim of the camp guards, by anything up to 50% of the standard allowance.

There were no rest days and the work day would begin at six thirty a.m. with *reveille* and end at seven thirty p.m. when each barrack was locked.

Later, when a more 'objective and pragmatic' view of the status of prisoners was adopted, then the diet was substantially reduced, deliberately creating endemic and chronic ill health and, of course, premature death, usually by starvation.

The first group of internees were detailed to construct barracks and were supplied with adequate quantities of lumber and tools which were retrieved at the end of each day and counted; the loss, or theft of any item would immediately result in the 'work gang' being denied their evening ration and made to stand outside the accommodation overnight.

To avoid the possibility of disease there was adequate sanitation and shower facilities, but no hot water (even in winter!). The purpose of the camp was punishment and re-education, not hospitality!

As the re-education camps received more inmates, it became obvious and self evident that their capacity and use would greatly exceed the temporary housing for a few hundred men and when, finally, the construction had been completed there was accommodation at each camp for about five and a half thousand internees (one hundred to one hundred and twenty barracks, each holding fifty people).

Escape, and capture, was treated as a disciplinary offence subject to a minimum of three months incarceration in solitary confinement, again dependant on the whim of the prison guards and the difficulties and inconveniences encountered capturing the fleeing prisoner.

Whether or not the terror and the purges were a deliberately planned operation to stifle and destroy any and all opposition was, for those who were caught in the web, an irrelevant conjecture, for their plight exposed the total absence of any legal protection or natural justice. The first group to be rounded up and ultimately 'disposed of' were the renegade leaders, prominent supporters of, and the focus of their support, Bill Martin.

Arrests were made, not in the dead of night, when the noise would attract the cautious raising of curtains and the slight opening of front doors (with the lights, of course, dimmed or darkened to avoid the attention of the security forces) but in the full glare of daylight so that the event was clearly seen by the community.

There were no minor irrelevancies such as arrest warrants signed by a magistrate for such procedures had been swept away . The powers of a Regional Commissioner were awesome, for martial law was in force because of the national emergency and the 'open ended' order had been signed by the Queen herself.

Remember!?

The mass trial, or what passed as a trial, was purely cursory. They were charged, *en masse*, under various sections of the State Of Emergency-Martial Law. Second Edition:

(One)   Organise, promote, support, join or assist in the act of Sedition, Revolution or Treason

(Two)   Withhold knowledge of any intention, act, statement or assistance from a Regional Commissioner, his deputy or the military authorities concerning any individual or body of persons who wish or intend to harm the State by Sedition, Revolution or Treason

(Five) Disseminate information, whether true or false, that could be reasonably expected to create public unrest, distress or disquiet

(Six)   Organise, promote, support, join or assist a strike or the withdrawal of labour

(Eleven)Membership or support of the Communist Party which has been proscribed as an illegal organisation

And finally...

(Twelve)Membership of a Trades Union unless that body has been sanctioned by a Regional Commissioner or his deputy.

The men had little time to assess their situation, for early on the following morning, without even being given the opportunity to wash or be provided with breakfast or fluids, they were taken by a coach, which had had all of its windows, both inside and out covered, including even the driver's windscreen, except for a small area only adequate for the driver to see out of, and to follow a pilot vehicle ahead of him. Thus to add to the occupants' concerns were the reasons and purpose of their new predicament and after a pedestrian journey of nearly three hours the vehicle manoeuvred through a narrow gate and into the quadrangle of an old , crumbling Victorian era building.

The hearing was held in a former, decommissioned Magistrate's Court - in camera - and whether it was intended to promote a facade or veneer of legality is now unimportant, though under the State of Emergency - Martial Law. Second Edition, the hearing was entirely legal and no doubt the location had been chosen as it was able to accommodate such a large number of defendants - twenty three and the three military officers who formed the tribunal together with a civilian legal advisor (believed to have been a clerk in a local law practice), the prosecuting counsel and *ONE* [author's emphasis] military defence counsel who were all adequately accommodated inside the large court. Hopes raised by the defendants, when they entered the courtroom, that the location symbolised the natural rule of law were immediately dashed when the single defence counsel identified himself, gave each one of the twenty three a copy of the charges and naively asked if...

"Any of the defendants were prepared to plead not guilty to *ALL* [again the author's emphasis] of the charges, for the death penalty would be applied for conviction on any one of the offences?"

Apparently there was an ominous silence as each man read his copy of the charges realising individually and collectively that they were doomed. Bravely, Bill Martin announced that:

"He alone would make a pleading on both his own account and the group, once the defence counsel had made his final submission."

Such was the contempt for the due process of law that the document authorising the tribunal's verdict of guilty (on all charges, for each defendant) and the death penalty, in accordance with the conditions of the State Of Emergency- Martial Law. Second Edition *WAS ALREADY PREPARED* [yet again the author's emphasis], signed by the Regional

Commissioner and in the possession of the prosecuting counsel, which only required the date to be inserted.

The prosecuting counsel did not present any witnesses and relied solely on a number of signed statements where, on each, the signatures had been redacted on the grounds that the authors were intelligence officers in the former M.I. 5and 6 departments of the nation's intelligence service, which had now been subsumed into the new national intelligence organisation, BoNSal., and for security purposes their identities had to remain anonymous.

It is only a casual observation but had the procedures of a normal court of justice been followed, then any half competent defence counsel could, and would, have dismembered the prosecuting counsel's evidence, however the defence counsel did not pursue this line of argument. The defence counsel's apathetic argument that certain of the *ALLEGED* [author's own emphasis] offences had taken place before the Second Edition had been made public and that two statements, amongst many, were only allegations (that the 'ring leaders' had been financially supported by 'foreign' or 'hostile' interests and their actions fermented revolution or sedition) should be deemed inadmissible on the grounds that the Intelligence officers supported their statements by circumstantial and secondary source (hearsay) reports were acknowledged by the tribunal, who then adjourned the proceedings to deliberate.

After no more than ten to fifteen minutes the court was reconvened and the tribunal announced that the statements were all to be deemed admissible for the defence's argument had at no time raised doubts about the integrity or validity of the statements.

The outcome was now a formality and the defence counsel, baulked by the decision, rapidly lost any incentive to pursue a lost cause.

It was left to Bill Martin to present an explanation that was doomed to failure but must have so impressed the tribunal that they referred to his presentation in their brief summing up. He was warned not to make a political speech and to deal solely with the prosecution's case, matters which conventionally should have been dealt with by the defence counsel. On one, possibly two occasions he was warned and cautioned that his presentation was becoming a political platform, however despite little preparation, he was able to morally justify his , and his co-defendants' actions...

"He and all the other defendants had campaigned, fought and on more than one occasion gone on unofficial strike, in conflict with their supine and ineffectual Union, with one goal and desire... to improve the safety and quality of life of the miners that supported and followed them. Only those in the room that had been down the mines, that had suffered the frightening experience of claustrophobia, the coal dust swirling around them and in their lungs, the fear of darkness and above all the ever present fear of an industrial accident, could understand what was incorrectly called their militancy. Safety and any measure to protect them could never be enough, whether the mines were owned and controlled by the 'Capitalists' or now, by the nation. They could never be adequately compensated for their dirty, dangerous job.

Yes, they received anonymous donations to support their cause (he was, of course, aware of the source of one major contributor but judiciously did not identify that source) which was not a crime *per se* and he challenged the prosecutor to name and identify the many various sources of the donations.

The clarion call of the New Order and of its leader, John Tyndall, had been about a fairer nation and I again challenge you all to experience the life of what was almost a troglodyte!"

But it was ,inevitably, all in vain. The preordained verdict of the tribunal, which was supported by Martin's own admission and confession that all the defendants had been on more than one unofficial strike, was guilty and almost immediately after they were sentenced, the men were taken in the same coach that had brought them to the court, along the A 635, to an isolated part of the moors where a group of soldiers waited, passing the time smoking and coarsely laughing, whilst lounging beside a lorry draped in tarpaulin, adjacent to a bulldozer and a mechanical digger carried on the back of a military transporter painted in camouflage. It was now late afternoon and the temperature was becoming cooler; the tarpaulin was raised exposing a machine gun and its operator, who proceeded to execute the tribunal's sentence. Within a few minutes the bulldozer and mechanical digger had buried and covered any evidence of the event, only leaving the marks of their caterpillar treads which the weather would erode and the growth of new vegetation soon hide. A few pieces of gritstone scattered on the site or even a simple cairn could have been erected but it was getting uncomfortably cold and a hot meal must have been beckoning the participants and the executioner.

The incident took place somewhere on Saddleworth Moor where the vegetation is overwhelmingly of cotton grass and some heather, but beneath the surface, or where the surface has been eroded, are areas of peat which might preserve evidence of the event for future generations to accidentally discover and ponder on its significance.

For every day that followed, the State's grip on power strengthened.

John Tyndall arrived at the mansion and was personally met by the general manager on the steps that led to the main entrance. His life had profoundly changed beyond recognition and had exceeded all his hopes and expectations since that first time when, it seemed a lifetime ago, he had been invited to the exclusive golf club and his reception was a cogent recognition of his political status, his reputation and national prominence. As he entered the building and walked towards the reception area the staff visibly stood in awe of his presence and clearly awaited an opportunity to assist him in any trivial or humble way. The general manager, with consummate diplomacy, confirmed that his suite was ready for him and the tedious necessity of registration was unnecessary in view of his reputation and his contribution to the well being of the nation.

The twelve members of the National Council and the two non voting members now assembled at the golf club had allocated up to three full working days to resolve the various problems that had arisen and to agree policies and decisive action to implement their policies. There was overwhelming agreement that for the time being the Queen's flight, along with the rest of the Royal family, remain a State secret, though, at the suggestion of the Council member nominated by the media, the press would maintain the facade and illusion that she and Prince Philip continued to attend various functions and events and also to perform her more formal responsibilities which would be supported by historical photographs that would be rigorously checked before publication.

The former Prime Minister's treachery would be further publicised alongside details of new, necessary restrictions that were being currently planned as if to personally associate Harold Wilson with the unfortunate necessity to implement such harsher conditions.

Manny Gold was effusively praised for his work bringing in the combined identity, ration and internal passport and that the first signs and anecdotal evidence proved that rationing had been welcomed by the nation at large bringing with it guaranteed supplies of food and banishing at a stroke, the profiteers and regional shortages some of which had been deliberately engineered by the R.Cs. themselves.

The Bureau of National Security and Intelligence (BoNSaI.) through its three representatives, confirmed that control of the country's borders, which included the ports which serviced shipping to the Iberian Peninsula, Scandinavia, Ireland, North America, South Africa and their staunch allies, New Zealand and Australia were being ruthlessly tightened to prohibit the flight of any unauthorised British nationals and the punishment for the offence and more so for those who assisted any attempt, was covered under the State of Emergency - Martial Law. Second Edition, Items (Two) and (Ten).

Withhold knowledge of any intention, act, statement or assistance from a Regional Commissioner, his deputy or the military authorities concerning any individual or body of persons who wish or intend to harm the State by Sedition, Revolution or Treason.

Enter a zone or area designated as prohibited unless permitted by a duly authorised official.

One hundred and eight people were currently being detained, ninety nine of whom had been caught trying to flee the country and the rest who had been complicit assisting them.

Since every port and technically the country's coastline had been declared a prohibited zone, a successful prosecution could be pursued (under Item Ten) since as certain representatives argued, a prosecution under the other section might not be proved. The three representatives of BoNSal. acknowledged the argument and confirmed that they were preparing further lists of offences which could be included in a new public announcement and which might consolidate all or some of the previous Editions (provisionally to be allocated as the State of Emergency - Martial Law. Sixth Edition).

Manny Gold, who had allowed the other Council members to comment on certain aspects of the Second Edition reminded everyone present that the internal passport of the new identity card completely covered what was a potential flaw or loophole in their control of an individual's movement or freedom. The document clearly, in absolute terms, stated that:

'It was an offence to travel outside of the area or areas permitted by the document without prior written permission.'

...and only the nature of the penalty had to be determined.

It was announced that thirty–seven people were also under arrest and were presently being held in the new detention centre on Dartmoor for offences under Items Four and Five of the State of Emergency - Martial Law. Second Edition...

Disseminate information prejudicial to the security and interests of the State and

Disseminate information, whether true or false, that could be reasonably expected to create public unrest, distress or disquiet.

Little time was spent on the subject, but later the local Regional Commissioner (whose area of authority included Dartmoor) arbitrarily imposed a period of imprisonment, without the right of remission, of ten years, instead of the mandatory death penalty.

It was at this meeting that the twelve new deputy Regional Commissioners were to be appointed and the National Council was at an *impasse* in their choice of appointees, for cliques or groups had coalesced and were championing their own choices.

Finally the log jam was broken because the dominant, major group comprising the representatives of the three military Services, combined with the Intelligence Services, John Tyndall (who astutely saw where power would ultimately rest) and the Commissioner of the former Metropolitan Police agreed, as a temporary measure and in view of the crucial necessity to...

"Clean and purify the nation of the endemic bacillus of 'subversives' and internal 'fifth columnists'" (a verbatim extract of a remark and an argument made by the authorised representative of the head of the former M.I.6).

It was then unanimously agreed that the twelve be drawn, four from each of the armed forces which would mirror the recent allocation for their immediate superiors but if and when any Commissioner or deputy was replaced for any reason, then his replacement would normally, but not absolutely, be chosen from their original military branch. An honest arrangement but in the future, following intrigues, power struggles and coups the military - intelligence-security axis asserted and maintained their dominance and power.

The Council member and Commissioner of the former Metropolitan Police representing the nation's previous civilian police forces confirmed that he had been informed and was receiving ongoing reports and intelligence from all over the country that there was swelling anger against the militarisation of what had been unarmed civilian forces which many officers feared might be used against their own communities. There was no empirical evidence to identify which specific groups were clamouring against the new direction that the lightly armed forces were being inexorably directed but anecdotally they were in the middle ranks where members had been serving for anything up to two decades whilst the younger officers were more amenable to more active and aggressive methods of control.

There was, however, unanimous agreement that ruthless action was ill advised and the sensible advice of the representative of the 'media' was accepted and promptly acted upon. The various police forces were to be amalgamated into larger and greater territorial constituencies roughly approximating to the twelve regions of the Regional Commissioners, resulting in an unnecessary layer of middle ranking officers who would be prematurely retired on very generous pension terms which cynically, when their influence had waned and was exhausted, and using the excuse of a future economic crisis, would find their generous pensions irrevocably scaled back. Furthermore it was agreed that members of the new paramilitary forces would be located in areas outside of the regions where they had family or community ties.

Two major decisions were also reached which were to have wide ranging consequences for the nation. The Trade Union movement had to be ruthlessly controlled and its existing leadership 'replaced' - a euphemism for a wholesale purge of its leaders and of the more aggressive 'firebrands' based at grass level. This was a step 'too far' for the Council member, who had been plucked from the ranks of the moderate mining union, who rendered a spirited argument in defence of pragmatic and modern trade unionism. He had literally issued his own death warrant as would others, for later the National Council would turn inward and without emotion or sentiment purge their body of those whose vision of the future and the pathway to its goal did not coincide with the destiny perceived by the military–intelligence - security group of members.

The representative of the former M.I.5 announced that BoNSaI already held lists compiled earlier by M.I.5 of 'subversives' and were drawing up secondary and tertiary lists. Those on any of the three lists could, or would form a potential obstruction to their plans and would have to be 'disposed of'. Journalists currently under arrest following the closing down of the Communist supporting newspaper, the *Morning Star*, were also to be 'disposed of' once the Intelligence Services were satisfied that they had been squeezed dry of any information and that the necessity of a trial or series of trials be dispensed with.

Documents that had been seized from the newspaper's offices, combined with lists recovered from the home of the former editor, his solicitors and, he could now reveal that for some time they had had a 'mole' buried deep in the heart of the newspaper, allowed them to compile a list of members of the now banned Communist Party and that mass arrests could be made in the next few days including subscribers to the closed newspaper whose particulars could and would be obtained from every local newsagent or identified by newsvendors.

He made a further announcement, the ramification of which was to have even wider ranging consequences both for the nation and the National Council itself. The former M.I.5 was being fundamentally restructured under the 'umbrella' of BoNSal and was to be designated the Special State Internal Security Service (S.S.I.S.S.) and would be responsible for internal security and, of course, responsible to BoNSal.

It was at this moment, when the intended direction of the Council's policy was clearly exposed, that apparently a minor number of Council members independently and then jointly objected to arbitrary execution or conviction without trial, claiming that the innocent might be gathered in with the guilty. The 'hard liners', who in reality were the grouping of the military – Intelligence services, supported by Tyndall, but not now the former Commissioner of the Metropolitan Police, realised that in the future those who were obstructing their plans would themselves be victims of the regime.

And what of Manny Gold who had sold his conscience? He also detected the seismic shift but temporarily remained neutral, deciding to act as an arbitrator, endeavouring to reconcile the two factions and differing interests, but he recognised where real power lay and he was aware of the precedent and events in post war Eastern Europe and how the Communists had insidiously and cunningly developed their power bases before they usurped and destroyed the existing democratic governments.

An unrealistic and cumbersome temporary compromise was reached, primarily to avoid a damaging schism in the National Council. The 'hard liners' appeared to back down and agreed that any conviction or execution for 'political offences' had to be approved by three R.Cs. comprised of pre determined different elements and if only one disagreed with the evidence, then the defendant would be held in prison until he (or she) appeared before a tribunal composed of three other Commissioners or their deputies, an arrangement that the 'hardliners ' resented for they saw in the liberal democratic process a return to the tried and failed methods of recognising defendants' rights ahead of the protection of the community's best interests.

It was doomed to failure and with its demise would follow the second purge of the leadership.

NINE

There then followed a brief period of consolidation while the S.S.I.S.S. prepared the groundwork for the 'disposal' of the trade union leadership and various 'trouble makers' whilst at the same time the new paramilitary force was being built up and indoctrinated in the use of force and applied violence, unfettered by the archaic and anachronistic considerations of responsibility to the community.

For the population at large a serene calm had descended. Their confidence in the reliability and availability brought on by food rationing and almost immediately afterwards the surprise de -rationing of milk, but not of cream, which the government, no, the new concept of national leadership, the New Order, confirmed was not healthy because of its high fat content, left the people confident that their new leaders genuinely had their best interests at heart, especially as a rumour suggested that shortly bread would also be de-rationed.

Furthermore the fear of, and potential threat of further nuclear attacks had subsided, as promised by a leadership where decisive action and honesty had become their hallmark.

True, there had also been an ugly rumour circulating that was discounted by the overwhelming bulk of the nation as being maliciously inspired and even more preposterous and baseless in fact; that every Commissioner and their deputies had been purged and shot, purely on the grounds that they had originally been appointed by the totally discredited Harold Wilson.

But the leadership, or more specifically the 'hardliners', essentially both led and propelled by the single mindedness of the representative from the recently formed S.S.I.S.S., Andrew Duggan, were only waiting and preparing for the moment when they felt confident that their plans could and would succeed. Central to their strategy was the conversion of the civilian police force to a lightly armed security force supported (when necessary) by the new paramilitary force whose members were drawn, in the main, from the three armed services and politically screened for their enmity, and perhaps pathological even rabid, hatred of communism, socialism, liberalism and the organisations that projected their policies. Nuclei of the nascent forces were being built up nationwide and would support the evolving former police forces in their new role protecting the State from its enemies and not in its archaic and obsolete role protecting the community from crime or disorder. Perhaps the new style police force wore a velvet glove over an iron fist whilst the new paramilitary force that would be brought in as support (for any eventuality from ruthless riot control to mass arrests of subversives) exhibited a callous, cold iron fist devoid of human emotion or humanity.

The Trade Union leadership and members of the Communist Party were to be their first targets whilst, in hushed tones, the fate of three members of the National Council were being weighed.

John Tyndall, his status and power continually increasing, was securely based in London assisted by the young, former senior Civil Servant who had been allocated to him when he had first achieved power and was proving to be an indispensible tower of strength, support and advice. It had been his suggestion that Tyndall remain in the capital where the real power lay, though Tyndall independently took the opportunity to fulfil a promise to his former mentor and installed Colin Jordan, together with his small band of sycophantic thugs, and out of the gaze of his fellow Council members ,to command the expanding system of prison camps in Scotland ,which Jordan sarcastically described as...

"Five star hotels waiting for their new guests."

TEN

The Trades Union Congress was due to convene, in Brighton, during September and the 'hard liners' agreed that whilst the new paramilitary forces would not have sufficient numbers to satisfactorily complete their trawl of the trade union leaders and other militants, the opportunity to arrest so many officials concentrated in one small area over a short period was an opportunity that could not be missed.

Early in August the Trade Union movement received an unexpected but welcome overture from their former comrade who had been surprisingly promoted to the status of member of the National Council. Of course the hard liners on the National Council had absolutely no intention of reaching a compromise but needed the time to prepare for the arrests and the purge of the union movement whilst the union representatives inferred that the National Council, like previous governments, were bending to the will and arguments of the unions. And yet a third perspective on the negotiations was adopted by the former mining leader who naively believed that not only did he have the authority that was mandated to him by his fellow Council members but the honourable good faith of the union negotiators and that, perhaps, once and for all they could resolve and end the nation's long outstanding history of industrial strife and differences.

Andrew Duggan (and behind him, the shadowy Intelligence services) was manipulating, orchestrating and pulling the strings of the National Council like a puppeteer.

During the protracted period of negotiations, when the union negotiators exposed their unrealistic, uncompromising and intransigent posture (which was described in the press and on radio and T.V. as 'groundbreaking negotiations that all parties recognised as the foundation of a partnership that would create a long term relationship between the National Council, workers and management') the S.S.I.S.S. was updating and expanding its lists of firebrands, union leaders and senior executives some of whom were originally on the primary list that had been bequeathed by the old M.I.5, whilst secondary and tertiary lists were being regularly updated and extended. Bookings for accommodation were regularly furtively checked from the five star 'Grand' down to the most humble 'Bed and Breakfasts', identifying the location of the many targets that would be arrested.

The first action of the new Special State Internal Security Service was planned for the early morning of the final day of the Conference when every available member of the new paramilitary force would be assembled overnight in London and would be brought down, not by train with the strong possibility that railway workers would alert their masters that there was something most unusual taking place, but by coaches which were commandeered on the Friday morning. They would arrive before dawn the next day and in conjunction with the local security force, seal off the town and especially the A 23 and 24 roads and would begin their arrests around seven a.m.

In all, a successful trawl would amount to approximately nine hundred and eighty men including some thirteen women, who would immediately be sent to London by the very same coaches that had brought their captors to Brighton. On arrival in London they would then be transferred onto trains that would terminate in Edinburgh before the final part of the journey, which would end the following day in the prison complex, overseen by the ruthless Colin Jordan and his henchmen who would only be notified of the prisoners' imminent arrival whilst they were en route to Edinburgh.

This was to be the crucial test of the resolve and power both of the National Council and of their public image, the New Order. Railway workers, ranging from signalmen to train drivers might refuse to facilitate the movement of the trains taking their union leaders, but in anticipation and in consummate preparation, agents of the S.S.I.S.S. had already visited Kings Cross station and had even noted the location of some horizontal beams that were not only accessible but conveniently located to be used as...

At the personal request and insistence of Andrew Duggan, the Commissioner of the former Metropolitan Police and a member of the National Council was under discreet observation, for he had shown his hand when the matter of automatic convictions had been raised. The consensus was that a replacement could be found from amongst his senior officers but even to instigate enquiries might alert him, though two candidates were already prominent, both eager for power and dissatisfied with the current nature of policing which they professed to be too tolerant of left wing political activists such as those who had supported the Campaign for Nuclear Disarmament(C.N.D.) and their marches and rallies, whilst members of the notorious and secretive Committee of 100 which subsequently became Spies for Peace (and had been infiltrated by an agent provocateur personally known to the author) were already prominently included on the secondary list of arrests .

The third was not unexpectedly Manny Gold, especially as he was a *protege* of Wilson and even though he had been a party to his betrayal and arrest. Despite his administrative contribution the hard liners were only prepared to accept total commitment to their goals and cause and Gold`s neutrality and attitude was seen and interpreted as being less than total commitment. No one was aware of his duplicity and ultimate loyalty to the United States or even doubted his loyalty to the State but what he apparently did not display was total dedication to the cause. Whether a 'six-sense' alerted him or if he was warned is now irrelevant but he decided on an act of treachery to show his loyalty and to divert any attention away from his relationship with the United States.

Within days of the National Council conference, Gold had indirectly passed to the ambassador a summary of the three day meeting and his assessment of their future plans but since he was not aware of the ongoing and imminent secret plan to purge both the trade union movement and the banned Communist party he could only observe and advise that punitive action was intended.

Gold realised that there was one obvious candidate who was expendable, plausible and readily available for sacrifice and by his actions he could ingratiate himself with the dominate faction in the National Council.

In an apparent act of hospitality, friendship and reconciliation, he invited the isolated and vulnerable man to a discreet lunch where he wined and dined him and made a proposition that he could not refuse, in the light of his current dire situation, caused by his association with Harold Wilson which had effectively totally ruined his career. Gold would give him an immediate introduction to the United States ambassador, who they both already knew, and he was to deliver certain documentation, personally to him, which the man eagerly agreed to. In the meantime Gold arranged to meet the ambassador and warned him that whilst he should receive the man with courtesy, that the whole purpose was to implicate him in a fraudulent scenario that the man wanted to pass secrets to the American government in exchange for asylum. The ambassador recognised the simplicity of the plan and in order to give the whole affair added credence suggested that he would contact a member of the National Council (Andrew Duggan), identify the potential traitor and then immediately contact Gold who would arrange for the arrest and disposal of Gerald Kaufman.

His 'disposal' was prompt, thus avoiding an independent interrogation that might cast suspicion on Manny Gold, however in the brief time before his execution, no doubt Gerald Kaufman was able to muse on his loyalty to the former Prime Minister and the urgency of his death unlike the fate that was to confront the trade union leadership.

ELEVEN

The early morning strollers, walking along the promenade and the pier, took little notice of the coaches being lined up outside of the Grand Hotel, but on closer inspection they would have observed that all the windows, both inside and out, had been obscured by black paper that had been firmly fixed by adhesive tape. Even the driver's windscreen had been partially covered, though it only slightly limited his field of vision. Their attention was addictively focussed on the unusual sight, and sound, of a helicopter hovering over the hotel.

Inside, the reception area was suddenly inundated by a vast body of security forces brandishing pistols and some machine guns, whilst a second wave rushed in and positioned themselves at what must have been pre determined strategic points including the entrance to the restaurant which even at two minutes past seven was full of diners enjoying both the excellent breakfast and the company of their fellow trade unionists. At the rear of the hotel further security forces had positioned themselves to seal off the building, whilst others entered and permeated through, and into, the working heart of the building.

Seemingly unobserved, three, or was it four men? (but definitely including Andrew Duggan), such was the unexpected chaos that no one was certain, sat themselves down inside the main lobby and extricated from briefcases, books that could have been, under different circumstances, collections of holiday photographs, but were in fact mainly portrait photographs, or in some cases full length photos of their intended victims, whilst from another bulging briefcase one of the men produced a file which contained personal physical details of the many men and women who were about to be detained, including information such as scars, tattoos (especially applicable to former members of the merchant and Royal navy), circumcisions, war wounds and visible disabilities.

Then, without warning, an ominous, sinister, almost evil spectre appeared from within the coaches as some two hundred black uniformed troops emerged; their black, calf length leather boots exactly matching their black helmets which had a unique design and shape not unlike a teardrop, and finally their black uniforms had an eerie similarity to the uniforms worn in the pre war science fiction film made by Alexander Korda, 'Things To Come'. But there was one final macabre part of their outfits which was almost frightening in itself: their faces were covered by black balaclavas or in a few cases the men wore sunglasses, the lenses tinted also black which completely obscured their eyes.

The planned shock of their unexpected arrival, their dispersal and subsequent actions make a full report of the ensuing events difficult to record but most, with great athleticism, leaped and bounded up the stairs, whilst a few, who had commandeered the lift, went up in small groups. They were armed mainly with machine guns, but others carried and wielded, and used with vicious devastating effect, a variety of instruments on angry residents who, with a knee jerk reaction, objected to their heavy handed actions. They did not realise that these men were unencumbered or unconstrained by the rule of law or the courtesies of civil conduct and their behaviour was both horrific and frightening both for their victims and other hotel guests.

The end justifies the means and the narrow gauge of the mesh would catch their victims with great success, proving the value of surprise, their ruthlessness and meticulous planning.

A few were caught, *in flagrante*, and some of those were photographed with their partners-of both sexes-possibly as evidence or to be used for the gratification of their captors. They were given an inadequate period to dress, the process being accelerated by the use of coshes, truncheons and the boot after which every prisoner was hooded, the only orifice being a small hole approximating to the area of the mouth but without any slits adjacent to the eyes or nose.

Mainly from the restaurant, but also from the lounges and bedrooms, some four hundred and twenty-five men and some women were detained, identified then hooded, before they were marched to the waiting coaches which began their journey to Kings Cross. For the next three hours or so, paramilitary forces brought in a further four hundred and forty overwhelmingly men but some eight women who had been arrested in various hotels, 'bed and breakfasts' and a few private homes, many, when their hoods were temporarily lifted, appeared dazed and unable to express their protestations and as they were marched out into the street and towards a constant stream of blacked out coaches, were unable to see four bodies, covered by blankets, of men who had, on the spur of the moment, decided to commit suicide instead of suffering an uncertain future.

Later, those who had to endure incarceration, would ask if...

"The living envied the dead?"

The S.S.I.S.S. had been cunning, devious and contemptible. At ten twelve a.m. they had suddenly closed, with the cooperation of the station authorities, Kings Cross, on the grounds, which were plausible, that there was to be a terrorist outrage and they suspected that explosives were to be used to kill, maim and disrupt the efficient running of the station. S.S.I.S.S. men dressed as army bomb disposal officers appeared to comb various parts of the cavernous complex, deliberately planting three devices and after having declared those areas safe and permitting railway staff to return, strategically exploded the three devices by radio, killing some twenty to thirty and injuring seventy to eighty other expendable people, a few minutes before the first coach arrived.

They then had the complete, dazed cooperation of the staff and it was unnecessary to use the horizontal beams for the execution of any of the staff if they had objected to the transportation of the trade union leaders and other members, whose identities remained anonymous as they were embarked, still hooded, into the empty carriages.

Later that day leading members, prominent and former supporters of the Campaign for Nuclear Disarmament and 'Spies for Peace', including the following (though the author has not been able to substantiate the identities of many of those who were alleged to have been were arrested) were transported to Dartmoor charged under Item Three of the State of Emergency- Martial Law. Second Edition...

Organise, promote, support, join or assist in an act or series of acts of terrorism.

> Gerald Holtom – the man who designed the C.N.D. symbol

> The historian, A.J.P. Taylor, who was a prominent founding member as was Fenner Brockway who was one of the few surviving M.Ps. and therefore a tangible link to the past and his leader, the now dead, deposed P.M., Harold Wilson

> The film director Lindsay Anderson (who apparently was singled out for the most cruel treatment) because of his documentary film, March to Aldermaston, a record of the Easter 1958 march.

> Canon John Collins, Kingsley Martin (editor of the New Statesman), Peggy Duff, Ritchie Calder, James Cameron, Michael Foot and J.B. Priestley- some of the original founders and members of C.N.D`s first executive committee.

Various sponsors including:

> John Arlott, actors and actresses Peggy Ashcroft, Dame Edith Evans, Miles Malleson and Flora Robson. Luminaries from the world of music, Benjamin Britten and Michael Tippett and from the Church, journalism, academia and the arts, the Bishop of Birmingham Dr. J .L. Wilson, Victor Gollancz, E.M. Forster, Rev.Trevor Huddleston, Henry Moore and the cartoonist 'Vicky' whose arrest and disappearance would later be the catalyst for an unsuccessful protest by sections of the emasculated media.

> Olive Gibbs - the then current chairwoman of C.N.D.

Some of the group of intellectuals and activists who founded the Committee of 100 including Ralph Schoenman, April Carter, Hugh Brock and Ralph Miliband.

Michael Randle- its first secretary.

Three of the notorious 'Wethersfield Six'- Ian Dixon, Trevor Hatton and Pat Pottle. Helen Allegranza and Terry Chandler died 'whilst resisting arrest' and Michael Randle was 'netted' in his administrative capacity.

Donald Rooum, Peter Cadogan and Diana Shelley were definitely arrested, the former in malicious response to an earlier incident when he proved that an offensive weapon had been planted on him, forcing a public inquiry and the eventual imprisonment of three police officers.

Some of the original signatories to the Committee of 100, many of whom had resigned as early as 1963 including:

An anonymous female who had, in reality, been a mole and is known to this author as well as being an agent of Joel Ben Yitzhak, John Braine, George Melly, Bernard R. Miles, John Neville and John Osborne.

TWELVE

The reality of the totalitarian and authoritarian state, unfettered by the constraints of the rules of natural law and justice, was clearly and tragically expressed, but not exposed, by the events at the complex of prison camps in Scotland, overseen and administered by Colin Jordan and his sadistic henchmen. Such were their indiscriminate, extreme and effective draconian methods that whilst their operation became the principle and standard upon which other camps later based their systems, there is empirical evidence, supported by some heavily redacted documentary reports, that in view of the perverted and totally inhuman methods employed (and even applied to some of the older females), that other camps literally moderated the degree of violence as they were unable to employ men, and sometimes even women, who were capable or willing to perform acts of unimaginable violence and sadism.

The horror began the moment the first batch of prisoners arrived at the camp, ironically numbered eighty-eight, after suffering the physical exhaustion of a forced eleven mile walk.

They were lined up, in rows, and made to stand erect for some two hours before any further action took place. Those, there were nearly thirty, three of whom were women, who succumbed and collapsed, were dragged away and summarily executed, deliberately in full view of the prisoners, on a set of raised gallows prominently situated in the centre of the parade ground, which formed the focus of the camp, and which were flanked on either side by the symbol of Christianity and brotherly love, two crosses, each some eleven feet in height and constructed of wood, the horizontal beam being subtly joined with the expertise of a master craftsman and joiner.

The cruel and callous executions instantaneously announced a message that was unambiguous and unequivocal. The inmates were at the mercy of their jailors.

The exhausted and frightened survivors were confronted by one of Jordan's most vicious followers who literally screamed out that every man and woman (there were, apparently, two women left in the initial group) had to take off all their clothes, be fumigated (of their obscene political opinions) and then report to give their name, their trade union affiliation and date of birth when they would be provided with their prison uniform which would prominently display their identification number on both their chest and back and that henceforth any communication between the jailors and prisoners and, if permitted , between prisoner and prisoner was by number only.

Thus the programme of dehumanisation had begun.

Communication between prisoners was only allowed and permitted by prior authority of the prison staff (and usually only at refreshment times) and on the absolute understanding that names were never to be used - only the prisoner's identification number - and that any violation would incur an appropriate punishment which was normally determined by the supervising jailor and could range from common assault with a convenient implement and always reduction to half rations to, including a case which appeared, but was redacted in a previously mentioned report, to breaking of both legs and then forcing the woman to crawl to her barracks and then her bunk.

They were not fed that evening, but for many the gift of sleep, on wooden bunks, without a blanket, was a refuge from the hell of their incarceration.

The purpose of the camps was punishment and re-education, since the social ideal of, and discredited concept of rehabilitation, was deemed unachievable. In reality the end product was death and disposal, for the calorific value of the prisoners` diet, set by the camp head, was never adequate for heavy manual labour and averaged, at best, one thousand four hundred calories per day, an amount that was grossly insufficient.

Whilst each camp in the complex was managed by one of Jordan`s acolytes, the day to day administration was run by former, or current non political prisoners who had completed or were serving terms for crimes of violence or those who were employed in the offices, who would have been convicted of commercial offences such as fraud or dishonest conduct.

If there is any doubt whatsoever in *YOUR* mind as *YOU* read this harrowing part of my investigation, do not hesitate to accept that the methods used were to remorselessly and utterly, by brutality, pulverise their victims, without conscience, demoralising the prisoners and totally subjugating their minds and bodies. Thus the endemic bacillus of subversion would be wiped clean unless death interrupted the process of cleansing.

The first morning at camp Eighty-Eight clearly and transparently exposed the nature of the horror and regimen that was to confront the beleaguered prisoners. They were woken at six -thirty a.m. and forced to shower (for hygiene purposes), assembled in the parade ground and counted, barrack by barrack. By the first morning, two had died in their sleep and mercifully never learned the daily routine.

They would be given one meal a day that would be served before returning to their barracks in the evening and during the day in a thirty minute hiatus when, subject to availability, water would be provided, *HOWEVER* [again the author`s own emphasis] this was conditional on each barrack meeting its quota and in default they would be provided with half rations only.

They were to construct a road that would ultimately terminate at a road junction, some eleven miles away.

Every prisoner, irrespective of sex, age or health was obliged to contribute their labour since this was no longer the Socialist Utopia where labour could be withdrawn, threatening the economic strength and vitality of the nation. Those who were unable to work or who were seen to avoid their fair contribution would automatically be placed on half rations which could not be supplemented by other prisoners` contributions and no medication would be provided, for what little was being manufactured, after staff had withdrawn their labour in the recent unofficial strikes that *THEY* had condoned or supported, was being issued to the nation's armed forces who had valiantly risked their lives defending the country.

There are few, if any monuments, to those who succumbed to the regimen. Those who died or were executed were removed from the camp, for hygiene reasons, and were buried in the foundations of the road that their comrades began to build with their own hands. Notification of death - there was a schedule of reasons used - was not sent to the next of kin but to their trade union affiliation (presumably for onward transmission) and included such stock reasons as:

Shot whilst attempting to escape

Executed for a major violation of prison rules

Cardiac infarction, diabetic coma or epileptic fit (despite compulsory regular daily administration, under supervision, of appropriate medication)

Consequence of injuries inflicted by other prisoners

Natural causes- usually defined as age, for anyone over sixty

Starvation was never cited, however the reason hunger strike was sometimes used was to falsely imply the victim's 'stand' against the authorities.

Some notifications even promised to forward on medical reports which, of course, never materialised and finally all correspondence bore the contact address of a Post Office Box Number (1663) in Wrexham which did not exist and letters were posted bearing a Wrexham franking making it impossible to locate the origin and location of the Scottish camps.

At that time the classical methods of torture were not employed for there was adequate evidence that the methods of violent brutality and remorseless demoralisation and intimidation were not only maintaining order but were re-educating the inmates, or those who were still alive.

But the continuous attrition and the casualty rate was inexorable and within four months all of the original prisoners had died, or been executed, the younger, fitter ones surviving the longest whilst the older, and usually overweight and unhealthy, died first. Their only tangible memorial being graffiti scratched on the walls of their barracks or the humble stone cairns which were placed at the side of the road and which were soon recognised for their true purpose by the next and subsequent generations of prisoners.

Most poignant was a brief inscription scratched on the wall of one of the barracks which stated that:

God have mercy on our souls,

and was signed...

Ray Buckton, ASLEF.

The 'success' and efficiency of the Scottish complex of prison camps was recognised by the decision to temporarily close down the two other complexes on Dartmoor and the Yorkshire Moors, necessitating the transfer of their remaining inmates, though less than a year later, the Dartmoor group of camps was reopened to take in the new and growing flood of civilian subversives and enemies of the State who would be subjected to a less harsher regime but still violent and brutal. The second generation of prisoners included and mainly comprised the trawl of C.N.D., Committee of 100 and 'Spies for Peace' members and supporters and Communist Party members (including subscribers to the Morning Star) who had been arrested in December, three months after the 'Brighton' sweep.

Interestingly, the worst fears of some members of the National Council were being proved correct for amongst the detainees were a group whose only connection was, as a matter of common kindness, that they had regularly purchased, for friends or work associates, the Morning Star from newsagents or vendors because of their convenient availability and had been later identified by the vendors as regular purchasers of the newspaper. Their protestations were in vain for there was no longer anyone to hear their pleas and their arguments were met by unbridled sadistic violence and if they were lucky a relatively quick death by crucifixion, though their legs were bent at the knee since it was found, by trial and error, that this posture increased the pain and placed greater strain on the lungs and heart.

Classical, and more modern methods of torture were never generally used in the camps, but were increasingly employed, on the unwritten authority of the S.S.I.S.S. by 'civilian' auxiliaries of the militarised former civilian police forces in their unremitting and incessant pursuit, not of confessions, but of information.

The relief of pain, by the body's own methods of unconsciousness or coma, or by confession was never tolerated. Only the admission of new information not yet known to the authorities was acceptable and even then was not a sufficient reason to cease the implementation of torture for usually more information would be forthcoming.

THIRTEEN

The perversion and suppression of news, information or knowledge was becoming an important demand of the New Order applied to the state controlled media, and necessitated, and created, an ever expanding bureaucracy dedicated exclusively to the control, supervision, dissemination and later the revision of any inconvenient, 'obsolete' or contradictory history.

The origins and concept lay in pre war Nazi Germany and the Soviet Union of Stalin. Adolf Hitler's brilliant Propaganda Minister ,Joseph Goebbels, oversaw a programme of propaganda based on the premise that society could and would be persuaded to believe any lie, if that lie was consistently repeated as a fact. In the Soviet Union, history was rewritten, supplemented by ,for example, the falsification of old photographs where new enemies of the State were literally erased from existence and the photographic evidence was reconstructed to hide the alteration.

The actual origins or genesis began in a series of articles and letters in *The Times* of November nineteen sixty-five, but no evidence now exists in the country of its original publication, for its genesis has been rewritten and reprinted, but it suggested, in an interview with the head of the New Order, John Tyndall, that the will of the people be heard in the form of a national survey so that the New Order could pursue policies that reflected the nation's demands and wishes. There then followed a deluge of letters , most of which could not be published, because of the continued (and deliberately engineered) shortage of newsprint, advocating different policies and priorities whilst some suggested, for economic frugality, that opinion polls be used again.

Of course the entire plan was a complete fabrication but allowed the State, through 'researchers', to openly approach, directly or indirectly, targeted 'subversives' for information included in a schedule of apparently bland but diverse subject matters, relating to the general concerns of the community, whilst as a facade other people were approached for their opinions to give credibility to the plan.

The 'results' of the 'Opinion Polls' began to be published late in February nineteen sixty-six and continued for six or seven weeks, whilst further 'polls' were 'taken' over the next six months or so.

The foundation of the deception was the intention to deceive and mislead the nation, creating a false perspective of the country's attitude to various problems. Thus the first and most dramatic result showed that eighty–three percent of the nation believed that the Queen and the Royal family were a cultural anachronism in the twentieth century (compared to another spurious figure of thirty-nine percent in an alleged poll taken four years before) and that a Republic, led by an elected President, would best represent the nation's real interests and image and be more representative of the country's values. The article generated an avalanche of letters, most of them genuine, though they were edited because of the restriction on space and in order that as many readers as possible could contribute to the debate in support of a Republic, whilst to give the appearance of balance a few letters were published supporting the Monarchy which were denigrated by a series of editorials supporting the people's will and suggesting a referendum on this most important of decisions.

The second poll result, published at the same time, was an overwhelming wish to end rationing of bread.

With supplies of refined flour and wheat constantly flowing from North America, much of which had been purchased at concessionary prices and stored in overflowing granaries, the New Order and John Tyndall were able to announce that the leadership had listened to the people and their wishes and were able to immediately de-ration bread and also to make available cream in a number of forms, for its health benefits, as a source of fat in winter was, and always had been, recommended as beneficial.

The hypocrisy and duplicity was compounded by an apology from John Tyndall, in a television interview, that he personally recognised the inconvenience of bread rationing which had been caused by Harold Wilson refusing to buy grain, spending the allocation on the purchase of computers from the United States which had no functional purpose in a modern state and were machines with no future in view of their limited capabilities.

By the end of nineteen sixty-five, the S.S.I.S.S. and the paramilitary civilian police forces had been firmly established, closely coordinated with an embryonic helicopter force and in the future the nation would, with dread and fear, associate the sound and sight of a helicopter with the ruthless black clad organisation.

Opposition from within the paramilitary civilian police forces had been cunningly neutralised by the implementation of the recommendation that the local forces be reorganised and reduced to twelve independent forces whose authority roughly approximated to the areas under the jurisdiction of the twelve Regional Commissioners.

The national 'daily newspapers' had been reduced to four in number, *The Times* (which absorbed both the *Daily Telegraph* and the *Guardian*), *Sun* (which had united with the left leaning *Daily Mirror*), *Daily Mail* (which, with undisguised pleasure, incorporated the *Daily Express*) and a new title, *The Peoples` Daily*, the official journal of the New Order with, allegedly, the largest national circulation. *The Evening News* became the only London evening paper, whilst nationwide, regional 'dailies' became virtual carbon copies of their London counterparts except for items of local interest.

The importation of foreign newspapers was strictly forbidden and only made available to the political elite whilst, where permitted, imported goods were *ALWAYS* [author's emphasis] examined for the wrapping paper might include pages from banned newspapers.

With ingenious deviousness and deceit, the *Sun* positioned and portrayed itself as the focus, not of an anti government front, but as an independent journal that questioned the policies of the New Order, receiving a continuous flood of correspondence in support of their position and at the other extreme a massive postbag accusing them of heresy and disloyalty. It will come as no surprise to *YOU*, the reader, to learn that details of those who openly supported the newspaper's stand became known to the S.S.I.S.S. with obvious later consequences.

There was no publicity or even reports in the press, radio or television when two members of the National Council were replaced on January first, nineteen sixty-six, as an Assistant Commissioner of the former Metropolitan Police, known for his very strong views on aggressive methods of control, replaced his superior and a recently retired Army Officer became responsible for the management of industrial affairs and workers` rights.

Relentlessly, the pendulum of political policy was swinging ever further towards the extreme right of the spectrum.

Whilst superficially the vast bulk of the people appeared satisfied, the S.S.I.S.S. was beginning to receive ominous and sometimes alarming reports of dissention and even dissatisfaction, including lists from the 'Sun' newspaper and in February nineteen sixty-six at a conference of the National Council, two matters received major attention resulting in decisions that would further change the nature of the country.

The National Council recognised that at some time in the future the nation might learn of the Queen's flight but they agreed that the situation be pre-emptied by a change in the hierarchical leadership and the creation of a figurehead President devoid of any executive power.

To resolve the problem a number of scenarios were proposed and considered, amongst which the first being the most simple, that the Queen unexpectedly abdicated leaving the country with her family, but that would expose the New Order to explain her reasons.

The second was feasible being her death in an accident (a plane or car crash was suggested) along with her son, who was second in line to the throne, though this scenario would again not resolve the problem, or thirdly, a scandal of epic proportion that might disgrace the Monarchy. With total control of the media the leadership could supervise any possible options however there always was the problem that an unexpected and therefore unpredictable element could arise and they could lose control of events.

It was then that the venal, corrupt and cynical Manny Gold put forward a suggestion that was above all simple, convincing, plausible and realistic. The demand for the abolition of the Monarchy and its replacement by a Republic and a titular head of state, a President, had to come from the people themselves and not from the New Order. A series of opinion polls, published during a dramatic crisis and scandal in the Royal family, would express the nation's increasing and overwhelming dissatisfaction and disgust of the Monarchy, whilst the media would begin a parallel campaign which would increase in magnitude and even viciousness, culminating in a national referendum, which for appearances sake, would be overseen and supervised by representatives of two neutral European states, Switzerland and Sweden, the former a Republic and the latter, a monarchy.

The campaign to vilify and humiliate the Queen and Royal family would have to be extremely thorough and scrupulously punctilious. It could, and did, begin with obtuse and obscure references and comments in the national newspapers, seemingly unfathomable and incomprehensible cartoons and captions, paragraphs or photographs missing from articles, reports of misbehaviour by unnamed, well known, public faces and the implication that the freedom of the press was being strangled , which, in their perverted sense of irony, was true The options could be limitless and required the leadership of a great conductor and an experienced first violin.

The representative of the media was the obvious choice and he readily agreed to accept the task, though he demanded and received approval that he 'chair' a small group of politically reliable like minded journalists, advertising executives, public relations consultants and even an author of political fiction to produce a plan which was presented within ten days, approved and by the beginning of March nineteen sixty-six had begun insidiously and perniciously to undermine the absent monarchy.

At the heart of the deception was the fraudulent allegation that a member of the Royal family had been involved in a fatal accident which they had, through their influence, bribery and corruption 'covered up' and that a female passenger in the car had suffered a miscarriage. The perpetrators of the deception intended to use and actually resorted to every obscene and vile method to poison the people's minds and influence their opinions, despite the fact that it was a capital offence under Items Four and Five of the State Of Emergency - Martial Law. Second Edition:

Disseminate information prejudicial to the security and interests of the State, and,

Disseminate information, whether true or false, that could be reasonably expected to create public unrest, distress or disquiet.

The second matter which concerned the National Council were the S.S.I.S.S. and BoNSal reports on growing dissention and dissatisfaction combined with the 'lists' supplied by the' *Sun'* newspaper.

It was apparent that their efforts to placate the nation could never be totally or absolutely successful however it was imperative that they remain fully vigilant and allow their enemies some very limited leeway to express their dissatisfaction and therefore expose their disloyalty.

The 'terrorist' explosions and subsequent chaos at Kings Cross station had shown how an event could be managed and turned to an advantage and further acts of alleged terrorism would be employed to place the nation in a continuous state of alert against internal 'fifth columnists' and external infiltrators.

Bombings of public places, interference with public transport vehicles such as buses and trains causing them to crash and the malicious spreading of untrue rumours were approved, but more ominously it was agreed that individuals and whole groups could be observed by telephone 'tapping', the opening of mail, the 'bugging' of targeted individuals' homes, places of work and at social centres such as public houses, restaurants (or what passed as restaurants as living standards had begun to deteriorate) or cinemas which could become targets for surveillance without a court order for the courts had been dissolved. This observation, when made by Andrew Duggan, received applause and sarcastic comments of mockery as the vestiges of democracy stood like broken ruins of ancient and long forgotten cities.

An even more threatening development to the individual's liberty which, in truth, had ceased to exist, was the formation of a new nebulous organisation of individuals, whose only allegiance was to the New Order and who would act as the eyes and ears of the Party and who would report any acts of disloyalty and whose only reward was the appreciation of the Party.

Malicious rumours were later sown throughout the country alleging that the underage heir to the throne was the drunken driver of a vehicle involved in the fatal accident, that his sister (other names were mentioned) was the passenger but above all were the ludicrous and, of course, wholly spurious and mendacious suggestions that the Royal family, and the Queen and her advisors in particular, were acting in a morally corrupt manner, suppressing details of the incident.

At the same time the National Council decided to find a compliant and malleable candidate who could fulfil their criteria as a future figurehead President. In order to give his office status and respect it was agreed that a national ballot would be held offering two candidates, once again supervised by independent representatives from Switzerland and Sweden, and that the preferred candidate would receive a substantial, but credible majority. Since the identities of the current twelve members of the National Council were not known to the general public, and indeed no group photograph of the twelve together or photographs of individual members had ever been published, it was agreed that one member might be chosen to oppose the successful candidate and that he would not lose his place on the National Council.

John Tyndall was the most obvious candidate, well known and highly regarded, but his candidature *MIGHT* generate too much popular support and therefore defeat the whole purpose of the exercise.

Fate conspired to present the members of the National Council with a potential candidate who fulfilled their requirements for he was mature, urbane, well read, educated and experienced in various aspects of power for he had been, at one time, a government minister and who confided in his *protégé* that he would be amenable to the position of President even though it was devoid of power. However his name and reputation might render him unacceptable to the British people.

FOURTEEN

The formal purpose of the reception was to introduce the two new members of the National Council to the international diplomatic community and the representatives of the many 'governments in exile', however the event was eclipsed and overshadowed by the arrival, with his *protégé* John Tyndall, of the infamous, even notorious Sir Oswald Mosley. He very quickly became the focus of attention for many of the guests and for some he was viewed as an historical relic of an age and of events that were now totally irrelevant to the world of the nineteen-sixties, whilst many others, who were aware of his reputation and record, in general considered his presence and philosophy repugnant. But there were also those who, out of interest, were prepared not only to tolerate his presence but also to listen to him.

He told them not only what they wished to hear but also aired views and opinions on some matters that they were not prepared to confront.

Over the next few days, many, a majority, of the Regional Commissioners, together with most of the deputy Regional Commissioners who were also present at the reception, convened unofficial *ad hoc* meetings and communicated their surprise considered findings with one another.

His charismatic personality but above all the persuasiveness of his cogent arguments created a dilemma which revolved around two basic questions that could only be answered by the man himself and by the nation. Was he sincere and was the country prepared to accept him in view of his record and reputation?

They overwhelmingly concurred that he had radiated an almost magical charisma and still, mysteriously, was able to hypnotically mesmerise his audience with his personality, charm and, above all, the force of his arguments. No wonder a generation had been seduced by his compelling arguments three decades before. But history and events had proved him woefully wrong and for the nation the raw memories of family members who had given their lives and who lay in unmarked graves in the Far East, North Africa, in the bitterly cold seas of the North Atlantic and on the beaches of Normandy, Dunkirk and Dieppe, together with still vivid recollections of their own sacrifices on the Home Front were memories that could be quickly raised and would scupper his possible re-emergence.

His comments and observations had drawn an ever increasing audience that evening and his apparent sincerity and ability to answer unscripted questions pleased certain interested listeners.

But actions and deeds speak louder than words.

"Yes, He had been profoundly wrong about the Jewish contribution to society and the cause of freedom and democracy... He had confused Jewish involvement in the leadership of the Bolsheviks under Lenin as part of a nonexistent Jewish-Zionist conspiracy when Communism was then and remained to this day the enemy of freedom... How right Winston Churchill was in the nineteen thirties to speak out alone as he warned a complacent Government, Parliament and a nation still traumatised by the horrors of the First World War and the savage blow of the Depression, of the 'Gathering Storm'...His incarceration, early in the war under Defence Regulation, section 18B... How, like millions of others, he had been totally sickened when the reality of National Socialism was exposed as forces from both East and West begun to liberate the Death Camps...There was so much in his life and career that he would alter but he was unable to turn back the clock."

Referring, with deep emotion, to the great Persian poet and mathematician Omar Khayyam and his epic work, The Rubaiyat, he recited a Quatrain with the immense power of a respected Shakespearean actor, almost magnetically drawing them to his beating guilty heart...

"The Moving Finger writes; and, having writ,

Moves on: nor all thy Piety nor Wit

Shall lure it back to cancel half a Line,

Nor all thy Tears wash out a Word of it."

It was as though he was confessing his failures and that he was using the opportunity to reach out both to all those who were in that immediate circle of listeners and the nation at large.

"It was crucial that the New Order and above all the National Council stood by their principles for it was necessary to cleanse the nation of the infection which had permeated and infected the body politick. He had been right, for Communism was an infection that had imprisoned and destroyed much of Western, Central and Eastern Europe and was now only being contained and held at bay by the determined forces of freedom and democracy.

He respected the values of Socialism and he would remind his audience that many years before he had been drawn to the values of the Fabian society. It was not that Socialism was wrong, it was that the nation had been insidiously infected and undermined by enemies whose loyalties lay in Moscow and Peking and to men whose agenda was anathema to everything that the British people stood for."

For some of those who had been present, they specifically remembered his closing comments, as if they were an answer to their search, for here was a man who could lead the nation as a caring shepherd, whilst the National Council could remould the nation and create a society and authority unaffected by either the ballot box or any ground swell of popular opinion and opposition, for any isolated dissidents would be unable to muster support or be able to communicate or broadcast their ideas. Less than three days later John Tyndall received an unexpected telephone call from Andrew Duggan and the owner of the *Sun* newspaper asking if he could set up a meeting with Sir Oswald Mosley to discuss his possible contribution to the nation's future and wellbeing.

The meeting was held in John Tyndall's suite and possibly consisted of five people only. I would emphasise that no records of the meeting, if recorded, now exist and the fact of the meeting and the cynical and squalid agreement that was reached are the reports of secondary and tertiary sources.

The fifth person at the meeting was Tyndall's personal assistant and previously his senior civil service advisor who had been trained in the morally corrupt art of both facilitating his master's wishes whilst at the same time being able to guide him in the most prudent and pragmatic direction.

Whether or not they actually believed in Mosley's profound change of political direction or, if in the privacy of the meeting, he confessed his dishonesty, we will never know, for the only tangible result of the meeting was that the owner of the *Sun* newspaper and chairman of the committee recently set up to disseminate false information to defame the Queen and Royal family also, unofficially, begin a parallel process to promote Sir Oswald Mosley as President elect ,a *de facto* action that was later retrospectively approved and endorsed at the next formal meeting of the National Council.

As a postscript to these events it is alleged, that in a secret report personally delivered to the United States ambassador by Manny Gold, and now buried deep in the National Archives in Washington, that Mosley openly admitted at the meeting that his political philosophy was ruled by pragmatism and opportunism but above all by the views espoused by his *protégé* in his nineteen sixty-two work, The Authoritarian State, which in part, had been inspired and based on their conversations. Indeed, if anything, he truly believed, from remarks made by his *protégé* , that the National Council intended, and the direction would receive his total endorsement, to create or even turn back the clock to a political feudal society where the people would be ruled, absolutely, by a new generation of barons, who, in no way would ever subscribe to a modern day version of the Magna Carta.

Manny Gold is also alleged to have reported that Mosley claimed that the concepts of democracy, elections and above all secret ballots were a Utopian dream, for the nation was not fit to benefit from such a system because they were always bound by short -sighted and short-term self interests and not the best interests of the nation as a whole and that the most successful states were ones where power was concentrated in the hands of the few who also were the most competent to rule the many.

Mosley, in conclusion, according to Gold`s report, stated that it would be necessary to destroy the so called 'middle classes', business people, professionals, journalists and above all intellectuals who might create opposition to the new hierarchy, for between the elite leadership and the vast bulk of the nation would be a vast bureaucracy of workers loyal not to the state but to the New Order which in reality was the visible face of the National Council and as a figurehead, he Sir Oswald Mosley, would lead and guide the people.

The National Council agreed that by July a referendum would be held to abolish the Monarchy and by September a second referendum would take place to elect a popular President as head of the new democratic Republic. In the meantime the security force, helped when necessary, by the paramilitary force and assisted by intelligence obtained from sources such as the '*Sun*' newspaper and the new embryonic surveillance organisation of loyal New Order members, who, at the lowest level, but closest to the beating heart of the country, would identify disloyalty, dissent and the worst crime of all, opposition to the absolute rule of the Party.

FIFTEEN

BOLSHEVISM from MOSES to LENIN by DIETRICH ECKART, subtitled...

A DIALOGUE BETWEEN ADOLF HITLER and ME.

The following are sequential excerpts...

"And I will set the Egyptians against the Egyptians: and they shall fight every one against his brother and every one against his neighbour; city against city and kingdom against kingdom. And the spirit of Egypt shall fall in the midst thereof; and I will destroy the counsel thereof: and they shall seek to the idols, and to the charmers, and to them that have familiar spirits, and to the wizards"...

"Remember how it was here in Munich during the communist takeover? "I interjected." The houses of the Jews certainly weren't marked with blood, but there must have been a secret arrangement, because among all those who suffered the misfortune of a house search not one was a Jew. As a matter of fact, one of the stupid Red troopers who had me by the hair answered my sarcastic question by explaining that it was forbidden to search the Jewish houses"...

"And in all eternity nothing will change," he proceeded," so far as the attitude of the Jews toward our kings and our leaders is concerned. To destroy them is their eternal sin, and when they can't accomplish this by force, then they will use cunning. Whenever we have a strong leadership, the Jews are obliged to keep their noses clean. Our leadership can be truly strong, however, only if it is based completely in our people"...

"Tell me", I interrupted him:" strictly speaking, do you consider the Jew to be national, or international?"

"Neither", was the answer. "One who really feels international has as much regard for the rest of the world as he does for his own nation. Were our so-called international swarms really like that - fine. But I fear that they are secretly more concerned with the attitude of the rest of the world toward themselves than with their own attitude toward the world. Internationalism requires basically good intentions. But The Jew fundamentally and completely lacks these. He hasn`t the remotest idea of classifying himself with the rest of humanity. His aim is to dominate others in order to extort from them at his leisure"...

"In the year 1870", he rejoined," we Germans had the privilege of being a great people. The Jews considered that the time had arrived for replacing the French emperor, who had become undependable, with a pliable president"...

"The press, 'that select tool of the Anti- christ', as Bismarck called it, has designated us as 'Boches' and as 'Huns'"...

"Giordano Bruno called the Jew 'such a pestilential, leprous, and publicly dangerous race that they deserved to be rooted out and destroyed even before their birth'. This genial philosopher was burned at the stake. For his heresy? Opponents of the Church were swarming in Italy during his time, yet he, the most impartial of them, was seized"...

"I really doubt that there is any sort of medical encyclopaedia which contains terms suitable for describing the Jewish megalomania", he said. "But what an incredible talent they have for disguising it!"...

"Some religion! This wallowing in filth, this hate, this malice, this arrogance, this hypocrisy, this pettifogging, this incitement to deceit and murder - is that a religion? Then there has never been anyone more religious than the devil himself. It is the Jewish essence, the Jewish character, period!"...

"The truth", he said," is, indeed, as you once wrote: one can only understand the Jew when one knows what his ultimate goal is. And that goal is, beyond world domination, the annihilation of the world. He must wear down all the rest of mankind, he persuades himself, in order to prepare a paradise on earth."

Author`s note: Some of the *MORE* vicious, vindictive, violent, vile, lurid and perverted extracts have not been included.

The full resources of the state were urgently employed, both to denigrate the monarchy and at the same time promote, first the image, and later the potential candidature of the nation`s caring shepherd. But there were hurdles and objections to overcome, even though the National Council had total control of the media and a pool of various options to direct and persuade the people.

The National Council, through its political image and arm, the New Order, could have presented the nation with a *fait accompli*, but Gold`s bold and wise suggestion that the overthrow of the monarchy must appear to be the democratic will of the people, should equally if not more so apply to the election, by a democratic vote, of a president, albeit if necessary, by some injection of additional votes to produce the exact required result.

Oswald Mosley`s first public 'appearance' was preceded by major articles in *The Times* and the *Sun* essentially 'promoting' a recorded radio broadcast that their correspondents had previewed. You will note that the title 'Sir' had been dropped at the outset of the campaign in order to present him as a man of the people, and not of the Aristocracy, to gain the nation`s support, but in any case a plan was put in place to guarantee the required outcome at the forthcoming poll which would be announced when the leadership considered the time to be opportune and, of course, after an earlier plebiscite or referendum had overwhelmingly supported the abolition of the Monarchy.

The interview was an extended and carefully scripted and edited version of the remarks that he had recently made at the private reception, placing great emphasis on his fundamental change of heart and regrets on the harsh and bitter legacy of his pre war record but especially his new attitude towards the Jews and his recognition of the war time leadership of Winston Churchill, especially during the darkest days of nineteen forty to forty one. Almost seven minutes of the sixteen minute interview concentrated on the threat and evil of Communism, including a sincere statement that some days before he had anonymously travelled around parts of London and the suburbs and been shown the damage caused by the nuclear attacks and how, with the practical help of the New Order, the local communities were physically rebuilding both their lives but also the infrastructure.

The committee carefully analysed the public`s response to the broadcast, relying mainly on the *Sun`s* 'postbag', noting that the newspaper had cleverly, initially positioned itself against Mosley by reminding their readers, in an editorial the day after the broadcast, of Mosley`s 'pedigree' whilst accompanying the editorial were archive photographs of both one of his infamous rallies in London and the notorious and brutal 'battle of Cable Street'.

The 'postbag' was enormous, reflecting Mosley`s reputation and iconic place in the history of extreme Right wing politics. Over twelve thousand letters were received of which over half confirmed  the authors` continued ,vehement opposition both to the man and the sincerity of his new found values, indeed there was a common thread running through the letters which exposed the writers` contempt for the false sincerity of MOST [ author`s emphasis] politicians irrespective of their party allegiance. Significantly ,whilst more than half were against him , a sizeable minority, some forty four percent, either expressed neutral views or were prepared to accept his profound change of heart, but when combined with his attack on Communism , were in full support of his position.

More importantly, an in depth analysis, using the residential areas of their correspondents, showed that 'working class' readers and correspondents were, in general, in opposition to Mosley whilst the ' middle classes', the very group that Mosley wished to destroy , were his largest supporters, possibly mirroring events thirty–five years before in Weimar Germany and the middle classes` support for Adolf Hitler and the Nazis struggle against the left of centre political parties (together with uncontrolled Trade Union power) and above all Communism which was seen as the potential destroyer of middle class values and property rights.

Oswald Mosley was then placed in the proven, capable hands of the same group that had earlier coached his protégé in the art of modern communication techniques and the presentational skills associated with television, concentrating on softening his image and calming his now obsolete and unattractive, messianic, tyrannical and dictatorial style.

His first pre recorded television appearance was to be a 'live' interview followed by questioning from an 'invited' audience made up of various segments of the general public who had responded to requests shown earlier on television (and broadcast on the radio) for tickets.

Of course, unless YOU the reader are totally naive, the audience was made up of actors and proven supporters of Mosley, whilst only a few places were made available to the public and as you will soon read, virulent anti Mosley questions were permitted, even encouraged, for the vast bulk of the audience, the interviewer and Mosley himself had been previously prepared in order to MANIPULATE [author`s emphasis] the difficult probing questions that his detractors put to him.

The first half of the hour long programme, which was constantly interrupted by the boos and almost infantile heckling of his detractors - and which would ultimately play into the hands of their more disciplined and organised opponents - was a probing interview of questions that Mosley had had earlier notification and had prepared or had assistance preparing his answers. Great emphasis was laid on his leadership of the British Union of Fascists, their, and his anti-Semitism and his failed bid as recently as nineteen fifty-nine to re-enter Parliament on an extreme 'right wing' agenda of policies.

The questions and the questioner allowed him the broad latitude and freedom to apologise for his mistakes both personal and...

"As the leader of many decent people who, after the British Union of Fascists had been proscribed, had given their lives and future for King, country, freedom and liberty."

He emphasised that in the six years since he had stood at Kensington North he had had much time to reflect on his career but more importantly on the reality of the new world order which was simply the confrontation of the Western world`s concept of freedom and justice which now stood resolutely against a political concept and force that had consistently represented political oppression and the asphyxiation of individual liberty, advocated central state control but above all the forceful imposition of a single, centrally controlled ideology which would not tolerate intellectual dissention or even questioning [Thus he had unwittingly, succinctly described the nightmare that was like an insidious, uncontrollable cancer destroying the fabric of Britain and its heritage].   He had been right in nineteen thirty–five to oppose Communism and all it stood for and he would stand up, it need be alone, to defend his principles and those of the British people.

The pre-prepared questions concerning the Monarchy were cleverly and cunningly answered, for he believed that the New Order genuinely represented the people, whilst the old political parties, which had now been proscribed [therefore immediately confronting his television audience with the intellectual comparison of the New Order's actions banning other political parties with the Communists' banning any opposition], had an inherent loyalty to the Queen and more importantly the oath that an M.P. had to swear incorporated their loyalty to the Crown.

He believed that the New Order was listening to the heartbeat of the nation and if they demanded a democratic vote to resolve the future of the Monarchy then he felt certain that their demand would be met.

In response to a 'planted' question on his own personal attitude to the future of the Monarchy, he cleverly avoided a direct answer, only saying that:

"He had ambiguous, conflicting and contradictory thoughts on the matter, but certain facts had been made known to him in the last few days, which were not in the public domain because malevolent forces had maliciously tried to keep them from the nation and even the New Order. He intended to have them made public, including a car..."

The transmission had been deliberately crudely edited at this most crucial juncture in order that the viewers would be alerted to the propaganda which would allow gossip and hearsay to amplify and circulate further wild speculation.

As anticipated, the few genuine members of the 'loaded' and biased audience were aggressively hostile and as previously stated booed and heckled Oswald Mosley, indeed they had been chosen solely for these expected actions as it would give an impression of neutrality by the broadcaster. Two questions were raised, each vindictive and malicious, both in their wording and the manner of their delivery, generating a pre planned verbal torrent of abuse in reply from the rest of the audience.

Was he an Anti-semitic bastard? and the other question concerned the integrity of his opinions without accusing him of being a liar.

But the questions, amongst others that were not asked, had, in general, been anticipated and his answers had been carefully planned and the audience coached in their response.

Mosley quietly replied to his antagonists, reminding them not only of their responsibilities in a democratic state but that their questions would never be allowed in the totalitarian state that their behaviour indicated where their loyalties really lay. But they lived in a new society where tolerance and the genuine interests of the people were paramount and not where the bullies or the loudest held sway...

"Yes, to my eternal shame I was a rabid Anti-semite but events and history have shown me how wrong I was and that thank God what happened in Europe never happened on our soil because we were led by Churchill and a government that truly represented the people and our Christian values which also answers your other nasty question."

The room reverberated to the sound of the majority as they vigorously applauded Mosley and their hoots of derision which were directed towards the cowering group of men and two women who symbolised the cancer within the nation.

An immediate crude analysis by telephone showed a surge in support and popularity for Mosley which was substantiated by later, more intense, wider polling and which confirmed an even greater degree of support and which was published without adjustment, though the National Council feared an increase would not appear credible.

SIXTEEN

The British embassies in Bern and Stockholm were instructed to open secret discussions with the Swiss and Swedish governments to provide monitoring facilities for a possible referendum and subsequently of a popular vote to elect a President, if and only if the nation had previously voted in favour of abolishing the Monarchy.

Two members of the National Council led the discussions, assisted by the local ambassadors and their diplomatic staff. One of the two was later identified as the proprietor of the *Sun*, the other, tentatively, as the new head of what was formerly the Metropolitan Police. They realised that both governments were aware that the Queen and members of the Royal family had fled to Canada and that possibly they had also been informed by their London embassies that a propaganda barrage was in full swing intended to destroy the Monarchy`s reputation. They explained that there was a growing tidal wave of anger against the Monarchy and it was believed inevitable that the National Council would have to announce and hold a referendum on the future of the Monarchy and it was essential that the voting and counting was not only conducted to the highest traditions of British integrity but was seen, by independent observers to be, despite its archaic procedures, completely honest. The Monarchy was the fulcrum upon which the stability of the nation rested but they were determined to accede to the wishes of the people and avoid any destabilisation or civil strife, such being the present volatile and potentially anarchic atmosphere.

Two weeks later, which coincided with a further strengthening of Mosley`s position, and the secret approval of another presidential candidate, confirmation was received, agreeing to provide some one thousand observers to supervise, if requested, initially only the Referendum.

The die had been cast. In mid June, the latest proclamation,

STATE OF EMERGENCY- MARTIAL LAW.
SEVENTH EDITION

appeared, announcing that on Saturday, July 30th (which also was to be a national holiday) a Referendum would be held throughout England, Wales and Scotland (Northern Ireland was not included, not for constitutional reasons but intentionally, as the authorities did not wish to inflame passions between the Protestants and Roman Catholics) to determine the future of the Monarchy. Voting would be open to anyone aged eighteen and over and they could vote at any polling station on production of their identity card which would be stamped on entry between the voting hours of six-thirty a.m. to ten-thirty p.m.

The Referendum would comprise one question and the nation's wishes would be decided by a simple majority:

DO YOU WANT THE INSTITUTION OF THE MONARCHY TO CONTINUE OR DO YOU WANT IT ABOLISHED IN PERPETUITY? CONTINUE / ABOLISHED

Unreported and overshadowed by the momentous consequences of the forthcoming Referendum, which had caught the mood and imagination of the nation and fanned by biased statements and opinions from the Republican leaning media, with the minimum of fuss, the first arrests of dissidents had begun under the STATE OF EMERGENCY- MARTIAL LAW. SECOND EDITION, Item Twenty including all of the hooligans who had been seen on television, maliciously interrupting free speech by their constant interventions during Oswald Mosley's interview.

John Tyndall had been selected as the second candidate to stand in the Presidential election which would take place after the proclamation:

STATE OF EMERGENCY- MARTIAL LAW.
EIGHTH EDITION

was published and which would formally announce and confirm the result of the Referendum but would also confirm both the abolition of the Monarchy and the sequestration of all their lands, property and chattels some of which, by historical convention, had been held in trust for the benefit of the nation. The proclamation would conclude with the announcement that henceforth, the Nation, in consequence of the democratic will of the people, had now been reconstituted as a Republic to be headed by a President who would be elected by a popular majority vote of the people.

John Tyndall had been selected to oppose his mentor, not because of his reputation or to give the false appearance that the election was a genuine choice but because the National Council had effectively few other choices. They had discredited the now defunct Houses of Parliament and whilst there were still alive a band of mainly geriatric members of the abolished House of Lords none could be put forward, because of their former membership and the desire of the National Council to sever all and any links with the *ancien regime.*

The net had been cast wide to find a candidate who was not only prepared to stand, but was acceptable (to the National Council and the people) and suitable for the figurehead role.

Bernard Law Montgomery, the hero of El Alamein, was thought a most suitable candidate (even though he had been ennobled a Viscount and had been a member of the House of Lords) but was in declining heath and more importantly, because of his independent nature, it would not be possible both to control his utterances or to impose upon him the duty of making pre-prepared rigid public statements; but above all he had seen through the true nature of the New Order and the National Council and was not prepared to become, for him, a betrayer of all his values. Even a footballer was suggested!, thus potentially reducing the position of President to that of an entertainer. Bobby Moore, captain both of England and West Ham United was considered in view of his reputation and the fact that he would have led England in the cancelled World Cup finals, though every pundit and informed commentator believed that the team would not have survived the opening round.

In the end there was no one to turn to other than John Tyndall.

Polling would take place at nearly three thousand centres throughout England, Wales and Scotland, and for administrative purposes the twelve Regional Commissioners would supervise polling centres within their jurisdiction, which would be manned by members of the New Order. It was estimated that the Referendum could produce a potential electorate of some twenty million voters, whilst it also meant that the operation could *NOT* be properly supervised by an adequate number of observers provided by the Swiss and Swedish governments therefore permitting some vote rigging or creative counting.

Each and every polling centre would be open for sixteen hours and would have a minimum of fifteen desks (and the same number of ballot boxes) manned by loyal, specially trained members of the New Order who would work in four, four hour shifts, whilst the overstretched observers would not be expected to supervise each and every centre for the whole period. Voters could be promptly processed, for it was only necessary to identify them against the photograph on their identity card which would then be stamped as there was now no necessity to check the Electoral Registers which were, in the main, now out of date.

It was calculated, based on nearly five hundred voting centres nationwide, that by infiltrating around eighty voters to each centre (staggered and spread out through the sixteen hour day), each with no more than twenty-five fraudulent votes that bore the correct stamp, then the vote to abolish the Monarchy would be increased by about one million .

Production of some twenty thousand hand held mechanical counting devices, which would be used by the poll clerks to record each voter was put in hand, but a few days before the distribution of the devices they were found to be both unreliable if not faulty and the Referendum was saved by the assistance of the Swedish Government who came to the rescue, supplying at the last moment four thousand units from their own factories. The number of people who were a party to the fraud was reduced for instead of the poll clerks recording the number of voters handed ballot papers, responsibility passed to the marshalls (who were also supervised by the presiding officers) and who controlled the queues, for they would perform the counting, allowing errors to be deliberately made.

Counting of the votes under the careful, watchful eyes of the independent observers and the presiding officers took place on the following day, Sunday July thirty-first, and at each centre the total number of votes cast was checked against the total of the mechanical counting devices and whilst there were minor deviations, the Presiding officers were satisfied to confirm and verify the matches and since the electorate were permitted to vote at any centre there could be *no* check on the number of voters against the obsolete and unused Electoral Registers.

Each polling centre would then, by telephone, confirm to its Regional Centre, which was one of twelve nationally (the Scottish region was divided and incorporated in two of the other regions) the total number of votes cast, the number of spoiled votes and then the total number either in favour of abolition or continuation of the Monarchy.

These figures would then be collated and when all the outlying polling centres had reported their figures then each of the twelve Regional Centres would confirm, by secure telex, their final figures to the London centre.

The twelve members of the National Council were informed of the final result some time before they ascended the plinth at the base of Nelson`s Column, satisfied with the emphatic outcome which rendered their chicanery unnecessary. This was the first time that the National Council had been seen in public though their presence remained unannounced and the only member who was readily identifiable was John Tyndall and the prime subject of attention from the live television, radio and film coverage.

On Monday, August first, at one-seventeen p.m., from the plinth of Nelson`s Column in Trafalgar Square (which was clad in scaffolding awaiting the repaired statue of the great sailor), the National Returning Officer, a man of impeccable honesty, who had last performed a similar task at the Kensington North Parliamentary constituency at the nineteen fifty-nine General Election, rose from his seat and looked out onto an awesome sea of humanity and began his brief statement.

Trafalgar Square, St. Martin in the Fields and Whitehall, as far South as the Cenotaph, was a seething mass of foaming humanity, their sweat, exacerbated by the warm August day and their density combined to ferment an almost putrid odour. The foreign film cameras which were on site to record the momentous occasion would become, for posterity and historians, the sole true recorders of the event, the only untainted evidence of the identities of the then current twelve National Council members and the two 'non voting' members, for in years to come, after internal purges and political manoeuvrings, the use of doctored film would show, retrospectively, the latest members of the National Council as having been in power ON THAT DAY [Author`s emphasis] in nineteen sixty-six.

Viewers would also see the apparent overwhelming support and sympathy for the abolition of the Monarchy as professionally produced and manufactured placards and banners dominated the cameras` field of view. They had, of course, been supplied by the New Order with not only their full logistical support but also of the creative expertise of the same group, or their staff, that had been set up by the National Council, under the chairmanship of the owner of the Sun newspaper.

Even the slogans on some of the placards would be substituted by doctored film to support and verify the status of the new National Council members.

Support for the Monarchy, both in terms of the number of representatives and their valiant, but futile propaganda, was literally swamped by the abolitionists who paraded massive banners which required a number of carriers and which were used to hide the Monarchists' banners from the view of the T.V. and film cameras.

The National Returning Officer (N.R.O.) was not overawed by the heaving mass which pressed forward, all around the plinth, or by the presence of the N.C. members, all dressed in expensive lounge suits, who had achieved their goal, but only by the presence of Oswald Mosley, for he had last come across this man at the nineteen fifty-nine General Election and was well aware of his pedigree.

Once the result had been announced and the expected, almost hysterical frenzy had subsided, Mosley would deliver a very brief, carefully crafted statement to enflame the people and to raise his credentials as a forthcoming Presidential candidate which would be formally announced in the Eighth Proclamation that was to be imminently published and circulated, incorporating the Referendum result.

The N.R.O. carefully checked the sheet of paper which he held in his outstretched right hand whilst holding a microphone in the left, more to maintain his stability than for effect, and, with the confidence of experience, began. Silence temporarily gripped the immense gathering...

"As National Returning Officer for the Referendum I confirm that the total number of votes cast in support of the continuation of the Monarchy is three million, nine hundred and twelve thousand, nine hundred and sixty; for the abolishment of the Monarchy, twelve million... A roar, which one journalist compared to the sound of an erupting volcano, of delight and satisfaction, drowned the rest of the number and continued for some five or six minutes... three hundred and twenty-nine thousand, eight hundred and eleven votes whilst the number of spoiled votes totalled seven hundred and forty–two thousand, three hundred and ten."

Sometime later and before the Presidential vote, he realised that he had omitted to begin his statement with a note of the total number of votes cast.

Oswald Mosley was an experienced orator and remained in his seat despite the exhortations of Andrew Duggan, who sat next to him, to rise and address the crowd.

And when he did, as he slowly rose, he instinctively knew that this was the culmination of a journey that had taken over three decades to reach its inevitable fulfilment. His perseverance, his unwavering resolve but above all his shrewdness had now borne a ripe fruit and that fool Winston Churchill was no longer able to witness his victory, the victory of his superior intelligence and cunning.

There would be no pompous moralising for he intended to pander and exploit the deepest emotions of the crowd and the television viewers and radio listeners...

"The British people, by their actions, have not yielded to obsolete and archaic loyalties but have expressed their desires and hopes in the future of this nation, of the people, by the people and for the people... the future is now in your hands and you will hold accountable your leaders for you are truly the masters of your own destiny and future... the yoke of feudal rule has been forever lifted from off of your bowed shoulders."

The eighth edition of the STATE OF EMERGENCY- MARTIAL LAW was published some two weeks later and announced not only the result of the Referendum but confirmed that:

"The Monarchy has been abolished in perpetuity and that all their property, lands and chattels have been sequestrated and would now become assets of the nation. Henceforth a democratically elected President would represent and head the nation which, following the democratic will of the people had been reconstituted as a Republic.

On Sunday, September the fourth, an Election would be held between two candidates who had offered themselves for election... Oswald Ernald Mosley and John Hutchyns Tyndall, the winner being the one who secured the larger vote."

The proclamation concluded with details which confirmed a repetition of the same eligibility and voting procedures.

The Swedish government immediately used the opportunity to withdraw its cooperation following pressure from the Swedish Royal family and national public opprobrium, leaving the Swiss isolated, but they were able to raise over five hundred independent observers which might have allowed the National Council far greater freedom to rig the voting however it was decided by them to control the aggregation of the votes as the results were telexed to London.

Cynics had often said of dubious elections conducted in certain South American states that the system permitted ..."one man, one vote, once", which explains why the election of a President was a significant landmark, in more than one way.

The actual campaign lasted just under three weeks, long enough for the electorate to become bored with the 'hustings', which were stage managed giving the impression of a dramatic confrontation between two opposing candidates, but the outcome had already been determined and the whole procedure was a callous and cynical deception of the greatest magnitude. *YOU*, the reader, should have by now come to expect and you would be correct that audiences and crowds were carefully seeded with specially chosen participants and more importantly the questions posed to both candidates were, in the main.pre-prepared and the answers even more so crafted for maximum effect, thus their utterances lacked substance only offering vague superficial memorable phrases which were more like advertising slogans. Opinion Polls were frequently conducted for the benefit of the National Council in order to anticipate and prepare for the outcome. Mosley consistently held a three to six point advantage and as Andrew Duggan was quoted, but not of course publicly...

"It was for Oswald Mosley to lose."

The *Sun* came out in favour of John Tyndall whilst the *Times* supported Mosley and the Opinion Polls that they published were skewed in favour of their preferred candidate. The British public had been deluded that they were living through and experiencing a democratic and honest election but the truth was exactly opposite. Both candidates appeared in public, unannounced, though ,of course, prior notice had been given to New Order members to appear and ask predetermined questions with already prepared answers, at venues such as High Streets, outside of schools and especially at football matches, for the new season had just begun, though the wags and wits could be relied upon to make acerbic and derogatory comments which unbalanced both candidates since they expected a well organised , pre prepared number of questions.

Television and radio coverage was extensive, with constant repeats of interviews, statements and comments culminating in a 'live', face to face confrontation which was recorded earlier in the day, therefore permitted the editing out of any *faux pas*, chaired by John Freeman (a former Labour M.P., Government Minister and more recently, until the fall of Parliamentary democracy, the presenter of 'Face to Face', a hard hitting, innovative interview programme which created a veneer of genuine political balance and authenticity) and which lasted ninety minutes, allowing a number of questions, some of which had been solicited from the general public, that both men had prior knowledge.

Central to the discussion *AND APPROVED BY THE NATIONAL COUNCIL* [author's emphasis] was to be Tyndall's acknowledgement that not only was he the leader of the New Order but a member of the recently formed National Council, who were responsible to the New Order and who were liable to report to it, which was a perversion of the truth, especially as there did not exist a body which was the ultimate authority within the New Order.

Mosley, with his long experience of oratory and debate was a formidable speaker and with the prior knowledge of his opponent, who at best had been originally a street corner demagogue and who had only recently been tutored in the arts of modern communication (as had Mosley), in an elegantly constructed argument confronted Tyndall on his potential grasp of power as the leader of the New Order, member of the National Council and potentially, additionally, as President.

"It would be a dangerous combination in a democratic state if you held three different positions of power, whilst if I was elected my primary duty would be to supervise and watch over the new embryonic Council to protect the interests of all the people whether they had voted for me or not."

John Freeman had been cunningly deceived and mislead about the basic integrity of the discussion and his reputation suffered a blow when he was offered and accepted a diplomatic post in Washington where he was ambassador from 1969 to 1971, however at the end of the period, he and his wife, Catherine Dove, applied for, and were granted asylum, creating a minor incident which was not made public to the British people.

The nation was yet to learn that the forthcoming Presidential election was to be the final time that they would be consulted in the government of the country for as time and events unfurled they would become more concerned with having enough food on the table or the constant fear and worry of the knock on the door and the sudden disappearance of neighbours, friends, family and work colleagues.

The result was announced at the same location, again in front of the twelve members of the National Council (and the two 'non voting' members), including the man who was destined to be the defeated opponent, the same, for the last time, National Presiding Officer and the President elect, though the crowd was ignorant of the connivance and deception which had placed Mosley in the orbit of, and close to, the cockpit of absolute real power.

Undoubtedly it was the weather that deterred some of the candidates' supporters from attending and it was now possible to walk from the Cenotaph to the steps of St. Martin in the Fields without encountering any of the crowds.

The Election produced both a reduced turnout and an increased number of spoiled ballot papers indicating an underlying dissatisfaction with both candidates as only some twelve million votes were cast of which just over one and a half million were either deliberately or unintentionally spoiled. Of the valid votes, the result was much closer, but the result fully satisfied both candidates and the National Council, for Mosley received just over five million, four hundred and fifty thousand votes and his opponent, John Tyndall, just a fraction under five million .

Colin Jordan was not privy to the machinations that had secured such a prestigious position for his mentor but his ruthless, and successful, methods had not gone unnoticed in London so his approaches to Oswald Mosley (whilst concealing his envy of Mosley's and Tyndall's meteoric success), combined with his growing reputation, on the back of his, and his gang of sadists' violence, would propel his career back to London and the seat of power.

SEVENTEEN

Monday, February first, nineteen seventy-one.

Monday morning of a brave new world. Rumours had very quietly been circulating for two or three weeks, fuelled by speculation that the New Order had themselves disseminated the news, for reasons that people could not comprehend, that the currency was to be radically changed and on Monday, February first, a new proclamation appeared which confirmed the rumour.

STATE OF EMERGENCY - MARTIAL LAW
TWENTY-SEVENTH EDITION.

It was now dangerous to pass on even a snippet of gossip for the Security forces could, would and did arrest anyone who they alleged had been a party to rumour mongering and it was commonly agreed, but in hushed tones, that arrest would ultimately result in incarceration in the special camp complex which was supposed to be on Dartmoor. Friends, neighbours, family and fellow workers would just disappear. Fear dominated peoples` lives because of the uncertainty that their friends, neighbours, fellow workers and even their family members *COULD BE* [author`s emphasis] agents of the security forces and could act as *Agent Provocateurs*.

The first major round of purges which had begun in nineteen sixty-seven hoovered up members of the legal profession and judiciary and which was highlighted by two high profile trials alleging that, in the first, some judges and barristers had colluded to convict innocent defendants who were aware that the self same judges and barristers were involved in a homosexual prostitution scandal. The second trial was even more sensational for the defendants, four former High Court Judges, admitted receiving bribes via defendants` legal representatives to either have cases dismissed, on technical grounds, or for the Judges to direct the confused juries to find the defendants not guilty.

But completely overshadowing these two trials, held before Military Tribunals, was the mass trial of thirteen former heads of the armed forces in nineteen sixty-eight.

Such were the devastating nature of their crimes that the hearing was held in camera but in the interests of openness there was, originally, wide, edited coverage in the newspapers and excerpts were shown on the television news a week after the tribunal`s guilty verdicts of those offences where the defendants had pleaded not guilty.

During the trial ,the *London Evening News*, in a spectacular 'exclusive scoop' and in banner headlines, first confirmed that the heads of the three armed forces had planned a *coup d`etat*, the assassination of the President and the murder or arrest of as many as possible of the twelve Regional Commissioners and of their twelve deputies.

Secret negotiations had also been uncovered in the United States to reinstate the Monarchy under a 'puppet' King, for Charles had become the uncrowned King following the death of his mother in a horse riding accident after she had been thrown and broken her neck.

The list of crimes to which some of the defendants had confessed or where they were found guilty, traumatised and shocked the country and justified, in part, the electoral decision to abolish the Monarchy.

Their treachery and treason was even traced back to nineteen sixty-three and their contact and collusion with agents of the Warsaw Pact. They had admitted individually and as a group intentionally undermining the then legal government in preparation of an earlier attempted *coup d'etat*. The list of charges was breathtaking in the scope of their crimes and included, according to the sensational Evening News scoop...

Withholding intelligence from the government that the Warsaw Pact was imminently about to attack in November nineteen sixty-three.

Withholding intelligence from the government that the Warsaw Pact was to use, in contravention of the Geneva Convention, chemical weapons.

Placing, in jeopardy, the lives of their own British forces.

Placing in jeopardy, the lives of N.A.T.O. Forces, including forces from the United States,

Dereliction of duty.

That the head of the Air Strike Force (formerly at the time known as the Royal Air Force) and his immediate staff had placed the security of the nation in mortal danger, by, without the knowledge of the government and therefore without their approval, sending abroad the 'V' bomber force to South Africa, thereby laying open to attack, the country.

Supplying information to agents of an enemy state that would assist them prosecute acts of war against the United Kingdom ...For the purpose of overthrowing the legitimate government and setting up a military dictatorship.

Facilitating the escape of the Royal Family, together with some of the ring leaders of the unsuccessful coup (who had been arrested abroad and had been extradited back to Great Britain for trial).

In November nineteen sixty-eight, newsreel coverage at the cinema, and briefer, edited highlights on the two television channels showed the mass execution which took place within the grounds of the Tower of London. The convicted men were previously shown walking to an open space led by a priest, their hands tied behind them before being crushed to death by a tank, and the unedited film shown at the cinema included one of the traitors, who had shortly before rushed towards the film camera shouting...

> "Save yourselves, it is the National Council who are your
> enemy, for what they tell you are lies."

At which moment most cinema audiences burst out in laughter and jubilation at such a perversion and distortion of the truth.

In December nineteen sixty-nine, on Christmas eve, a mass purge began of ordinary members of the community. People would simply just disappear. Arrests seemed to be random and friends or family would attempt to visit the barracks of the Security forces or before that, to the local hospitals in an ever more desperate attempt to locate their missing friend or family member.

Cooperation by the authorities was nonexistent, indeed the Security forces were known to threaten arrest of the enquirers and the hospitals were overwhelmed, understaffed and short of every conceivable facility and drugs to cope with the majority of their patients who, it was claimed, had been fighting against the Warsaw Pact forces on the Balkan front.

But the purge had a logical and evil purpose, organised and operated by a new Directorate responsible to the S.S.I.S.S., under the vile, corrupt, cruel, malicious and vindictive Colin Jordan. His mandate was brief and specific: The arrest and 'processing' of any individual who had shown dissent or could be the focus, by their leadership or example, of groups in the community that might create opposition to the National Council. To secure information the methods used could, would and promptly secured confessions but what was always required was new information or information that could be ' cross- checked' to confirm its authenticity.

No statistical analysis is available, but of the early waves, arrests prominently featured those individuals who had communicated their support to the *Sun* newspaper which had fraudulently stood on a platform which whilst not openly opposing the leadership, certainly strongly implied that it questioned the National Council`s actions.

In recorded history, great cities, nation states, empires and civilisations have risen and then returned to the dust. As well as leaving details of their history, some, if not all, also bequeathed achievements that still formed part of modern (civilised) society where such bastions still existed such as in Canada, Australia and New Zealand. Art, architecture, science, mathematics (for example, use of the base number sixty for time and geometry), wonderful poetry and even, for the epicure, details of extravagant menus.

The use of torture probably goes back as far as pre-history and the eras of National Socialism in Germany between 1933 and 1945 or Stalinist Russia was not the end of the darkest side of 'civilisation'.

In the sixteenth and seventeenth centuries a titanic struggle took place between the new force of Protestantism and the established Roman Catholic Church. The Holy Roman and Universal Inquisition had been created in fifteen forty –two to proceed against those whose allegiance was in question and amongst those many that stood before them was Galileo Galilei for the crime of writing, and having published his great work, The Dialogue on the Great World Systems, though his confrontation with the Papal authorities had gone back decades.

Ultimately the dissident scientist was to be humiliated, confronted by the awesome power of the Papacy, forced to retract and finally shown , but not the subject of its violence, the instruments of torture.

The following testimony dates from sixteen – twenty and is the statement of an Englishman who was racked by the Spanish Inquisition...

"I was brought to the rack, then mounted on the top of it. My legs were drawn through the two sides of the three- planked rack. A chord was tied about my ankles. As the levers bent forward, the main force of my knees against the two planks burst asunder the sinews of my hams, and the lids of my knees were crushed. My eyes began to startle, my mouth to foam and froth, and my teeth to chatter like the doubling of a drummer's sticks. My lips were shivering, my groans were vehement, and blood sprang from my arms, broken sinews, hands and knees. Being loosed from the pinnacles of pain, I was hand-fast set on the floor, with this incessant imploration: `Confess! Confess! `".

The following list (incorporating my investigation report references) catalogues details of tortures *DIRECTLY AUTHORISED* by Colin Jordan or acts committed by some of the paramilitary forces whilst supporting certain operations under his regime. Unfortunately I have been unable to substantiate the lurid and frightening allegation which is listed first, (although there have been many accusations and rumours in the United States and consequently much speculation) or the second, an *ALLEGED* conversation:

01 M 31 211 170D

Breeding of rats specifically to populate prisons in order to spread Weil's disease (which is also known as Leptospirosis or mud fever) and can be fatal.

02 T 20 117 030 S

"Well, then you just walk out of the room. T hen you won't have seen anything. You will not have been party to anything."

"What about the Geneva conventions?"

"Which flag do you serve?" came the tart reply.

04 T 21 600 192 S

"A report prepared by his GP reveals how his torturers repeatedly thrust batons and bottles into his rectum...during his six-month imprisonment he claims he was strung up, whipped across the soles of his feet with thick cables and beaten with batons. On one occasion, a guard used pliers to wrench a nail from his finger. On another, a bottle was forced into his rectum."

05 T 12 604 003 S

"Six men tied to the walls or gym equipment moaned in agony. They had been beaten. One was half naked, his chest festering from scorch marks inflicted with a blowtorch. Another had a broken jaw. All were covered in blood and bruises. At least two were to be executed. He [name redacted by the author] discovered later.

(His) wrists were handcuffed to the leg of a billiard table in the middle of the gym. A rope was tied to his ankles then pulled and attached to some weights, leaving his body stretched on the floor. Six of [name of man redacted by the author]'s men began beating him.

"They punched and kicked me in my face and all over my body" (he recalled). "They broke my nose and I lost three teeth. Then they clubbed me and struck me in the chest with the end of a billiard cue. My face was covered in blood. Every time I passed out they'd stop for a few minutes and then start again.

They attached electric cables to my toes. Then they started giving me shocks, mild at first and then more and more powerful until the current going through my body was so strong that I was jumping off of the floor. It felt that all my nerves and muscles were being ripped apart. "

06 T 40 602 101 S

"Noxious fumes would be introduced to his room causing his eyes and nose to run. The temperature of his cell would be manipulated, making his cell extremely cold for long stretches of time. He [name redacted by the author] was denied even the smallest and most personal shreds of human dignity by being deprived of showering for weeks at a time, yet having to endure forced grooming at the whim of his captors...He was threatened with being cut with a knife and having alcohol poured on the wounds. He was also threatened with imminent execution. He was hooded and forced to stand in stress positions for long periods. He was forced to endure exceedingly long interrogation sessions, without adequate sleep, wherein he would be confronted with false information, scenarios and documents to further disorientate him. Often he had to endure multiple interrogators who would scream, shake and otherwise assault (him)."

07 T 72 211 092 S

"The men who carried his body from the square said police had gouged out one of his eyeballs with a knife and then forced it back through the empty socket into his brain."

08 T 13 112 181 S

"We used to give thirsty prisoners salty water to drink, one time, two times,three times, then give them pure water. When they wanted to urinate we put a rubber band around the penis so they couldn't. So whatever we wanted, they would be ready to confess.

He will never forget the time his jailor used electricity on his genitals, however:" he came back with the electricity stick and jabbed it into my testicles saying, `This is to cull your race`".

09 T 213 081 S

"...Sprayed him with water and applied the electrodes... of a car battery to (his) chest and other parts of (his) body.

He witnessed other detainees being sexually abused with glass Pepsi bottles.

I was on a wooden board like a table, face up, in underpants and blind-folded. I don`t know how the ends are raised but some mechanism makes it go up. I suffered terrible pain in my lower neck as my body was forced into a V-shape."

10 T 03 214 080 S

"The Tyre. A large one into which the victim is forced and beaten on the feet, and the ` flying carpet` , where the prisoner is strapped face-up on a wooden board that is bent to stretch his spine.

Children are tortured alongside adults and are even subject to more brutal torture as interrogators believe children could crack faster and give them names."

11 T 03 211 111 S

"In front of his children they cut his legs off at the knee, both of them."

12 T 82 211 152 S

"A witness, who was 17 at the time, told how he was ordered to go out in a small boat and collect bodies, many naked, headless and bound together by wire. One woman had a dead infant in her arms."

13 T 212 120 S

"I've known them take a blowtorch to the kids of (farm) workers to make them scream.

Attackers have used boiling water on their prisoners, or dripping molten plastic. In some cases victims have been asphyxiated with plastic bags and had hot clothes irons used on them while others have had a noose placed round their necks and then been dragged for long distances behind their own vehicles."

14 T 72 314 070 S

"Pumping. A sexual torture to find money in women's vaginas. Pregnant women are assaulted and forced to have abortions. Foetuses are finished off by being smothered in plastic wrap.

A renegade official was (reportedly) executed by having a mortar shell fired at him.

Prisoners were skewered through the palm of the hands with barbed wire and yoked (together) like animals."

15 M 60 315 051 D

"Raped her, injected her with drugs, beat her and urinated over her."

16 M 02 319 072 D

"Hostages were dismembered, had their eyes gouged out and were left hanging from hooks in the ceiling.

Men were SAID [author's emphasis] to have been castrated and had fingers removed with pliers before being blinded and hanged.

They drive knives inside a child's body. If you look at all the bodies, fingers are cut by pliers, the noses are ripped by pliers.

17 M 92 411 040 D

"[Name redacted by the author] was said to have been thrown into a cage with his five closest aides, after which 120 hounds which had been starved for three days were released, eating the men until there was nothing left."

18 T 20 411 021 S

"They are abused and deprived of basic rights such as going to the lavatory and washing."

19 M 04 412 022 D

"Inmates who were pregnant usually gave birth to dead babies, but there was one case when the baby was born alive. The security agent came in (and) told us to put the baby in the water upside down. The mother was begging... (and) with her shaking hands picked up the baby and put the baby face-down in the water. The baby stopped crying.

The unhappy being who walked to his death seemed no longer a member of the family of man. It would have been easy to mistake him for an animal, with his wild hair, his bruises, his crusts of dried blood, his bulging eyes. They had stuffed his mouth full of rocks (to shut him up).

Pigeon Torture. You are handcuffed behind your back and hung (up) so that you are not able to stand or sit. Then you are kicked and beaten with clubs and you are hung up for three, four days. You urinate and defecate and you are totally dehydrated."

20 M 23 415 071 D

"Raping hundreds of women and burning children after pouring kerosene down their throats.

" 21 M 40 416 091 D

"(He) buried victims alive. He tortured others with red-hot irons and electric shocks. A favourite method was to drip hot oil into the eyes of prisoners."

There are documents and witness statements to substantiate his(Jordan's) basic venal moral corruption. He accumulated great material wealth, along with the only currencies that had a commercial value and were convertible, the United States Dollar, the Swedish Kroner and the Swiss Franc. The pound Sterling was, in his eyes, fundamentally worthless. In exchange for property, works of art or desirable goods (such as classic cars and stamp collections) that could be lucratively sold to wealthy foreigners, he arranged the release and travel permits for those unfortunate to have been caught in his web, to Sweden, the United States or Canada which would leave the recipients destitute, alive but free. His integrity fulfilling his side of the agreement was exemplary (possibly because intermediaries acting on behalf of the prisoners were always adamant that goods would not be passed over until their clients were actually released) though his ingrained and fanatical anti-Semitism meant that Jewish emigrants paid more, much more.

His immediate staff were just as venal, though on a smaller scale, lucratively selling 'dispensations' and taking advantage of their position for sexual gratification, whilst Jewish prisoners were subject to 'special' attention.

The foregoing now conveniently brings us to the next few chapters which will concludes this extensive, but not comprehensive, unauthorised investigation and report, however whilst it is outside of the chronological history that is the subject of this work and will be the subject of a future, in depth analysis, of the career and influence of Colin Jordan, mention MUST [author's own specific emphasis] be raised, of his foiled attempts to introduce an English language version of the nineteen thirty-eight calumny, Der Giftpilz.

Der Giftpilz (or The Poisonous Mushroom) was written by Ernst Hiemer and was published by the notorious Julius Streicher's Nuremberg publishing house to influence children and was sometimes even used in schools.

My vocabulary or even my old Concise Oxford (English) Dictionary cannot adequately describe this totally sickening work which Jordan unsuccessfully attempted, in nineteen seventy-four, to be used in British schools as a crude propaganda work but was stopped, though it appeared later in a modified and toned down form to vilify and disparage the Slav nations, their heritage, culture ,traditions and racial pedigree.

Extracts from a nineteen thirty-eight English version, issued by the 'Friends of Europe', an organisation which has apparently disappeared, now follows :

"From a Jew`s face

The wicked Devil speaks to us,

The Devil who, in every country,

Is known as evil plague.

Would we from the Jew be free,

Again be gay and happy,

Then must youth fight with us,

To get rid of the Jewish Devil."

THE EXPERIENCE OF HANS AND ELSE WITH A STRANGE MAN.

"Here, kids, I have some candy for you. But you both have to come with me."

"You are a Jew!" He cries, and seizing his sister, runs off as fast as his legs will carry him. At the corner of the street he meets a policeman. Quickly Hans tells his story. The policeman gets on his motorbike and soon overtakes the strange man. He handcuffs him and takes him to prison.

HOW THE JEW TREATS DOMESTIC HELP

The Jew is a devil. I shall hate him as long as I live. And I shall always think of the saying I heard yesterday:

"German woman, great or small.

The Jew calls you simply : Goja.

He hates you, corrupts you,

Treats you worse than cattle.

If a girl wants to keep herself pure

Let her steer clear of the Jews!

If she wants to make good in life`s struggle,

Let her have no truck with the Jews!"

EIGHTEEN

Sunday, February seventh, nineteen seventy-one.

STATE OF EMERGENCY- MARTIAL LAW.
TWENTY-SEVENTH EDITION.

On Monday February fifteenth new currency regulations would apply.

President Mosley spoke on the Sunday evening of the fourteenth to the nation, on both television channels and on the radio.

His statement was unexpectedly buoyant, upbeat, surprising and above all, welcome.

"The nation`s forces have won a massive victory, on land, at sea, and in the air against the vile sub human forces composed of cretins from the Warsaw Pact, in the Balkan peninsular, therefore securing the seaway to Cairo and the Middle East and not only loosening, but throwing off the noose and shackles of their piratical actions. Without fear, our mercantile fleet can bring to our shores the necessary fuel to promote industrial production and increase the nation`s wealth.

The strength of our nation can now be quantified in the new currency which you will be able to use as from tomorrow, when, coincidentally, I am assured, goods and food, that have been in short supply because of the recent military activity should be available in abundance.

Together we have all suffered the deprivation of shortages. Now, together, let us enjoy and appreciate the fruits of victory and your sacrifices."

The Twenty-seventh Edition clearly spelt out the procedure concerning the new currency but not the rationale behind the change:

Henceforth it became a capital offence to possess Sterling notes or coins, United States and Canadian Dollar notes or coins or currency from Switzerland or Sweden (again both notes and coins).

A new non convertible currency, for internal use only, the United Kingdom Dollar (divided into one hundred cents) would be used and in the preceding week, post offices were overwhelmed by the general public in an almost hysterical rush to dispose of their Sterling and collect their new, pristine notes and coins. The former was printed on eighty gramme paper through which was weaved a delicate thread for security purposes and which was quietly described by experts as shoddy and reflected the true commercial value of the non convertible currency. The coins of various denominations were, if not more so, both shoddy and easily forged though the consequences following detection were literally fatal.

On Monday February fifteenth, Radio Moscow announced, to a rousing peal of bells and then patriot military music, that Warsaw Treaty forces, supported by five divisions of Soviet ground forces and massive air cover, had encircled, overwhelmed and accepted the surrender of eighty-five thousand N A T O troops in the now liberated Yugoslavia allowing the population to return to their domestic lives and the pursuit of democratic Socialism.

On the first of March the...

STATE OF EMERGENCY- MARTIAL LAW
TWENTY-EIGHTH EDITION

appeared without comment but was received with great excitement. Salary tax was to be reduced from twenty-five to ten percent. But behind all these actions and others that have been mentioned was a concerted, callous plan, Machiavellian in concept, to remorselessly and methodically bludgeon the British people into subjugation, primarily by consistently reducing their food ration, limiting medical treatment, allowing epidemics to flourish (especially in Winter) and destroying the resolve of the people by the continuous use of arrests, deportation to anonymous re-education centres and an almost hysterical climate of fear.

NINETEEN

Saturday, October sixth, nineteen seventy-three.

A regional conflagration had yet again broken out in the Middle East, this time Egypt and Syria had apparently, for once, efficiently coordinated their forces and had attacked the surprised Jewish state of Israel, on what was the anniversary of their most important and sacred religious festival. Unconfirmed first reports dramatically stated that Egyptian troops had crossed, and liberated, the vital Suez Canal, that Syrian troops were successfully storming the Golan Heights and that the Syrian High Command was confident that the Zionist State would soon be vanquished and the...

"Contagious bacillus of Judaism and Zionism would, once and for all, be cleansed and exterminated."

The news would not be announced in London because it was of no interest to the public.

Of the twelve original members of the National Council only four remained, and very soon two of them would be toppled, leaving only Andrew Duggan as one of the two survivors and the only member who had witnessed *ALL* the dramatic changes and above all the change in philosophy of the Council's principles and values.

Underpinning the National Council's policies was the accumulation and expansion of their power which was projected through the image of the New Order and a figurehead President, devoid of any real power, who was satisfied with minute authority but more importantly the image and trappings of his office. Even so plans had been put in hand, with his knowledge and consent, that would literally perpetuate both his image and presence.

The armed forces, at their highest level, were now centres of intrigue where the pursuit of power and political influence dominated their actions and, where once they had been loyal to the Crown and therefore Parliament, senior officers now had the junior officers watched and the junior officers watched their seniors who appeared more concerned to protect and expand their power bases than to carry out their duties.

Since the creation of the National Council there had been two major internal coups in the absolute top level of the three military services where currently an equilibrium now held sway under the authority of a ruthless officer corps.

The National Council was now dominated by a Military–Intelligence service axis symbolised by their uniforms which had changed from civilian lounge suits to a military style suit.

Israel was perhaps the only truly democratic nation (other than the 'old' nations of the former British Commonwealth) that existed and their position both geographically and strategically was significant in the confrontation with the Soviet Union and Warsaw Pact. The 'Middle East', in a vast symbolic crescent from Morocco on the Atlantic coast, along the Southern Mediterranean coast and as far East including Afghanistan was a permanent foaming sea of minor power struggles, a maelstrom of tribal, inter religious (Sunni versus Shi`ite) strife and local national enmity (Persia versus Iraq, Syria versus Iraq and above all Syria versus Persia) whilst the permutations involving Egypt and other nations appeared to change and interweave, as regularly as the seasons changed.

Britain's only interest was a continuous, guaranteed supply of oil which was secured by the military might of Israel who recovered from their initial losses and with the support of the United States, who supplied much needed equipment, regained the initiative and lost ground but above all their regional dominance.

The British people were ignorant of these events and circumstances. The average person, if such a definition is applicable and true, was primarily concerned to have enough food on the table, to avoid illness at any cost, for medical treatment was all but impossible to secure and *NOT, UNDER ANY CIRCUMSTANCES*, to invite the interest or scrutiny of the Paramilitary, or the black uniformed, cycloid helmeted Security forces and finally the shadowy, ethereal army of eavesdroppers and loyal members of the detested New Order who were believed to betray even friends or family members.

The only person who could now be trusted was the President, paternal and kind, who would literally turn up unannounced, to meetings or even private homes, though NOTHING was now private because of the constant fear of infiltration by alien, foreign fifth columnists (whatever that meant) and the installation in private and public places of listening and more recently, viewing devices to protect the community from terror attacks.

TWENTY

He thought that he was immune from the ever more violent storm that raged outside of his hermetically sealed and insulated world and the unexpected tremors that shook his local community but he was to learn that no one was exempt from the power and authority of the National Council and its control of every aspect of society`s life.

He had rarely bothered, like most others, to read, let alone grasp the consequences of the posters that the National Council published and had displayed on every public building, and their sheer volume meant that the original posters, which had not survived the ravages of time and the weather, had been covered over.

The...

STATE OF EMERGENCY-MARTIAL LAW TWELFTH EDITION,

had been, for him, yet another manifestation of the pomposity of the authorities and he was unaware that it confirmed a national 'Direction of Labour' order. The State could now, without explanation, compel and send any and everybody to a place and any type of employment throughout the country.

Thus an item (number eight) of the

STATE OF EMERGENCY-MARTIAL LAW
SECOND EDITION

had been extended to encompass any non-military, civilian occupation.

Dr. John Wrighton had only once before been confronted by the authority and power of the new regime and had assessed the experience as an aberration and the misuse of power and authority. He was therefore visibly shocked when he received notice that, with immediate effect, he was to be sent to University College Hospital in Gower Street, London, but was to continue his profession as a trauma surgeon. He, and his wife Jean, would be separated as she characteristically, emphatically refused to move back to London and the *ALLEGED* [author's emphasis] shortages and deteriorating housing conditions. She would stay in their new home in Weymouth where their children would have safer, healthier lives and, despite rationing, fish and farm produce seemed for them, in gratitude of medical services rendered, still readily available in quality and generous quantity.

He had been plunged' into the deep end, immediately on his arrival and was only just familiarising himself with the names and abilities of his surgical team, whilst literally learning of the shortages and excuses which covered up a lack of resources. The operating theatres were effectively working on a twenty-four hour shift basis and his patients were nearly exclusively injured forces, and from what he could glean, they had been serving on the Balkan Front and were the ones that had been deemed suitable(as eligible elite forces) for treatment. He had quickly learned not to too closely listen to rumours, however it was alleged that many injured troops had been left to die of their wounds following a ruthless programme that weeded the inoperable (or superfluous enlisted infantry) from the potential valued survivors.

Clearly there were no 'Florence Nightingales' to administer humanitarian kindness.

He had been resident in the hospital for less than a week and was living in a second floor flat near Judd Street and his stomach was slowly acclimatising itself to the poor and bland hospital food which was the only available food following the strict enforcement of rationing, and once again, to use the now hackneyed word, alleged, inferior to the special food allowance for the patients but he could not discern any difference in their diet compared to his.

He was woken by the telephone around twelve–twenty in the morning and told, without any thought as to his situation and inconvenience, that he was urgently needed at an accident site and that he would be....at which moment he heard an almost deafening series of bangs on his front door which was ominous in its portent of things to come. He walked over to the front door and could distinctively hear his name being called with an urgency and tone that worried him.

Two well dressed men stood at the opened entrance and courteously questioned the tenant`s identity and in response confirmed that he was to accompany them, without delay or explanation, adding a postscript that:

"Should he have a professional bag of equipment that he could bring it along."

Two nearly identical black coloured vehicles were parked outside the front entrance to the block of flats and passing pedestrians deliberately avoided their gaze for none wished to be noticed by the men in the first car, which bore the unique registration double five, double five at the beginning and at the end of the registration plate, though perhaps , since his view had been brief and cursory, they could have been the letter S.

Concerned for his own safety and security he was only slightly reassured when one of the two men courteously opened the rear nearside door for him to enter the vehicle though it could have been a prelude to his arrest, however the man entered the front passenger seat and immediately picked up a microphone and attentively listened to a two way radio.

Dr., actually by his qualifications, Mister Wrighton, soon realised that there were two differently positioned rear view mirrors fixed to the inside of the front windscreen and the one nearer to the passenger`s side was so positioned as to observe him. He deliberately moved and in response the passenger reset his mirror before continuing his duty receiving and sending messages to the other, lead car.

Mr. Wrighton was to begin a journey of less than one hour which would not only have a destination but would also be a Damascene revelation that would awaken and illuminate his blinkered and closed concept of the real nature of the totalitarian, authoritarian state.

The two vehicles turned into Judd Street and he intentionally looked out for the old Police section house which, on more than one occasion, had been the venue for some uninhibited partying with other medical students and their police officer friends but that was a long time ago, in the early nineteen–fifties, and the world and his life had changed immeasurably. The front entrance to the section house appeared unaltered and exempt from the changes outside, however, as the car flew past, he noted the presence of two guards from the Security force carrying sub-machine guns and the pavement outside was covered by large blocks of concrete interspaced by steel pylons buried into the ground and most gruesome of all, barbed wire wound around the pylons.

The car turned left into the Euston Road, igniting old, half forgotten memories and he was immediately struck by the paucity of traffic, the absence of any black taxicabs and the occasional buses which he noted were no longer red , but painted mainly green as if camouflaged, however before he could make a definitive assessment the two vehicles made a right hand turn into Eversholt Street passing, on the left hand side, Euston Railway Station which was very busy like an ant hill. The vehicles continued North towards Camden Town tube station and he realised that the traffic lights or where the lights should be situated, at the junction with Pratt Street, were either no longer operating or had been taken away. He was reliving his youth for this was the route that he followed, if he was able to cadge a lift, in the direction of his family home. But something had changed, something fundamental, something that he had taken for granted: he couldn`t put his finger on the pulse but something tangible was very different. The station was passed on the left hand side and as the car continued relentlessly North past Kentish Town and no doubt towards Archway he suddenly recognised the great change that had taken place that seemed to pervade and permeate the streets and the people.

There was an overwhelming greyness, an absence of colour and vitality and whilst he could just about remember, even in the years that immediately followed the Second World War, the shortages and rationing, that there was at least an atmosphere of hope for the future and the appearance of colour in the people's clothes, their surroundings but above all in their attitude. Now everything appeared in monochrome and the people seemed sullen, subdued and depressed, shuffling along as if they had no energy, purpose or if they were resigned to their fate. And their weakness, which probably was also physical, was mirrored by their surroundings, for the buildings around them and the shops within the buildings were dull, decaying and dilapidated. It was as if the very life force was being sucked from the whole environment.

The two vehicles reached the Archway gyratory and the lead car unexpectedly stopped for a few moments before the following car received a message which was translated into instructions to pass the Highgate Hill entrance and then to turn immediately left into the Archway Road passing, on the left hand side, the Whittington Hospital which still looked Victorian and in keeping with the surroundings, still depressingly miserable and in need of modernisation. He decided to look behind for as long as physically possible for he knew that as the vehicle drove up the hill, the view behind him would become magnificently panoramic but he was unable to maintain his posture.

As he turned round, the impressive bridge spanning the road loomed up but its appearance was unlike anything that he had seen before. He was totally unprepared for the vision that confronted him. A giant poster was draped across the bridge roughly thirty feet wide and by the same amount in depth. The first words that came into his mind were stunning and awesome. Staring at him was the face of President Mosley, strikingly life like and dynamic but his eyes looked at him and him alone. The portrait had captured the very essence of the man and no caption was necessary or slogan required. And then, most unexpectedly, the driver broke his self imposed silence and stated that:

"He envied Dr. Wrighton and the challenge that confronted him."

There was little traffic to delay them. Highgate tube station was soon passed as was Highgate Wood and at the junction with Aylmer Road the two vehicles took the right hand fork towards East Finchley and after that they reached The Bald Faced Stag. Every turn of the four wheels brought him closer to his roots and memories of his youth but he was not prepared nor could he for the incident that was soon to take place. As they reached The Green Man their inexorable journey to as yet an unknown destination was suddenly halted, without apparent reason, by a young member of the Military, as they prepared to cross the almost deserted North Circular Road. John Wrighton's view was obscured but he was certain that the passenger in the lead car got out, began to argue with the young man who was soon joined by a superior officer. Suddenly, unexpectedly, the tranquillity was broken by the unmistakeable sound of a shot and John was certain that he saw, or did he?, the officer spin round one hundred and eighty degrees and collapse on the ground. He was absolutely certain that the passenger re-entered the lead car which drove off followed by their vehicle.

As he passed the site of the altercation he saw the lifeless body strewn across the road but just as chillingly the driver and his associate seemed oblivious to the incident, crossing the North Circular Road and continuing North, passing the Lido on the right hand side which John remembered was a venue for the nineteen forty-eight Olympic Games, before shortly reaching The Tally Ho! He was nearly home but every moment was now filled with dread and foreboding.

"These people are capable of anything!"

He distinctively remembered glancing to his left and just catching sight of Totteridge and Whetstone tube station, but his mind was focused on his own precarious situation. Suddenly, almost subconsciously, he cast a momentary glance again to his left; he caught sight of the " Hole in the Wall" cafe and greedily remembered the bacon sandwiches which fuelled his sporting prowess. He then looked both to the left and right and was confronted by the calamitous and macabre vision of the massive destruction of the housing on both sides of the road. It was as if a giant from a child's fairy tale had huffed and puffed and blown down everything in the path of his breath. And then, immediately next, on both sides of the road, the two parades of shops were similarly devastated, reduced to rubble and the cinema, a haven of pleasure for him and his old school friends, was a pile of rubble, but the pub next door was undamaged!, indeed he could see what must have been the regulars having a drink ... or two.

Turning his head forward again he saw ahead of him ,draped from the bridge, yet another but smaller, dramatic picture of President Mosley but this one was more compassionate and paternal and was captioned 'The Great Shepherd'.

As the two vehicles drove up Barnet Hill, he chanced, one final time, to look to his left towards the Dollis Valley and the brook that gave the area its eponymous name. It was the site of total and absolute desolation. It had the appearance of a desert, arid and sterile, the brook no longer a geographical feature.

The rumours that he had ignored, disbelieved or thought impossible, must be true. It was, without doubt, the epicentre of a nuclear explosion and the cause of the chaotic devastation that he had just witnessed.

The two vehicles reached the apex of the hill and bore right passing the prominently located church on their left, which appeared to have considerable structural damage almost certainly caused by the nuclear explosion, and proceeded onwards as he realised that the junction was no longer controlled by traffic lights. Very shortly afterwards, at the junction with the old St. Albans Road, the lead vehicle hesitated but then continued straight on, soon passing, again on the left hand side, the local war memorial. He knew they were travelling in the direction of the quaintly named Potters Bar and he still did not know the origin of the name, when suddenly, like a revelation, a distant memory, nearly thirty years old, became as vivid and lucid as the road ahead of him was clear of traffic.

It was a Sunday morning, the first one in June nineteen forty-four, the fourth. He was eleven years of age walking towards Barnet with his parents when they met, coming from the opposite direction, the local milkman, who must have just finished his round and was returning home. They stopped and briefly chatted. He had one item of news...

"They've all gone. It must be on."

Two days later the American forces who had been based in the fields adjacent to the Barnet – Potters Bar Road (the A 1000) were landing on French soil.

How could he have forgotten such a minor but momentous incident?

The vehicle gently, but emphatically, turned left and he instinctively knew, without looking, that they were entering the Wrotham Park Estate.

TWENTY-ONE

He was initially drawn to the impressive Palladian facade of the magnificent building which was sparsely populated by observers looking out onto the vast, immaculately mown lawn in front of the house. He looked to his left and saw two fire engines, an ambulance and about fifty or seventy-five black uniformed Security forces standing in an undisciplined circle. The convoy, John wondered what to correctly call two vehicles, a brace?, drew up, and the passenger in the front seat exited the vehicle and courteously opened the rear door quickly stating that:

"We are only concerned with the health and well being of the passenger."

The five men unceremoniously breached the circle of troops and were confronted by the shocking sight of a Bell 47(G-2, produced under license, in England, by Westland Aircraft) helicopter lying on its back, its two bladed rotors beneath it, broken and irregularly positioned. A small group of firemen and civilians were clustered next to the bubble which served as the passenger pod.

Two young doctors, in white coats, (he later discovered that they were from the nearby Barnet General Hospital) were endeavouring, with little success, to move, let alone extricate the pilot, who was awkwardly and unnaturally positioned over the only passenger who clearly, by his pleas, was in extreme pain and was still waiting for treatment. The pilot, on the other hand, was silent.

He had had little recent experience of onsite accident procedures and drew the two young casualty doctors aside for a brief report on the medical condition of the two men. For some, as yet unknown reason, they were terrified, not of their responsibilities, but of failure.

They could not reach the passenger who clearly was the sole concern of everyone present. Two shots suddenly rang out and a silence descended over everyone present. A shocked John Wrighton turned round to see the man who had just previously shot the Army officer, withdraw from the Perspex bubble and the sight of the dead pilot who had sacrificed his life. His stomach almost retched both in horror and revulsion (for an instance reviving memories of a painful but happier earlier time) and, without thought, he automatically rushed up to the pod calling for the firemen to immediately demolish the Perspex canopy, after which the pilot's body was dragged away, enabling the hero of the hour, who was shielding the face of the passenger from any splinters ,the opportunity to assess the patient's condition. As he drew his hand back, the identity of the passenger was self evident and unmistakeable. He had saved the life of the President.

TWENTY TWO

His clinical experience, and the immediate diagnoses by the two junior casualty doctors, was that both legs had been broken, both probably single, simple fractures of the femur but they concurred that there was the potential danger that there could be internal damage to the soft tissue and bleeding if the fractures were multiple. Furthermore it appeared that three or four ribs had also been fractured and the President's face had been heavily bruised.

He had not been inside Barnet General Hospital for well over a decade and his initial impression was, like the Whittington Hospital, that it should be razed and rebuilt, but circumstances dictated otherwise. The ambulance, accompanied by the two cars, arrived outside a small block of buildings not immediately connected to the main hospital which was a private wing and the patient, covered by a blanket, to hide his identity, was carefully carried on a stretcher by four porters with the care and respect that would be accorded to a rare and valuable classical marble statue, under the supervision and care of the three doctors.

Temporary splints, hastily fashioned by Mr. Wrighton were adjusted in the presence of the two men who had chauffeured him from Central London and who introduced themselves as members of the President's personal bodyguard. Earlier that morning they had supervised his departure from Regents' Park in a surveillance Bell 47 helicopter which was part of the Security forces' fleet and which they had kindly offered to give him a demonstration. Awkwardly landing on a slope, it had been caught by an unexpected gust of wind and they had been immediately informed, just as they were leaving on their journey to Barnet, temporarily diverting to Gower Street and University College Hospital, where they demanded the services of a senior surgeon.

Thus fate, like the Sword Of Damocles, invisibly hanging over events, had caused him to be involved in a matter that he would have preferred not to have been a part of.

Whilst their two associates were ruthlessly supervising the evacuation of the private wing and the summary removal of the patients, their visitors and the medical staff (as well as being confronted by their futile protestations) to the main building, which was occupied in the main by injured military forces, the two men stood guard over the isolated, anonymous President, securing him from any possible unwanted interest. Mr. John Wrighton was informed, with the greatest courtesy, but with an underlying sinister implication, that failure was not an option, that he was in sole charge of the patient's health and recovery and that he could have available any necessary facility to aid him in his task.

He now realised why the two junior doctors were terrified and he requested that, accompanied by one of the two bodyguards, they were to commandeer any necessary facility including X Ray equipment and one operating room which was to be urgently and meticulously deep cleaned and held on standby.

Shortly afterwards, the President's wife, Diana, arrived and was allowed a few minutes privacy with her husband before Mr. Wrighton returned to the room.

Quietly, and with a measured tone, he explained to the semi conscious patient and his concerned wife what he proposed to do, both immediately and during the long night that lay ahead, and whilst painful, his condition was not critical or dangerous but would require his immediate attention, to which his plan received, to his relief, not only the approval of the President but his humorous, if weak response, including the remark that nearly fifty years before [actually in nineteen twenty-six - author's observation] when he had flirted with the Socialist Fabian Society, he had met a former member, the writer and author Herbert Wells, about whom he could recount some stories that could not be published, but the author of the Invisible Man would have been thrilled by one of his suggestions. The immediate fear of failure and the dire consequences temporarily receded but he still remembered what he had thought earlier in the day...

"These people are capable of anything!"

Clearly, the ribs had been, at a minimum, badly bruised which meant that as the President laughed he felt a sharp pain across his chest. One of the casualty doctors completely bound his head in bandages, leaving only slits for his eyes and mouth whilst the other doctor wrapped his two hands to the amusement of Diana Mosley.

Just as dusk was descending, the President was wheeled out of his room accompanied by his wife, his doctor and an entourage of bodyguards who were currently superfluous and some ninety minutes later, following a comprehensive series of X Rays, the original diagnoses were confirmed.

Still bandaged, to protect his anonymity, the President was moved to the operating theatre, passing a knot of surgeons and their teams who seemed more concerned that they had been deprived of one of their theatres, than the identity of the bandaged man and perhaps piqued that two young casualty doctors and not them, seemed to be deeply involved in the treatment.

By eleven forty-five that evening the patient was back in his room, still swathed in bandages at his own request, but also encrusted by plaster casts to protect his legs. He was told, before he slipped into a deep sleep, assisted by a sleeping pill, that his incarceration would last some six to eight weeks and that he should only receive immediate family members for the next forty–eight hours after which he could receive other visitors .

At twelve–sixteen precisely the two young doctors prepared to leave the confines of the hospital, leaving Mr. Wrighton with the responsibility and duty of looking after the patient overnight, but they were stopped and warned that they were forbidden to leave the complex. They too, no all three of them would be incarcerated and then what?

At around six a.m. John Wrighton stirred from his deep sleep, alerted by primitive senses developed over hundreds of thousands of years, by an intrusion into the room, for indeed it was one of the two doctors who had been unable to sleep, deeply concerned and rightly so, as to his future and circumstances. The security officer accompanying him was only interested in the safety of the patient and therefore rapidly removed the young man as the resident doctor resumed his deep sleep.

He was woken, not by the rays of sunlight streaming through the window as dawn broke, but later around nine twenty when Diana Mosley arrived followed by her chauffeur who was carrying a magnificent bouquet, radiant in reds, yellows, pinks and surrounded by green foliage. He excused himself and walked along the corridor where he was confronted by the two young men who insisted on urgently speaking to him.

John realised that their predicament also applied to him, but even more so. They were, in effect prisoners, unable to leave the building, their 'cells' were former patients' rooms supervised by three security officers. Breakfast, or what served as breakfast, was uninspiring and not particularly nutritious and was avoided by him. John thought that was the least of their worries. The question that was important was what did the future have in store for them?

The immediate answer were two events with totally contradictory interpretations. As he attempted to leave the building a feminine voice called him by his title and he instinctively turned round. It was Diana Mosley, her face ecstatically happy and radiant.

Her remarks inspired both confidence in the future and immediate relief from the unknown possibilities that could confront them.

"My husband was so effervescent and optimistic about the future and even asked when he could walk again. I could say that he looked the picture of health but he insists on wearing that stupid bandaging in order to surprise his visitors. Please could you do something about removing all the bandages? I, we, are indebted to you, and certainly there must be something that my husband can arrange to show his appreciation and gratitude?"

At which propitious moment two waiters miraculously appeared bearing, with the art of many years experience and expertise, two large trays, thoughtfully covered by ironed linen cloths which they, with artistic and theatrical effect, as if taunting a raging bull in a bullring, pulled away to reveal a magnificent display of the finest breakfast ingredients that the best hotels, in the old days, could produce.

Taunting her husband, she began to spoon feed him porridge which had been generously covered with double cream and sprinkled with Demerara sugar, allowing him to drink, through a straw that had been thoughtfully provided, blood red orange juice though it was obvious that he was having difficulty holding the equisite and elegant crystal glass in his bandaged hands. Diana Mosley turned to Mr. Wrighton and, with a sincere tone of genuine interest, asked if he had eaten.

John thought carefully, not wishing to offend her or more importantly the unknown forces that were lurking outside .His answer was honest and surprising for he had not eaten or drunk since the evening before last, such was the speed of events since yesterday morning. He could not speak for the other two young men and had no intention of mentioning the hospital's fare.

Nearly an hour later the same two waiters returned, laden with a number of trays which were presented with the same professionalism and verve and which were covered with a vast array of superb freshly and excellently cooked hot and cold dishes which were gratefully appreciated.

During the morning the President received a small number of visitors and their presence spurred him to have the bandages removed by one of the junior casualty doctors who was on his allocated shift.

Early that afternoon, the three doctors, still sated by the magnificent breakfast, were formally requested by Diana Mosley to join her for lunch and, ominously, to meet the President's head of security. The three men knew, instinctively, that their future was literally in his hands.

He was charming, erudite, even witty in the presence of the President's wife but the three doctors independently recognised that beneath the image, designed and tailored to meet the President's approval, lay a cold, ruthless and pragmatic streak that would not be assuaged by petty personal emotion. They dined frugally and awaited the true nature of the person to emerge from the chrysalis of his image. Some thirty minutes later in the privacy of his temporary office he clearly, lucidly and unequivocally summarised their position:

"You are all in protective custody as you are not only responsible for the health and recovery of the President but are custodians of a State secret which may not ,at any time, be made public. You will, of course, be given at your request, any medical facility to assist the President return to full health and during this period every reasonable facility will be made available for your comfort. Ultimately your future will be determined by my superiors."

Their immediate fate was now clear, but the man continued...

"As an urgent imperative and with the sole aspect of security in mind, I intend to have the President moved to another location, most likely the Wrotham Park Estate, where you will accompany him and give ongoing medical treatment, but I recognise that a further period in this hospital may, or will, be necessary."

John Wrighton responded confidently and confirmed that he understood the man's concerns and it was his intention to err on the side of caution, in view of the patient's age, and that he was to be given fourteen days rest after which a series of X Rays were to be repeated, which he hoped, would confirm that the healing process had begun, then the patient could be taught to use his crutches. Once he had regained his confidence he could be moved, preferably to a ground floor location, thus avoiding the necessity or potential danger of using stairs.

Dr., Mr Wrighton also suggested that this time scale could give the Estate an opportunity to make adequate arrangements and was pleased that Wrotham Park had been chosen for it was conveniently near to the hospital in the event of an emergency or for routine treatment such as a further course of X Rays. In answer to the man's questions he confirmed, of course, that X Rays could be taken through the plaster casts but he would check the equipment and consult his technical records though he felt that he, and his two associates, who were acquitting themselves well, should be allowed some latitude and freedom.

John's parents and family had recently left the area and he now no longer had any immediate connections with the Hagley Wood suburb of Barnet though he still nurtured great nostalgia for Priddeon's Hill and above all the adjacent Hagley Common where the former Olympic Champion, the late Jack Lovelock, like him but a generation before had trained and where he had felt the exhilaration of the wind and rain in his face, had seen the wild rabbits scurrying around and where he had felt at peace with life and nature.

The man would consider, and if need be refer, his request that the three men be permitted some liberty- the word freedom seemed anathema to him-even if it were under discreet supervision. The three realised that their ultimate future could rest in the hands of Diana Mosley and sometimes the memory of grateful people is both short and fickle.

The days – and nights – fell into an unofficial, even predictable, routine that went someway to satisfy the three doctors and most important of all, their sole and exclusive patient, but they were still effectively confined to the private wing, however an unspoken freedom was permitted which allowed them to leave the building and to wander briefly around, but not beyond, the immediate vicinity. They had been forbidden to speak to, or communicate with, anybody not connected with the private wing which could be considered as an isolation ward.

But above all they could not pursue their professional careers and were, in reality, little more than menial servants assisting, and supervising, the day to day essential needs of their sole patient.

Their primary pleasure, and the highlight of each day, were the three visits and delivery from the Wrotham Park Estate of their superb and lavish meals, always presented and served by two highly experienced waiters once they had satisfied the dietary needs of the patient, but this was no substitute or amelioration that could justify the interruption to the challenge and service that the practice of medicine, in its many diverse forms, could give.

Despite the fact that their embargo on visits by non immediate family members had passed, the President was still only visited by family members and his wife Diana, and their concern for his well being and recovery was the only time that any one of the three doctors, who were always in imminent attendance, were contacted by the visitors or Diana Mosley who appeared to have forgotten her earlier appreciation of their work.

The patient's day had become as regular as the swing of a metronome. He would wake at eight-thirty and at nine o'clock precisely, a courier would arrive with all the national newspapers which would subsequently only receive a cursory glance and almost at the same time his breakfast would be delivered which, like his other meals, was consumed with the same enjoyment and relish as by the three doctors who always ate separately from him.

They therefore did not notice that his interest never focused on the headline articles which he visibly dismissed with a cynical and wry smile but he concentrated his attention on the day's forthcoming television programmes and the crossword puzzles which temporarily absorbed his concentration.

If there was a highlight to his day it was probably around eleven a.m. when a different courier arrived and delivered the *New York Times, the Washington Post and the Stars and Stripes.*

On the first Friday, the twelfth, during lunch, the younger of the two casualty doctors commented, in passing, that whilst the *Stars and Stripes* was always the same day's edition, the other two journals were always consistently one day late and that day were the editions for Thursday October eleventh and both had led with details of the new Middle East war which was not being reported in any of the British newspapers. The doctors concurred, but did not pursue the subject further, that the President was currently obtaining news of events from the United States journals which explained why he gave them his meticulous attention even occasionally marking specific sections and sometimes making notes in a book.

On the first Monday, two different television sets had been installed, one which would receive the approved national channels, the other, more interestingly, the American forces television network in the United Kingdom and Oswald Mosley would brook no interruption, even by his wife, when an interesting film was being broadcast or if he was viewing a news cast on the United States military channel which would receive his almost addictive and undivided attention.

On that Friday, after lunch, the President was immersed in a 'soap opera', *General Hospital*, and was unconcerned that his attendant physician was at a loss how to use his valuable time. John Wrighton casually began to read the previous day's edition of the *Washington Post* having exhausted the vacuous contents of Friday's *Times*. Apolitical, his reading habits had been limited to the Lancet, which now was a shadow of its former formidable self, now being published only quarterly and much reduced both in size and information.

The contents of the *Washington Post* were a dramatic revelation and in contradiction to the British newspapers. Factual and objective, in a manner that domestic papers were blatantly and obviously propaganda outlets in the 'national interest', articles were intelligently written but above all were incisive and informative.

The leading article on the front page was coverage of the war in the Middle East and was accompanied by a striking aerial photograph of a column of Israeli tanks, charging across the Sinai desert, creating a storm of dust in their wake . The banner headline confirmed a massive and ruthless counter–attack against an inferior and smaller number of Egyptian tanks though none of this news was in the British papers. Inside the journal he chanced upon a further article, also accompanied by a photograph, combined with a caustic and blistering editorial opinion.

The photograph recorded the visit, led by Hugh Stephenson, of a delegation of five members of the National Council including John Tyndall and Andrew Duggan to Washington which was received by a confident and ebullient Vice-President, Spiro Agnew, who that same day apparently had successfully rebutted malicious and fraudulent accusations by the now disgraced Attorney- General, Elliot Richardson, that he had ,over an extensive period, criminally filed incorrect income tax returns.

The purpose of the meeting was to negotiate supplies of the latest military equipment but the journal`s defence correspondent intimated that the President, Richard Nixon, who had yet again deliberately snubbed his ally's delegation, was only prepared to lease some of their fleet of obsolete Polaris submarines and their missiles, which would still be under the ultimate control of American naval officers assigned to each vessel.   The editorial was scathing.   It asked how representatives of the British Government could appear and act in such a positive manner when yet again it had been snubbed and humiliated.

The article quoted Hugh Stephenson who spoke on behalf of the representatives of the 'Air Strike' and 'Sea Strike' forces, the organisations that had superseded the now obsolete and redundant Royal Air Force and Navy. The former was endeavouring to procure the installation of the powerful Titan Two missile system fitted with the nine megaton W53 series thermonuclear weapon whilst Sea Force hoped to secure four, or possibly five, of the new generation submarines and their missiles(the awesome Poseidon system)...

"They were confident that their requirements (and shopping list) would be met in full, enabling them to continue the joint equal partnership as the defenders and leaders of the free world."

TWENTY-THREE

During the late afternoon of Friday the twelfth, whilst one of the casualty doctors, watched by John Wrighton, was giving the patient a routine, but thorough examination, that the duty security officer, not having received a response to his knock on the door, entered the room, sincerely apologised both to the patient and the two attendant doctors, and then discreetly and quietly spoke to Oswald Mosley. As he left the room the two doctors were informed by their patient that an important visitor, known for his impatience, was waiting outside but would have to wait until the examination had been satisfactorily completed.

Ten minutes later, just as the examination was being concluded, a violent noise was heard outside, followed by a scuffle and the door being hurriedly opened. The opened door revealed a man, clearly and visibly agitated, and dressed in a military outfit who then, with complete disregard for the circumstances, in a voice that expressed his arrogance, demanded that:

"The two visitors [sic] immediately leave the room as he needed to discuss an urgent matter of national importance and for which action was long overdue."

Oswald Mosley had had previous skirmishes with the man`s impetuous and aggressive nature which were intensifying and becoming almost implacable as he relentlessly acquired more and more power and he responded, in measured tones, addressing him by his first name (Colin), defusing a potentially explosive situation.

"I am aware of the nature of the matter, which has been on my mind since before the helicopter crash, for as we both know, was the reason and purpose of my unfulfilled visit to Wrotham Park and that most importantly I am grateful and appreciative of your interest in my health."

There then followed a brief hiatus, a tranquil interruption, when the visitor must have sensed that his blunt approach had been parried and rebuffed, which permitted him to courteously respond to the President`s diplomatic reply. Shortly after which the younger doctor left the room, his task completed, leaving Mr Wrighton to follow him but he was stopped by the President, who possibly required him as a barrier that could obstruct any possible intimidation by the visitor.

In the background, the state controlled television channel broadcast its presence but only received the President's partial attention, however his visitor was strangely infuriated and insisted, much to the suppressed anger of his host ,that:

"He had no intention of competing against such a device, despite the recent invention, by their scientists, of a device connected to the cathode ray tube that could soon transform the set into a surveillance camera able to watch and monitor the viewer and his surroundings."

He was obscure and indirect when he presented his facts, clearly uncomfortable at the presence of a witness, but the doctor was able to construct the essential outline of the problem, though the fundamental matter was alluded to as if his very presence precluded the two men from directly referring to the substance of this clearly highly confidential situation. Colin Jordan had procured a sixteen millimetre film which he had intended to screen in the presence of the President at Wrotham Park the previous Saturday and whilst both men were aware of the contents, the President freed himself from any inhibitions and candidly commented that:

"He did not have the power, influence, or any authority to persecute the man for coprophilia and that any resolution of the problem would have to be taken by the man's peers in the National Council. Indeed whilst the habit was grossly unnatural and abhorrent to most people he felt certain that the members of the National Council would balance the man's previous contributions to the success of the revolution and his future potential contribution against the inconvenience and any minor suffering caused to the vulnerable and wretched young boys shown in the film."

Mr Wrighton had been facing his patient when he heard the triumphal cords that preceded the national news. Colin Jordan must have turned the sound up for the newscaster was clearly heard to state that:

"Earlier that day, the President returned to his duties, following a heavy cold, and is seen opening a new extension to the Jaguar car factory which will enable the manufacturer to increase production levels and the export of Jaguar sports cars to the United States which eagerly absorbs this exciting car and its sister saloon models. Here the President is seen speaking to factory floor staff before joining fellow workers in the canteen for lunch."

His Latin was somewhat rusty but he could still construct a translation which disgusted him. Less than four feet away from him lay the President, who in the next seven days would commence the next stage of his recuperation and recovery. This was no absurd fantasy. The revolution, the end of Parliamentary government and perhaps even the 'democratic' vote to abolish the Monarchy could all have been a fraudulent deception, but the image of the President was incontrovertibly a sham, a theatrical illusion and he, unlike the rest of the nation, now knew of a deception to perpetuate the image and status of the President. Oswald Mosley was superfluous, but his image and paternal influence over the nation could be eternal. Metaphorically, but of course not literally, the apolitical surgeon was pole-axed by the cynical and evil truth.

TWENTY-FOUR

The following day, the national press carried wide coverage of the President's visit, including a number of photographs and it was impossible for his two junior casualty doctors not to read or be unaware of the event. John Wrighton sensed that they all now shared a new secret, the consequences of which were too dangerous to contemplate.

Two weeks later, the three doctors and their patient moved to the heavily, but discreetly guarded, tranquil setting of Wrotham Park. A week earlier, a series of X Rays had confirmed that the healing process had successfully begun and the patient quickly acquired the skills and confidence to use crutches giving him a new freedom and his carers a new concern that the President might overextend himself and prejudice his recovery.

Whilst the three physicians now enjoyed greater liberty, magnificent catering facilities and the freedom of the estate, they would soon be confronted by their separate fates and for John Wrighton, he would become an unwitting witness to the final chapter of a journey that had begun in the secret, conspiratorial, pre revolutionary world of the underground cafes of Moscow before the outbreak of the First World War and the dying days of the autocratic Russian Tsarist Monarchy. Through a meandering, sometimes random chain of events, British Parliamentary democracy had been destroyed and a Monarchy, that in various forms, had survived for over a thousand years was ended, and the ultimate result was not a utopian socialist society, but its anathema, a totalitarian right wing Fascist state.

TWENTY-FIVE

It is said that all roads lead to the eternal city of Rome, but my journey of discovery conveniently terminated, not at the end of the Appian Way, but off of the A1000 in the Wrotham Park Estate where, ironically, the last vestige of Parliamentary democracy was destroyed by John Tyndall, who was in the forefront of the arrest of the final British Prime Minister, Harold Wilson. Ironical, for at the same location and in the same room, John Tyndall would be arrested for an offence that was not on the Statute Book, for *ALL* [author's own emphasis] Parliamentary Acts had been swept away and none of the State of Emergency-Martial Law proclamations *SPECIFICALLY* defined his actions as an offence.

My report is based on observations from impeccable primary and secondary sources of the actual events, which overlapped each other and are described below.

Furthermore, the spectre, shadow and myth of the discredited Jewish conspiracy, allegedly revealed in the notorious and fraudulent Protocols of the Learned Elders of Zion, was again maliciously raised because of the appearance of the ethereal Joel Ben Yitzhak and his attempted manipulation of those who were a party to some of the events, but his presence was the result of a more pressing and important matter.

Wrotham Park and the surrounding estate was a convenient location, both for members of the National Council and their guests, to relax, unobserved, close to Central London, without them having to travel to their private estates located further away from the metropolis.

The three doctors had been in residence for nearly three weeks when a group of American travel agents, antique dealers and businessmen arrived. The National Council was determined to earn American Dollars by any means possible (including, for example, overlooking male and female prostitution in brothels and leisure centres specially opened for American servicemen based in the country, provided that payment was collected in U.S. Dollars, however this measure was not entirely successful for some enterprising British residents, close to the many bases scattered throughout the country, used their own initiative to entice the servicemen to part with their dollar bills even though possession was a capital offence).

From where the original idea sprung, or who even first conceived the basis of the plan, is now lost in the mists of subsequent events, however the National Council no longer had any interest in the history or traditions of the nation, indeed they had a contempt for the artefacts, whether valuable or not, that identified or represented events in the history of the country. They were, however, interested in raising, as much as possible, U.S. Dollars to be used for the purchase of military equipment. The party of Americans were the vanguard that would precede selected groups of wealthy tourists or representatives of institutions or organisations who would be permitted to bid, in exclusive auctions, for the nation's heritage which would be leased to the successful bidders, whether they be individuals, institutions or organisations, for a fixed period, normally restricted to fifteen years, after which they would revert back to the British authorities. Thus the wealth and heritage of the nation, acquired and accumulated over hundreds of years was now in jeopardy of being temporarily or permanently lost if their new custodians were inclined to be dishonest.

And some of the country's rapacious leaders were not disinclined to privately permit the export of any goods, be they rare fossils, paintings plundered from private ownership, or exotic cars if the conditions of what was effectively private *PURCHASE* [author's specific emphasis] were attractive.

Of course none of the three doctors were privy to the minutae of the group's plans and the exact reason for their hosts' lavish hospitality, but they had been informed, in general terms, of the purpose of the visit whilst, in response, they had parried the group's enquiries concerning the health of the President, whose accident had been covered in the American press but had not been the subject of much interest.

She however was the focus of the group's attention and also attracted the interest of the three doctors, but any normal male would be excited, even fired, by her vivacity, her personality or her stunning natural beauty. John Wrighton was also drawn to admire her and the professional opinion of the three men was that she was in her early fifties but, according to the older of the two casualty doctors, she could pass for a woman in her late thirties. She exuded the glamour, elegance and sophistication that Hollywood portrayed so well, especially the way she dressed and the aura of glamour that her appearance created and which was now no longer shown on the British cinema screens or on the state controlled television channels.

In a rare instance of disagreement the senior doctor considered that the appearance of her skin was finer than Alabaster but the younger of the two junior doctors both trumped and corrected him when he responded with an almost erotic desire that:

"She was the living embodiment of a classical Greek statue carved with passion from the finest marble that could be hewn from the quarries."

The incoming new guests unexpectedly arrived twenty-four hours early and would have been allocated some of the rooms that the outgoing party of Americans were to vacate. Their arrival caused great consternation and administrative confusion until the General Manager was located and effortlessly resolved, to everyone's satisfaction, the dilemma.

It was an insignificant and understandable complication that was readily resolved. They had travelled on an earlier connecting flight from neutral Sweden, deliberately to reach London as soon as possible, and the change had not been registered with the aviation authorities in England, however Presidential suites at the Dorchester Hotel in central London had been urgently arranged and chauffeur driven cars would arrive after dinner to transport them on the fifty minute journey and most impressively, the central London store Harrods (now subject to restricted entry and U.S. Dollar currency payments only), would open exclusively for them, early the following morning, to meet their shopping requirements.

There was not one murmur of dissatisfaction, only of appreciation which was later enhanced, when over dinner, they were informed that following their visit to Harrods and during their return to Wrotham Park, a short diversion would take place giving them a special viewing of the tomb of Karl Marx in Highgate Cemetery where they could place wreaths of red roses that Harrods would have ready for them.

The party of four Soviet 'diplomats', accompanied by two 'translators', travelling under Swiss diplomatic documentation, were in Britain ostensibly on a mission to develop trade links - despite the fact that since November nineteen sixty-three a state of war had, *de facto*, existed - and that although currently military action was restricted to both sides harassing the other in the Mediterranean and supporting skirmishes and confrontations through their surrogates in the Balkans, the reality was that direct military conflict had ceased. But trade had continued and flourished since the assassination of the American President ten years before, through the initiative of entrepreneurs based in neutral Sweden, who acted as conduits and agents between the two sides and had permitted Sweden to swiftly overtake Switzerland as the focal point of trade between the old 'West' and 'East'.

At the root of the present *status quo* and its corollary was the realisation that neither side could win an all out war and it would be catastrophic for either side to launch a pre-emptive thermonuclear first strike because their enemy, although perhaps even mortally wounded and with its leadership probably dead within an hour of the first missiles being launched, would still have a battle plan and adequate reserves, in the air ,on land, and at sea (in reality *UNDERNEATH* – author`s very special emphasis) based on the Polaris and now the Poseidon nuclear submarines or their Russian equivalents to devastate their enemy. In one word it would be suicide.

Thus the world now lived in equilibrium, though both sides secretly feared the intentions of the 'Great Helmsman', the dying Mao Tse Tung and his unknown successor since his proclaimed heir, Lin Piao had been killed in unusual and still unclear circumstances. The country was in turmoil, being politically cleansed, in what was known as the 'Cultural Revolution' and it had been publicly announced, rather chillingly, that the regime was prepared to use their arsenal of hydrogen bombs to promote their social revolution. Mao`s Prime Minister, Chou En Lai, had categorically stated that they were prepared to sacrifice *SEVEN HUNDRED AND FIFTY MILLION* or even a *BILLION*(Author's emphasis) of their own countrymen to bring Socialism to the oppressed people outside of their orbit of influence which would now even include the Soviet Union who had been branded as 'Revisionist' but above all had...

"Betrayed Marxist-Leninism."

The Soviet delegation would soon have informal meetings with members of the National Council including Manny Gold, Hugh Stephenson and Andrew Duggan who just returned from the United States and the 'Manchurian' question would, no doubt, be raised by both sides and for the British perhaps this was a once only, golden opportunity to create the foundations of an arrangement that could rectify and end the decade long estrangement with the incumbent American President and his predecessor.

But one member of the Soviet delegation, responsible only to First Secretary Leonid Brezhnev, had brought knowledge of the final hours of Lin Piao: how he and his party had fled from China with details of their nuclear arsenal and more importantly of their delivery platforms of bombers and missiles and that fifteen minutes away from the protection of Soviet fighters, which had flown into sovereign Chinese territorial space, their plane had been shot down by Chinese fighters. He was empowered to disclose these and other facts and an offer from the First Secretary that was so implausible but could alter the future balance of power.

They dined early, their dinner representing the best of British cuisine beginning with grilled lobster, followed by Scottish Aberdeen Angus roast beef with traditional Yorkshire Pudding and finishing with bread and butter pudding drowned in double cream and the diners showed their appreciation by demanding not only each a second portion of the dessert, but in one case, a third. Their conversations, in Russian, were subdued until their hosts presented them with ice cold vodka which was consumed with gusto and which fuelled their joviality.

Manny Gold had been urgently summonsed to receive the party of premature visitors and he arrived just as the party of Americans returned from their final full day of meetings and viewings of potential auction artefacts.

However, behind the facade of the potential promise of future cooperation, the leaders of the Soviet delegation knew that any negotiations could not begin until one further interested party had arrived, the man who had proposed and promoted the meeting, and whose own agenda would form part of the discussions. He represented an organisation that was unincorporated, unpublicised and was even ethereal, but its aims, by its actions were clear and specific. Both the Politburos of the Union of Soviet Socialist Republics and the People's Republic of China, now ideologically in opposition, both actually trusted the coiled snake, the Jew, Joel Ben Yitzhak .

And one member of the delegation also had an item that the head of the K G B had entrusted to him an hour or so before his departure from Moscow: An envelope that had to be handed to Andrew Duggan and no one else. It was to be, in the words of the head of the K G B, Yuri Andropov...

"A sign of their good faith."

The two 'translators' were, in fact, in addition to their skills as fluent English speakers, K G B officers whose primary responsibility was to protect the delegation both from unnatural local influences and their own human frailties. Of the four men, one had replaced a diplomat at the last possible moment, though this had been planned from the outset and it was claimed that he was a specialist military officer and of the four was the only one unable to speak any English.

TWENTY-SIX

John Wrighton followed the party of sixteen or seventeen Americans into the dining room and was shown a table made up for three guests on the periphery, which allowed him an excellent view, both of the whole room including a vast specially made up table which accommodated the effervescent party of Americans, and of the vivacious American woman who again was the centre of attention for her fellow compatriots, who could not be unaware of their new fellow guests whose behaviour became more rowdy and boisterous as the flow of vodka generously continued.

Purely, for professional purposes, he observed her and whilst the rest of her party seemed to deliberately ignore the presence of men with whom they were notionally at war, she, strangely, seemed drawn, not only to their presence, but their behaviour and loud conversation. There was something in her attitude that he could not quantify.

Not surprisingly, the sound of the spoken Russian language revived memories of the only time he had been in the Soviet Union, some fourteen years before in September nineteen fifty-nine, and he wondered about the fate of the men and women that he had briefly met,' on both sides'.

Suddenly his view was obscured, as a contingent of waiters converged on the banquet table carrying two large turkeys, accompanied by all the trimmings that an American would expect, for the restaurant manager announced, to the delight of his guests, that their hosts were providing an early feast in anticipation of the forthcoming Thanksgiving Day Holiday, which he hoped they would all enjoy at home, with their families and friends and remember this early celebration. The inviting smell of the cooked birds wafted over as he noted that generous portions of corn bread and cranberry sauce were being distributed with the meat.

His interest and attention was distracted when unexpectedly a voice asked ...

"May I join you?"

John looked up and saw the pleasant smiling face of a man whom he recognised but was unable to identify. The man clearly sensed that the doctor did not know his identity and to put him at his ease, stated that:

"I know who you are, you are the surgeon who performed the remarkable act of bravery that saved the life of the President and who has been attending to him ever since. You have our gratitude. Incidentally my name is Manny Gold, but I am most adamant that you call me by my first name, it would be an honour.

Oswald Mosley may be down later to meet our two sets of guests but I understand that he has been drawn into a meeting with..."

He stopped abruptly as if he wanted to say something, but was constrained by discretion.

The opening introductions having been completed, Manny Gold showed great interest in the health and recovery of the President, but the response was guarded and unspecific for the doctor was discreet and did not wish to disclose what might be determined a state secret, answering briefly, but honestly, that:

"He was making an excellent recovery" (without stating ...for a man of his age).

Gold judiciously changed the subject, noting that Mr Wrighton had shown great interest in the premature Thanksgiving Day feast and the two turkeys that were currently being carved .

"Perhaps I could ask the restaurant manager if he could prepare two additional plates for two salivating guests who wished to join in the celebrations? "

At which point John signalled his approval and his fellow guest rose and walked assuredly the few steps across the room to talk to the manager, immediately drawing his attention, and a smile which confirmed that their wishes would soon be met. Then Gold turned round, his face as white as a sheet. He unsteadily walked back to the table, sat down and slowly began to recover his composure as if the circulation of blood was returning, but the doctor immediately could sense the man's unexpected distress. Asked if he needed his professional attention, he emphatically confirmed that it was unnecessary but strangely sat with his back to the banquet table of Americans.

They were enjoying their Thanksgiving Day feast and a conversation that was devoid of any contentious matters when the party of Russians rose from their table and began to march out of the dining room, but one of the party, probably, but most likely the worse for wear, accidentally brushed past Manny Gold causing him to drop his fork which the Russian picked up and returned to him, speaking in Russian and presumably apologising. Dr. Wrighton, coincidentally at that very moment, looked across the room at the American woman and realised, or convinced himself, that she not only understood what had just been said but it was not an apology.

Shortly afterwards the sequence of unconnected events continued when the President, expertly using his pair of crutches, entered the room and was immediately met by the manager who offered to prepare the table that had just been vacated by the six Russians and moments later one of the American delegation presented himself and offered his own place as a sign of the party's goodwill. Mosley turned, clearly saw the stunning American travel agent, hesitated, but stated...

"Your hospitality is deeply appreciated but the duties of office must come first and therefore, with sincere regret, I must decline your kind offer and the company of such an attractive young lady."

The President sat down between his doctor and Gold, smiling at the former but addressing his remarks to the latter. They were frank, candid, hushed but indiscreet clearly demonstrating his trust in the doctor and the urgency of the matter.

"I have just seen the film that Colin Jordan has, I believe, hawked round some members of the National Council and he has demanded that I take some immediate, urgent action against the person involved."

At which moment John Wrighton correctly sensed that it would be prudent to excuse himself and he rose, citing the necessity to leave the room for a few minutes.

What he would not hear, for he was outside the room and the comment was spoken in hushed tones, was an assessment and warning...

"He is dangerous, incorrigible, but above all, venal. I fear that I was the catalyst that first promoted his aspirations to the levers of power and that I am now unable to halt or derail his progress. I found the film degrading, humiliating and embarrassing. The acts upon the young boys, disgusting, however it appears that Jordan wishes to usurp Tyndall in his pursuit of power. I, we, may have to choose between the lesser of two evils."

He shivered in the cold mid November evening air but felt that it was both wise and prudent to suffer this minor inconvenience than have knowledge of an unwanted and possibly dangerous state secret. Like the famous scene in the 'Third Man', which was currently being shown again in British cinemas, he stood hidden in an alcove, a shadow masking his presence, but the brilliant light from the reception hall, which flooded onto the carriageway outside, suddenly illuminated a fleeing woman, the woman, who exited the building and begin to search for something or someone when, without warning, they both heard an incorporeal voice call out, in Russian, and he watched, unobserved, as she walked towards the source and origin of the call. Then, unexpectedly, he heard the voices of a man and a woman speaking in Russian. There was no doubt in his mind of the language that was being spoken and the conversation continued for what seemed minutes until it came closer and closer when suddenly the two were illuminated by an upstairs light. It *WAS* the woman and he was the man who had accidentally brushed past Gold and had then apologised. They were holding hands, not like lovers but like a brother and sister and they spoke only in Russian.

He would never know that for a few minutes, together with their old and dear friend, they would be reunited and for the three of them, after three decades, the random years would be ended, but the fear of discovery was permanently hanging over them, for each bore secrets that could, or would, destroy them.

Manny Gold decided that the President's dilemma would give him an ideal opportunity to excuse himself and perhaps meet, for the last time, his two dear old friends. Excusing himself on the grounds that he wished to mull over the dilemma, he quickly left the building in response to the hurried message that had been clumsily passed to him and which he hoped she had also heard.

Once he left the building he soon located his friends but he had also been observed by a man who would never know the origins and reasons for this unusual *rendez-vous*.

Like undisciplined children they all rapidly spoke at the same time, disregarding the priority of the other two but absorbing the others' comments and remarks, temporarily discarding the cloak of secrecy that had covered much of their lives and protected them from their actions both present or past.

The truth could destroy them all. Lavrenti Beria's orders, the existence and real purpose of the camp and the massacre of the former American residents, another Katyn Forest manifestation of the evils and horrors of war. Presumably the American authorities were still unaware of the final fate of all those idealistic American Socialists who had emigrated in the nineteen–thirties, during the Great Depression, to the promised land of opportunity and social equality. But above all even they did not realise that each one of them had been complicit planning and organising the assassination of the thirty-fifth President of the United States. Kashkarov, who had originally requested his friend, Goldburgh, to devise a plan which he then passed to Nikita Khrushchev, which was refined and which finally had been transmitted for action to Natalia Koenigsberg .

One slip could fatally destroy their lives but the shock of their unexpected meeting was the catalyst that unleashed the avalanche of emotion that overwhelmed their discretion and caution.

A car pulled into the carriageway illuminating all the participants in its beam which scanned across the front of the building, suddenly compelling the three friends to turn away from each other and to separately re enter the house. John Wrighton, whose presence had also been exposed, watched these events and the arrival of Joel Ben Yitzhak.

TWENTY-SEVEN

She could not travel for at least seventy-two hours, because of a mild stomach infection. How she managed either to deceive the impressionable young doctor or to create the symptoms will never be known: perhaps she used Senna which would have caused a laxative effect and if she knew that she was mildly allergic then, conveniently its side effects might confuse a doctor blinded by her dishonest description of her symptoms, but she seemed pleasantly reconciled to his diagnosis and instructions.

The young doctor left the room and promised to visit her again, within a few hours, when he would bring suitable medication, but rest, plenty of fluid and a rigid abstention from all but the most simplest of foods would accelerate her recovery. The General Manager was most cooperative and immediately put him in contact with the United States Navy offices off of Grosvenor Square and its medical department which promised, for a distressed American citizen, to immediately dispatch a courier with the prescription.

Late that morning Andrew Duggan arrived, accompanied by Hugh Stephenson, just in time to meet the departing American delegation, and they were then introduced to Ben Yitzhak by Manny Gold. In the absence of the Soviet delegation who, they were informed, were enjoying the decadent luxuries of 'Harrods', the three men had a preliminary meeting with Ben Yitzhak who they all found to be extremely well informed, competent but unwilling to divulge his own position. Duggan trusted neither Ben Yitzhak or Manny Gold, both because they were Hebrews, but also because the former seemed able to ingratiate himself with the leaders of so many regimes whose values and policies were in contradiction to each other and his motives were unfathomable, and the latter, because he never and still did not believe the story of his time in wartime Russia and the inconsistencies which went back to their first meetings in the Middle East during the war. However, because of their status as joint members of the National Council, it was unfortunately necessary to work with, but still not to trust him.

Andrew Duggan was unaware of the heavy drinking session that his six guests had survived the previous evening, for their appearance and well being could have been that of six abstainers and the two 'translators' introduced, in near impeccable English, the four 'diplomats' to Duggan only, in the temporary absence of Hugh Stephenson who had been urgently summonsed by the President on a matter of great urgency and he was therefore unaware of their identities and the fact that the fourth member was a late replacement and, unfortunately , the only one who was unable to speak any English at all.

Of all those present, only Manny Gold seemed to know Ben Yitzhak and only very slightly and with consummate ease the intermediary, switching effortlessly between the two languages, confirmed that a discreet rapprochement could not only bring economic benefits to both sides, but, in the longer term, perhaps could be the foundation of a more secure political relationship. Cleverly playing on their greed, he argued, without denigrating his connections with the Swedish government, that they could bypass the myriad of entrepreneurs based in Sweden who had grown wealthy on the schism between the two powers.

He also spoke of the fragile peace between the three major powers, flattering his British hosts as to their status in the world order, though of course, he was well aware of their true insignificant role. But Duggan was no fool and it was he who first raised the spectre of China, without admitting the truth: that in depth knowledge of their military capabilities, economic performance and above all the policies of the leadership, which were determined by the enigmatic and reclusive Mao Tse Tung, were sparse and which therefore meant that the British (and their

American protectors) were unable to develop a comprehensive and viable policy.

It was at this moment, that unexpectedly the President and Hugh Stephenson quietly entered the room and whilst Stephenson took his place opposite the four 'diplomats', the President ,aided by his crutches, stood erect and confident before courteously introducing himself to the Russian party and apologising for his lapse not welcoming them on their arrival the previous evening, however on turning round and being confronted by the Jew, Joel Ben Yitzhak, it was universally apparent that they had met before and that their relationship was certainly not amicable or warm, but he had no alternative but to go through the motions of hospitality and welcome.

The meeting, now in the presence of the President, returned to the question of trade and commerce and it was self evident that both parties wanted to expand their direct mercantile dealings and to ultimately bypass the army of intermediaries, by squeezing them out, to their joint financial benefit.

Thus it could be intellectually argued that the Chinese claim that the Soviet Union had betrayed Marxist- Leninism was true or was about to fulfil their analysis. And for the British, for financial gain, they were prepared not to raise the fate of those troops that had been captured, or surrendered, in response to the diabolical chemical warfare attack ten years before, if any of them were still alive. Thus the true, venal nature of politics and expediency clearly expressed itself.

Joel Ben Yitzhak was satisfied with the progress of the meeting and would soon raise the question of relations with China but he first intended to deliver a secret message and dramatic offer from the Prime Minister of Israel, Golda Meir, but events were to take an unexpected course that would change the purpose and direction of the face to face meeting.

TWENTY-EIGHT

DER RING DES NIBELUNGEN:

GOTTERDAMMERUNG

VON RICHARD WAGNER

VOLLSTANDIGER KLAVIERAUSZUG

VON KARL KLINDWORTH

ACT THREE, SCENE TWO,

A WOODED PLACE ON THE RHINE,

GUNTHER`S HALL.

THE DEATH OF SIEGFRIED.

Andrew Duggan joined the parade of delegates eagerly leaving the conference room for the restaurant where a single table had been carefully laid for fifteen guests which was more than sufficient when, delicately, his shoulder was tapped and automatically turning, he saw the hand of one the two Soviet 'translators' who then discreetly indicated, by a hand gesture, for him to remain in the room. The translator, in full view of Duggan, passed to Kashkarov, who was the only other person left in the room, a large envelope, before announcing that the diplomat had a confidential matter to discuss and that he would act as the interpreter since Kasahkarov was unable to speak any English at all.

Kashkarov spoke slowly as his words were translated and at the same time he opened the envelope. Duggan was totally unprepared for the revelation that was to shortly unfold.

"This envelope was sealed in my presence by the Chairman of the Committee for State Security, Yuri Andropov, less than three days ago, and who instructed me to deliver an enclosed smaller envelope to you personally with a request that I should emphasise that the contents were a sign of his good faith and that whilst you review the contents I was to read certain instructions for only I would be able to fulfil the answer to your question. Therefore, I am as intrigued as you are about this whole affair."

Inside were two further envelopes, the larger one addressed to Duggan and a small envelope, hand written by Andropov, addressed to Kashkarov which he eagerly opened. Inside was a brief hand written note but he recognised the author's distinct handwriting.

They each silently read and perused the enclosures whilst a pregnant, electrified air of expectation and anticipation was fulfilled by the contents. The note to Kashkarov, written on expensive headed plain paper, was brief and absolutely specific:

"You are only to identify the person concerned and not to discuss the matter further. After which you may threaten to abort the negotiations if your host pursues the subject, however your identification will be sufficient."

The documentation supplied to Duggan consisted of five separate parts which he reviewed with mounting shock, but ultimately with excitement and satisfaction.

The first, in triplicate, were photocopies of a short letter written in Cyrillic which he could not understand. The second, typed on plain but expensive paper, was a copy, presumably of the photocopies and again in Cyrillic, whilst the next, third document, was a poor quality envelope, inside which was a brief hand written letter, in black ink, neatly folded and annotated in a different coloured ink with a short note and fourthly, on a further piece of plain but expensive paper was, presumably, a translation in English which he avidly read before suddenly noting the author's identity. He was nearly in shock, such were the contents of the letter, but with justified satisfaction he momentarily placed his two elbows on the table and placed his opened palms on his lowered forehead. The investigation which had begun nearly thirty years before and which he had pursued intermittently had proved to be justified; his instincts had been right all along, his inspired intuition combined with an insight into the man's nature were now independently confirmed. He was about to dispose of the envelope when he noted inside a small pack held together by a paper clip and as his hand 'fished' inside to take out the package he caught his finger which he rapidly withdrew and automatically placed inside his mouth to relieve the sharp pain. He tipped over the envelope which ejected the package.

The quality of the shiny paper identified the three small sheets as photographs, each stamped with a Cyrillic inscription and a number (nineteen forty-four). He turned each picture over, the first was a profile, the second a portrait and the final one, a full frontal portraiture of the poorly dressed man taken standing up.

Astutely, Duggan handed one photocopy to the translator and asked him to read out the letter, including the annotation in Russian, which he did not understand. Then he asked the man to translate the document, including the annotation, whilst he compared the oral translation with the typed translation. They not only matched, but he noted that Kashkarov was taken aback when the contents were read out, especially when the translator mentioned, both in Russian and English, the name Lavrenti Beria. He sensed that the Soviet 'diplomat' was strangely shaken by the whole incident including the involvement of the former head of the N K V D. Then unexpectedly, in perfect English, in a tone that more than anything betrayed his true rank and status he ordered the surprised translator to leave the room.

He stood up, took out from his pocket a packet of cigarettes which he offered to Duggan and subsequently lit two cigarettes with a match before wearily sitting down. Perhaps a minute passed in total silence after which he gave to Duggan the hand written note from Andropov and which he promised to shortly translate.

"When I enter the restaurant I will put my right hand on the man's shoulder to identify him...but no more than that. May I please read the original of the letter?"

Duggan hesitated, intending to comply with Kashkarov's request but instead passed over one of the photocopies which he read and then repeated the translation which the official translator had accurately given but he also added...

"This is on official N.K.V.D. notepaper and reads...Comrade Beria.

I pledge my loyalty to the First Secretary, the Party and the N K V D. I am returning to England and when you need me no doubt your agents will contact me with your (he paused for a moment, leaned over and pointed out on the photocopy that the Russian word for your had been underlined for emphasis, and then continued)...orders.

On my return to Landon (he stopped, smiled, again leaned over, pointed to the misspelt word and again continued after explaining his second interruption) I will, if necessary, give a cover story to deflect any information being divulged about the events of the last twelve months. I also hope to trace and meet my parents. And it is signed by a man that I only met once and it was in Lavrenti Beria`s private office a year or so before...Mandel Goldburgh... What had he been doing?"

Wisely, Duggan requested the return of the photocopy and the room was enveloped in total silence. Both men must have been wondering what the other was thinking. Duggan was in a reflective mood, excited and proud that his instincts had been proved correct but he was concerned how deep had been the infiltration of the government by this man and if any of the cancer remained. Wilson had been disposed of but for some years before there had been persistent, even malicious rumours about his true political orientation and it was now imperative that the National Council investigate anyone who had been connected, directly or indirectly, with the final corrupt and disloyal government of the old regime. Immediately he remembered another Wilson appointee, Gerald Kaufman, a Socialist like Goldburgh (or Gold), a Wilson *protégé* who Goldburgh had ruthlessly disposed of without permitting anyone to question him. It was unlikely, but possible, that Kaufman could also have been an agent, sacrificed by a man so devoid of pity or compassion as Gold, to cover his treachery. This could be the excuse that he had waited for, for so long and...

His thoughts were suddenly interrupted by Kashkarov who emerged from his own silence to announce that:

"I forgot to confirm that the annotation was in the handwriting of Beria, ending with his initials and stating...File with my personal papers to be used against Kaganovich and, perhaps in the future, against the other Yid."

Duggan decided to hold back arresting Gold for his treachery because whilst he realised that an offence or offences might have been committed under Items One, Two and Eleven ,Part One of the State of Emergency-Martial Law. Second Edition, he would first consult with his fellow National Council Member Hugh Stephenson who had every reason to harbour antagonism towards Gold, for more than anyone he knew that Gold and Kaufman were Wilson`s *protégés* and *HE* had been the subject of Wilson`s vengeance which had temporarily obstructed and retarded his career. The documents, now safely back in the envelope, were handed to members of his staff with strict instructions to guard them, literally on pain of death.

Duggan entered the restaurant and sat, most conveniently, adjacent to Stephenson, whilst Gold sat almost opposite them, with vacant seats either side of him. It was as if the process of ostracism had begun. The two Russians, after a suitable period, jovially entered, and were shown to places near both Gold and Stephenson by the restaurant manager. Duggan's excitement was barely concealed as he watched Kashkarov stop behind Gold and firmly, but amicably, place his right hand on Gold's right shoulder. The act of involuntary betrayal had been completed.

The conviviality was fuelled by perhaps the last remaining stock of ten bottles of 1950 Petrus Pomerol Grand Vin in the country which permitted Stephenson to propose a toast to the Presidents of both countries, closer links which could facilitate the renewed supply of the best French vintages and, strangely, the resumption of old friendships.

The banquet, for it was far grander than a luncheon, and it is not necessary to itemise the menu for the author has no interest in the first four courses, ended with the astonishing and spectacular arrival, carried by three waiters, of a thirty inch high tower of profiteroles (from which cascaded down chocolate which must have been added at the last moment) and which the guests were soon to discover were filled with double cream and infused with vanilla.

Perhaps it was just before four when Stephenson asked Duggan to join him for a 'breath of fresh air', just as the last embers of sunlight were dying in the twilight but once outside he made a dramatic statement that for Duggan was to sully and to cast into doubt the veracity of the documentation which less than three hours before had shaken him to his very core and created an euphoria of satisfaction.

Duggan was about to hint that he had been given certain information by Kashkarov when Stephenson made his dramatic announcement:

"Amongst the Russian party is a man called Kashkarov-if that is his real name - who I met once, in Paris, in nineteen sixty-three. Despite what you might have been told, or led to believe, his command of English is excellent and by his actions he is not to be trusted. He purported to be a messenger but I suspect his role and motives then and now are more complex and labyrinthine."

Duggan suppressed the desire to confide in Stephenson until he could consider all his options for the very act of Gold's impeachment could well rebound on him.

Kashkarov had recognised Stephenson as the representative of the British government who he had met in Paris during the summer of nineteen sixty-three and he was confident that the recognition had been reciprocated for he had obliquely referred to the meeting in the final concluding part of his toast. He carried a message from the First Secretary to the British President concerning the death of Lin Piao and the information that he was bringing to his new masters, but above all it concerned an offer of cooperation that would primarily involve the United States. The concept was so incredible that only a meeting at the highest level could validate the integrity of the proposed plan.

Even the messenger could not believe that for a further time in his career a plan conceived by him would be taken up by a First Secretary. It had been prepared by his planning department in response to a list of potential military or political scenarios. It was for a joint American and Soviet pre emptive thermonuclear first strike against China and to thwart, in the long term, China's plans for global revolution. He knew that the Chinese limited arsenal of nuclear and thermonuclear weapons paled into insignificance when compared to the joint stock of the only two super powers but more importantly, strategically, the Chinese currently did not have a viable delivery system of missiles and that there was a window of opportunity to decimate the rapidly industrialising China before it was too late. It was imperative that he pass a message to Oswald Mosley.

For Joel Ben Yitzhak the time was now propitious for him to pass on a message both to the Soviet delegation and the British President from his political mistress, the Israeli Prime Minister, Golda Meir, that offered the defeated Arab axis an honourable comprehensive peace settlement, the return of all their lost lands in return for unconditional recognition, secure, defendable boundaries, equitable water rights and the opportunity to create a tranquil harmony between former implacable enemies. He would involve Oswald Mosley despite an almost vicious, violent, vindictive, visceral vendetta that had its roots in the Cable Street battle nearly forty years before, for he knew that the President would inform his American masters of the offer, therefore ingratiating himself and the National Council with the Washington executive.

TWENTY-NINE

But all their masters' plans and expectations were doomed to failure for the prevailing wind in Washington, where the real power lay, would continue to be influenced by the Industrial-Military complex, President Nixon's inherited distrust of London as a source of intelligence or even as a trusted, equal partner but above all by new, circumstantial evidence which pointed to those who were behind the assassination of President Kennedy.

The richly stocked library, luxuriously filled with elegant, antique furniture was an ideal location for what could have been the venue and cauldron of two acts which might have changed the future of the world order, however despite the two messengers conveying their unexpected and striking offers, old prejudices and current insecurities ultimately overrode the potential of a new direction.

The Soviet 'translator' sat strategically outside the door leading into the library, dutifully reading the previous day's Washington Post, alert to any unwanted visitors and enjoying a lemon tea with Demerara sugar. Unfortunately Kashkarov was a prisoner of a rigid and inflexible system for his instructions were to deal exclusively with the British President who was both unaware of the earlier revelation concerning Gold that had been conveyed to Duggan, and then shortly afterwards, the even more spectacular disclosure made again to Duggan, but by Stephenson. Had Mosley known of these two incidents earlier in the day then his attitude might have been more cynical and objective however when the 'bomb shell' of the message was announced, his first reaction was that the British could turn the matter to their advantage with their American allies.

They were the only people in the room, for Mosley had not been originally present when it was announced that Kashkarov did not speak English, however he began the meeting by confiding in his Russian guest that his status as President was essentially ceremonial and that the real power lay in the twelve members of the National Council and not the New Order just as in the Soviet Union ultimate power lay in the hands of the Politburo and not the Communist Party. He also suggested, perhaps rather arrogantly, that he had been chosen, not for his charisma and political expertise but for his acquired wisdom and diplomacy that on more than one occasion had been used to stop various factions destroying themselves in internecine strife.

"Democracy, as a political concept, was a failure and the rights allegedly granted by Magna Carta at Runnymede, obsolete and anachronistic."

Kashkarov, apparently attracted by the justification for the political regime, based on a logic that was as elegant as an Euclidian proof in geometry, was further told that the National Council believed that their purpose was comparable to a human gyroscope that was designed to maintain a harmonious equilibrium. Kashkarov, who was fascinated by this profound statement, was junior to Mosley by some two decades but was aware of his interesting, but chequered history which compelled him to consider a response. Having discharged his message and noting that Mosley had hurriedly began to make notes he threw caution and diplomacy to the wind and in the absence of any witnesses he asked a dangerous and most provocative question to his host when unexpectedly the restaurant manager, who had either been permitted entry by the gate-keeper or had circumnavigated him, came in bearing an ornate salver on which were three exquisite goblets and an unopened bottle of 1811 Chateau de Fontainbleau "Cave de L`Empereur" Vieille Fine Napoleon Cognac and after having described the bottle and its contents with almost reverential respect confirmed that Joel Ben Yitzhak was waiting to meet the two men. Thus the question that had been asked and that the recipient was prepared to answer honestly was never, ever answered.

Mosley went through the courtesy of formal introductions despite his hatred of the Yid Zio, Ben Yitzhak, who he knew had described him, over forty years before, as a ...'Pig snorting in the trough of power' but he correctly sensed that the two men were aware of each other and probably had met before .

The conversation was conducted in English though the two guests sometimes wandered off in Russian and once or twice in another language that Mosley correctly recognised as a bastard version of German, which was Yiddish, and which Kashkarov had learned from his Jewish wife. Whilst they both sincerely apologised for their occasional digressions, Mosley had used the opportunity to vigorously make notes, sometimes interrupting his guests for clarification of certain points and at others, his attention was lost as the enormity of the two messages engulfed his thoughts.

Perhaps each one believed that their offers would be received not only at their face value but more importantly would be positively acted upon, however when Mosley met Duggan the following day together with Hugh Stephenson, a different complexion was placed on the veracity of Kashkarov`s message and as for Gold, Mosley`s ancient hatreds temporarily overwhelmed him and henceforth Gold would be addressed by his birth surname and not by his new Anglicised name. However he still intended to consider the man`s wise counsel and looked forward to his recommendations about the struggle between Tyndall and Jordan.

And finally he promised himself that he would endeavour to repay a debt of gratitude but he was unable to completely fulfil the act of thanks for he was only an instrument of the National Council`s orders.

THIRTY

The following morning the three old friends ate separately in the restaurant, only a few steps from each other but it could have been the actual distance between Moscow, London and Atlanta. John Wrighton sat with his two junior casualty doctors and deliberately watched them. He knew that there was a bond which united them together but it was secret and so unnatural that the very act of contact was forbidden, an act of social incest. And as she left the room he saw a tear rolling down her cheek and he would never know what anguish and distress was hidden behind the aura of beauty, glamour and elegance.

The message was brief. It was a request, a command to meet President Mosley for a brief walk in the gardens.

They unknowingly followed the exact same path that Harold Wilson had regularly trodden during his incarceration nearly a decade before, his thoughts directed to an uncertain future and probably his own demise. John Wrighton correctly conjectured that the President was about to break the news of his fate, not knowing that Stephenson had intimated to President Mosley that the National Council had unanimously decided the destiny of the three doctors.

But before he disclosed their future he began to talk about the world outside of the unreal existence which was the Wrotham Park Estate.

THIRTY-ONE

Dr., Mr John Derek Wrighton was to be astounded by the President's contradictory candour, perversion of the truth and rank hypocrisy concerning the subject and nature of his comments which emphatically strengthened his earlier cynicism and insight into, and about, the New Order.

"I have endeavoured to serve my country throughout my life and have been both rewarded and imprisoned for my loyalty and patriotism. At the age of twenty-one, shortly after the end of the First World War, I was elected as a Conservative M.P. and a decade later became Chancellor of the Duchy of Lancaster in a Labour government under Ramsey MacDonald. By nineteen thirty-two, when I founded the British Union of Fascists, I had recognised the self evident, incontrovertible truth that was clearly visible but was temporarily obscured by the ineffective policies of the existing political parties and which have been the foundation of my principles for the last forty years.

The concept of democracy, of one man -or woman-with one vote each, of universal suffrage, resulted in the inevitable weakening of the very foundations of the nation. And combined with the post war creation of the so called 'Welfare State' and a universal 'National Health Service', undermined the very strengths that gave this country the basis and will both to work and the initiative to create wealth.

But fundamentally, the problem has been, and will ever be that the people, the masses, the proletariat, like herds of wild animals, were both short sighted and only concerned with short term goals, as the herds , scenting water, would rush headlong to the next watering hole, so the electorate would blindly rush to the largest bribe that the politicians of the Right and Left would offer them in their manifestos which they knew that they could not fulfil.

Adolf Hitler recognised the degenerate forces that had destroyed the Weimar Republic and especially the demonic evil of Jewish Bolshevism and with the authority of the German Parliament that spoke on behalf of the people, who had themselves recognised the basic faults in the so called democratic system, gave the leader absolute freedom to direct the nation. Thus we have the precedent that the people consent to devolve total power to the leadership, in their own best interests.

More specifically he recognised the threat of Bolshevism both as an ideological concept and as we have seen by its expansion, its intention to absorb and subjugate alien free nations. Adolf Hitler proclaimed to a world that did not wish to confront the truth that:

"We are your bulwark against Bolshevism! "

However President Roosevelt, the cripple in the White House, and Prime Minister Churchill, the alcoholic who ordered my imprisonment, along with my wife, in May nineteen-forty under section 18B of the Defence Regulations, were politically blind to the real danger and the true enemy of the individuals' rights.

Adolf Hitler was a great visionary who conceived of a major political union, governed from the new capital of Germania, which would stretch from the Atlantic Ocean to the Ural Mountains, a European Union ruled by technocrats in Germania who would be able to neutralise the threat of Soviet Communism. History and events record otherwise and now the world order and the arsenals of military power have changed.

My crime, and again history and events have proved both my innocence and prescience was, that I did not, or was unable to persuade the British people of the dangers of Communism which greatly exceeded Hitler's desire for secure borders, in the East against Russia and in the West against the belligerent French and the Maginot Line which would permit them to launch an aggressive attack on Germany, believing that they were secure behind fortifications of concrete and steel.

During the struggle to secure the future of the New Order and my Presidency I was accused of being a political apostate but I have remained faithful to my values. It became, and continues to be necessary, in the short term, for the whole nation from the President down to the humblest citizen to sacrifice a part of their existence for the good of the state because the reward for success was and is, not only our continued independence but that each citizen would be able to fulfil their destiny. However failure will result in the capitulation to the forces of Bolshevism, the international Jewish conspiracy and all that we striven for.

Unfortunately there are still (fewer and fewer) isolated dissident forces and intellectual concepts that are endemic in the country and it was necessary to identify their roots and the misguided citizens that were still prepared to support and disseminate these ideas which corrupt and distort the education that guides the overwhelming majority and which our enemies, at home and abroad, brazenly and erroneously still describe as propaganda and indoctrination.

The prime duty of any government, or its leaders, since society evolved from wandering, nomadic tribes herding domesticated animals, into permanent fixed settlements and the rise of agriculture, expanding first into villages and then into towns and finally cities has been, and will ever be, its duty to defend its citizens from external enemies and internal subversion and we have been successful carrying out our duty .

But there has been a price that has been shared nationwide. The annual expenditure of our military and security budget absorbs such a vast amount of the country`s resources that unpalatable cuts have had to be made elsewhere: medical services have been cut back, whilst doctors have been directed into compulsory military service and the nation's production of food has been primarily directed to our forces who have valiantly defended our frontiers, and in the Middle East and in the Balkans where, as I speak, they are expelling the forces of extreme Islamic nationalism and communism from both areas .

We are not the first, and I hope that we will not be the last to defend the values of our nation against the hideous beast of Bolshevism and its bastard scion, Socialism. Nearly forty years ago, contemporary to the time when I was struggling to warn our country of the gathering storm of rising Socialism and the Jewish- Bolshevik conspiracy that would internally destroy all that we cherished and valued, Francisco Franco led the Nationalist cause in Spain on a crusade against the evil of the Republicans who were openly supported by agents from Moscow. Franco, by single minded devotion, defeated his enemy in nineteen thirty-nine but it became necessary to cleanse the nation in which an insidious venal virus had become endemic. Thus enemies of the state were hunted down, the infection cleansed and the bastion of Spanish values restored.

This can be the only way forward. Again, at a similar time, in nineteen thirty-four, Chang Kai Shek in China was involved in a titanic struggle with the forces of communism led by the treacherous Mao Tse Tung and he was on the cusp of a monumental and total victory after the aptly named Fifth Annihilation Campaign, but for reasons that are still obscure he allowed his beaten enemy to escape in what was known as the 'Long March' and over a decade later Chang was ousted, and expelled, from the country that he had nurtured and defended, by the perfidious communists.

Despite continuous and concerted action, we face an ongoing struggle against the lies of our enemies who claim that the continued spiral downwards in the ration allowance is a concerted attempt to subjugate the nation by creating malnutrition, lethargy and exhaustion in the people, but nothing could be further from the truth.

I acknowledge that some years ago John Tyndall presented an extremely cogent and persuasive argument (which I believe, in truth, had been conceived, and prepared by his personal assistant, a former 'high flying' top civil servant in the old regime) but accusations that we have and continue, as a matter of policy, to deliberately claim to increase the allowance of certain rationed goods after having previously reduced the allowance ,exposes the lies and hypocrisy of our enemies for we always endeavour to provide for the weak, the pregnant mothers and those who are unable to represent themselves, by making available food when it is plentiful. But.."

John Wrighton had been intently listening, at times confused, at others, shocked at the justification of what was effectively a totalitarian dictatorship and the hypocrisy of the leadership's luxurious lives compared to the living standards of the people. His mind wandered as Mosley continued and he therefore did not absorb the President's further comments until, subconsciously, he heard the phrase...

"After you leave here."

He found them both sitting on a bench beneath the branches of a horse chestnut tree, denuded of its leaves which in the height of Summer would have created a pleasant umbrella against the sun's rays but on that November day it was bitterly cold and exposed them to a biting wind that attempted to search for any and every available orifice. He listened to Mosley who continued, unaware that his companion had temporarily lost his concentration and attention.

"...your two young associates will immediately be conscripted and given, despite their youth, a senior rank and shortly sent to the Middle East, where, I am afraid to tell you, the casualty rate is statistically high. I will personally warn them that the purpose of their assignment is to both utilise their professional skills and ultimately to dispose of them for they and you are parties to secrets that cannot be broadcast.

John, I have in my power the ability and will both to thank you for your care, and to offer you, and close members of your family, emigration rights, though my assistance could place even me in jeopardy. Thus I am making an offer that you accompany me on my next official journey abroad (which, I believe, is to Chicago, before Christmas), as my personal physician, after which you may, if you so wish, seek local asylum, supported by a fund of local currency that you will conveniently steal from me. Thank you for your professional attendance during the last few weeks."

As they resumed their walk John`s mind was swimming with conflicting loyalties, to his profession and the country of his birth, but he calculated that the unwelcome knowledge that he had accrued would, at some time result, in the words of Mosley, in his 'disposal' for the rules of law and order and natural justice had been breached and washed away and that he, and many like him, who could have protested or even halted what was now a nightmare could have saved what they had previously taken for granted, democracy and freedom.

They both instinctively turned round when they heard Mosley's first name being called out by a male voice that was clearly 'out of breath' and they saw Gold rushing towards them and from his disposition, it was clear that he was the bearer of bad or dramatic news.

Mosley addressed him by his birth name, Goldburgh, and his interest was curt and inquisitive...

"Yes?"

The reply was interrupted by Gold searching for breath, a matter which concerned the doctor...

"John Tyndall was arrested very early this morning by Duggan, Stephenson and Jordan and for reasons that I do not know, my informant also tells me that they intend to arrest me ,if only to consolidate their hold on power."

THIRTY-TWO

It was Thursday, November the twenty-second and Wrotham Park was an empty shell devoid of any guests save for the President, his wife and personal physician. The two young casualty doctors had left following a very brief formal meeting with Oswald Mosley who had handed to each of them a group photograph of the three doctors surrounding the President which he had personally signed and dated but he had delegated to John Wrighton the unenviable task of outlining their immediate and long term futures, however he had persuaded himself that their strengths' of character and resilience might just promote their survival. Thus he had washed himself clean of any moral responsibility.

Goldburgh had also been arrested, as the traitor himself had anticipated, and his and Tyndall`s whereabouts had not been disclosed even to the President, a matter that gave him little loss of sleep but he was more concerned that the flow of official documentation had become a trickle and that visits by members of the National Council were like Albatrosses in a game of golf which he had determined to take up again, when the plaster cast had been removed, for there were a number of moribund local clubs that he could reinvigorate, especially for the flow of American visitors who would soon be arriving to bid and if successful ,lease , at a price, the nation`s unwanted treasures.

But it was clear that his prime concern was the impending and ever imminent moment when his physician would confirm the removal of his plaster.

He had recently become very frisky, a situation which was resolved with the discreet assistance and knowledge of the General Manager, and had continued without the knowledge of his wife though her unexpected arrival was too coincidental.

He was bored, but events would soon galvanise him and confirm that even for him tomorrow was insecure.

His ordered and compartmentalised day meant that he did not watch the British television channels until the early afternoon, preferring to watch the American Forces Network for news that was not tainted or perverted as was the B.B.C. and he was literally shocked to learn that that evening the President was to address the nation and he spent the next hour or so futilely endeavouring to contact members of the National Council for details of his participation.

His wife noted his agitation and shared his concern when she heard of the imminent broadcast and that her husband had not been forewarned of his appearance or more importantly of the contents of the speech.

They, the President, his wife and John Wrighton were equally impressed and deceived by the actor, for the man purporting to be the President was not the President as he was shown, on a number of occasions, in full profile and was not encased in a plaster , but then , as it was pointed out, the country had been kept in the dark concerning the helicopter crash and Oswald Mosley`s injuries. Whoever he was, he performed superbly, his appearance, the way in which he carried off the mannerisms and tiny character traits were impressive, even confusing its real subject ,and his voice convincingly also captured the tone and timbre of the part that he was playing, but for its subject it was a betrayal of his status and position, exemplified when the President, in a show of exasperation and anger, accused the man or those who had organised the pretence of stealing his clothes both in a literal and figurative sense.

And then he realised that not only was he potentially redundant and superfluous but that the consequences could be fatal. He ,they, had concentrated on the appearance of the man but not what he had to say and when they at last listened to his speech they were filled with a foreboding about the immediate future and for John Wrighton, the fulfilment of the promise that had been recently made to him.

"...They have betrayed the revolution, but above all Tyndall betrayed you all, secretly working in collusion ,conspiring and conniving , hand in glove, although with different goals, together with the arch traitor Manny Gold, for many of the sacrifices that you made were in vain, whilst he filled his own coffers with profits made from the abundant supplies of food that he had stored in granaries and warehouses that had been designated for national emergencies. Unknown even to his closest associates and shrouded in a cloak of secrecy and obfuscation he had carried out practices and perversions at his residence near the famous city of Winchester that are too despicable and heinous for me to elaborate upon. At the same time we discovered, after a long investigation, during which time many thousands of lives were needlessly lost, both at home and abroad, that the Jew, Mandel Goldburgh, who had blatantly and falsely projected his patriotism under the name of Manny Gold, had been a sworn agent of our bitter enemies, the Bolsheviks, the Soviet Union.

A perfidious coward, spy and traitor, he has fled the country, his current location unknown, but he has been pursued by loyal , indefatigable agents of our nation, determined to bring him back to face the wrath and justice that his crimes justify.

Have no illusions about the task ahead. The New Order has to cleansed and purified of the treacherous infections that these two traitors have introduced into the rank and file of the party and we have entrusted this duty to a loyal patriot, Colin Jordan, who will lead the purification of any vindictive, vicious, venomous, virulent viruses that the two traitors may have secretly introduced. Expect further traitors, spies and fifth columnists to be unearthed and any corruption eradicated.

We will go forward together, for when in the course of the destiny of a nation it is confronted by a crisis of such magnitude that the very fabric of its values are tested to its limits then the leadership, by virtue of its benign strength and integrity, will defend the weak against the tyrannical enemy`s malevolent actions, for victory will be assured.

Victory at all costs, victory in spite of all terrors, victory however long and hard the road may be, for without victory there is no survival."

How many times did I warn you that freedom was fragile and should not be taken for granted?!

The Author.

THE END

THE PREQUEL: IT HAPPENED HERE

AN ALTERNATIVE TRUE HISTORY

EPILOGUE

Thursday November 22nd 1973

ONE

The clandestine meeting was intentionally not held in the Oval Office where the participants might be observed either entering or leaving, but in a nondescript and insignificant office on the third floor of the otherwise little known Watergate office complex in the nation's capital, Washington. Republican President Richard Nixon, successor to the former Democratic President Lyndon Baines Johnson, who had died earlier in the year, was brought to the building in strict secrecy and stealth and was welcomed by the executive editor of the Washington Post, who introduced him to two young journalists who stood in awe of their unexpected visitor.

The office and its contents appeared chaotic but the two young men standing behind an old wooden desk that had seen better days, gathered their composure whilst quietly realising that their coup was to be fully exposed to the President and soon to an amazed nation. Ben Bradlee, the executive editor of the Washington Post, formally introduced his two young investigative journalists, Robert 'Bob' Woodward and Carl Bernstein.

A small number of secret servicemen posing as bomb squad officers were assisting the police, who patrolled and searched the corridors of the deserted building, whilst outside could be seen hundreds of evicted occupants milling aimlessly around as firemen and fire trucks waited patiently for the building to be searched following a hoax bomb threat. When, two hours later, the building was declared safe, two of the men had been spirited away and vanished as if they had never been to the building and as for the other two they temporarily basked in the knowledge that soon their names and revelation would be known nationwide.

One week earlier Ben Bradlee had visited the President in the Oval Office bearing a single sheet of paper on which were typed two very similar, but different series of numbers and letters. But it was the story behind the identification of the numbers and letters that both intrigued and propelled Nixon to institute a treasure hunt amongst dusty and damp long forgotten boxes of files clothed in cascading, intricately weaved cobwebs, which almost hid, but not quite, the evidence and dramatic truth. And then detectives urgently began a search which conclusively confirmed what the two young journalists had earlier reached, an identical result. Absolutely nothing. Two men had been allocated virtually consecutive Social Security numbers and had never existed prior to their applications. Furthermore, discreet parallel enquiries with the two men's families and associates could not definitely produce any firm, tangible evidence fof their early lives.

Ominously, chillingly, one fact did emerge. The man who had committed suicide in Dallas, on Friday, November the twenty-second 1963 and had everything to live for, had owned and used, very effectively, an Italian Mannlicher-Carcano 91/38 6.5 millimetre rifle.

The other man, who had died in a motor accident less than twenty-four hours after the first had committed suicide, had left few clues as to his life since he obtained his Social Security number but one tantalising clue was half remembered by his small circle of friends, two of whom had been quickly located, for they were both in prison, that:

"He was visiting Dallas to meet an old friend whom he had not seen since nineteen forty-four and was interested in how well he had coped with life and to thank him for nursing him back to health."

They both independently remembered his remark for it was perhaps the only time that he had alluded to his early life; and his sudden death, combined with the Presidential assassination, made his remark all the more memorable.

Very little further germane evidence became available and the two journalists were reassigned on more mundane matters until...

TWO

Mandel Goldburgh, also known as Manny Gold, looked outside the double glazed window at a cold, Thursday morning in Chicago, Illinois and tried to adjust to the 'jet lag', for twenty-one hours earlier he had been held incommunicado in an army base somewhere in the Home Counties, a few cells away from a now empty repository that had housed John Tyndall, who was now dead and not, as a sympathetic guard had intimated to him, been moved closer to London for interrogation.

His own arrest had been unexpected and brutal. He was visiting the President to discuss the consequences of either supporting Tyndall or Jordan, an almost impossible choice, but he was siding in favour of John Tyndall, the better of two bad options, when unannounced, Duggan entered the room, accompanied by Hugh Stephenson and an arrogant and contemptible Colin Jordan. Obviously events had overtaken his rational deliberations, for Duggan ignored the President and walked up to him waving a sheet of paper for him to read. It was a photocopy of his letter. All he remembered was the shock recollection of a memory that had been buried so deep that the fact of his communication with Beria had all but been forgotten but before he could even explain the circumstances that had obliged him to falsely declare his loyalty, Jordan barged across the path of Oswald Mosley, called him a...

"Fucking traitor, fifth columnist,sub numan Hebrew monkey and Yid scum",

before hitting him with a cosh so violently that apparently it was some sixteen hours before he awoke in an isolation cell. Although he had been imprisoned for nearly a week he was not aware of Tyndall`s presence until he heard him speaking rather plaintively, a few cells along the passageway and immediately afterwards, the voice of Jordan, and for a few moments he dreaded the sound of a key in the lock of his cell and then the door opening and finally...

Two days later there was a commotion in the passageway, the sound of a key in the lock and then the door opened. He was bungled out of the room where he suddenly saw a small detachment of...

For the first time in just over a week he looked at himself in the mirror and saw a gaunt face staring at him, and as he examined himself he realised that he was still wearing the same suit and shoes which he had so carefully chosen for his important meeting with the President.

He ate breakfast which was a muffin and savoured the strong, sweet coffee. He would have a bath and, if possible, a shave.

But there was only a shower and whilst he luxuriated in the cleansing force of the hot water cascading down, his mind wandered and he realised that his liberation would come at a price. They, the Americans, would require to debrief him and no doubt their British allies would show them the copy letter. He had to protect her, whatever her identity was now and his great friend who would protect him if the situation was reversed but he was undoubtedly back in Russia whilst she was somewhere in the United States.

He was yet to learn that he was staying in a 'safe house' at 5712 Kenwood Ave., Chicago, Illinois but that information would be divulged within the hour when washed, dressed and mentally refreshed he walked into the lounge and was confronted by the man who had earlier delivered his breakfast and an elegant, mature man with immaculately manicured nails, exquisitely dressed, who, with impeccable manners and breeding, 'welcomed home' his guest and began the debriefing by suggesting that his tailor (who he had 'rescued' from England some years before) would be immediately summonsed to measure him for some bespoke suits whilst in the meantime he would urgently arrange for an 'off the peg' complete wardrobe to be delivered.

"It has been an extremely long time since we last met and I am certain that your story is both exciting and interesting. Where would you like to begin?"

THREE

She was woken by the joyous and boisterous sounds of children laughing, giggling, running and jumping on the wooden floor in the corridor outside of her bedroom. She smiled as the door opened accompanied by the muted sounds of giggling and only her three younger grandchildren entered, in single file, for the eldest was now at university studying mathematics and beginning his journey through life.

They congregated around the bed and she reminded them all about the first time that the four grandchildren had simultaneously stayed with their grandparents and how they had tickled the soles of their late grandfather's feet and eventually woken him when he suddenly bellowed...

"Who has woken me from my slumber?!"

It was a very happy home and apart from the withdrawal of the elite K G B troops who had been replaced by a rota of normally no more than three local police officers, *HER* world had not changed.

But for the British people, indefatigable, stoic and immensely brave, starved of the truth and fed a diet of lies, they would only learn a perverted version of the fate of the two former members of the National Council, however their own future had been tragically and incorrectly foretold in poetic terms just over two hundred years before by Thomas Arne ...

"Rule, Britannia! Britannia rule the waves: Britons never will be slaves".

POLITICAL CONTROL BY THE TOTALITARIAN STATE IN THE FORMER 'GREAT BRITAIN'

A BRIEF REVIEW.

In the winter of nineteen sixty-six to sixty-seven, the National Council was confronted by its first major crisis, when external pressure from the 'old' Commonwealth countries of Canada, South Africa, Australia and New Zealand, together with Anglophile organisations in the United States began to raise strong objections to the perceived and actual policies being enacted in the former 'Great Britain'. Primarily they were the restrictions on personal freedom exemplified by the issue of the 'Internal Passport', which incorporated a ration card, and evidence of a policy of blatant and untrue propaganda which hid the truth about the International political balance of power and above all the wanton destruction of democratic and legal institutions and procedures.

Foreign journalists based in London and confidential diplomatic reports enabled Britain's 'friends' to grasp the tragedy of the country's descent into a right wing single party state echoing and reflecting Germany, post January nineteen thirty-three. Pressure was placed on, and then by the five governments, to act decisively with the leadership in London, though the United States government, under President Johnson, was half hearted in its diplomacy for it had already made clear to the leadership that it was not concerned with their internal policies, only that their military bases and commercial operations were not interfered with by British dissidents, citing the historical example of adverse influence by such organisations as C N D, the Committee of 100 and Spies For Peace.

The old Commonwealth countries had been supporting the 'Mother Country' by the export of basic and essential food supplies at rates which were far below the normal commercial tariff on the (now limited) international market, whilst the United States, with the cynicism and commercial consideration for profit, echoed the 'generous' terms of Lend-Lease during the Second World War. Thus the twelve members of the National Council were confronted with a dilemma that could expose them to unwanted pressure.

Intellectually, John Tyndall did not possess those qualities that had, and still distinguish many erudite and well educated politicians, but he was existing in an environment and atmosphere where those attributes

175

were not the primary tools and qualities needed by men who sought power for the purpose and callous intention of maintaining uninterrupted, continuous control. At that time he was at the apex of his power, influence and reputation though the solution that he proposed was undoubtedly the concept of his assistant, who we have already seen in my report was a former 'high-flying' civil servant who had been assigned to him when, and before the revolution, he had first achieved power under Harold Wilson. We can be certain that once *HIS* plan had been approved, and later, when it had proved to be immensely successful, that its origins and concept were solely claimed by him.

Control of the individual, by the issue of the Internal Passport, administered and operated by the paramilitary authorities with ruthless efficiency, could now be coordinated with a new additional policy which with Kafkaesque cruelty would actually effectively control the body of the individual.

By a ruthless policy of food rationing and malnutrition ,mental apathy would be induced, thus simplifying the state's ability to control the individual and thus any attempts at opposition.

At the root of the plan, as Tyndall first explained to the other almost incredulous members of the National Council, based on the proposition Thomas Malthus put forward in his work 'An Essay On The Principle Of Population', was that (put simply) the expansion of population would exceed the increase in agricultural production. Malthus, a trained mathematician argued that the former was geometric and the latter, arithmetic, thus inevitably leading to food shortages and subsequently to famine. It was this proposition that inspired two Victorians, Alfred Wallace and Charles Darwin to independently conceive the idea of 'Natural Selection' and in the context of Tyndall's proposition that the engine of survival, competition, *ASSISTED* by selective food rationing would kill off the weak but leave the survivors weakened.

Tyndall conveniently limited his intellectual explanation, emphasising his argument which he supplemented with the well received comment that they, the National Council, did not have a responsibility to maintain and raise the nation's diet and above all, concomitant, its standard of living, citing the war time rationing of food under the Churchill National government and post war research which had conclusively shown the fairness of rationing but above all that the nation's general health had improved. If their allies in the so called 'Old Commonwealth' were not prepared to understand and accept their dire situation, standing alone against the forces of tyranny and the potential threat of either an all out attack or invasion, the consequences of any reduction or withdrawal of supplies, for whatever reason, would primarily fall on the British people who had borne and were prepared to continue their sacrifices in the cause of peace and freedom. But fundamentally, as he continued, the crucial reason for a draconian regime of rationing was to reduce the nation's will by their physical exhaustion.

The supply and control of the food chain could (and would) be selective, regional and with sophisticated modifications, targeted against and for certain groups. Thus the old and generally unhealthy and therefore unproductive were essentially a drain on the nation's wealth and would therefore be subject to a reduced ration allowance whilst young pregnant women would receive an increased allowance. Workers, in certain industries, necessary for the nation's production of military equipment or export of goods such as motor vehicles or Scotch Whisky would receive increased rations. On the other hand, prisoners who were enemies of the state, in the labour camps, would receive specially reduced allowances, since their sole purpose was to atone for their guilt, by the contribution of their labour, and probably, by the expiry of their sentences, if they were still alive, they might still not be successfully reintegrated into society and were therefore expendable.

Combined with the deliberate, reduced availability of medical services, medicine and the presence of the omnipotent paramilitary former police force, the individual and the will of the individual would be crushed.

It would be crucial and imperative to monitor many aspects of the community's environment for the ever dangerous possibility of an outbreak of infectious, contagious diseases which might get out of control. Mortality rates could be subtly increased and manipulated. In effect there could be a cull of the population that could be promoted by, amongst other circumstances,premature deaths of the 'old', infanticide of children with defects therefore not putting a burden on the state, domestic violence victims and fatalities from illnesses where previously, by the administration of drugs or correct nursing, the patient would have survived.

Apparently, at this juncture, another National Council member-believed to be the representatives of the Air Strike Force - interrupted the presentation and suggested, to much laughter and subsequent applause, that the existing embryonic propaganda system could be massively expanded and refined and that the ration allowances could, for example, be reduced and then, to the plaudits of the propaganda system, raised but to a level beneath its previous allowance.

The same National Council member also suggested that an artificial 'Black Market' could be created, ultimately operated and controlled by the state, but represented by unsuspecting members of the community, selling rationed or unobtainable goods which could be recovered by the paramilitary forces and the parties arrested therefore exposing further enemies of the state. Fear and fear of the unknown, combined with the draconian powers of the authorities would destroy any potential opposition and fuel distrust in the community of their fellow citizens.

But ultimately, it was control of the food supply that could determine the state's iron grip on the community.

THE PREQUEL: IT HAPPENED HERE

AN ALTERNATIVE TRUE HISTORY

AUTHOR'S COMMENTS

Reader,

As you have been able to obtain the three parts of my unauthorised investigation and report which, by necessity, was printed outside of the Republic of Great Britain **AND THEN UNDER DIFFICULT CIRCUMSTANCES FOR SECURITY REASONS** (which is reflected in the errors that you may have noted or the quality of the printing), you will now realise that much of the history that you have learned, following that dramatic Friday, November the twenty-second, nineteen sixty-three, the newspapers and books that you may have read and the information broadcast on radio, film, television and other media is a **TRAVESTY AND PERVERSION OF THE TRUTH.**

Now **YOU** are able to decide if this work really answers those questions about the inconsistencies which you may have detected in the many 'facts' or, for example, the photographs and films that have been published which have up to now formed the basis of your opinions. What you have read, by necessity, included some very unpleasant content matter that my investigations uncovered. I endeavoured to be meticulous and absolutely scrupulous in my presentation of **HISTORICAL FACTS** but certain situations and events were sometimes best described using a flexible, liberal licence. It is also imperfect (but uncorrupted by others' involvement!) and, if I am permitted, I welcome readers' constructive comments, **HOWEVER, ALWAYS BE AWARE OF ECHELON (MENWITH HILL), TEMPORA (G.C.H.Q. CHELTENHAM) BUT ABOVE ALL THE UNITED STATES NATIONAL SECURITY AGENCY AND THE PRISM PROGRAM!**

My report, which was an objective but not comprehensive account of the **TRUE HISTORICAL EVENTS** which shaped our country, included certain descriptions and incidents that were necessary to expose and illuminate both the nature of the totalitarian state and the actions of its original founders and their successors and their disregard and contempt for (the now obsolete concept of) democracy and the basic rights of the individual which were swept away in the former United Kingdom of Great Britain and Northern Ireland .

Because this narrative is **NOT** a novel which would therefore include items of fiction, **YOU**, the reader, should now be able to understand the origins and nature of the totalitarian state. Freedom of an unfettered press, free speech and eternal vigilance were three of the bulwarks that formerly defended our democratic values and institutions.

The primary theme of this work is of betrayal, both of the individual and of a once proud nation, but is also an attempt to examine human nature and how people can, and invariably are, corrupted by power or money or how the weak can be suppressed by the strong or those without moral integrity.

I would like to state that the work that you have now finished reading was in part written (but not researched) under the magnificent cupola of the Duomo in Florence, the Basilica di Santa Maria del Fiore; the awe inspiring Colosseum in Rome (truly a wonder of the world); also whilst enjoying coffee in St. Mark's Square, Venice observing the seemingly unending throng of sightseers; in the university library or Hayward Field stadium of the University of Oregon, Eugene, and finally during a stay in the Alhambra Palace in Granada whilst relaxing in its tranquil gardens, rich with the fragrant smells of exotic plants adjacent to a pomegranate bush bursting with ripe fruit cascading from its branches, but in truth is the culmination of nearly six decades of thought, contemplation and probably frustration as I grappled to understand the complexity and contradictions of human nature.

I have deliberately included extracts from five virulently anti-Semitic publications (and am absolutely unrepentant in their inclusion): the infamous Protocols of the Meetings of the Learned Elders of Zion (both a plagiarism and a fraudulent fabrication) ,which is frequently depicted, in illustrations, as a coiled snake or an octopus, its tentacles enveloping the earth; My Struggle (Adolf Hitler's pseudo-philosophical declaration of faith and a portent of things to come), the vicious and scurrilous tract, The Authoritarian State by John Hutchyns Tyndall, the evil, depraved and perverted Der Giftpilz (The Poisonous Mushroom) from the Nuremberg publishing house of the notorious Julius Streicher and finally, Bolshevism from Moses to Lenin by Dietrich Eckart (who, in January 1919, co founded the Deutsche Arbeiterpartei which, in February 1920, changed its name to the Nationalsozialistische Deutsche Arbeiterpartei- the NSDAP). He was the original publisher of the Volkischer Beobachter and wrote the lyrics of Deutschland erwache. Please believe me, the contents of his work 'Bolshevism' are ugly, repugnant and vile in the least.

In isolation, and as a class of literature, they all serve as a warning never to allow intolerance and bigotry to breathe and flourish, which in itself is a contradiction to the theme of free speech. However, perhaps the right to free speech is not absolute and in a democratic society it could be sowing the seeds of its own destruction by tolerating and allowing unbridled free speech, which actually was permitted in the old United Kingdom with disastrous results. Thus the slogans of the 'Left' and their appeal to the workers of the world and the call of, and for equality, like the sirens' song of the 'Right's' arguments may both appear beguiling and their programmes to resolve society's ills, plausible, however power without accountability **LED** to what you have just read. Costa-Gavras' dramatic nineteen sixty- nine film, Z, (He lives) is a chilling example of the consequences of the asphyxiation of a democracy resulting in a totalitarian state and its influence on the judicial process.

I received conflicting advices concerning editing of the work but finally decided to initially edit the work and correct any punctuation errors **MYSELF,** though when the work was finally formatted , reviewed and partially checked by my younger son-in-law, Peter and by my wife,Sandra, errors were discovered and corrected Therefore I must still be held responsible for any mistakes (as is the responsibility for the transcription and accuracy of information that I have obtained from various source material which is listed in the bibliography and acknowledgements at the end of the work) I would appreciate notification and comments concerning specific errors, supported where appropriate by documentary evidence.

I was anxious that an independent editor might delete or alter certain parts in order to give the work a style and format which was more commercially attractive and 'popular', consequently excluding facts which were relevant to my report. Most important of all, their potential deletion and exclusion would deprive a voice to those who are no longer with us and who are unable to tell their stories or present the evidence which has been suppressed or perverted; thus may the innocent be revenged and the guilty exposed.

It was also suggested that I should include a brief autobiography but, on reflection, since I have lived an extremely dull, uneventful, bland, colourless, dreary and exceedingly boring life, without any highlights, that there could be no information that would interest the reader. However I am drawn to an observation on human frailty by

Shakespeare, in Hamlet, which I am informed, partially summarises one of my **MANY** faults and failings.

Now that **YOU** have read this report, **YOU**, yes you the reader, have **ONLY** to look around at the surveillance cameras-both overt and covert or to learn that your private electronic communications and records **COULD** or have been penetrated at any time or that Central or Local government takes it upon themselves to unnecessarily invade the individual's privacy **WITHOUT** reasonable cause, should give you **EVERY** reason to realise that your personal freedom is at risk.

I end these observations and comments with a request that you share with me, and enjoy, the following extracts from Edward Fitzgerald's magnificent free translation of the Rubaiyat of Omar Khayyam (a work that I consider includes some of the most sublime verses ever written).

For me the epic work symbolises the beauty of life.

YOUR journey of discovery has nearly ended...

HAMLET PRINCE OF DENMARK: AN EXTRACT FROM ACT 1, SCENE IV- THE PLATFORM

HAMLET...

So, oft it chances in particular men,

That for some vicious mole of nature in them,

As, in their birth,-wherein they are not guilty,

Since nature cannot choose his origin,-

By the o'ergrowth of some complexion,

Oft breaking down the pales and forts of reason,

Or by some habit that too much o'er-leavens

The form of plausive manners; that these men,

Carrying, I say, the stamp of one defect,

Being nature's livery, or fortune's star

Their virtues else, be they as pure as grace,

As infinite as man may undergo,

Shall in the general censure take corruption

From that particular fault

EXTRACTS FROM
THE RUBAIYAT OF OMAR KHAYYAM

FIRST QUATRAIN

Awake! for Morning in the Bowl of Night

Has flung the Stone that puts the Stars to Flight:

And Lo! the Hunter of the East has caught

The Sultan`s Turret in a Noose of Light.

ELEVENTH QUATRAIN

A loaf of Bread beneath the Bough

A Flask of Wine, a Book of Verse-and Thou

Beside me singing in the Wilderness-

And Wilderness is Paradise enow.

TWENTY THIRD QUATRAIN

Ah, make the most of what we yet may spend,

Before we too into the Dust descend;

Dust into Dust, and under Dust, to lie,

Sans Wine, sans Song, sans Singer, and-sans End!

TWENTY SIXTH QUATRAIN

Oh, come with old Khayyam, and leave the Wise

To talk; one thing is certain, that Life flies;

One thing is certain, and the Rest is Lies;

The Flower that once has blown for ever dies.

TWENTY EIGHTH QUATRAIN

With them the Seed of Wisdom did I sow?

And with my own hand laboured it to grow;

And this was all the Harvest that I reaped-

`I came like Water, and like the Wind I go`.

FIFTY FIRST QUATRAIN

The Moving Finger writes; and, having writ,

Moves on: nor all thy Piety nor Wit

Shall lure it back to cancel half a Line,

Nor all thy Tears wash out a Word of it.

FIFTY SECOND QUATRAIN

And that inverted Bowl we call the Sky,

Where under crawling coopt we live and die,

Lift not thy hands to IT for help-for IT

Rolls impotently on as Thou or I .

THOSE PARTS ARE IDENTIFIED IN THE FOLLOWING TABLES:

CHARACTER BIOGRAPHIES
(FIRST SECTION)

ABBOTT AND **COSTELLO**

WILLIAM "BUD" ABBOTT (1897-1974) AND LOU COSTELLO (1906-1959) WERE AN AMERICAN COMEDY DUO WHOSE WORK IN VAUDEVILLE AND ON STAGE,RADIO,FILM AND LATER TELEVISION MADE THEM THE MOST POPULAR COMEDY TEAM DURING THE 1940s AND 1950s.

https://en.wikipedia.org/wiki/Abbott-and-Costello

ABLETT   NOAH

04 10 1883   31 10 1935

TRADE UNIONIST AND POLITICAL THEORIST WHO IN 1912 WAS THE MAIN AUTHOR OF "THE MINERS' NEXT STEP" A TREATISE DEMANDING A MINIMUM WAGE FOR MINERS AND FOR CONTROL OF THE MINES TO BE HANDED TO THE WORKERS. BETWEEN 1921 AND 1926 HE WAS AN EXECUTIVE MEMBER OF THE MINERS` FEDERATION OF GREAT BRITAIN.

https://en.wikipedia.org/wiki/Noah-Ablett

AGNEW   SPIRO THEODORE

09 11 1918   17 09 1996

REPUBLICAN POLITICIAN, FIFTY-FIFTH GOVERNOR OF MARYLAND AND THE THIRTY NINETH VICE PRESIDENT OF THE UNITED STATES UNDER RICHARD NIXON (Q. V.) FROM 1969 TO 1973 WHEN HE RESIGNED FOLLOWING A TAX EVASION OFFENCE BUT IN REALITY HE HAD BEEN CHARGED AND WAS MOST LIKELY GUILTY OF OFFENCES INCLUDING EXTORTION, TAX FRAUD, BRIBERY AND CONSPIRACY.

https://en.wikipedia.org/wiki/Spiro-Agnew

ALI   MUHAMMAD

17 01 1942   03 06 2016

BORN CASSIUS MARCELLUS CLAY JNR. AND KNOWN AS THE
GREATEST OR THE LOUISVILLE LIP HE CHANGED HIS NAME ON
HIS CONVERSION TO SUNNI ISLAM IN 1975. HE WON THE GOLD
MEDAL IN THE LIGHT HEAVYWEIGHT BOXING DIVISION OF THE
1960 SUMMER OLYMPICS BEFORE TURNING PROFESSIONAL.
HE IS REGARDED AS ONE OF THE GREATEST HEAVYWEIGHT
BOXERS OF ALL TIME HAVING WON THE WORLD
CHAMPIONSHIP ON THREE OCCASIONS IN 1964, 1974 AND 1978
AND IS GENERALLY REGARDED AS THE GREATEST ATHLETE
OF THE 20TH CENTURY. HIS RECORD WOULD BE EVEN MORE
SUCCESSFUL FOR HE WAS STRIPPED OF HIS FIRST TITLE FOR
A DRAFT EVASION CONVICTION AND HE DID NOT FIGHT FOR
NEARLY FOUR YEARS DURING WHICH PERIOD HE APPEALED
AGAINST THE CONVICTION WHICH WAS FINALLY OVERTURNED
BY THE U.S. SUPREME COURT.

https://en.wikipedia.org/wiki/Muhammad-Ali

AMECHE   DON

31 05 1908   06 12 1993

AMERICAN ACTOR,VOICE ARTIST AND COMEDIAN BORN
DOMINIC FELIX **AMICI**. ATTENDED MARQUETTE UNIVERSITY.
AMONGST HIS FILMS WERE ALEXANDER`S RAGTIME BAND AND
THE STORY OF ALEXANDER GRAHAM BELL.

https://en.wikipedia.org/wiki/Don-Ameche

ANDERSON   LINDSAY GORDON

17 04 1923   30 08 1994

BEST REMEMBERED FOR HIS 1968 FILM 'IF', HE STUDIED
ENGLISH AT WADHAM COLLEGE, OXFORD AND WAS A
SOCIALIST, FILM, THEATRE AND DOCUMENTARY DIRECTOR
AND FILM CRITIC.

https://en.wikipedia.org/wiki/Lindsay-Anderson

ANDROPOV   YURI VLADIMIROVICH

15 06 1914   09 02 1984

FULL MEMBER OF THE 24TH, 25TH AND 26TH POLITBUROS AND CANDIDATE MEMBER OF THE 23RD AND 24TH POLITBUROS. FOURTH CHAIRMAN OF THE COMMITTEE FOR STATE SECURITY (K G B) 1967-1982. AGED SIXTEEN WAS A MEMBEROF THE ALL-UNION LENINIST YOUNG COMMUNIST LEAGUE AND DURING THE GREAT PATRIOTIC WAR TOOK PART IN PARTISAN GUERRILLA ACTIVITIES IN FINLAND.

IN 1956, AS SOVIET AMBASSADOR TO HUNGARY,PLAYED A PIVOTAL ROLE IN CRUSHING THE HUNGARIAN REVOLUTION AND IN 1968 WAS A 'HARD LINER' IN THE SUPPRESSION OF THE CZECHOSLOVAK 'PRAGUE SPRING'.

https://en.wikipedia.org/wiki/Yuri-Andropov

ARLOTT   LESLIE THOMAS JOHN

25 02 1914   14 12 1991

FROM 1930 TO 1934 HE WORKED AS A RECORDS CLERK IN A MENTAL HOSPITAL AND FROM 1934 TO 1946 AS A POLICEMAN IN THE SOUTHAMPTON COUNTY BOROUGH POLICE FORCE RISING TO THE RANK OF SERGEANT. HE BECAME A JOURNALIST, AUTHOR AND AN ICONIC B.B.C. CRICKET COMMENTATOR.

https://en.wikipedia.org/wiki/John-Arlott

ASTAIRE   'FRED'

10 05 1899   22 06 1987

BORN FREDERICK AUSTERLITZ HE WAS AN AMERICAN DANCER, CHOREOGRAPHER, SINGER, MUSICIAN AND ACTOR. THE AMERICAN FILM INSTITUTE NAMED HIM THE FIFTH GREATEST MALE STAR OF ALL TIME.

https://en.wikipedia.org/wiki/Fred-Astaire

BAKER   RICHARD

15 06 1925

BROADCASTER AND NEWSREADER FOR B.B.C. TELEVISION
NEWS FROM 1954 TO 1982.

https://en.wikipedia.org/wiki/Richard-Baker-(broadcaster)

BANNISTER   SIR ROGER GILBERT

23 03 1929

RETIRED BRITISH NEUROLOGIST AND FORMER MASTER OF
PEMBROKE COLLEGE, OXFORD. HOWEVER HIS IMMORTAL
CLAIM TO FAME WAS ACHIEVED ON THE 6TH MAY 1954 WHEN HE
RAN, AT IFFLEY ROAD, OXFORD, THE WORLD`S FIRST SUB
FOUR MINUTE MILE IN THREE MINUTES 59.4 SECONDS.

https://en.wikipedia.org/wiki/Roger-Bannister

BARBIE   NIKOLAUS 'KLAUS'

25 10 1913   23 09 1991

S.S. OFFICER AND MEMBER OF THE GESTAPO. HE WAS
KNOWN AS 'THE BUTCHER OF LYON' FOR HAVING PERSONALLY
TORTURED FRENCH PRISONERS OF THE GESTAPO WHILST
STATIONED IN LYON, FRANCE AND HE ARRESTED JEAN
MOULIN, ONE OF THE HIGHEST RANKING MEMBERS OF THE
FRENCH RESISTANCE AND HIS MOST PROMINENT ENEMY.

AFTER THE WAR, UNITED STATES INTELLIGENCE SERVICES
EMPLOYED HIM FOR THEIR ANTI MARXIST EFFORTS AND LATER
ASSISTED HIS ESCAPE TO SOUTH AMERICA. IN 1983 HE WAS
EXTRADITED FROM BOLIVIA TO FRANCE, WHERE HE WAS
CONVICTED OF WAR CRIMES AND DIED IN PRISON.

https://en.wikipedia.org/wiki/Klaus-Barbie

BELL   ALEXANDER GRAHAM

03 03 1847   02 08 1922

BORN IN SCOTLAND BUT SPENT MOST OF HIS LIFE IN THE UNITED STATES, HE WAS AN INVENTOR AND ENGINEER WHO CREATED THE FIRST PRACTICAL TELEPHONE AND WAS AWARDED THE FIRST U.S. PATENT IN 1876.

LATER HE DID GROUNDBRAKING WORK IN OPTICAL TELECOMMUNICATIONS, HYDROFOILS AND AERONAUTICS AND IN 1888 BECAME ONE OF THE FOUNDING MEMBERS OF THE NATIONAL GEOGRAPHIC SOCIETY.

https://en.wikipedia.org/wiki/Alexander-Graham-Bell

BEN-GURION   DAVID

16 10 1886   01 12 1973

HE WAS THE FIRST PRIME MINISTER OF ISRAEL FROM 1948 TO 1954 AND AGAIN FROM 1955 TO 1963. HE WAS ALSO MINISTER OF DEFENCE FROM 1948 TO 1954 AND PRIOR TO THESE POSITIONS, CHAIRMAN OF THE PROVISIONAL STATE COUNCIL OF ISRAEL IN 1948.

A PASSIONATE ZIONIST, HE WAS BORN IN POLAND WHICH THEN WAS PART OF THE RUSSIAN EMPIRE AND IN 1906 EMIGRATED TO PALESTINE WHICH THEN WAS PART OF THE OTTOMAN EMPIRE. HE TOOK THE NAME BEN–GURION AFTER THE MEDIEVAL HISTORIAN JOSEPH BEN GORION AND STUDIED LAW AT ISTABNBUL UNIVERSITY HAVING EARLIER STUDIED AT WARSAW UNIVERSITY.

AS HEAD OF THE JEWISH AGENCY EXECUTIVE HE WAS THE DE FACTO LEADER OF THE JEWISH COMMUNITY IN PALESTINE FROM 1935 AND ON THE FOURTEENTH OF MAY 1948 HE FORMALLY PROCLAIMED THE ESTABLISHMENT OF THE STATE OF ISRAEL AND WAS THE FIRST TO SIGN THE ISRAELI DECLARATION OF INDEPENDENCE WHICH HE HAD HELPED TO WRITE. HE LED THE COUNTRY BOTH IN THE 1948 ARAB – ISRAELI WAR AND THE WAR OF 1956.

https://en.wikipedia.org/wiki/David-Ben-Gurion

BERIA   LAVRENTI PAVLOVICH

29 03 1899   23 12 1953

SOVIET POLITICIAN, DE FACTO MARSHALL OF THE SOVIET
UNION AND STATE SECURITY ADMINISTRATOR, CHIEF OF THE
SOVIET SECURITY AND SECRET POLICE APPARATUS (N K V D).
SUCCEEDED NIKOLAI YEZHOV (Q.V.). AFTER THE WAR HE
ORGANISED THE COMMUNIST TAKEOVER OF CENTRAL AND
EASTERN EUROPE WHILST ALSO SUPERVISING THE
DEVELOPMENT OF THE SOVIET NUCLEAR WEAPONS
PROGRAMME AND THE FIRST EXPLOSION IN 1949 WHICH WAS
ASSISTED BY ESPIONAGE AGAINST THE UNITED STATES.

https://en.wikipedia.org/wiki/Lavrentiy-Beria

BERLIN   IRVING

11 05 1888   22 09 1989

BORN ISRAEL ISIDORE BEILIN, IN THE RUSSIA EMPIRE AND
TAKEN TO AMERICA IN 1893 BY HIS FATHER, A SYNAGOGUE
CANTOR, HE BECAME A COMPOSER AND LYRICIST AND IS
WIDELY CONSIDERED AS ONE OF THE GREATEST
SONGWRITERS IN AMERICAN HISTORY.

https://en.wikipedia.org/wiki/Irving-Berlin

BERNSTEIN   CARL

14 02 1944

AMERICAN INVESTIGATIVE JOURNALIST AND AUTHOR. ALONG
WITH "BOB" WOODWARD (Q.V.) UNCOVERED THE 'WATERGATE
SCANDAL' RESULTING IN THE EVENTUAL RESIGNATION OF
PRESIDENT NIXON (Q.V.). SINCE WATERGATE AND HIS
DEPARTURE FROM THE WASHINGTON POST HE HAS
CONTINUED TO FOCUS ON THE THEME OF THE USE AND
ABUSE OF POWER.

https://en.wikipedia.org/wiki/Carl-Bernstein

BLISS   SIR ARTHUR EDWARD DRUMMOND

02 08 1891   27 03 1975

ENGLISH COMPOSER AND CONDUCTOR. IN THE 20S AND 30S
HE COMPOSED EXTENSIVELY FOR THE CONCERT HALL,
BALLET AND FILMS.

https://en.wikipedia.org/wiki/Arthur-Bliss

BORODIN   ALEXANDER PORFIRYEVICH

12 11 1833   27 02 1887

AS WELL AS BEING A DOCTOR AND CHEMIST HE WAS A
NOTABLE ADVOCATE OF WOMEN'S RIGHTS; OF GEORGIAN
ORIGIN HE IS BEST KNOWN AS A ROMANTIC COMPOSER AND
HIS WORKS INCLUDE HIS SYMPHONIES AND "IN THE STEPPES
OF CENTRAL ASIA" AND THE OPERA , PRINCE IGOR.

https://en.wikipedia.org/wiki/Alexander-Borodin

BOSCH   HIERONYMUS

BO RN   1450   09 08 1516

BORN JHERONIMUS VAN AKEN, HE WAS AN EARLY DUTCH
PAINTER WHO FLOURISHED IN THE LATE FIFTEENTH AND
EARLY SIXTEENTH CENTURIES AND WHOSE WORK WAS
WIDELY COPIED, ESPECIALLY HIS MACABRE AND DARK
DEPICTIONS OF HELL. HIS WORK IS RECOGNISED FOR ITS`
FANTASTIC IMAGERY, DETAILED LANDSCAPES AND
ILLUSTRATIONS OF MORAL AND RELIGIOUS CONCEPTS.

https://en.wikipedia.org/wiki/Hieronymus-Bosch

BOTVINNIK   MIKHAIL

17 08 1911   05 05 1995

SOVIET AND RUSSIAN INTERNATIONAL CHESS GRANDMASTER
AND THREE - TIME WORLD CHESS CHAMPION, 1948 TO 1957,
1958 TO 1960 AND 1961 TO 1963.

https://en.wikipedia.org/wiki/Mikhail-Botvinnik

BOWEN   EVAN RODERIC

06 08 1913   19 07 2001

A BARRISTER AND LIBERAL M.P. FROM 1945 TO 1966. HE WAS
ON THE RIGHT OF THE PARTY AND DURING THE 1956 SUEZ
CRISIS SUPPORTED THE GOVERNMENT OF EDEN (Q.V.).

https://en.wikipedia.org/wiki/Roderic-Bowen

BRADLEE   BENJAMIN CROWNINSHIELD "BEN"

26 08 1921   21 10 2014

EXECUTIVE EDITOR OF THE 'WASHINGTON POST' FROM 1968
TO 1991. HE ROSE TO NATIONAL PROMINENCE OVERSEEING
THE PUBLICATION OF WOODWARD (Q.V.) AND BERNSTEIN`S
(Q.V.) STORIES DOCUMENTING THE WATERGATE SCANDAL. HE
WAS A GRADUATE OF HARVARD, IMMEDIATELY RECEIVING HIS
NAVAL COMMISSION, JOINING THE OFFICE OF NAVAL
INTELLIGENCE AND SERVED AS A COMMUNICATIONS OFFICER.

https://en.wikipedia.org/wiki/Ben-Bradlee

BRAINE   JOHN GERARD

13 04 1922   28 10 1986

NOVELIST, HE IS CHIEFLY REMEMBERED FOR HIS FIRST WORK
'ROOM AT THE TOP'. HE WAS ASSOCIATED WITH THE ANGRY
YOUNG MEN MOVEMENT.

https://en.wikipedia.org/wiki/John-Braine

BREZHNEV   LEONID ILYICH

19 12 1906   10 11 1982

SUCCEEDED NIKITA KHRUSHCHEV (Q.V) AS FIRST
SECRETARY.GENERAL SECRETARY OF THE CENTRAL
COMMITTEE OF THE COMMUNIST PARTY OF THE SOVIET UNION
1964 TO 1982.FULL MEMBER OF THE 20TH TO 26TH POLITBUROS
1956 TO 1982.FULL MEMBER OF THE 19TH TO THE 26TH CENTRAL
COMMITTEES 1952 TO 1982.

https://en.wikipedia.org/wiki/Leonid-Brezhnev

BRITTEN   EDWARD BENJAMIN, BARON BRITTEN

22 11 1913   04 12 1976

COMPOSER, CONDUCTOR AND CELEBRATED PIANIST. HE STUDIED AT THE ROYAL COLLEGE OF MUSIC AND IN 1948 HELPED FOUND THE ANNUAL ALDEBURGH FESTIVAL. HE WAS A CENTRAL FIGURE IN 20TH CENTURY BRITISH CLASSICAL MUSIC.

https://en.wikipedia.org/wiki/Benjamin-Britten

BROCKWAY   ARCHIBALD FENNER,

            BARON BROCKWAY OF ETON AND SLOUGH

01 11 1888   28 04 1988

IN 1907 JOINED THE INDEPENDENT LABOUR PARTY AND WAS A REGULAR VISITOR TO THE FABIAN SOCIETY. BY 1913 HE WAS A COMMITTED PACIFIST, A POSITION HE HELD FOR THE REST OF HIS LIFE, GOING TO PRISON ON A NUMBER OF OCCASIONS THOUGH HE ASSISTED IN THE RECRUITMENT OF BRITISH VOLUNTEERS TO FIGHT AGAINST FRANCO (Q.V.) AND THE NATIONALISTS DURING THE SPANISH CIVIL WAR. HE WAS A LABOUR M.P. FROM 1929 TO 1931 AND FROM 1950 TO 1964.

https://en.wikipedia.org/wiki/Fenner-Brockway,-Baron-Brockway

BROWN   GEORGE ALFRED, BARON

02 09 1914   02 06 1985

BRITISH LABOUR POLITICIAN WHO SERVED AS DEPUTY LEADER OF THE LABOUR PARTY FROM 1960 TO 1970 AND ALSO IN A NUMBER OF CABINET POSITIONS, MOST NOTABLY AS FOREIGN SECRETARY. HE WAS A LEADER OF THE PARTY`S TRADE UNION RIGHT WING HOWEVER HE WAS UNABLE TO COPE WITH THE PRESSURES OF HIGH OFFICE WITHOUT EXCESSIVE DRINKING.

https://en.wikipedia.org/wiki/George-Brown,-Baron-George-Brown

BUCKTON   RAYMOND WILLIAM

20 10 1922 07 05 1995

LABOUR LEADER OF YORK COUNCIL AGED 24, GENERAL SECRETARY OF ASLEF 1970 TO 1987 AND PRESIDENT OF THE TRADES UNION CONGRESS 1984.

https://en.wikipedia.org/wiki/Ray-Buckton

BUKHARIN   NIKOLAI IVANOVICH

09 10 1888 15 03 1938

RUSSIAN BOLSHEVIK REVOLUTIONARY, POLITICIAN AND AUTHOR ON REVOLUTIONARY THEORY. AS A YOUNG MAN HE SPENT SIX YEARS IN EXILE, WORKING CLOSELY WITH FELLOW EXILES, LENIN (Q.V.) AND TROTSKY (Q.V.). ONE OF THE ORIGINAL LEADERS, AFTER STALIN`S (Q.V.) RISE AND CONSOLIDATION OF POWER HE WAS OUSTED AND WAS A VICTIM OF THE PURGE.

https://en.wikipedia.org/wiki/Nikolai-Bukharin

MANNINGHAM-BULLER

        REGINALD EDWARD, FIRST VISCOUNT DILHORNE

01 08 1905 07 09 1980

CONSERVATIVE POLITICIAN AND LAWYER, HE WAS LORD HIGH CHANCELLOR FROM 1962 TO 1964 AND HAD PREVIOUSLY SERVED AS SOLICITOR GENERAL AND THEN ATTORNEY-GENERAL FOR ENGLAND AND WALES.

https://en.wikipedia.org/wiki/Reginald-Manningham-Buller,-1st-Viscount-Dilhorne

BUTLER   JOYCE SHORE

13 12 1910 02 01 1992

LABOUR M.P. 1955- 1979.

https://en.wikipedia.org/wiki/Joyce-Butler

BUTLER   RICHARD AUSTEN,

BARON BUTLER OF SAFFRON WALDEN

09 12 1902   08 03 1982

CONSERVATIVE POLITICIAN AND M.P. FOR THIRTY-SIX YEARS DURING WHICH PERIOD HE WAS THE CHANCELLOR OF THE EXCHEQUER, HOME SECRETARY AND FOREIGN SECRETARY.

https://en.wikipedia.org/wiki/Rab-Butler

CALDER   PETER RITCHIE,

BARON RITCHIE–CALDER OF BALMASHANNER

01 07 1906   31 01 1982

SCOTTISH SOCIALIST AUTHOR, JOURNALIST AND ACADEMIC. DURING THE SECOND WORLD WAR HE WAS APPOINTED DIRECTOR OF PLANS AND CAMPAIGNS AT THE POLITICAL WARFARE EXECUTIVE BRANCH OF THE GOVERNMENT AND WROTE PROPAGANDA POSTERS AND LEAFLETS AND SPEECHES FOR ALLIED LEADERS. HE BECAME THE SCIENCE EDITOR OF THE NEWS CHRONICLE, WAS PRESIDENT OF THE NATIONAL PEACE COUNCIL AND AS A HUMANIST CO SIGNED THE HUMANIST MANIFESTO.

https://en.wikipedia.org/wiki/Peter-Ritchie-Calder

CAMPBELL   SIR DAVID CALLENDER

29 01 1891   12 06 1963

ULSTER UNIONIST M.P. FROM 1952 TO 1963 AND LIEUTENANT – GOVERNOR OF MALTA FROM 1943 TO 1952.

https://en.wikipedia.org/wiki/David-Campbell-(British-politician)

CAMUS   ALBERT

07 11 1913   04 01 1960

HE WAS A FRENCH NOBEL PRIZE-WINNING AUTHOR, JOURNALIST AND PHILOSOPHER.

https://en.wikipedia.org/wiki/Albert-Camus

CARTER   HORATIO STRATTON'RAICH'

21 12 1913   09 10 1994

PROFESSIONAL FOOTBALLER WHO ALSO PLAYED, FOR A
SHORT WHILE, FIRST CLASS CRICKET AND IS THE ONLY MAN
TO HAVE WON A CUP WINNER'S MEDAL BOTH BEFORE AND
AFTER THE WAR.

https://en.wikipedia.org/wiki/Raich-Carter

CASTLE   BARBARA ANNE,

              BARONESS CASTLE OF BLACKBURN

06 10 1910   03 05 2002

NEE BETTS, LABOUR POLITICIAN AND M.P. FROM 1945 TO 1979
AFTER WHICH SHE SERVED AS A MEMBER OF THE EUROPEAN
PARLIAMENT FROM 1979 TO 1989.

SHE HELD A NUMBER OF CABINET POSTS IN THE WILSON (Q.V.)
GOVERNMENTS OF 1964 TO 1970 AND 1974 TO 1976 RANGING
FROM MINISTER FOR OVERSEAS DEVELOPMENT 1964 -1965 TO
SECRETARY OF STATE FOR SOCIAL SERVICES 1974-1976. SHE
IS PERHAPS BEST REMEMBERED FOR HER 1969 WHITE PAPER,
WHILST FIRST SECRETARY OF STATE, 'IN PLACE OF STRIFE'
WHICH PROPOSED TO REDUCE THE POWER OF THE TRADE
UNIONS, HOWEVER THE UNIONS 'NEGOTIATED' A DEAL WHICH
DROPPED MOST OF THE CONTENTIOUS CONDITIONS.

https://en.wikipedia.org/wiki/Barbara-Castle

CHAMBERLAIN ARTHUR NEVILLE

18 03 1869   09 11 1940

BRITISH CONSERVATIVE POLITICIAN WHO SERVED AS PRIME
MINISTER BETWEEN 1937 AND MAY 1940 WHEN HE WAS
SUCCEEDED BY WINSTON CHURCHILL (Q.V.) HE WAS BEST
KNOWN FOR HIS POLICY OF APPEASEMENT AND IN
PARTICULAR THE MUNICH AGREEMENT OF 1938.

https:/en.wikipedia.org/wiki/Neville-Chamberlain

CHANEY JR. LON

10 02 1906   12 07 1973

LON CHANEY JR., BORN CREIGHTON TULL CHANEY WAS A FILM ACTOR WHO TOOK HIS STAGE NAME FROM HIS FATHER WHO WAS A FAMOUS SILENT FILM ACTOR.

https:/en.wikipedia.org/wiki/Lon-Chaney-Jr.

CHAPLIN   SIR CHARLES SPENCER "CHARLIE"

16 04 1889   25 12 1977

AN ENGLISH COMIC ACTOR AND FILM MAKER WHO ROSE TO FAME IN THE SILENT FILM ERA. HE BEGUN HIS CAREER IN ENGLAND TOURING MUSIC HALLS, THEN LATER WORKED AS A STAGE ACTOR AND COMEDIAN. AT 19 HE WAS SIGNEDTO THE PRESTIGIOUS FRED KARNO COMPANY, WHICH TOOK HIM TO AMERICA AND ULTIMATE GLOBAL FAME. IN 1919 HE CO-FOUNDED THE DISTRIBUTION COMPANY UNITED ARTISTS.

HIS REPUTATION RESTS ON HIS FAMOUS CHARACTER *THE TRAMP* AND HIS WORK FIRST IN THE SILENT FILM ERA AND THEN SOUND FILMS, WHICH HE EMBRACED LATE IN HIS CAREER AND WHICH INCLUDED *THE GREAT DICTATOR* WHICH SATIRISED ADOLF HITLER (Q.V.) AND BROUGHT TO PROMINENCE HIS LEFT WING VIEWS.

https://en.wikipedia.org/wiki/Charlie-Chaplin

CHAUCER   GEOFFREY

BO RN.   1343   25 10 1400

AUTHOR, POET, PHILOSOPHER, ASTRONOMER, HE ALSO MAINTAINED AN ACTIVE CAREER IN THE CIVIL SERVICE AS A BUREAUCRAT,COURTIER AND DIPLOMAT. KNOWN AS THE FATHER OF **ENGLISH** LITERATURE, IS WIDELY CONSIDERED THE GREATEST ENGLISH POET OF THE MIDDLE AGES AND A CRUCIAL FIGURE IN THE DEVELOPMENT OF MIDDLE ENGLISH.

HIS MOST FAMOUS LITERARY WORK WAS *THE CANTERBURY TABLES.*

https://en.wikipedia.org/wiki/Geoffrey-Chaucer

CHIANG   KAI-SHEK

31 10 1887   05 04 1975

CHINESE POLITICAL AND MILITARY LEADER WHO SERVED AS
THE LEADER OF THE REPUBLIC OF CHINA FROM 1928 TO HIS
DEATH. COMMANDANT OF THE WHAMPOA MILITARY ACADEMY
HE BECAME LEADER OF THE K.M.T. (KUO MIN TANG) IN 1925.IN
1927 A MAJOR SPLIT OCCURRED BETWEEN HIS NATIONALISTS
AND THE COMMUNISTS RESULTING IN A CIVIL WAR BUT AFTER
THE JAPANESE INVADED CHINA IN 1937. A TEMPORARY TRUCE
WAS AGREED IN ORDER THAT THEY COULD FIGHT THE
COMMON ENEMY WHICH BROKE DOWN AFTER THE JAPANESE
SURRENDER IN 1945.

THE CIVIL WAR RESUMED ULTIMATELY RESULTING IN THE
DEFEAT OF THE NATIONALISTS WHO RETREATED TO TAIWAN.

https://en.wikipedia.org/wiki/Chiang-kai-shek

CHOU   EN LAI

05 03 1898   08 01 1976

ALLY OF MAO TSE TUNG (Q. V.), HE WAS THE FIRST PREMIER
OF THE PEOPLE`S REPUBLIC OF CHINA SERVING FROM 1949
TO HIS DEATH.HE WAS ALSO THE FIRST FOREIGN MINISTER
BUT ONLY TO 1958. HE WAS ONE OF THE SURVIVORS OF THE
LONG MARCH AND IS **BELIEVED** TO HAVE KNOWN JOEL BEN
YITZHAK EITHER IN LONDON OR PARIS HAVING POSSIBLY MET
HIM DURING A STAY IN EUROPE IN THE EARLY 1920S THOUGH
THIS HAS NEVER BEEN CONFIRMED.

https://en.wikipedia.org/wiki/Zhou-Enlai

CHUIKOV   VASILY IVANOVICH

12 02 1900   18 03 1982

SOVIET LIEUTENANT GENERAL IN THE RED ARMY DURING THE
GREAT PATRIOTIC WAR, COMMANDER OF THE 62ND ARMY
DURING THE BATTLE OF STALINGRAD AND RESPONSIBLE TO
NIKITA KHRUSHCHEV(Q.V.). AFTER THE WAR HE WAS A
MARSHALL OF THE SOVIET UNION.

https://en.wikipedia.org/wiki/Vasily-Chuikov

CHU TEH   (MARSHALL)

01 12 1886   06 07 1976

CHINESE GENERAL,WARLORD,POLITICIAN, REVOLUTIONARY WHO AROUND 1909 JOINED THE TONGMENGHUI SECRET POLITICAL SOCIETY (THE FORERUNNER OF THE KUO MIN TANG) BUT LATER, UNDER THE SPONSORSHIP OF CHOU EN LAI (Q.V.), WHO HE HAD ORIGINALLY MET AT GOTTINGEN UNIVERSITY AROUND 1922, JOINED THE YOUNG COMMUNIST PARTY.

https:/en.wikipedia.org/wiki/Zhu-De

(SPENCER-) CHURCHILL

CLEMENTINE OGILVY, BARONESS

01 04 1885   12 12 1977

WIFE OF SIR WINSTON CHURHILL (Q.V.).

https://en.wikipedia.org/wiki/Clementine-Churchill

(SPENCER-) CHURCHILL

SIR WINSTON LEONARD

30 11 1874   24 01 1965

ARMY OFFICER, WAR CORRESPONDENT, JOURNALIST, AUTHOR AND STATESMAN WHO WAS AT THE FOREFRONT OF BRITISH POLITICS FOR HALF A CENTURY.

OUT OF OFFICE AND POLITICALLY' IN THE WILDERNESS' DURING THE 1930S HE WAS IN THE VANGUARD WARNING THE NATION ABOUT GERMAN REARMAMENT AND THEIR SINISTER INTENTIONS. ON THE TENTH OF MAY 1940 HE BECAME PRIME MINISTER LEADING A NATIONAL GOVERNMENT THROUGH MANY CRISES TO ULTIMATE VICTORY.

REGARDED BY MANY AS THE GREATEST ENGLISHMAN OF ALL TIME.

https://en.wikipedia.org/wiki/Winston-Churchill

CLARK   WILLIAM GIBSON HAIG,

BARON CLARK OF KEMPSTON

18 10 17 . 06 10 04

CONSERVATIVE POLITICIAN AND M.P.1959 TO 1966 AND 1970 TO 1992.

https://en.wikipedia.org/wiki/William-Clark,-Baron-Clark-of-Kempston

CLIFFE   MICHAEL

?? 03 1904   09 08 1964

BRITISH LABOUR POLITICIAN, UNION ACTIVIST AND M.P. NATIONAL EXECUTIVE MEMBER OF THE NATIONAL UNION OF TAILORS AND GARMENT WORKERS.M.P. 1958 TO 1964.

CHAIRMAN OF THE WARSAW GHETTO UPRISING MEMORIAL COMMITTEE.

https://en.wikipedia.org/wiki/Michael-Cliffe

COUSINS   FRANK

08 09 1904   11 06 1986

BRITISH TRADE UNION LEADER AND LABOUR POLITICIAN. HE WAS GENERAL SECRETARY OF THE TRANSPORT AND GENERAL WORKERS` UNION FROM 1956 TO 1969 AND MINISTER OF TECHNOLOGY UNDER HAROLD WILSON (Q.V.) FROM 1964 TO 1966.

https://en.wikipedia.org/wiki/Frank-Cousins

COWARD   SIR NOEL PEIRCE

16 12 1899   26 03 1973

AN ENGLISH PLAYWRIGHT, COMPOSER,DIRECTOR, ACTOR AND SINGER, HE ACHIEVED GREAT SUCCESS AND RECOGNITION WITH MANY OF HIS STAGE PLAYS INCLUDING *HAY FEVER,PRIVATE LIVES* AND *BLITHE SPIRIT.*

https://en.wikipedia.org/wiki/Noel-Coward

CRIPPS   RICHARD STAFFORD

24 04 1889   21 04 1952

ALTHOUGH HE STUDIED CHEMISTRY AT UNIVERSITY COLLEGE , LONDON HE LATER BECAME A SUCCESSFUL BARRISTER, HIS CAREER BEING INTERRUPTED BY THE FIRST WORLD WAR WHEN HE SERVED AS A RED CROSS AMBULANCE DRIVER IN FRANCE.

HE WAS A LABOUR M.P.SERVING FROM 1931 TO 1950 AND DURING THAT PERIOD HE WAS SOLICITOR GENERAL FOR ENGLAND AND WALES (1930-1931).

HE WAS AMBASSADOR TO THE SOVIET UNION FROM 1940 TO 1942 AND BOTH LORD PRIVY SEAL AND LEADER OF THE HOUSE OF COMMONS IN 1942.

IN THE POST WAR LABOUR GOVERNMENT, HE WAS PRESIDENT OF THE BOARD OF TRADE, MINISTER FOR ECONOMIC AFFAIRS AND CHANCELLOR OF THE EXCHEQUER (1947 TO 1950) WHERE, IN 1949, HE WAS INVOLVED IN THE DEVALUATION OF THE POUND.

https://en.wikipedia.org/wiki/Stafford -Cripps

CRONKITE   WALTER LELAND JNR.

04 11 1916   17 07 2009

AMERICAN RADIO, TELEVISION BROADCASTER AND THEN A 'NEWS ANCHORMAN'. HE BECAME ONE OF THE UNITED STATES LEADING REPORTERS IN THE SECOND WORLD WAR COVERING ACTION IN NORTH AFRICA AND EUROPE EVEN FLYING OVER GERMANY IN BOMBING RAIDS. HE IS HOWEVER BEST KNOWN AS ANCHORMAN FOR THE CBS EVENING NEWS FROM 1962 TO 1981.

https://en.wikipedia.org/wiki/Walter-Cronkite

DARWIN   CHARLES ROBERT

12 02 1809   19 04 1882

HE WAS AN ENGLISH NATURALIST AND GEOLOGIST FAMOUS FOR HIS CONTRIBUTIONS TO EVOLUTIONARY THEORY WHICH WITH COMPELLING EVIDENCE APPEARED IN HIS 1859 BOOK, *ON*

THE ORIGINS OF SPECIES. HE ESTABLISHED THAT ALL SPECIES IN LIFE HAD DESCENDED OVER TIME FROM COMMON ANCESTORSAND IN A JOINT PUBLICATION WITH ALFRED RUSSEL WALLACE (Q.V.) INTRODUCED HIS SCIENTIFIC THEORY THAT THIS BRANCHING PATTERN OF EVOLUTION RESULTED FROM A PROCESS WHICH HE CALLED NATURAL SELECTION, IN WHICH THE STRUGGLE FOR EXISTENCE FAVOURS THE BEST ADAPTED.

https://en.wikipedia.org/wiki/Charles-Darwin

DEEDES   WILLIAM FRANCIS 'BILL', BARON

01 06 1913   17 08 2007

BRITISH CONSERVATIVE POLITICIAN, ARMY OFFICER WHO WON THE M.C. IN 1945, JOURNALIST AND NEWSPAPER EDITOR. HE WAS AN M.P. FROM 1950 TO 1974.

https://en.wikipedia.org/wiki/Bill-Deedes

DE GAULLE   CHARLES ANDRE JOSEPH MARIE

22 11 1890   09 11 1970

HE WAS A FRENCH GENERAL,WRITER, POLITICIAN AND STATESMAN.

LEADER OF THE FREE FRENCH (1940-44) AND THE HEAD OF THE PROVISIONAL GOVERNMENT OF THE FRENCH REPUBLIC (1944-46). IN 1958 HE FOUNDED THE FIFTH REPUBLIC AND WAS ELECTED THE 18TH PRESIDENT OF FRANCE UNTIL HIS RESIGNATION IN 1969. HE WAS A DECORATED OFFICER IN THE FIRST WORLD WAR, WOUNDED SEVERAL TIMES AND LATER TAKEN PRISONER AT VERDUN FAILING ON A NUMBER OF OCCASIONS TO ESCAPE.

DURING THE 'COLD WAR' HE ARGUED THAT FRANCE, AS A MAJOR POWER, SHOULD NOT RELY ON OTHER COUNTRIES, SUCH AS THE UNITED STATES, FOR ITS' NATIONAL SECURITY AND PROSPERITY. HE PERSUED A POLICY WHICH LED HIM TO WITHDRAW FROM NATO AND TO LAUNCH AN INDEPENDENT NUCLEAR WEAPONS PROGRAMME.

https://en.wikipedia.org/wiki/Charles-de-Gaulle

DEMICHEV   PYOTR NILOVICH

21 12 1917   10 08 2010

SOVIET POLITICIAN AND CANDIDATE MEMBER OF THE 22ND TO 27TH POLITBUROS.MINISTER OF CULTURE FROM 1974 TO1986.

https://en.wikipedia.org/wiki/Pyotr-Demichev

DIOR   MARIE FRANCOISE SUZANNE

07 04 1932   20 01 1993

WEALTHY FRENCH SOCIALITE AND POST-WAR NAZI SUPPORTER. IN 1963 SHE MARRIED COLIN JORDAN (Q.V.) SHORTLY AFTER HIS RELEASE FROM PRISON, THOUGH SHE HAD BEEN RECENTLY ENGAGED TO JOHN TYNDALL (Q.V.) WHO WAS STILL IN PRISON. THE MARRIAGE ENDED EARLY IN 1964 BUT THE EVENT CAUSED A LIFELONG SPLIT BETWEEN THE TWO MEN.

https://en.wikipedia.org/wiki/Francoise-Dior

DIVINE   ARTHUR DURHAM (DAVID) C B E ,D S M

27 07 1904   30 04 1987

BORN IN CAPE TOWN, SOUTH AFRICA, BETWEEN 1922 AND 26 AND AGAIN BETWEEN 1931 TO 35 WORKED AS A JOURNALIST ON *THE CAPE TIMES*. HE WAS A PROLIFIC BOOK WRITER ON A VARIETY OF SUBJECTS, WAR CORRESPONDENT AND AFTER THE SECOND WORLD WAR, THE DEFENCE CORRESPONDENT OF *THE SUNDAY TIMES, A* POST HE HELD TILL 1975.

HE CROSSED THE ENGLISH CHANNEL THREE TIMES DURING OPERATION DYNAMO, THE EVACUATION OF THE B. E. F. IN MAY 1940, AND ON THE THIRD JOURNEY WAS WOUNDED.HE WAS AWARDED THE D S M AND WROTE A BOOK IN 1941 BASED ON HIS EXPERIENCES WHICH IN 1958 WAS THE BASIS FOR HIS FILM SCREENPLAY, *DUNKIRK*.

HIS POSTWAR BOOKS WERE CRITICAL OF BRITAIN'S AND THE MINISTRY OF DEFENCE'S ATTITUDE TO MODERNISATION.

https://en.wikipedia.org/wiki/David-Divine

DOUGALL   ROBERT

27 11 1913   19 12 1999

ENGLISH RADIO AND TELEVISION ANNOUNCER AND
NEWSREADER.IN 1939 AS SENIOR ANNOUNCER FOR THE B.B.C.
EMPIRE SERVICE HE ANNOUNCED TO THE WORLD BRITAIN`S
DECLARATION OF WAR ON GERMANY. HE WAS A PRESIDENT
OF THE RSPB.

https://en.wikipedia.org/wiki/Robert-Dougall

DOUGLAS-HOME

ALEXANDER FREDERICK

(BARON HOME OF THE HIRSEL)

02 07 1903   09 10 1995

BRITISH CONSERVATIVE PRIME MINISTER WHO SUCCEEDED
HAROLD MACMILLAN (Q.V.) HE IS BEST REMEMBERED AS THE
PARLIAMENTARY AIDE TO NEVILLE CHAMBERLAIN (Q.V.) WHO
HE ACCOMPANIED TO MUNICH IN 1938 AND WITNESSED
SIGNING OF THE MUNICH AGREEMENT.

https://en.wikipedia.org/wiki/Alec-Douglas-Home

DRAKE   SIR FRANCIS

CIRCA 1540   27 01 1596

ENGLISH SEA CAPTAIN, PRIVATEER, NAVIGATOR AND
POLITICIAN DURING THE REIGN OF QUEEN ELIZABETH 1. FROM
1577 TO 1580 HE CARRIED OUT THE SECOND
CIRCUMNAVIGATION OF THE WORLD IN A SINGLE EXPEDITION
AND WAS SECOND-IN–COMMAND OF THE ENGLISH FLEET
AGAINST THE SPANISH ARMADA IN 1588.

https://en.wikipedia.org/wiki/Francis-Drake

DZERZHINSKY FELIX EDMUNDOVICH

11 09 1877   20 07 1926

HE ESTABLISHED THE SOVIET SECRET POLICE FORCES
(CHEKA), SERVING AS ITS HEAD FROM 1917 TO 1926 AND ALSO
HEADED THE GPU WHICH BECAME THE OGPU (1922 TO 1923
AND THEN 1923 TO 1926 RESPECTIVELY). HE WAS FLUENT IN
YIDDISH AND KNEW JOEL BEN YITZHAK (Q.V.).

https://en.wikipedia.org/wiki/Felix-Dzerzhinsky

ECKART   (JOHANN) DIETRICH

23 03 1868   26 12 1923

JOURNALIST,PLAYRIGHT,POET AND POLITICIAN WAS ONE OF
THE FOUNDERS OF THE *DEUTSCHE ARBEITERPARTEI*
(GERMAN WORKERS' PARTY-DAP)WHICH LATER EVOLVED INTO
THE NAZI PARTY (NSDAP). HE WAS A KEY INFLUENCE ON
ADOLF HITLER (Q.V.) IN THE EARLY YEARS OF THE PARTY AND
WAS A PARTICIPANT IN THE 1923 MUNICH BEER HALL PUTSCH.

https://en.wikipedia.org/wiki/Dietrich-Eckart

EDEN   ROBERT ANTHONY,FIRST EARL OF AVON

2 06 1897   14 01 1977

BRITISH CONSERVATIVE POLITICIAN AND PRIME MINISTER
(WHO WON THE M.C. DURING THE FIRST WORLD WAR) FROM
1955 TO 1957 DURING WHICH PERIOD, IN 1956, HE COLLUDED
WITH THE FRENCH (AND ISRAELIS) TO REGAIN CONTROL OF
THE SUEZ CANAL FROM THE EGYPTIANS. HOWEVER UNDER
PRESSURE FROM THE AMERICANS AND PRESIDENT
EISENHOWER (Q.V.) HE WAS FORCED TO WITHDRAW.

https://en.wikipedia.org/wiki/Anthony-Eden

EICHMANN   OTTO ADOLF

19 03 1906   01 06 1962

WAS A GERMAN NAZI SS LIEUTENANT COLONEL AND ONE OF
THE MAIN ORGANISERS OF THE HOLOCAUST. HE FACILITATED
AND MANAGED THE LOGISTICS OF THE MASS DEPORTATION
OF JEWS TO GHETTOS AND THEN TO THE EXTERMINATION

CAMPS IN GERMAN OCCUPIED EASTERN EUROPE. AFTER THE WAR, IN 1950, HE MOVED TO ARGENTINA BUT IN 1960, THE ISRAELI SECRET SERVICE KIDNAPPED HIM, BRINGING HIM TO ISRAEL WHERE HE WAS CONVICTED OF CRIMES INCLUDING WAR CRIMES, CRIMES AGAINST HUMANITYAND CRIMES AGAINST THE JEWISH PEOPLE. HE WAS HUNG ON JUNE FIRST 1962.

https://en.wikipedia.org/wiki/Adolf-Eichmann

EINSTEIN   ALBERT

14 03 1879   18 04 1955

IN 1921 HE RECEIVED THE NOBEL PRIZE FOR PHYSICS FOLLOWING HIS TWO REVOLUTIONARY PAPERS –THE SPECIAL THEORY OF RELATIVITY (1905) AND GENERAL RELATIVITY (1915) IN WHICH THE FORMER, AMONGST OTHER CONCEPTS RELATED ENERGY TO MATTER (HIS FAMOUS EQUATION E = MC2) AND THE RELATIONSHIP BETWEEN SPACE, TIME AND THE CONSTANT VELOCITY OF LIGHT. IN THE LATTER PAPER HE DEFINED THE NATURE OF GRAVITY.

HE WAS VISITING THE UNITED STATES IN 1933 ,WHEN HITLER – Q.V. – CAME TO POWER AND, BEING JEWISH, DID NOT GO BACK TO GERMANY AND IN 1940 HE BECAME AN AMERICAN CITIZEN.

HIS CONTRIBUTION TO THEORETICAL PHYSICS, SCIENCE AND INTELLECTUAL THOUGHT CANNOT EVER BE BRIEFLY SUMMARISED IN ANY ABBREVIATED BIOGRAPHY.

https://en.wikipedia.org/wiki/Albert-Einstein

EISENHOWER DWIGHT DAVID

14 10 1890   28 03 1969

KNOWN AS 'IKE',WAS THE THIRTY-FORTH PRESIDENT OF THE UNITED STATES BEING THE FIRST TERM LIMITED PRESIDENT IN ACCORDANCE WITH THE 22ND AMENDMENT TO THE CONSTITUTION. **IN HIS 1961 FAREWELL ADDRESS TO THE NATION HE EXPRESSED HIS CONCERNS ABOUT FUTURE DANGERS OF MASSIVE MILITARY SPENDING, ESPECIALLY DEFICIT SPENDING AND GOVERNMENT CONTRACTS TO PRIVATE MILITARY MANUFACTURERS, AND COINED THE TERM 'MILITARY-INDUSTRIAL COMPLEX'.**

HE WAS A FIVE STAR GENERAL DURING WORLD WAR TWO AND SERVED AS SUPREME COMMANDER OF THE ALLIED FORCES IN EUROPE BEING RESPONSIBLE TO ORDER THE INVASION AND LIBERATION OF THE OCCUPIED NATIONS IN JUNE 1944.

IN 1956 HE WAS RESPONSIBLE FOR FORCING FRANCE , BRITAIN AND ISRAEL TO WITHDRAW FROM THE SUEZ CANAL ZONE AND THE SINAI PENINSULA.

https://en.wikipedia.org/wiki/Dwight-D.-Eisenhower

EISENSTEIN SERGEI MIKHAILOVICH

22 01 1898   11 02 1948

RUSSIAN FILM DIRECTOR WHO SERVED IN THE RED ARMY IN 1918. HE IS FAMOUS FOR HIS SILENT FILMS INCLUDING STRIKE AND THE BATTLESHIP POTEMKIM AND HIS HISTORICAL (SOUND) WORKS INCLUDING ALEXANDER NEVSKY AND IVAN THE TERRIBLE.

https://en.wikipedia.org/wiki/Sergei-Eisenstein

ELGAR SIR EDWARD WILLIAM, FIRST BARONET

02 06 1857 23 02 1934

ENGLISH COMPOSER WHO WAS APPOINTED MASTER OF THE KING`S MUSICK IN 1924 .

https://en.wikipedia.org/wiki/Edward-Elgar

ERLANDER TAGE FRITIOF

13 06 1901   21 06 1985

SWEDISH SOCIAL DEMOCRATIC POLITICIAN AND TWENTY-FIFTH PRIME MINISTER FROM 1946 TO 1969.

ACTIVELY INVOLVED IN STUDENT POLITICS AT LUND UNIVERSITY HE GRADUATED IN POLITICAL SCIENCE AND ECONOMICS IN 1928.

AS STATE SECRETARY AT THE MINISTRY OF SOCIAL AFFAIRS HE WAS ONE OF THE SENIOR OFFICIALS RESPONSIBLE FOR THE ESTABLISHMENT OF INTERNMENT CAMPS DURING THE SECOND WORLD WAR EVEN THOUGH THE COUNTRY WAS

NEUTRAL. KNOWLEDGE OF THE EXISTENCE OF THE CAMPS WAS KEPT FROM THE SWEDISH PEOPLE AND INTERNEES INCLUDED VARIOUS ETHNIC MINORITIES AS WELL AS POLITICAL DISSIDENTS, ESPECIALLY COMMUNISTS AND SOVIET SYMPATHISERS.

https://en.wikipedia.org/wiki/Tage-Erlander

ESHKOL   LEVI

25 10 1895   26 02 1969

HE WAS THE THIRD ISRAELI PRIME MINISTER FROM 1963 TO 1969 AND DURING THAT PERIOD, FROM 1963 TO 1967, THE MINISTER OF DEFENCE.

BORN LEVI SHKOLNIK IN THE KIEVGOVERNATE OF THE RUSSIAN EMPIRE HE MOVED TO PALESTINE IN 1914 AND DURING WORLD WAR ONE VOLUNTEERED FOR THE JEWISH LEGION. PRIOR TO, AND IMMEDIATELY AFTER THE ESTABLISHMENT OF THE STATE OF ISRAEL HE WAS A MEMBER OF THE HAGANAH HIGH COMMAND AND WAS PRIME MINISTER DURING THE 'SIX DAY WAR' OF 1967.

https://en.wikipedia.org/wiki/Levi-Eshkol

FAYE   ALICE

05 05 1915   09 05 1998

BORN ALICE JEANE LEPPERT, SHE WAS AN AMERICAN ACTRESS AND SINGER. ONE OF HER MOST FAMOUS FILMS WAS THE 1938 PRODUCTION OF IRVING BERLIN`S (Q.V.) ALEXANDER`S RAGTIME BAND WHICH ALSO STARRED TYRONE POWER AND DON AMECHE (Q.V.).

https://en.wikipedia.org/wiki/Alice-Faye

FISHER   ALAN

20 06 1922   20 03 1988

GENERAL SECRETARY OF THE NATIONAL UNION OF PUBLIC
EMPLOYEES FROM 1968 TO 1982 AND PRESIDENT OF THE
TRADES UNION CONGRESS IN 1981, HE SPENT HIS ENTIRE
WORKING LIFE AT THE N.U.P.E.

https://en.wikipedia.org/wiki/Alan-Fisher-(trade-unionist)

FLEMING   IAN LANCASTER

28 05 1908   12 08 1964

ENGLISH AUTHOR, JOURNALIST AND NAVAL INTELLIGENCE
OFFICER (DURING THE SECOND WORLD WAR) AND FAMOUS
FOR HIS CREATION OF THE JAMES BOND SPY NOVELS.

https://en.wikipedia.org/wiki/Ian-Fleming

FORD   GERALD RUDOLPH 'JERRY' JNR.

14 07 1913   26 12 2006

BORN LESLIE LYNCH KING JNR., HE WAS THE 40TH VICE
PRESIDENT OF THE UNITED STATES UNDER NIXON (Q.V.) AND
SUCCEEDED HIM TO BECOME THE 38TH PRESIDENT ON HIS
RESIGNATION, GRANTING HIM A CONTROVERSIAL
PRESIDENTIAL PARDON FOLLOWING NIXON`S ROLE IN THE
WATERGATE SCANDAL.

FORD HAD EARLIER SERVED NEARLY 25 YEARS AS THE
REPRESENTATIVE FROM MICHIGAN`S 5TH CONGRESSIONAL
DISTRICT, EIGHT OF THEM AS THE REPUBLICAN MINORITY
LEADER.

https://en.wikipedia.org/wiki/Gerald-Ford

FORD   JOHN 'BULL'

01 02 1894   31 08 1973

AN AMERICAN FILM DIRECTOR WHOSE CAREER SPANNED
OVER FIFTY YEARS FROM THE SILENT ERA TO SOUND. HE
WON FOUR ACADEMY AWARDS FOR BEST DIRECTOR IN 1935,
1940,1941 AND 1952. AMONGST HIS MANY FILMS WAS THE MAN

WHO SHOT LIBERTY VALANCE, THE GRAPES OF WRATH AND HOW GREEN WAS MY VALLEY WHICH WON THE BEST PICTURE AWARD.

BORN JOHN MARTIN FEENEY HE EARNED THE NICKNAME 'BULL' FOR HIS STYLE WHILST PLAYING HIGH SCHOOL FOOTBALL. HE MOVED TO HOLLYWOOD FROM MAINE FOLLOWING HIS ELDER BROTHER IN 1914 AND BEGAN HIS CAREER AS A SILENT FILM ACTOR AND AMONGST HIS ROLES WAS AN UNCREDITED APPEARANCE IN THE 1915 CLASSIC, THE BIRTH OF A NATION AS A KLANSMAN.

https://en.wikipedia.org/wiki/John-Ford

FRANCO   (CAUDILLO-HEAD OF STATE)

FRANCISCO BAHAMONDE

04 12 1892   20 11 1975

SPANISH GENERAL AND DICTATOR OF SPAIN FROM 1939 TILL HIS DEATH. IN 1936 JOINED WITH OTHER GENERALS IN A PARTIALLY SUCCESSFUL COUP AGAINST THE REPUBLIC WHICH LED TO THE SPANISH CIVIL WAR WHICH ENDED IN 1939.

https://en.wikipedia.org/wiki/Francisco-Franco

FREEMAN   JOHN

19 02 1915   20 12 2014

HE SAW ACTIVE SERVICE IN THE SECOND WORLD WAR AND SERVED IN THE FAMOUS 'DESERT RATS'. HE BECAME A LABOUR M.P. IN 1945 AND SERVED FOR TEN YEARS BEFORE STANDING DOWN TO BECOME A T.V. JOURNALIST. HE WAS APPOINTED HIGH COMMISSIONER FOR INDIA AND THEN AMBASSADOR TO THE UNITED STATES. HIS DISTINQUISHED CAREER LATER INCLUDED THE CHAIRMANSHIP OF LONDON WEEKEND TELEVISION, PRESIDENT OF I.T.N. AND A VISITING PROFESSORSHIP AT UNIVERSITY OF CALIFORNIA, DAVIS.

https://en.wikipedia.org/wiki/John-Freeman-%28British-politician%29

FROST   SIR DAVID PARADINE

07 04 1939   31 08 2013

JOURNALIST, COMEDIAN, WRITER, MEDIA PERSONALITY AND
TELEVISION HOST. AFTER GRADUATING FROM GONVILLE AND
CAIUS COLLEGE CAMBRIDGE WITH A THIRD IN ENGLISH, HE
WAS CHOSEN BY NED SHERRIN (Q.V.) TO HOST THE NEW
SATIRICAL T.V. PROGRAMME 'THAT WAS THE WEEK THAT WAS'
LEADING TO WORK IN THE UNITED STATES AS A HOST ON U.S.
TELEVISION.HE DEVELOPED A REPUTATION FOR INTERVIEWS
WITH LEADING U.S.POLITICIANS INCLUDING RICHARD NIXON
(Q.V.).

https://en.wikipedia.org/wiki/David-Frost

GAGARIN   YURI ALEKSEYEVICH

09 03 1934   27 03 1968

HE WAS A RUSSIAN SOVIET PILOT WHO BECAME THE FIRST
HUMAN TO JOURNEY INTO OUTER SPACE WHEN HIS VOSTOK
SPACECRAFT COMPLETED ONE ORBIT OF THE EARTH IN ONE
HOUR AND FORTY-EIGHT MINUTES ON APRIL 12TH NINETEEN
SIXTY-ONE. HE BECAME AN INTERNATIONAL CELEBRITY BUT
WAS KILLED IN A TRAINING ACCIDENT PILOTING A M I G 15.

https://en.wikipedia.org/wiki/Yuri-Gagarin

GALILEO   GALILEI

15 02 1564   08 01 1642

AN ITALIAN ASTRONOMER, ENGINEER, PHYSICIST,
PHILOSOPHER AND MATHEMATICIAN, HE PLAYED A MAJOR
ROLE IN THE SCIENTIFIC REVOLUTION DURING THE
RENAISSANCE AND IS WIDELY REGARDED AS ONE OF THE
GREATEST SCIENTISTS OF ALL TIME. OF HIS MANY
ACHIEVEMENTS AND CONTRIBUTIONS TO SCIENCE ARE THE
IMPROVEMENT TO THE NEWLY INVENTED TELESCOPE AND
SUPPORT FOR COPERNICANISM AND HIS ADVOCACY OF
HELIOCENTRISM WHICH BROUGHT HIM INTO CONFLICT WITH
THE CHURCH.

IN 1615 HE WAS FORMALLY DENOUNCED TO THE ROMAN
INQUISITION AND AFTER AN INVESTIGATION WAS WARNED TO

ABANDION HIS SUPPORT FOR THE THEORY WHICH HE PROMISED TO DO BUT LATER DEFENDED HIS VIEWS IN HIS MOST FAMOUS WORK, 'DIALOGUE CONCERNING THE TWO CHIEF WORLD SYSTEMS' PUBLISHED IN 1632, RESULTING IN HIM BEING TRIED BY THE INQUISITION, FOUND GUILTY OF HERESY AND HE SPENT THE LAST YEARS OF HIS LIFE UNDER HOUSE ARREST.

https://en.wikipedia.org/wiki/Galileo-Galilei

GALLACHER WILLIAM 'WILLIE'

25 12 1881   12 08 1965

SCOTTISH TRADE UNIONIST, SOCIAL ACTIVIST AND COMMUNIST.HE WAS ONE OF THE LEADING FIGURES OF THE SHOP STEWARDS` MOVEMENT IN WARTIME GLASGOW AND A FOUNDING MEMBER OF THE COMMUNIST PARTY OF GREAT BRITAIN.

A LIFELONG TEETOTALLER. IN 1916 AS CHAIRMAN OF THE CLYDE WORKERS` COMMITTEE, THEIR JOURNAL,'THE WORKER', WAS PROSECUTED UNDER THE DEFENCE OF THE REALM ACT FOR AN ARTICLE CRITICISING THE WAR AND HE WAS SENT TO PRISON FOR SIX MONTHS.

IN 1919 HE RETURNED TO PRISON FOR A FURTHER FIVE MONTHS BEING CONVICTED AS PART OF A GROUP OF UNION LEADERS FOR 'INSTIGATING AND INCITING LARGE CROWDS OF PERSONS TO FORM PART OF A RIOTOUS MOB'.

IN 1925 HE WAS ONE OF TWELVE MEMBERS OF THE COMMUNIST PARTY CONVICTED UNDER THE 1797 INCITEMENT TO MUTINY ACT AND WITH FOUR OTHERS WAS SENTENCED TO TWELVE MONTHS IMPRISONMENT.

HE WAS A COMMUNIST M.P. FROM 1935 TO 1950.

https://en.wikipedia.org/wiki/Willie-Gallacher-(politician)

GEHLEN   REINHARD

03 04 1902   08 06 1979

FIRST PRESIDENT OF THE FEDERAL INTELLIGENCE SERVICE UNTIL 1968.

https://en.wikipedia.org/wiki/Reinhard-Gehlen

GLADSTONE   WILLIAM EWART

29 12 1809   19 05 1898

BRITISH LIBERAL POLITICIAN WHO SERVED AS PRIME MINISTER FOUR TIMES AND ALSO FOUR TIMES AS CHANCELLOR OF THE EXCHEQUER.

https://en.wikipedia.org/wiki/William-Ewart-Gladstone

GOEBBELS   PAUL JOSEPH

29 10 1897   01 05 1945

GERMAN POLITICIAN AND MINISTER OF PUBLIC ENLIGHTENMENT AND PROPAGANDA, MARCH 1933 TO THE DAY BEFORE HE COMMITTED SUICIDE WHEN HE WAS BRIEFLY, FOR ONE DAY, CHANCELLOR. HE WAS VEHEMENTLY ANTISEMITIC AND STRONGLY SUPPORTED THE 'FINAL SOLUTION'. ONE OF HIS FIRST ACTS ON ASSUMING OFFICE WAS TO AUTHORISE THE NOTORIOUS BURNING OF 'UN GERMAN ' BOOKS FOLLOWED SHORTLY AFTERWARDS BY A ONE DAY BOYCOTT AGAINST JEWISH BUSINESSMEN, DOCTORS AND LAWYERS.

https://en.wikipedia.org/wiki/Joseph-Goebbels

GOTTWALD   KLEMENT

23 11 1896   14 03 1953

CZECHOSLOVAK COMMUNIST POLITICIAN WHO WAS A CABINET MAKER BY TRAINING. HE WAS, PERHAPS, THE CLASSIC EXAMPLE OF A LOYAL SERVANT TO 'MOSCOW'. IN THE FIRST WORLD WAR HE DEFECTED FROM THE AUSTRO-HUNGARIAN ARMY TO THE RUSSIANS.

IN 1921 HE WAS A CHARTER MEMBER OF THE KSC (COMMUNIST PARTY OF CZECHOSLOVAKIA) AND EDITED THE PARTY`S NEWSPAPER TO 1926.

FROM 1938 TO 1945, FOLLOWING THE MUNICH AGREEMENT, HE WAS EXILED IN MOSCOW BUT IN MARCH 1945 HE AGREED TO FORM A NATIONAL FRONT GOVERNMENT WITH EDVARD BENES WHO HAD BEEN DEMOCRATICALLY ELECTED PRESIDENT IN 1935 AND WHO HAD HEADED, IN LONDON, A GOVERNMENT IN EXILE SINCE 1941. FROM 1945 TO FEBRUARY 1948 HE DELIBERATELY UNDERMINED THE DEMOCRATIC GOVERNMENT FINALLY OUSTING THE NON COMMUNIST MEMBERS IN AN EFFECTIVE COUP.THERE THEN FOLLOWED A CONSOLIDATION OF POWER AND A SERIES OF PURGES AND TRIALS INCLUDING FORMER MEMBERS OF THE GOVERNMENT MOST PROMINENTLY RUDOLF SLANSKY (Q.V.).

HIS MAJOR OFFICES WERE CHAIRMAN OF THE COMMUNIST PARTY OF CZECHOSLOVAKIA FROM 1945 TO 1953, THE FIFTH PRESIDENT OF CZECHOSLOVAKIA FROM 1948 TO 1953 AND FOURTEENTH PRIME MINISTER FROM 1946 TO 1948.

https://en.wikipedia.org/wiki/Klement-Gottwald

GRECHKO   ANDREI ANTONOVICH

17 10 1903   26 04 1976

SOVIET GENERAL, MARSHALL OF THE SOVIET UNION AND MINISTER OF DEFENCE FROM 1967 TO HIS DEATH.A FULL MEMBER OF THE 23 RD AND 24TH POLITBUROS. HE JOINED THE RED ARMY IN 1919 AND THE COMMUNIST PARTY IN 1928. AMONGST HIS MANY POST WAR APPOINTMENTS FROM 1960 TO 1967 HE WAS THE COMMANDER IN CHIEF OF WARSAW PACT FORCES.

https://en.wikipedia.org/wiki/Andrei-Grechko

GREENE   SIDNEY FRANCIS,

BARON GREENE OF HARROW WEALD

12 02 1910   26 07 2004

GENERAL SECRETARY OF THE NATIONAL UNION OF RAILWAYMEN FROM 1957 TO 1975 AND PRESIDENT OF THE TRADES UNION CONGRESS IN 1970.

https://en.wikipedia.org/wiki/Sidney-Greene,-Baron-Greene-of-Harrow-Weald

GRIFFITHS   JAMES 'JIM'

19 09 1890   07 08 1975

LABOUR POLITICIAN AND TRADE UNION LEADER WHO WAS AN M.P. FROM 1936 TO 1970 AND DEPUTY LEADER FROM 1955 TO 1959. A PACIFIST, HE CAMPAIGNED AGAINST THE GREAT WAR.BEFORE COMING AN M.P. HE WAS PRESIDENT OF THE MINERS` FEDERATION OF SOUTH WALES.

IN THE ROLE OF MINISTER FOR NATIONAL INSURANCE IN THE 1945 ATTLEE (Q.V.) GOVERNMENT HE WAS RESPONSIBLE FOR CREATING THE MODERN STATE BENEFIT SYSTEM.

https://en.wikipedia.org/wiki/Jim-Griffiths

GRISHIN   VIKTOR VASILYEVICH

18 09 1913   25 05 1992

FIRST SECRETARY OF THE MOSCOW CITY COMMITTEE OF THE COMMUNIST PARTY 1967 TO 1985

FULL MEMBER OF THE 24TH, 25TH AND 26TH POLITBUROS 1971 TO 1986

FULL MEMBER OF THE 19TH, 20TH AND 22ND TO 26TH CENTRAL COMMITTEES 1952 TO 1986.

https://en.wikipedia.org/wiki/Viktor-Grishin

GROMYKO   ANDREI ANDREYEVICH

18 07 1909   02 07 1989

FULL MEMBER OF THE 24TH TO 27TH POLITBUROS, STATESMAN AND AMBASSADOR DURING THE COLD WAR. AS SOVIET FOREIGN MINISTER HE PLAYED A DIRECT ROLE IN THE CUBAN MISSILE CRISIS AND LATER HELPED NEGOTIATE ARMS LIMITATION TREATIES SUCH AS THE ABM TREATY, THE NUCLEAR TEST BAN TREATY AND SALT S ONE AND TWO.

https://en.wikipedia.org/wiki/Andrei-Gromyko

GUDERIAN   HEINZ WILHELM

17 06 1888   14 05 1954

NICKNAMED SCHNELLER HEINZ, HE WAS A GERMAN GENERAL DURING WORLD WAR TWO AND IS NOTED FOR HIS SUCCESSFUL LEADERSHIP OF PANZER/TANK UNITS IN POLAND, FRANCE AND RUSSIA.

DURING THE INTER WAR YEARS HE PIONEERED MOTORIZED TACTICS AND PROMOTED THE USE OF RADIO COMMUNICATIONS BETWEEN TANK CREWS AND DEVISED SHOCK TACTICS THAT PROVED HIGHLY EFFECTIVE.

https://en.wikipedia.org/wiki/Heinz-Guderian

GUSTAF VI ADOLF OF SWEDEN

OSCAR FREDRIK WILHELM OLAF GUSTAF ADOLF

11 11 1882   15 09 1973

KING OF SWEDEN FROM OCTOBER TWENTY-NINETH 1950 TO HIS DEATH. HE WAS A LIFELONG AMATEUR ARCHEOLOGIST PARTICULARLY INTERESTED IN ANCIENT ITALIAN CULTURES AND BOTANY, BEING CONSIDERED AN EXPERT ON THE RHODODENDON.

DURING HIS REIGN WORK BEGAN MODERNISING THE LEGAL STATUS OF THE MONARCHY WHICH WAS COMPLETED AFTER HIS DEATH.

https://en.wikipedia.org/wiki/Gustaf-VI-Adolf-of-Sweden

HAMILTON   WILLIAM WINTER 'WILLIE'

26 06 1917   26 01 2000

LABOUR M.P. FOR CONSTITUENCIES IN FIFE, SCOTLAND
BETWEEN 1950 AND 1987 WHO HELD STRONG REPUBLICAN
VIEWS.

https://en.wikipedia.org/wiki/Willie-Hamilton

HAMMER   ARMAND

21 05 1898   10 12 1990

AMERICAN BUSINESSMAN, PHILANTHROPIST AND ART
COLLECTOR. RAN OCCIDENTAL PETROLEUM FROM 1957 TO
HIS DEATH. HE HAD CLOSE TIES IN AND WITH THE SOVIET
UNION.

https://en.wikipedia.org/wiki/Armand-Hammer

HARRIMAN   WILLIAM AVERELL

15 11 1891   26 07 1986

AMERICAN DEMOCRATIC POLITICIAN (BUT UP TO 1928, A
REPUBLICAN), BUSINESSMAN AND DIPLOMAT. HE SERVED
PRESIDENTS ROOSEVELT, TRUMAN, KENNEDY AND JOHNSON
(Q.V.) IN VARIOUS POLITICAL AND DIPLOMATIC ASSIGNMENTS
AND POSTS AND WAS AMBASSADOR TO THE COURT OF ST.
JAMES IN 1946 AND EARLIER FROM 1943 TO 1946 TO THE
SOVIET UNION.

https://en.wikipedia.org/wiki/W.-Averell-Harriman

HARRIS   SIR ARTHUR TRAVERS, FIRST BARONET

MARSHALL OF THE ROYAL AIR FORCE,
GCB,OBE, AFC.

13 04 1892   05 04 1984

COMMONLY KNOWN AS "BOMBER" HARRIS BY THE PRESS AND
WITHIN THE RAF AS "BUTCHER" HARRIS.

HE WAS AIR OFFICER COMMANDING –IN–CHIEF RAF BOMBER
COMMAND DURING THE LATTER HALF OF THE SECOND WORLD

WAR AND IMPLEMENTED THE GOVERNMENT'S POLICY OF AREA BOMBING OF GERMAN CITIES.

https://en.wikipedia.org/wiki/Sir-Arthur-Harris,-1st-Baronet

HEALEY   DENIS WINSTON, BARON

30 08 1917   03 10 2015

LABOUR POLITICIAN WHO WAS AN M.P. FOR JUST OVER FORTY YEARS.WHILST AT BALLIOL COLLEGE, OXFORD HE MET THE FUTURE CONSERVATIVE PRIME MINISTER EDWARD HEATH (Q.V.) AND DESPITE THEIR POLITICAL DIFFERENCES THEY BECAME LIFELONG FRIENDS. HE FOUGHT IN THE SECOND WORLD WAR RISING TO THE RANK OF MAJOR IN THE ROYAL ENGINEERS.

DURING HIS POLITICAL CAREER HE WAS DEPUTY LEADER OF THE PARTY FROM 1980 TO 1983 AND WHILST IN GOVERNMENT WAS SECRETARY OF STATE FOR DEFENCE AND CHANCELLOR OF THE EXCHEQUER.

https://en.wikipedia.org/wiki/Denis-Healey

HEATH   SIR EDWARD RICHARD GEORGE 'TED'

09 07 1916 17 07 2005

CONSERVATIVE POLITICIAN, LEADER OF HIS PARTY FROM 1965 TO 1975 AND PRIME MINISTER FROM 1970 TO 1974.

HE WAS AN M.P. FROM 1950 TO 2001, BECOMING THE 'FATHER OF THE HOUSE' DURING THE LAST NINE YEARS.

IN 1939 HE OBTAINED A SECOND CLASS HONOURS BA FROM BALLIOL COLLEGE, OXFORD IN PHILOSOPHY, POLITICS AND ECONOMICS AND IT WAS WHILST AT UNIVERSITY HE MET DENIS HEALEY (Q.V.) FORGING, DESPITE THEIR POLITICAL DIFFERENCES, A LIFE LONG FRIENDSHIP.

AS AN UNDERGRADUATE, HE TRAVELLED WIDELY IN EUROPE WITNESSING THE 1937 NUREMBERG RALLY WHERE HE MET, AMONGST OTHERS, JOSEPH GOEBBELS (Q.V.) STRENGTHENING HIS OPPOSITION TO APPEASEMENT AND IN 1938 HE VISITED SPAIN DURING THE CIVIL WAR.

DURING HIS PERIOD AS PRIME MINISTER HE OVERSAW THE DECIMALISATION OF THE CURRENCY IN 1971 AND IN 1973 TOOK THE COUNTRY INTO THE EUROPEAN ECONOMIC COMMUNITY. FRICTION BETWEEN THE CATHOLIC AND PROTESTANT COMMUNITIES IN NORTHERN IRELAND GAVE HIS GOVERNMENT MANY PROBLEMS, HOWEVER INDUSTRIAL PROBLEMS WITH THE TRADE UNIONS AND ESPECIALLY THE MINERS ULTIMATELY ENDED HIS YEARS OF POWER. HE HAD ATTEMPTED TO CURB THE POWER OF THE UNIONS WITH THE 1971 INDUSTRIAL RELATIONS ACT BUT TWO STRIKES BY THE MINERS IN 1972 AND 1974 RESULTED IN HIM CALLING A GENERAL ELECTION IN ORDER TO OBTAIN A MANDATE BUT THE OPPOSITION LABOUR PARTY UNDER WILSON GAINED MORE SEATS FORCING HIM TO RESIGN.

https://en.wikipedia.org/wiki/Edward-Heath

HELMS   RICHARD McGARRAH

30 03 1913   23 10 2002

AN INTELLIGENCE OFFICER HE BEGAN HIS CAREER IN THE WAR TIME OFFICE OF STRATEGIC SERVICES (O.S.S.). BETWEEN 1965 AND 1966 HE WAS THE DEPUTY DIRECTOR OF THE CENTRAL INTELLIGENCE AGENCY AND THE 8TH DIRECTOR FROM 1966 TO 1973.

FROM 1973 TO 1977 HE WAS THE UNITED STATES AMBASSADOR TO IRAN.

https://en.wikipedia.org/wiki/Richard-Helms

HIEMER   ERNST

05 07 1900   29 07 1974

JOURNALIST AND LATER EDITOR OF THE NOTORIOUS ANTI SEMITIC NEWSPAPER DER STURMER AND AUTHOR OF ANTI SEMITIC BOOKS FOR CHILDREN INCLUDING DER GIFTPILZ (THE POISONOUS MUSHROOM) AND DER PUDELMOPSDACKELPINSCHER UND ANDERE BESINNLICHE ERZAHLUNGEN (THE POODLE-PUG-DACHSHUND-PINSCHER AND OTHER CONTEMPLATIVE STORIES).

https://en.wikipedia.org/wiki/Ernst-Hiemer

HILTON   JAMES

09 09 1900   20 12 1954

ENGLISH NOVELIST AND ALSO HOLLYWOOD SCREENPLAY
WRITER BEST REMEMBERED FOR HIS NOVELS KNIGHT
WITHOUT ARMOUR, LOST HORIZON, GOODBYE, MR. CHIPS AND
RANDOM HARVEST.

https://en.wikipedia.org/wiki/James-Hilton-%28novelist%29

(EMPEROR) HIROHITO

29 04 1901   07 01 1989

124TH EMPEROR OF JAPAN, HE RULED FROM 1926 TO HIS
DEATH.AT THE START OF HIS REIGN JAPAN WAS THE WORLD`S
NINETH LARGEST ECONOMY. ALTHOUGH HEAD OF STATE
DURING THE SECOND WORLD WAR HE WAS NOT PROSECUTED
FOR WAR CRIMES THOUGH HIS DEGREE OF INVOLVEMENT
REMAINS CONTROVERSIAL.

https://en.wikipedia.org/wiki/Hirohito

HITLER   ADOLF

20 04 1889   30 04 1945

AUSTRIAN BORN GERMAN POLITICIAN WHO WAS LEADER OF THE NAZI PARTY, CHANCELLOR OF GERMANY FROM 1933 TO 1945 AND FUHRER OF NAZI GERMANY FROM 1934 TO 1945. AS EFFECTIVE DICTATOR OF GERMANY HE WAS RESPONSIBLE FOR CAUSING WORLD WAR TWO AND THE HOLOCAUST.

ALONG WITH STALIN (Q.V.) THEIR ACTIONS INFLUENCED AND DOMINATED EUROPEAN POLITICS FOR THE SECOND QUARTER OF THE 20TH CENTURY.

IN 1923 HE LED A FAILED COUP TO SEIZE POWER IN MUNICH RESULTING IN HIS IMPRISONMENT, DURING WHICH TIME HE WROTE HIS AUTOBIOGRAPHY AND POLITICAL MANIFESTO, MEIN KAMPF.

HIS ANTISEMITIC POSTURE WAS BASED ON HIS ERRONEOUS BELIEF OF AN INTERNATIONAL JEWISH CONSPIRACY INVOLVING BOTH CAPITALISM AND (BOLSHEVIK) COMMUNISM.

https://en.wikipedia.org/wiki/Adolf-Hitler

HO   CHI MINH

19 05 1890   02 09 1969

BORN NGUYEN SINH CON OR CUNG, HE WAS CHAIRMAN OF THE CENTRAL COMMITTEE OF THE COMMUNIST PARTY OF VIETNAM FROM1951 TO 1969, FIRST SECRETARY OF THE CENTRAL COMMITTEE OF THE COMMUNIST PARTY OF VIETNAM, 1956 TO 1960, FIRST PRESIDENT OF VIETNAM 1945 TO 1969 AND PRIME MINISTER OF VIETNAM FROM 1945 TO 1955.

HE WAS A VIETNAMESE COMMUNIST REVOLUTIONARY LEADER, A KEY FIGURE IN THE FOUNDATION OF THE DEMOCRATIC REPUBLIC OF VIETNAM AS WELL AS THE PEOPLE`S ARMY OF VIETNAM AND VIET CONG. HIS MOST FAMOUS MILITARY VICTORY WAS THE DEFEAT OF THE FRENCH AT DIEN BIEN PHU IN 1954.

https://en.wikipedia.org/wiki/Ho-Chi-Minh

HOLTOM   GERALD HERBERT

20 01 1914   18 09 1985

A PROFESSIONAL DESIGNER AND ARTIST HAVING GRADUATED FROM THE ROYAL COLLEGE OF ART, HE WAS A CONSCIENTIOUS OBJECTOR IN THE SECOND WORLD WAR. HE DESIGNED THE FAMOUS CND SYMBOL, BASED ON THE FLAG SEMAPHORE ALPHABET.

https://en.wikipedia.org/wiki/Gerald-Holtom

HONEYCOMBE

RONALD GORDON

27 09 1936   09 10 2015

AUTHOR, PLAYWRIGHT, STAGE ACTOR AND FORMERLY NATIONAL TELEVISION NEWSCASTER IN THE U.K.

https://en.wikipedia.org/wiki/Gordon-Honeycombe

HOOVER   HERBERT CLARK

10 08 1874   20 10 1964

RAISED AS A QUAKER, HE WAS A PROFESSIONAL MINING ENGINEER, A GRADUATE OF STANFORD UNIVERSITY (INDEED HE ENTERED THE UNIVERSITY IN 1891, ITS' INAUGURAL YEAR, AND CLAIMED TO BE ITS' VERY FIRST STUDENT, BY VIRTUE OF HAVING BEEN THE FIRST PERSON TO SLEEP IN THE DORMITORY). A REPUBLICAN, HE BECAME THE 31ST PRESIDENT OF THE UNITED STATES (1929-33) AND WAS PREVIOUSLY THE THIRD UNITED STATES SECRETARY OF COMMERCE FROM 1921 -28.

DURING HIS PRESIDENCY THE NATION SUFFERED THE WALL STREET CRASH IN OCTOBER 1929 WHICH, ALONGSIDE HIS SUPPORT FOR THE CONTINUATION OF PROHIBITION, WERE SIGNIFICANT ELECTORAL FACTORS IN HIS FAILED BID TO BE RE-ELECTED

https://en.wikipedia.org/wiki/Herbert-Hoover

HORNER   ARTHUR LEWIS

05 04 1894   04 09 1968

WELSH TRADE UNION LEADER AND COMMUNIST POLITICIAN, HE WAS PRESIDENT OF THE SOUTH WALES MINERS` FEDERATION FROM 1936 UNTIL 1946 AND IN AUGUST 1946 WAS ELECTED GENERAL SECRETARY OF THE UNIFIED NATIONAL UNION OF MINEWORKERS. A PROTEGE OF NOAH ABLETT (Q.V.) HE WAS A FOUNDING MEMBER OF THE COMMUNIST PARTY OF GREAT BRITAIN IN 1921 BUT IN 1931 HE BECAME DISSATISFIED WITH THEIR POLICY TOWARDS TRADE UNIONS COMPELLING HIM TO TRAVEL TO MOSCOW AND APPEAL TO THE COMINTERM AS HE FACED EXPULSION FROM THE PARTY IN GREAT BRITAIN. THE VERDICT, WHICH IDENTIFIED MISTAKES ON BOTH SIDES, WAS SUFFICIENTLY FAIR FOR HIM TO COMPLY WITH A PUBLIC ADMISSION OF HIS ALLEGED MISTAKES.

https://en.wikipedia.org/wiki/Arthur-Horner-(trade-unionist)

HUMPHREY   HUBERT HORATIO JNR.

27 05 1911   13 01 1978

DEMOCRATIC POLITICIAN WHO ORIGINALLY TRAINED AS A PHARMACIST AND PRACTISED FROM 1931 TO 1937 WHEN, AFTER RETURNING TO COLLEGE, HE ENTERED POLITICS. HE WAS A UNITED STATES SENATOR FROM 1949 TO 1964 AND AGAIN FROM 1971 TO 1978.IN 1947 HE WAS A CO FOUNDER OF THE LIBERAL ANTI- COMMUNIST GROUP AMERICANS FOR DEMOCRATIC ACTION.

FROM 1965 TO 1969 HE SERVED AS THE THIRTY-EIGHTH VICE PRESIDENT OF THE UNITED STATES UNDER JOHNSON (Q.V.) BUT LOST THE NOVEMBER 1968 PRESIDENTIAL ELECTION TO NIXON (Q.V.).

https://en.wikipedia.org/wiki/Hubert-Humphrey

HUXLEY   ALDOUS LEONARD

26 07 1894   22 11 1963

ENGLISH WRITER AND PHILOSOPHER BEST KNOWN FOR HIS NOVEL BRAVE NEW WORLD.

https://en.wikipedia.org/wiki/Aldous-Huxley

ISHII   SURGEON GENERAL SHIRO

25 06 1892   09 10 1959

JAPANESE ARMY MEDICAL OFFICER, MICROBIOLOGIST AND DIRECTOR OF THE IMFAMOUS UNIT 731, A BIOLOGICAL WARFARE UNIT OF THE IMPERIAL JAPANESE ARMY INVOLVED IN FORCED AND FREQUENTLY LETHAL HUMAN EXPERIMENTATION DURING THE SECOND SINO- JAPANESE WAR OF 1937 TO 1945.

https://en.wikipedia.org/wiki/Shiro-Ishii

JANNER   BARON BARNETT

20 06 1892   04 05 1982

LIBERAL THEN LABOUR POLITICIAN AND AN M.P. FOR TWENTY-NINE YEARS OVER A PERIOD OF THIRTY-NINE YEARS. PRESIDENT OF THE BOARD OF DEPUTIES OF BRITISH JEWS, 1955-1964.

https://en.wikipedia.org/wiki/Barnett-Janner,-Baron-Janner

JOHNSON   CLAUDIA ALTA TAYLOR

22 12 1912   11 07 2007

KNOWN AS 'LADY BIRD', THE WIFE OF THE THIRTY-SIX PRESIDENT, LYNDON B. JOHNSON AND FIRST LADY OF THE UNITED STATES.

https://en.wikipedia.org/wiki/Lady-Bird-Johnson

JOHNSON   LYNDON BAINES

27 08 1908   22 01 1973

KNOWN AS 'L B J' HE WAS THE 36TH PRESIDENT OF THE
UNITED STATES, SUCCEEEDING HIS ASSASSINATED
PREDECESSOR JOHN F. KENNEDY (Q.V.). HE WAS RENOWNED
FOR HIS DOMINEEERING, SOMETIMES ABRASIVE PERSONALITY
AND HIS STYLE OF AGGRESSIVE COERCION. DESPITE THIS
TRAIT HIS PROGRAMME OF SOCIAL REFORM PROMOTED
GREATER EQUALITY INCLUDING LEGISLATION IN THE FIELDS
OF MEDICAL SERVICES, ENVIRONMENTAL PROTECTION, THE
ARTS, EDUCATION AND A 'WAR ON POVERTY', HOWEVER HE
GREATLY EXPANDED THE WAR IN VIETNAM.

https://en.wikipedia.org/wiki/ Lyndon-B.-Johnson

JONES   JAMES "JACK" LARKIN

29 03 1913   21 04 2009

GENERAL SECRETARY, TRANSPORT AND GENERAL WORKERS`
UNION. FOUGHT IN THE SPANISH CIVIL WAR AND WAS
SERIOUSLY WOUNDED AT THE BATTLE OF THE EBRO IN 1938.

https://en.wikipedia.org/wiki/Jack-Jones-(trade-unionist)

JORDAN   JOHN COLIN CAMPBELL

19 06 1923 09 04 2009

A LEADING FIGURE IN POSTWAR NEO-NAZISM IN BRITAIN.
THIRD LEADER OF THE WORLD UNION OF NATIONAL
SOCIALISTS FROM 1968 TO HIS DEATH.

HE JOINED THE LEAGUE OF EMPIRE LOYALISTS AND BECAME
THEIR MIDLANDS ORGANISER AND IN 1956 LAUNCHED THE
WHITE DEFENCE LEAGUE WHICH IN 1960 MERGED WITH THE
NATIONAL LABOUR PARTY TO FORM THE BRITISH NATIONAL
PARTY.

WITH JOHN TYNDALL (Q.V.) HE FOUNDED THE NATIONAL
SOCIALIST MOVEMENT IN 1962.

LATER THAT SAME YEAR HE HOSTED AN INTERNATIONAL
CONFERENCE OF NATIONAL SOCIALISTS RESULTING IN THE
FORMATION OF THE WORLD UNION OF NATIONAL SOCIALISTS

OF WHICH HE BECAME THE COMMANDER OF ITS` EUROPEAN SECTION.

ON AUGUST 16TH WITH TYNDALL AND OTHERS THEY WERE CHARGED UNDER THE 1936 PUBLIC ORDER ACT WITH ATTEMPTS TO SET UP A PARAMILITARY FORCE AND HE WAS SENTENCED TO NINE MONTHS IMPRISONMENT.

ON HIS RELEASE HE MARRIED FRANCOISE DIOR (Q.V.) BUT THEY SEPARATED IN THE FOLLOWING JANUARY.

IN 1964 HE FORMED THE GREATER BRITAIN MOVEMENT HAVING POLITICALLY SPLIT WITH TYNDALL AND IN 1967 HE WAS AGAIN CONVICTED UNDER THE 1936 PUBLIC ORDER ACT FOR DISTRIBUTING A VITUPERATIVE LEAFLET AND ALSO SENTENCED TO EIGHTEEN MONTHS IMPRISONMENT FOR BREAKING THE 1965 RACE RELATIONS ACT BY CIRCULATING MATERIAL LIKELY TO CAUSE RACIAL HATRED.

https://en.wikipedia.org/wiki/Colin-Jordan

JOSEPH   KEITH SINJOHN, SECOND BARONET

17 01 1918   10 12 1994

BRITISH CONSERVATIVE POLITICIAN, CABINET MEMBER, BARRISTER AND M.P. FROM 1956 TO 1987

https://en.wikipedia.org/wiki/Keith-Joseph

KAFKA   FRANZ (HEBREW NAME ANSCHEL)

03 07 1883   03 06 1924

HE TRAINED AS A LAWYER AND FOUND WORK IN AN INSURANCE COMPANY, WRITING SHORT STORIES IN HIS SPARE TIME WHILST COMPLAINING ABOUT THE LITTLE TIME HE HAD TO DEVOTE TO WHAT HE CAME TO REGARD AS HIS CALLING. HIS WORKS HAVE A DARK PYSCHOLOGICAL UNDERTONE.

https://en.wikipedia.org/wiki/Franz-Kafka

KAGANOVICH LAZAR MOISEYEVICH

22 11 1893   25 07 1991

SOVIET POLITICIAN, ADMINISTRATOR AND **LOYAL** ASSOCIATE OF JOSEPH STALIN (Q.V.). CANDIDATE MEMBER OF THE 14TH TO 16TH POLITBUROS 1926 TO 1930 AND FULL MEMBER OF THE 17TH TO 20TH POLITBUROS 1930 TO 1957. IN 1922 STALIN PROMOTED HIM TO HEAD THE ORGBURO OF THE SECRETATIAT WHICH WAS RESPONSIBLE FOR ALL ASSIGNMENTS WITHIN THE APPARATUS OF THE COMMUNIST PARTY.

WITH MOLOTOV (Q.V.) WAS GIVEN THE TASK OF IMPLEMENTING THE COLLECTIVIZATION POLICY THAT CAUSED A CATASTROPHIC FAMINE DURING 1932 TO 1933 IN THE UKRAINE.

IN 1934, AT THE XVII CONGRESS OF THE COMMUNIST PARTY,HE CHAIRED THE COUNTING COMMITTEEE AND FALSIFIED VOTING FOR POSITIONS TO THE CENTRAL COMMITTEE RESULTING IN STALIN BEING REELECTED AS THE GENERAL SECRETARY INSTEAD OF SERGEI KIROV (Q.V.).

https://en.wikipedia.org/wiki/Lazar-Kaganovich

KAHN   HERMAN

15 02 1922   07 07 1983

HE WAS A FOUNDER OF THE HUDSON INSTITUTE BEFORE WHICH HE WORKED AT THE RAND CORPORATION. HIS REPUTATION RESTS ON HIS WORK 'ON THERMONUCLEAR WAR' WHICH IS AN ANALYTICAL VIEW OF THE CONSEQUENCES OF THERMONUCLEAR WAR.

https://en.wikipedia.org/wiki/Herman-Kahn

KAMENEV   LEV BORISOVICH

18 07 1883   25 08 1936

BORN **ROZENFELD,** WAS A BOLSHEVIK REVOLUTIONARY AND A PROMINENT SOVIET POLITICIAN. HE SERVED BRIEFLY AS THE FIRST HEAD OF STATE OF SOVIET RUSSIA IN 1917 AND FROM 1923-1924 WAS THE ACTING PREMIER IN THE LAST YEAR OF LENIN`S LIFE (Q.V.). THE BROTHER IN LAW OF LEON TROTSKY (Q.V.), UNDER THE LEADERSHIP OF JOSEPH STALIN (Q.V.) HE

FELL OUT OF FAVOUR AND, FOLLOWING A SHOW TRIAL, WAS EXECUTED.

HE WAS A FULL MEMBER OF THE 8TH TO THE 13TH POLITBUROS AND A CANDIDATE MEMBER OF THE 14TH.

PRIOR TO THE FIRST WORLD WAR AND FOR SOME YEARS HE HAD BEEN A CLOSE ASSOCIATE OF VLADIMIR LENIN THOUGH THEY SOMETIMES DIFFERED.

https://en.wikipedia.org/wiki/Lev-Kamenev

KARLOFF   BORIS

23 11 1887   02 02 1969

AMERICAN FILM ACTOR BORN IN THE UNITED KINGDOM. REAL NAME WILLIAM HENRY **PRATT**.

https://en.wikipedia.org/wiki/Boris-Karloff

KAUFMAN   SIR GERALD BERNARD

21 06 1930   26 02 2017

FROM THE 2015 GENERAL ELECTION UNTIL HIS DEATH HE WAS THE 'FATHER OF THE HOUSE' SERVING AS AN M.P. SINCE 1970.

HE GRADUATED FROM QUEEN`S COLLEGE, OXFORD WITH A DEGREE IN PHILOSOPHY, POLITICS AND ECONOMICS AND DURING HIS TIME AT UNIVERSITY HE WAS SECRETARY OF THE UNIVERSITY LABOUR CLUB.   FROM 1954 TO 1955 HE WAS ASSISTANT GENERAL SECRETARY OF THE FABIAN SOCIETY, FROM 1955 TO 1964 HE WAS A LEAD WRITER ON THE DAILY MIRROR AND FROM 1964 TO 1965 A JOURNALIST ON THE NEW STATESMAN.

FROM 1965 TO 1970 HE WAS THE PARLIAMENTARY PRESS LIAISON OFFICER FOR THE LABOUR PARTY BEFORE BEING ELECTED AS AN M.P.

BETWEEN 1974 AND 1979 HE WAS A JUNIOR MINISTER AND BETWEEN 1980 AND 1992 HE WAS AN OPPOSITION 'SHADOW' MINISTER.

IN 1962 AND 1963 HE CONTRIBUTED TO THE B.B.C. SATIRICAL PROGRAMME PRODUCED BY NED SHERRIN (Q.V.)'THAT WAS THE WEEK THAT WAS'.

https://en.wikipedia.org/wiki/Gerald-Kaufman

KENDALL   KENNETH

07 08 1924   14 12 2012

ORIGINALLY A SCHOOLMASTER, HE WAS LATER A CAPTAIN IN THE COLDSTREAM GUARDS AND WAS INJURED ON D-DAY. HE LATER BECAME A B. B. C. T.V. NEWSCASTER.

https://en.wikipedia.org/wiki/Kenneth-Kendall

KENNEDY   EDWARD MOORE 'TED'

22 02 1932   25 08 2009

YOUNGEST BROTHER OF PRESIDENT JOHN F. KENNEDY AND SENATOR ROBERT F. KENNEDY (Q.V.) WHO WERE BOTH ASSASSINATED. HIS PRESIDENTIAL ASPIRATIONS WERE FOREVER THWARTED BY THE 'CHAPPAQUIDDICK' INCIDENT IN 1969 AND THE DEATH, IN A MOTOR ACCIDENT, OF HIS PASSENGER AFTER WHICH HE PLEADED GUILTY TO A CHARGE OF LEAVING THE SCENE OF AN ACCIDENT. HE SERVED, WITH GREAT CREDIT, AS A SENATOR FOR NEARLY FORTY–SEVEN YEARS AND WAS RESPONSIBLE FOR BRINGING INTO LAW OVER THREE HUNDRED BILLS.

https://en.wikipedia.org/wiki/Ted-Kennedy

KENNEDY   JACQUELINE LEE 'JACKIE'

28 07 1929   19 05 1994

WIFE OF THE ASSASSINATED PRESIDENT JOHN F. KENNEDY.

https://en.wikipedia.org/wiki/Jacqueline-Kennedy-Onassis

KENNEDY   JOHN'JACK'FITZGERALD

29 05 1917   22 11 1963

THIRTY-FIFTH PRESIDENT OF THE UNITED STATES UNTIL HIS ASSASSINATION ON NOVEMBER 22ND 1963. SUCCESSFULLY

CONFRONTED NIKITA KHRUSHCHEV (Q.V.) OVER THE CUBAN MISSILE CRISIS IN THE PREVIOUS YEAR.

https://en.wikipedia.org/wiki/John-F.-Kennedy

KENNEDY   ROBERT FRANCIS 'BOBBY'

20 11 1925   06 06 1968

BETTER KNOWN BY HIS INITIALS '**RFK**' HE WAS THE CAMPAIGN MANAGER FOR HIS BROTHER JOHN IN THE SUCCESSFUL NOVEMBER 1960 PRESIDENTIAL ELECTION AND WAS APPOINTED ATTORNEY GENERAL WHERE HE ADVOCATED CIVIL RIGHTS FOR AFRO-AMERICANS AND CRUSADED AGAINST ORGANISED CRIME AND THE MAFIA. FOLLOWING THE CALIFORNIA PRESIDENTIAL PRIMARY HE WAS ASSASSINATED BY SIRHAN SIRHAN (Q.V.).

https://en.wikipedia.org/wiki/Robert-F.-Kennedy

KERENSKY   ALEXANDER FYODOROVICH

02 05 1881   11 06 1970

WAS A RUSSIAN LAWYER AND POLITICIAN WHO SERVED AS THE SECOND MINISTER-CHAIRMAN OF THE RUSSIAN PROVISIONAL GOVERNMENT BETWEEN JULY AND NOVEMBER 1917 BEFORE THE LENIN LED BOLSHEVIK COUP. HE SPENT THE REST OF HIS LIFE IN EXILE AND ALTHOUGH HE DIED IN THE UNITED STATES HE IS BURIED IN LONDON, ENGLAND.

INTERESTINGLY, HIS FATHER, WHO WAS A TEACHER, TAUGHT THE YOUNG LENIN AND BOTH FAMILIES WERE FRIENDS.

https://en.wikipedia.org/wiki/Alexander-Kerensky

KERR   ARCHIBALD CLARK, FIRST BARON INVERCHAPEL

17 03 1882   05 07 1951

BRITISH DIPLOMAT. WAS AMBASSADOR TO CHINA BETWEEN 1938 AND 1942, SOVIET UNION BETWEEN 1942 AND 1946 AND THE UNITED STATES BETWEEN 1946 AND 1948.

https://en.wikipedia.org/wiki/ Archibald-Clark-Kerr,-1st-Baron Inverchapel

KEYSTONE KOPS

FICTIONAL INCOMPETENT POLICEMEN, FEATURED IN SILENT FILM COMEDIES IN THE EARLY 20TH CENTURY AND PRODUCED BY MACK SENNETT FOR HIS KEYSTONE FILM COMPANY BETWEEN 1912 AND 1917.

https://en.wikipedia.org/wiki/Keystone-Kops

KHRUSHCHEV NIKITA SERGEYEVICH

15 04 1894   11 09 1971

FIRST SECRETARY OF THE CENTRAL COMMITTEE OF THE COMMUNIST PARTY OF THE SOVIET UNION 1953 TO 1964 WHEN OUSTED BY LEONID BREZHNEV (Q.V.). FULL MEMBER OF THE 18TH TO 22ND PRESIDIUM/ POLITBURO 1939 TO 1964. IN FEBRUARY 1956, AT THE 20TH PARTY CONGRESS HE DENOUNCED STALIN`S PURGES EVEN THOUGH HE WAS AN ACTIVE PARTICIPANT. IN 1962 HE WAS CONFRONTED BY THE UNITED STATES PRESIDENT, JOHN KENNEDY (Q.V.) OVER THE CUBAN MISSILE CRISIS AND HE BACKED DOWN.

https://en.wikipedia.org/wiki/Nikita-Khrushchev

KHRUSHCHEVA   NINA PETROVNA

14 04 1900   13 08 1984

THIRD WIFE OF NIKITA KHRUSHCHEV AND MOTHER OF THREE OF HIS CHILDREN, RADA, SERGEI AND ELENA. FIRST MET IN 1922 BUT ONLY OFFICIALLY MARRIED IN 1965.

https://en.wikipedia.org/wiki/Nina-Petrovna-Khrushcheva

KIRILENKO   ANDREI PAVLOVICH

08 09 1906   12 05 1990

SOVIET POLITICIAN WHO JOINED THE COMMUNIST PARTY IN EITHER 1930 OR 1931. FULL MEMBER OF THE 22 ND TO 26TH POLITBUROS AND CANDIDATE MEMBER OF THE 19TH POLITBURO.ALTHOUGH 'ALLIED'TO KHRUSHCHEV (Q.V.) HE SUPPORTED BREZHNEV (Q.V.) IN THE LATTER`S CONSPIRACY AGAINST KHRUSHCHEV BECOMING HIS 'CHIEF LIEUTENANT' WITHIN THE CENTRAL COMMITTEE, SECURING HIS POWER BASE.

https://en.wikipedia.org/wiki/Andrei-Kirilenko-(politician)

KIRKPATRICK SIR IVONE AUGUSTINE

03 02 1897   25 05 1964

BRITISH DIPLOMAT AND PERMANENT UNDER-SECRETARY OF STATE FOR FOREIGN AFFAIRS. IN 1918, WHILST STATIONED IN THE NETHERLANDS, HE WORKED AS A SPYMASTER RUNNING A NETWORK OF BRITISH AGENTS OPERATING IN GERMAN OCCUPIED TERRITORY AND IN 1941 HE WAS ENTRUSTED TO INTERVIEW HITLER`S (Q.V.) DEPUTY, RUDOLF HESS FOLLOWING HIS FLIGHT TO SCOTLAND.

https://en.wikipedia.org/wiki/Ivone-Kirkpatrick

KIROV   SERGEI MIRONOVICH

27 03 1886   01 12 1934

BORN SERGEI **KOSTRIKOV**, HE WAS A MEMBER OF THE 16TH AND 17TH POLITBUROS AND ROSE TO BECOME FIRST SECRETARY OF THE LENINGRAD CITY COMMITTEE OF THE ALL–UNION COMMUNIST PARTY BUT WAS ASSASSINATED, UNDOUBTEDLY ON THE ORDERS OF FIRST SECRETARY STALIN (Q.V.) THOUGH THIS WAS NEVER PROVEN.

https://en.wikipedia.org/wikiSergey-Kirov

KONAYEV   DINMUKHAMED AKHMETULY

12 01 1912   22 08 1993

FULL MEMBER OF THE 24 TH TO 26TH POLITBUROS AND CANDIDATE MEMBER OF THE 23RD POLITBURO. KHRUSHCHEV (Q.V.) APPOINTED BREZHNEV (Q.V.) AS THE SECOND SECRETARY OF THE COMMUNIST PARTY OF KAZAKHSTAN IN 1954 WHICH BEGUN A CLOSE FRIENDSHIP BETWEEN KONAYEV AND BREZHNEV.

https://en.wikipedia.org/wiki/Dinmukhamed-Konayev

KORDA   SIR ALEXANDER

16 09 1893   23 01 1956

BORN SANDOR LASZLO KELLNER IN HUNGARY, HE WAS A FILM PRODUCER AND DIRECTOR, FIRST WORKING IN HUNGARY THEN IN OTHER EUROPEAN CITIES BEFORE MOVING TO 'HOLLYWOOD' AND THEN TO BRITAIN BECOMING A LEADING FIGURE IN THE BRITISH FILM INDUSTRY, FOUNDING LONDON FILMS AND OWNING BRITISH LION FILMS, A FILM DISTRIBUTING COMPANY.

AMONGST THE MANY FILMS MADE AT THE DENHAM FILM STUDIOS WHICH WAS THE HOME OF LONDON FILMS WERE THE PRIVATE LIFE OF HENRY VIII AND THINGS TO COME, A VISION OF THE TWENTY-FIRST CENTURY AFTER A DEVASTATING WAR IN 1940.

https://en.wikipedia.org/wiki/Alexander-Korda

KOSYGIN   ALEXEI NIKOLAYEVICH

21 02 1904   18 12 1980

SOVIET POLITICIAN DURING THE COLD WAR. HE WAS CONSCRIPTED INTO THE LABOUR ARMY DURING THE RUSSIAN CIVIL WAR AND APPLIED FOR MEMBERSHIP OF THE COMMUNIST PARTY IN 1927. FULL MEMBER OF THE 18TH AND 22ND TO 25TH POLITBUROS AND CANDIDATE MEMBER OF THE 18TH TO 20TH POLITBUROS.

CHAIRMAN OF THE COUNCIL OF MINISTERS 1964 TO 1980.

https://en.wikipedia.org/wiki/Alexei-Kosygin

KOZLOV   FROL ROMANOVICH

18 08 1908   30 01 1965

FIRST DEPUTY OF THE COUNCIL OF MINISTERS OF THE SOVIET UNION, 1958 TO 1960, CHAIRMAN OF THE COUNCIL OF MINISTERS OF THE RUSSIAN SFSR 1957 TO 1958, FULL MEMBER OF THE 20TH TO 22ND POLITBUROS AND MEMBER OF THE 20TH TO 22ND SECRETARIAT 1960 TO 1964 WHEN HE WAS RELIEVED OF HIS DUTIES FOLLOWING THE OUSTING OF HIS MENTOR KHRUSHCHEV (Q.V.).

BETWEEN 1953 AND 1957 HE WAS THE FIRST SECRETARY OF THE LENINGRAD OBLAST CPSU AND FOR MANY YEARS WAS CONSIDERED KHRUSHCHEV'S LIKELY SUCCESSOR BUT HIS POSITION WAS UNDERMINED BY HIS ALCOHOLISM.

https://en.wikipedia.org/wiki/Frol-Kozlov

KRESTINSKY NIKOLAY NIKOLAYEVICH

13 10 1883   15 03 1938

HE WAS A RUSSIAN BOLSHEVIK REVOLUTIONARY AND POLITICIAN.

FULL MEMBER OF THE 8TH AND 9TH SECRETARIAT AND POLITBURO 1919 TO 1921, PEOPLE`S COMMISSAR FOR FINANCE OF THE RUSSIAN SFSR 1918 TO 1922 AND RESPONSIBLE SECRETARY OF THE RUSSIAN COMMUNIST PARTY 1919 TO 1921.

AFTER THE BOLSHEVIK VICTORY IN THE RUSSIAN CIVIL WAR HE SUPPORTED LEON TROTSKY`S (Q.V.) FACTION AND IN MARCH1921, FOLLOWING LENIN`S VICTORY AT THE TENTH PARTY CONGRESS HE LOST HIS PRESTIGIOUS POSTS BEING MADE AMBASSADOR TO GERMANY. IN 1928 HE BROKE WITH THE TROTSKYITE FACTION AND CONTINUED AS A DIPLOMAT TILL 1937 WHEN HE WAS ARRESTED DURING THE GREAT PURGES.

HE WAS PUT ON TRIAL AS PART OF THE TRIAL OF THE TWENTY-ONE, FOUND GUILTY AND EXECUTED.

https://en.wikipedia.org/wiki/Nikolay-Krestinsky

KURCHATOV IGOR VASILYEVICH

12 01 1903 07 02 1960

SOVIET NUCLEAR PHYSICIST AND DIRECTOR OF THE SOVIET ATOMIC BOMB PROJECT WHICH RESULTED IN THE FIRST SUCCESSFUL DETONATION IN 1949.

https://en.wikipedia.org/wiki/Igor-Kurchatov

KUUSINEN   OTTO WILHELM (WILLIE)

04 10 1881 17 05 1964

CHAIRMAN OF THE PRESIDIUM OF THE SUPREME SOVIET OF THE KARELO-FINNISH SOVIET SOCIALIST REPUBLIC, 1940 TO 1956, MEMBER OF THE 19TH PRESIDIUM AND MEMBER OF THE 20TH TO 22ND SECRETARIAT.

A FINN AND LATER A SOVIET POLITICIAN, LITERARY HISTORIAN AND POET WHO, AFTER THE DEFEAT OF THE REDS IN THE FINNISH CIVIL WAR, FLED TO THE SOVIET UNION WHERE HE WORKED UNTIL HIS DEATH.

HE WAS ORIGINALLY ACTIVE IN MAINSTREAM FINNISH POLITICS AND A MEMBER OF THE FINNISH PARLIAMENT BETWEEN 1908 AND 1913.

HE WAS INSTALLED AS THE HEAD OF THE 'PUPPET' GOVERNMENT IN FINLAND IN 1939 BY STALIN (Q.V.) DURING THE ULTIMATELY UNSUCCESSFUL WINTER WAR AND THE POST AND HIS GOVERNMENT WAS DISBANDED.

IN 1958 HE WAS ELECTED TO THE SOVIET ACADEMY OF SCIENCES.

https/en.wikipedia.org/wiki/Otto-Willie-Kuusinen

KVIRING   EMANUEL

13 09 1888 26 11 1937

SOVIET POLITICIAN AND LEADER OF THE COMMUNIST PARTY OF THE UKRAINE 1923 TO 1925. VICTIM OF THE GREAT TERROR AND EXECUTED. HE WAS HOWEVER REHABILITATED IN 1956.

https://en.wikipedia.org/wiki/Emanuel-Kviring

LANDAUER GUSTAV

07 04 1870   02 05 1919

WHILST HE TRANSLATED SOME OF THE WORKS OF WILLIAM SHAKESPEARE, OSCAR WILDE AND WALT WHITMAN INTO GERMAN, HE IS BEST REMEMBERED AS AN ADVOCATE OF SOCIAL ANARCHISM AND AS AN AVOWED PACIFIST. HE WAS BRIEFLY A COMMISSIONER IN THE SHORT LIVED BAVARIAN SOCIALIST REPUBLIC.

https://en.wikipedia.org/wiki/Gustav-Landauer

LEVER NORMAN HAROLD, BARON

15 01 1914   06 08 1995

BARRISTER AND LABOUR POLITICIAN WHOSE WAS AN M.P. FOR TWO DAYS **UNDER** THIRTY-FOUR YEARS. HE WAS CHANCELLOR OF THE DUCHY OF LANCASTER FROM 1974 TO 1979.

HE HELD A NUMBER OF PRESTIGIOUS POSITIONS INCLUDING GOVERNOR OF THE LONDON SCHOOL OF ECONOMICS AND THE ENGLISH SPEAKING UNION AND WAS A TRUSTEE OF THE ROYAL OPERA HOUSE.

https://en.wikipedia.org/wiki/Harold-Lever,-Baron-Lever-of-Manchester

LEVINE EUGEN

10 05 1883   05 07 1919

COMMUNIST REVOLUTIONARY AND LEADER OF THE SHORT LIVED BAVARIAN SOVIET REPUBLIC. HE ESCAPED FROM SIBERIA WHERE HE HAD BEEN EXILED FOLLOWING HIS PARTICIPATION IN THE FAILED1905 RUSSIAN REVOLUTION. HE SERVED, FOR A SHORT TIME, IN THE IMPERIAL GERMAN ARMY DURING THE FIRST WORLD WAR AND AFTERWARDS JOINED THE COMMUNIST PARTY OF GERMANY. HE HELPED TO CREATE A SHORT LIVED SOCIALIST REPUBLIC IN BAVARIA WHICH WAS REPLACED BY A SOVIET REPUBLIC UNDER ERNST TOLLER (Q.V.) WHICH VERY SHORTLY AFTERWARDS COLLAPSED FOLLOWING MILITARY ACTION BY THE GERMAN ARMY AND THE

FREIKORPS. ALONG WITH OTHERS INCLUDING ROSA
LUXEMBURG (Q.V.) HE WAS EXECUTED.

https://en.wikipedia.org/wiki/Eugen-Levine

LIN   MARSHALL PIAO

05 12 1907   13 09 1971

MINISTER OF NATIONAL DEFENCE 1959 TO 1971, VICE PREMIER
OF THE PEOPLE`S REPUBLIC OF CHINA 1954 TO 1971, VICE
CHAIRMAN OF THE COMMUNIST PARTY OF CHINA 1958 TO 1971
AND FIRST RANKING VICE PREMIER OF THE PEOPLE`S
REPUBLIC OF CHINA 1964 TO 1971.

HE WAS A MAJOR MILITARY LEADER PIVOTAL IN THE
VICTORIOUS CHINESE CIVIL WAR AND HE COMMANDED THE
DECISIVE LIAOSHEN AND PINGJINCAMPAIGNS. HE CO LED THE
MANCHURIAN FIELD ARMY OF THE P.L.A. INTO PEKING AND
CROSSED THE YANGTZE RIVER IN 1949.

IN THE EARLY 1960S HE WAS INSTRUMENTAL CREATING THE
FOUNDATIONS OF MAO`S (Q.V.) CULT OF PERSONALITY WHICH
EVOLVED INTO THE CULTURAL REVOLUTION AND WAS
REWARDED BY MAO IN 1969 BEING NAMED AS HIS SUCCESSOR
AS SOLE VICE CHAIRMAN OF THE COMMUNIST PARTY OF
CHINA.

HOWEVER IN 1971 HE WAS KILLED IN A PLANE CRASH IN
MONGOLIA AND WAS OFFICIALLY CONDEMNED AS A TRAITOR
BY THE COMMUNIST PARTY OF CHINA.THE REASONS BEHIND
THE EVENTS HAVE BEEN A SOURCE OF CONTINUED
SPECULATION.

https://en.wikipedia.org/wiki/Lin-Biao

LINCOLN   ABRAHAM

12 02 1809   15 04 1865

SIXTEENTH PRESIDENT OF THE UNITED STATES AND
CONSISTENTLY RANKED BY SCHOLARS AND THE AMERICAN
PUBLIC AS ONE OF THE GREATEST PRESIDENTS OF THEIR
NATION.HE LED THE COUNTRY THROUGH ITS CIVIL WAR,
PRESERVING THE UNION BUT SHORTLY AFTER VICTORY WAS
ASSASSINATED. PERHAPS HIS SUPREME ACHIEVEMENT WAS

THE EMANCIPATION PROCLAMATION OF 1863 ENDING SLAVERY.

https://en.wikipedia.org/wiki/Abraham-Lincoln

LINDBERGH   CHARLES AUGUSTUS

04 02 1902   26 08 1974

PRIMARILY KNOWN AS AN AVIATOR, HE WAS ALSO AN AUTHOR, INVENTOR, MILITARY OFFICER AND SOCIAL ACTIVIST.

HE SUDDENLY EMERGED FROM VIRTUAL OBSCURITY, AS A 25 YEAR OLD MAIL PILOT, TO WORLD FAME AS THE RESULT OF HIS SOLO NON STOP FLIGHT OF 33 HOURS 30 MINUTES IN MAY 1927 FROM THE ROOSEVELT FIELD IN GARDEN CITY ON NEW YORK`S LONG ISLAND TO LE BOURGET FIELD IN PARIS IN A SINGLE SEAT, SINGLE ENGINE PURPOSE BUILT MONOPLANE, THE SPIRIT OF ST. LOUIS.

IN THE LATE TWENTIES AND EARLY THIRTIES HE USED HIS FAME TO PROMOTE THE DEVELOPMENTOF BOTH COMMERCIAL AND AIR MAIL SERVICES.

https://en.wikipedia.org/wiki/Charles-Lindbergh

LLOYD   JOHN SELWYN BROOKE, BARON

28 07 1904   18 05 1978

KNOWN, FOR MOST OF HIS CAREER, AS SELWYN LLOYD AND LATER BARON SELWYN-LLOYD. A CONSERVATIVE POLITICIAN, HE WAS AN M.P.FOR NEARLY THIRTY-ONE YEARS AND SERVED AS FOREIGN SECRETARY, THEN CHANCELLOR OF THE EXCHEQUER AND FINALLY AS SPEAKER.

https://en.wikipedia.org/wiki/Selwyn-Lloyd

LOPEZ   JUSTO **(further and better particulars are required)**

LOVELOCK   DR. JOHN "JACK" EDWARD

05 01 1910   28 12 1949

IN 1929 HE WENT TO THE UNIVERSITY OF OTAGA TO STUDY MEDICINE AND IN 1931 HE BECAME A RHODES SCHOLAR AT EXETER COLLEGE, OXFORD TILL 1934, GRADUATING AS A

MEDICAL PRACTITIONER. HE PLACED SEVENTH IN THE 1932 OLYMPIC 1500 METRES IN LOS ANGELES AND THE FOLLOWING YEAR SET A NEW WORLD RECORD IN THE MILE. IN 1934 HE WON THE ONE MILE AT THE BRITISH EMPIRE GAMES.

IN 1936 IN THE BERLIN OLYMPIC GAMES HE WON THE 1500 METRES IN A NEW WORLD RECORD. TRAGICALLY HE WAS KILLED IN 1949 WHEN HE FELL UNDER AN ONCOMING TRAIN IN NEW YORK.

https://en.wikipedia.org/wiki/Jack-Lovelock

LUXEMBURG ROSA

05 03 1871   15 01 1919

MARXIST THEORIST, PHILOSOPHER, ECONOMIST AND REVOLUTIONARY SOCIALIST. A MEMBER OF VARIOUS LEFT WING ORGANISATIONS, SHE CO FOUNDED THE ANTI WAR SPARTAKUSBUND IN 1915 WHICH EVENTUALLY BECAME THE KPD (COMMUNIST PARTY OF GERMANY) AND DURING THE GERMAN REVOLUTION SHE CO FOUNDED THE NEWSPAPER DIE ROTE FAHNE (THE RED FLAG).

IN JANUARY 1919 SHE WAS SHOT AFTER THE SPARTACIST UPRISING WAS CRUSHED BY THE SOCIAL DEMOCRATIC GOVERNMENT IN CONJUNCTION WITH RIGHT WING PARAMILITARY GROUPS OF WORLD WAR ONE VETERANS KNOWN AS THE FREIKORPS.

https://en.wikipedia.org/wiki/Rosa-Luxemburg

MacARTHUR   DOUGLAS

26 01 1880   05 04 1964

A CAREER SOLDIER WHO ULTIMATELY ROSE TO BECOME A FIVE STAR GENERAL AND FIELD MARSHALL OF THE PHILIPPINE ARMY. HE WAS CHIEF OF STAFF OF THE UNITED STATES ARMY IN THE 1930S AND PLAYED A PROMINENT ROLE IN THE PACIFIC DURING THE SECOND WORLD WAR. HE LED THE UNITED NATIONS COMMAND IN THE KOREAN WAR UNTIL REMOVED BY PRESIDENT TRUMAN (Q.V.) IN 1951.

https://en.wikipedia.org/wiki/Douglas-MacArthur

MACHIAVELLI NICCOLO DI BERNARDO DEI

03 05 1469   21 06 1527

FLORENTINE HISTORIAN, POLITICIAN, DIPLOMAT, PHILOSOPHER AND WRITER WHO FLOURISHED IN THE LATE FIFTEENTH AND EARLY SIXTEENTH CENTURIES AND WAS FOR MANY YEARS AN OFFICIAL IN THE FLORENTINE REPUBLIC, WITH RESPONSIBILITIES FOR DIPLOMATIC AND MILITARY MATTERS.

HE IS FAMOUS FOR HIS MASTERPIECE, THE PRINCE, WHICH IS AN OBSERVATION ON THE USE OF POWER.

https://en.wikipedia.org/wiki/Niccolo-Machiavelli

MacLEOD   SIR JOHN

23 02 1913   03 06 1984

BRITISH ARMY OFFICER, TWEED DESIGNER AND POLITICIAN WHO SERVED AS AN M.P. FROM 1945 TO 1964. FOLLOWING THE DUNKIRK WITHDRAWAL IN 1940 HE WAS CAPTURED AND SPENT THE ENSUING FIVE YEARS AS A PRISONER.POLITICALLY HE WAS 'INDEPENDENT' AS A BACK BENCH M.P.

https://en.wikipedia.org/wiki/John-MacLeod-(politician)

MacMILLAN   MAURICE HAROLD, FIRST EARL OF STOCKTON

0 02 1894   29 12 1986

BRITISH CONSERVATIVE POLITICIAN AND STATESMAN WHO SERVED AS PRIME MINISTER, SUCCEEDING ANTHONY EDEN (Q.V.), FROM 1957 TO 1963, RESIGNING PREMATURELY BECAUSE OF A MEDICAL MISDIAGNOSIS AND POSSIBLY THE EFFECTS OF THE VASSALL AND PROFUMO SCANDALS.

IN THE FIRST WORLD WAR HE SERVED IN THE GRENADIER GUARDS, BEING WOUNDED THREE TIMES, MOST SEVERELY IN SEPTEMBER 1916, DURING THE BATTLE OF THE SOMME.

NICKNAMED 'SUPERMAC', HAUNTED BY MEMORIES OF THE GREAT DEPRESSION, HE CHAMPIONED A STRATEGY OF PUBLIC INVESTMENT TO MAINTAIN DEMAND, PRESIDED OVER AN AGE OF AFFLUENCE, MARKED BY LOW UNEMPLOYMENT AND HIGH, IF UNEVEN, GROWTH.

HE STRENGTHENED THE NUCLEAR FORCES BY ACQUIRING THE POLARIS SYSTEM AND PIONEERED THE NUCLEAR TEST BAN TREATY WITH THE UNITED STATES AND THE SOVIET UNION.

https://en.wikipedia.org/wiki/Harold-Macmillan

MALENKOV   GEORGY MAXIMILIANOVICH

08 01 1902   14 01 1988

FULL MEMBER OF THE 18TH, 19TH AND 20TH POLITBUROS FROM 1946 TO 1957 AND CHAIRMAN OF THE COUNCIL OF MINISTERS FROM 1953 TO 1955. A CLOSE ASSOCIATE OF JOSEPH STALIN, HE WAS DEEPLY INVOLVED IN THE PURGES OF THE 1930S AND AFTER STALIN`S DEATH WAS BRIEFLY LEADER BUT WAS DEPOSED AND ENDED HIS CAREER EXILED TO KAZAKHSTAN.

https://en.wikipedia.org/wiki/Georgy-Malenkov

MAO   TSE TUNG

26 12 1893   09 09 1976

CHINESE COMMUNIST REVOLUTIONARY, COMMONLY REFERRED TO AS CHAIRMAN MAO AND THE FOUNDING FATHER OF THE PEOPLE`S REPUBLIC OF CHINA.

HE WAS FIRST CHAIRMAN OF THE CENTRAL COMMITTEE OF THE COMMUNIST PARTY OF CHINA FROM 1945 TO 1976, FIRST CHAIRMAN OF THE CENTRAL POLITBURO OF THE COMMUNIST PARTY OF CHINA FROM 1943 TO1969 AND AMONGST OTHER APPOINTMENTS, MEMBER OF THE NATIONAL PEOPLE`S CONGRESS FROM 1954 TO 1959 AND 1964 TO HIS DEATH.

HIS POLITICAL THEORIES, MILITARY STRATEGIES AND POLITICAL POLICIES ARE COLLECTIVELY KNOWN AS MARXIST-LENINIST MAOISM.

LIKE HIS CONTEMPORARIES, HITLER AND STALIN (Q.V.) HIS IMPRINT ON NATIONAL AND GLOBAL HISTORY IS IMMENSE.

HE WAS A FOUNDING MEMBER BOTH OF THE CPC (COMMUNIST PARTY OF CHINA) AND LATER THE RED ARMY DURING THE CIVIL WAR WITH THE NATIONALIST KMT (KUO MIN TANG),

LEADING THE DEFEATED CPC AND RED ARMY FROM CERTAIN
ANNIHILATION IN THE FAMOUS LONG MARCH OF 1934-35.

AN UNEASY ALLIANCE EXISTED BETWEEN THE TWO GROUPS
WHO UNITED IN 1937 AGAINST THE JAPANESE INVADERS UNTIL
1945 WHEN THE CIVIL WAR RESUMED.

IN 1949 THE CPC TRIUMPHED EXPELLING THE NATIONALISTS
TO TAIWAN.

ON OCTOBER FIRST 1949, MAO PROCLAIMED THE FOUNDATION
OF THE PEOPLE`S REPUBLIC OF CHINA, A SINGLE PARTY
STATE CONTROLLED BY THE CPC, BRINGING IN LAND REFORM
TO CEMENT THE PARTY`S CONTROL. TO MAINTAIN
MOMENTUM OF THE REVOLUTION AND INDUSTRIALISATION HE
INITIATED, IN 1957, THE GREAT LEAP FORWARD AND IN 1966
THE GREAT PROLETARIAN CULTURAL REVOLUTION, THE
FORMER CAUSING WIDESPREAD FAMINE AND DEATH, THE
LATTER, DESTABILISATION OF THE WHOLE NATION.

https://en.wikipedia.org/wiki/Mao-Zedong

MARR   WILHELM

16 11 1819   17 07 1904

DESPITE THE FACT THAT THE FIRST THREE OF HIS FOUR
WIVES WERE JEWISH OR OF JEWISH ORIGIN HIS
REVOLUTIONARY, GERMAN NATIONALISTIC VALUES LED HIM
TO FOUND THE LEAGUE OF ANTISEMITES IN 1879 AND IN THE
SAME YEAR TO PUBLISH HIS PAMPHLET DER WEG ZUM SIEGE
DES GERMANENTHUMS UBER DAS JUDENTHUM.

https://en.wikipedia.org/wiki/Wilhelm-Marr

MARX   KARL

05 05 1818   14 03 1883

WAS A PHILOSOPHER, ECONOMIST,SOCIOLOGIST, JOURNALIST AND REVOLUTIONARY SOCIALIST. BORN IN PRUSSIA HE STUDIED POLITICAL ECONOMY AND HEGELIAN PHILOSOPHY. BECOMING STATELESS HE SPENT MUCH OF HIS TIME IN LONDON WHERE HE PUBLISHED VARIOUS WORKS INCLUDING JOINTLY THE 1848 PAMPHLET, *THE COMMUNIST MANIFESTO*

https:en.//wikipedia.org/wiki/Karl Marx

MAYHEW   CHRISTOPHER PAGET,BARON

12 06 1915   07 01 1997

LABOUR, THEN LIBERAL M.P. FROM 1945 -1950 AND THEN 1951-1974. 'WON' A CONTROVERSIAL HIGH COURT ACTION IN 1976, THE 'WARREN BERGSON' CASE .

https://en.wikipedia.org/wiki/Christopher-Mayhew

MAZUROV   KIRILL TROFIMOVICH

25 03 1914   19 12 1989

SOVIET POLITICIAN WHO JOINED THE COMMUNIST PARTY IN 1940 AND THE RED ARMY IN 1941. A FULL MEMBER OF THE 22ND TO 25TH POLITBUROS HE WAS PREVIOUSLY A CANDIDATE MEMBER OF THE 20TH AND 22ND PRESIDIUMS.

FIRST DEPUTY CHAIRMAN OF THE COUNCIL OF MINISTERS OF THE SOVIET UNION FROM 1965 TO 1978.

DURING HIS LATER RETIREMENT HE DISCLOSED DETAILS OF HIS INVOLVEMENT IN THE WARSAW PACT INVASION OF CZECHOSLOVAKIA IN 1968.

https://en.wikipedia.org/wiki/Kirill-Mazurov

Mc CONE   JOHN ALEXANDER

04 01 1902   14 02 1991

AMERICAN BUSINESSMAN AND REPUBLICAN POLITICIAN WHO
WAS THE SIXTH DIRECTOR OF THE CENTRAL INTELLIGENCE
AGENCY FROM 1961 TO 1965.

https://en.wikipedia.org/wiki/John-A.-McCone

Mc NAMARA   ROBERT STRANGE

09 06 1916   06 07 2009

AMERICAN BUSINESS EXECUTIVE AND SECRETARY OF
DEFENCE UNDER PRESIDENTS KENNEDY AND JOHNSON (Q.V.).
DURING WHICH TIME HE PLAYED A LARGE PART IN
ESCALATING THE NATION`S INVOLVEMENT IN VIETNAM.
BEFORE HIS ROLE IN GOVERNMENT HE WAS PRESIDENT OF
THE FORD MOTOR COMPANY.

https://en.wikipedia.org/wiki/Robert-McNamara

MEADOWS   EARLE ELMER

29 06 1913   11 11 1992

UNITED STATES TRACK AND FIELD ATHLETE WHO WON THE
1936 OLYMPIC POLE VAULT IN BERLIN AND IN 1937 BROKE THE
WORLD RECORD.

https://en.wikipedia.org/wiki/Earle-Meadows

MEIR   GOLDA

03 05 1898   08 12 1978

BORN GOLDA MABOVITCH IN KIEV, NOW IN THE UKRAINE AND
LATER, BY MARRIAGE, MYERSON.SHE WAS THE FOURTH PRIME
MINISTER OF ISRAEL LEADING HER COUNTRY IN THE 1973 YOM
KIPPUR WAR. AN **ALLEGATION** BRIEFLY SURFACED THAT THE
PARENTS OF HER MOTHER, BLUME NEIDITCH KNEW THE
FAMILY OF YOEL BEN YITZHAK.

https://en.wikipedia.org/wiki/Golda-Meir

MENASSEH   BEN ISRAEL

BO RN 1604   20 11 1657

BORN IN 1604 AS MANOEL DIAS **SOEIRO** HE WAS A
PORTUGUESE RABBI, KABBALIST, WRITER, PRINTER AND
PUBLISHER WHO FOUNDED THE FIRST HEBREW PRESS IN
HOLLAND IN 1626. THE JEWS HAD BEEN EXPELLED FROM
ENGLAND IN 1290 BUT HIS REPRESENTATION TO OLIVER
CROMWELL PERMITTED THEIR FORMAL RETURN.

https://en.wikipedia.org/wiki/Menasseh-Ben-Israel

MIKOYAN   ANASTAS IVANOVICH

25 11 1895   21 10 1978

CHAIRMAN OF THE PRESIDIUM OF THE SUPREME SOVIET OF
THE SOVIET UNION 1964 TO 1965, FIRST DEPUTY CHAIRMAN OF
THE COUNCIL OF MINISTERS OF THE SOVIET UNION 1955 TO
1964, MINISTER OF FOREIGN TRADE 1953 TO 1955, FULL
MEMBER OF THE 17TH TO 22ND POLITBUROS AND CANDIDATE
MEMBER OF THE 14TH TO 17TH POLITBUROS.

UNTIL HIS FORCED RETIREMENT IN 1965 HE WAS A LONG
SERVING MEMBER OF THE COMMUNIST PARTY HAVING, AT THE
AGE OF 20, FOUNDED A WORKERS' SOVIET IN GEORGIA AND
AROUND THE SAME TIME HE FORMALLY JOINED THE
BOLSHEVIK FACTION OF THE RUSSIAN SOCIAL DEMOCRATIC
LABOUR PARTY WHICH WAS LATER KNOWN AS THE
BOLSHEVIK PARTY.

https://en.wikipedia.org/wiki/Anastas-Mikoyan

MILES   BERNARD JAMES,

            BARON MILES OF BLACKFRIARS

27 09 1907 14 06 1991

ENGLISH CHARACTER ACTOR, WRITER AND DIRECTOR WHO
OPENED THE MERMAID THEATRE IN 1959, THE FIRST NEW
THEATRE IN THE CITY OF LONDON SINCE THE 17TH CENTURY

https://en.wikipedia.org/wiki/Bernard-Miles

MITFORD   DIANA, THE HON. LADY MOSLEY

17 06 1910 11 08 2003

BORN FREEMAN-MITFORD, SHE WAS MARRIED FIRST TO
BRYAN GUINNESS, HEIR TO THE BARONY OF MOYNE AND
SECONDLY TO SIR OSWALD MOSLEY (Q.V.). HER SECOND
MARRIAGE, IN 1936,TOOK PLACE AT THE HOME OF JOSEPH
GOEBBELS (Q.V.), WITH ADOLF HITLER (Q.V.) AS GUEST OF
HONOUR. HER INVOLVEMENT WITH RIGHT WING POLITICAL
CAUSES RESULTED IN THREE YEARS INTERNMENT DURING
THE SECOND WORLD WAR.

https://en.wikipedia.org/wiki/Diana-Mitford

MOLOTOV   VYACHESLAV MIKHAILOVICH

09 03 1890   08 11 1986

BORN VYACHESLAV MIKHAILOVICH **SKRYABIN**.FULL MEMBER
OF THE 14TH TO 20TH PRESIDIUMS / POLITBUROS FROM 1926 TO
1957 AND WAS THE PRINCIPAL SIGNATORY TO THE NAZI-
SOVIET NON AGGRESSION PACT OF 1939 (BETTER KNOWN AS
THE MOLOTOV- RIBBENTROP PACT) WHICH EFFECTIVELY
PAVED THE WAY FOR THE BEGINNING OF THE SECOND WORLD
WAR. HE WAS AWARE OF THE KATYN FOREST MASSARCE
PERPETRATED BY THE SOVIET AUTHORITIES.

https://en.wikipedia.org/wiki/Vyacheslav-Molotov

MONTGOMERY

FIELD MARSHALL BERNARD LAW "MONTY",

1ST VISCOUNT MONTGOMERY OF ALAMEIN

17 11 1887   24 03 1976

DURING THE FIRST WORLD WAR HE FOUGHT AT THE BATTLES
OF ARRAS AND PASSCHENDAELE. IN THE SECOND WORLD
WAR HE COMMANDED THE BRITISH EIGHTH ARMY IN NORTH
AFRICA AND WON THE DECISIVE BATTLEOF EL ALAMEIN
DEFEATING THE GERMAN AFRIKA CORPS WHICH
SYMBOLICALLY AND ACTUALLY WAS THE TURN OF THE TIDE IN
BRITISH FORTUNES. HE SUBSEQUENTLY COMMANDED THE
EIGHTH ARMY DURING THE ALLIED INVASION OF SICILY AND

THEN DURING THE INVASION OF ITALY.HE WAS ONE OF EISENHOWER`S (Q,V,) LEADING OFFICERS FOR THE OVERLOAD OPERATION(THE INVASION OF WESTERN EUROPE) AND ACCEPTED THE GERMAN SURRENDER AT LUNEBERG HEATH.

https://en.wikipedia.org/wiki/Bernard-Montgomery

MOORE   ROBERT FREDERICK CHELSEA "BOBBY"

12 04 1941   24 02 1993

ENGLISH PROFESSIONAL FOOTBALLER WHO PLAYED FOR WEST HAM UNITED FOR SIXTEEN YEARS AND WHO CAPTAINED THE VICTORIOUS ENGLAND SIDE IN THE 1966 WORLD CUP FINAL AT WEMBLEY.

https://en.wikipedia.org/wiki/Bobby-Moore

MOORE   SIR THOMAS CECIL RUSSELL,

              FIRST BARONET OF KYLEBURN

16 09 1886   09 04 1971

CONSERVATIVE M.P. FROM 1925 TO 1964. IN THE MID 1930S, WHILST A COLONEL IN THE BRITISH ARMY, HE WROTE WIDELY IN THE U.K.PRESS IN SUPPORT OF ADOLF HITLER (Q.V.) AND THE POLICIES OF NAZISM.

https://en.wikipedia.org/wiki/Sir-Thomas-Moore,-1st-Baronet

MORE   SIR THOMAS

07 02 1478   06 07 1535

ENGLISH LAWYER, SOCIAL PHILOSOPHER, AUTHOR , STATESMAN AND RENAISSANCE HUMANIST IN 1516 HIS WORK UTOPIA WAS PUBLISHED, ABOUT THE POLITICAL SYSTEM OF AN IDEAL AND IMAGINARY ISLAND SOCIETY.

HE WAS SPEAKER OF THE HOUSE OF COMMONS IN 1523, CHANCELLOR OF THE DUCHY OF LANCASTER (1525-1529) AND LORD CHANCELLOR FROM 1529 TO 1532.

A ROMAN CATHOLIC, HE OPPOSED THE PROTESTANT REFORMATION AND KING HENRY VIII`S SEPARATION FROM THE CATHOLIC CHURCH IN ROME, REFUSING TO ACCEPT HIM AS

SUPREME HEAD OF THE CHURCH OF ENGLAND AND WHAT HE SAW AS THE KING`S BIGAMOUS MARRIAGE TO ANNE BOLEYN. TRIED FOR TREASON, MORE WAS CONVICTED AND SUBSEQUENTLY EXECUTED.

https://en.wikipedia.org/wiki/Thomas-More

MOSLEY   SIR OSWALD ERNALD, SIXTH BARONET

16 11 1896   03 12 1980

FOR AN IN DEPTH BIOGRAPHY PLEASE REFER TO CHAPTER ONE OF THE ORIGINS AND BIRTH OF THE NEW ORDER

https://en.wikipedia.org/wiki/Oswald-Mosley

MUSSOLINI   BENITO AMILCARE ANDREA

29 07 1883   28 04 1945

KNOWN AS 'IL DUCE'(THE LEADER) HE WAS AN ITALIAN POLITICIAN, JOURNALIST AND LEADER OF THE NATIONAL FASCIST PARTY WHO RULED ITALY AS PRIME MINISTER FROM 1922 UNTIL OUSTED IN 1943.IN SEPTEMBER 1943 HE BECAME LEADER OF THE ITALIAN SOCIAL REPUBLIC, SUPPORTED BY THE GERMANS UNTIL HIS DEATH IN 1945.

FOLLOWING THE MARCH ON ROME IN OCTOBER 1922 HE BECAME THE YOUNGEST PRIME MINISTER IN ITALIAN HISTORY, SUBSEQUENTLY DESTROYING ALL POLITICAL OPPOSITION AND OUTLAWING LABOUR STRIKES.POWER WAS CONSOLIDATED THROUGH A SERIES OF LAWS THAT TRANSFORMED THE NATION INTO A ONE PARTY DICTATORSHIP.

https://en.wikipedia.org/wiki/Benito-Mussolini

MZHAVANADZE

VASIL PAVLOVICH

20 09 1902   05 09 1988

FULL MEMBER OF THE 20TH AND 22ND TO 24TH CENTRAL COMMITTEES AND CANDIDATE MEMBER OF THE SAME POLITBUROS.HE WAS A POLITICAL COMMISSAR IN THE RED ARMY DURING THE GREAT PATRIOTIC WAR.

IN JULY 1953 FOLLOWING THE DEATH OF STALIN (Q.V.) AND THE ARREST OF BERIA (Q.V.) THE GEORGIAN COMMUNIST PARTY WAS PURGED BY SUPPORTERS OF KHRUSHCHEV (Q.V.) AND HE BECAME FIRST SECRETARY OF THE GEORGIAN COMMUNIST PARTY. HE WAS IN POWER FROM 1953 TO 1972 WHEN HE RESIGNED FOLLOWING ACCUSATIONS OF CORRUPTION. HE WAS SACKED FROM THE POLITBURO AND RETIRED IN DISGRACE.

https://en.wikipedia.org/wiki/Vasil-Mzhavanadze

NASSER HUSSEIN

GAMAL ABDEL

15 01 1918   28 09 1970

SECOND PRESIDENT OF EGYPT, SERVING FROM 1956 TO HIS DEATH. HE PLANNED THE 1952 OVERTHROW OF THE MONARCHY AND WAS DEPUTY PRIME MINISTER IN THE GOVERNMENT. IN 1956 HE NATIONALISED THE SUEZ CANAL COMPANY RESULTING IN BRITAIN AND FRANCE OCCUPYING THE SUEZ CANAL ZONE WHILE ISRAEL INVADED THE SINAI PENINSULA. HOWEVER THE THREE ALLIES WITHDREW AMID INTERNATIONAL AND AMERICAN PRESSURE SIGNIFICANTLY BOOSTING NASSER`S POLITICAL STANDING.

https://en.wikipedia.org/wiki/Gamal-Abdel-Nasser

NEAL   HAROLD

03 07 1897   24 08 1972

BRITISH LABOUR POLITICIAN AND M.P. FROM 1944 TO 1970.

https://en.wikipedia.org/wiki/Harold-Neal

NELSON   HORATIO,FIRST VISCOUNT

29 09 1758   21 10 1805

HE WAS A BRITISH FLAG OFFICER IN THE ROYAL NAVY NOTED FOR HIS INSPIRATIONAL LEADERSHIP AND GRASP OF STRATEGY AND UNCONVENTIONAL TACTICS, WHICH RESULTED IN A NUMBER OF DECISIVE VICTORIES,

PARTICULARLY DURING THE NAPOLEONIC WARS. HE WAS WOUNDED SEVERAL TIMES IN COMBAT ,INCLUDING THE LOSS OF ONE ARM AND ONE EYE IN SEPARATE INCIDENTS.HE WAS SHOT BY A FRENCH SNIPER AND DIED OF HIS WOUND DURING HIS FINAL AND GREATEST VICTORY AT THE BATTLE OF TRAFALGAR ON OCTOBER 21ST 1805.

https://en.wikipedia.org/wiki/Horatio-Nelson,-1st-Viscount-Nelson

NIXON   RICHARD MILHOUS 'DICK'

09 01 1913   22 04 1994

THIRTY SEVENTH PRESIDENT OF THE UNITED STATES AND THE ONLY ONE EVER TO RESIGN THE OFFICE (FOLLOWING THE WATERGATE SCANDAL). HE MADE HIS REPUTATION IN THE EARLY NINETEEN FIFTIES AS A LEADING ANTI COMMUNIST FOLLOWING HIS PURSUIT OF THE HISS CASE.WAS PRESIDENT EISENHOWER`S (Q.V.)VICE PRESIDENT FROM 1953 TO 1961.

https://en.wikipedia.org/wiki/Richard-Nixon

OAKSHOTT   HENDRIE DUDLEY, BARON

08 11 1904   01 02 1975

BRITISH CONSERVATIVE POLITICIAN AND M.P. FROM 1950 TO 1964.

https://en.wikipedia.org/wiki/Hendrie-Oakshott,-Baron-Oakshott

OLIVIER   BARON LAURENCE KERR

22 05 1907   11 07 1989

WAS AN ENGLISH ACTOR WHO, IN 1930, HAD HIS FIRST IMPORTANT WEST END SUCCESS IN NOEL COWARD'S (Q.V.) PLAY, *PRIVATE LIVES*. HE ACHIEVED GREAT SUCCESS IN FILMS AND LATER ON IN HIS CAREER, IN TELEVISION.

https://en.wikipedia.org/wiki/Laurence-Olivier

OSWALD   LEE HARVEY

18 10 1939   24 11 1963

IN 1964 THE WARREN COMMISSION CONCLUDED THAT OSWALD ACTED **ALONE,** FIRING THE THREE SHOTS THAT KILLED PRESIDENT KENNEDY.

https://en.wikipedia.org/wiki/Lee-Harvey-Oswald

PAINE   THOMAS

09 02 1737   08 06 1809

BORN IN ENGLAND, HE WAS A POLITICAL ACTIVIST, PHILOSOPHER, POLITICAL THEORIST AND REVOLUTIONARY. HE WAS ONE OF THE FOUNDING FATHERS OF THE UNITED STATES AND HE INSPIREDTHE REBELS IN 1776 TO DECLARE INDEPENDENCE FROM BRITAIN. IN THE 1790S HE LIVED IN FRANCE BECOMING DEEPLY INVOLVED IN THE REVOLUTION. ALTHOUGH NOT BEING ABLE TO SPEAK FRENCH HE WAS ELECTED TO THE NATIONAL CONVENTION IN 1792.

HE IS MOST FAMOUS FOR HIS WORKS INCLUDING COMMON SENSE (1776), THE AMERICAN CRISIS (1776-83), RIGHTS OF MAN (1791) AND THE AGE OF REASON (1793-94).

https://en.wikipedia.org/.wiki/Thomas-Paine

PASTERNAK   BORIS LEONIDOVICH

10 02 1890   30 05 1960

POET, NOVELIST AND LITERARY TRANSLATOR.PERHAPS HIS MOST IMPORTANT WORK WAS 'DOCTOR ZHIVAGO', PUBLICATION OF WHICH WAS BANNED IN SOVIET RUSSIA IN VIEW OF HIS DEPICTION OF THE NASCENT COMMUNIST STATE.

https://en.wikipedia.org/wiki/Boris-Pasternak

PEARSON   LESTER BOWLES ' MIKE'

23 04 1897   27 12 1972

CANADIAN SCHOLAR, STATESMAN, SPORTSMAN, SOLDIER AND DIPLOMAT. HE WAS THE FOURTEENTH PRIME MINISTER OF CANADA FROM 1963 TO 1968, THE LEADER OF THE LIBERAL

PARTY OF CANADA FROM1958 TO 1968 AND THE SECOND
CANADIAN AMBASSADOR TO THE UNITED STATES FROM 1944
TO 1946.FROM 1948 TO 1968 HE WAS A MEMBER OF THE
CANADIAN PARLIAMENT.

IN 1952 HE WAS THE EIGHTH PRESIDENT OF THE UNITED
NATIONS GENERAL ASSEMBLY AND IN 1957 HE RECEIVED THE
NOBEL PRIZE FOR PEACE HAVING ORGANISED A UNITED
NATIONS EMERGENCY FORCE TO RESOLVE THE SUEZ CANAL
CRISIS.

DURING HIS PERIOD AS PRIME MINISTER HE INTRODUCED
AMONGST OTHER ACTS, UNIVERSAL HEALTH CARE AND A NEW
FLAG.

https://en.wikipedia.org/wiki/Lester-B.-Pearson

PELSHE   ARVID YANOVICH

07 02 1899   29 05 1983

LATVIAN NATIONAL, SOVIET POLITICIAN AND FUNCTIONARY.
FULL MEMBER OF THE 23RD TO 26TH POLITBUROS.

IN 1915 HE JOINED THE LATVIAN REGION OF THE BOLSHEVIKS
AND IN 1916 MET LENIN IN SWITZERLAND.PARTICIPATED IN THE
FEBRUARY REVOLUTION OF 1917 AND WAS A MEMBER OF THE
PETROGRAD SOVIET.

HE WAS ACTIVELY INVOLVED IN THE PREPARATION AND
CONDUCT OF THE 1917 OCTOBER REVOLUTION AND IN 1918
JOINED THE CHEKA.

IN NOVEMBER OF 1959 HE BECAME FIRST SECRETARY OF THE
LATVIAN COMMUNIST PARTY FOLLOWING A PURGE OF SOME
TWO THOUSAND OF THE PARTY LEADERSHIP AND ACTIVISTS
AND IN 1963 HEADED A COMMISSION WHICH INVESTIGATED
THE ASSASSINATION OF SERGEI KIROV(Q.V.).

https://en.wikipedia.org/wiki/Arvids-Pelse

PEREZ   ANDREU NIN

04 02 1892   20 06 1937

ALSO KNOWN AS ANDRES **NIN**. SPANISH COMMUNIST
POLITICIAN, JOURNALIST AND ACTIVIST. IN 1935 HE JOINTLY

FORMED THE WORKERS` PARTY OF MARXIST UNIFICATION
(P.O.U.M.), WHICH IDEOLOGICALLY WAS ANTI STALIN (Q.V.).
MURDERED BY AN UNIDENTIFIED PARTY BUT PROBABLY AT
THE INSTIGATION OF THE N K V D.

https://en.wikipedia.org/wiki/Andres-Nin

PILKINGTON   SIR RICHARD ANTONY

10 05 1908   09 12 1976

HE WAS AWARDED THE M.C. AFTER RETURNING WITH ONE OF
THE LAST GROUPS FROM DUNKIRK IN 1940. CONSERVATIVE
M.P. FROM 1935 T0 1945 AND 1951 TO 1964.

https://en.wikipedia.org/wiki/Richard-Pilkington-(politician,-born-
1908)

PINCHER   HENRY CHAPMAN

29 03 1914   05 08 2014

ENGLISH JOURNALIST, HISTORIAN, AND AUTHOR BEST KNOWN
FOR HIS WORKS ON ESPIONAGE. HE JOINED THE DAILY
EXPRESS IN 1946 AS A SCIENCE AND DEFENCE
CORRESPONDENT.

HIS BOOK, THEIR TRADE IS TREACHERY (1981) DISCLOSED
SUSPICIONS THAT MI5`S FORMER DIRECTOR GENERAL HAD
BEEN A SPY FOR THE SOVIET UNION. HE WAS ALSO
CONVINCED THAT THE FORMER BRITISH PRIME MINISTER,
HAROLD WILSON (Q.V.) HAD BEEN A SOVIET AGENT.

https://en.wikipedia.org/wiki/Chapman-Pincher

PIRATIN   PHILIP

15 05 1907   10 12 1995

HE WAS A MEMBER OF THE COMMUNIST PARTY OF GREAT
BRITAIN AND AN M.P. FROM 1945 TO 1950.

HE WAS A LEADING MEMBER OF THE STEPNEY TENANTS
DEFENCE LEAGUE AND A LEADER OF THE OPPOSITION TO
MOSLEY`S ANTI-SEMITISM AND HIS BRITISH UNION OF
FASCISTS` MARCHES THROUGH THE EAST END OF LONDON.
HE WAS AN ELECTED LOCAL COUNCILLOR AND GAINED A

REPUTATION DURING WORLD WAR TWO BY LEADING ONE HUNDRED PEOPLE TO SHELTER IN A LONDON UNDERGROUND STATION, A PRACTICE WHICH BECAME WIDESPREAD.

https://en.wikipedia.org/wiki/Phil-Piratin

PODGORNY   NIKOLAI VIKTOROVICH

18 02 1903   12 01 1983

FULL MEMBER OF THE 20TH TO 25TH POLITBUROS AND CANDIDATE MEMBER OF THE 20TH AND 21ST POLITBUROS, IN 1977 HE LOST HIS SEAT AND WAS FORCED TO RESIGN FROM ACTIVE POLITICS. HE JOINED THE COMMUNIST PARTY IN 1930 AND WAS A TECHNOCRAT.

https://en.wikipedia.org/wiki/Nikolai-Podgorny

POLYANSKY   DMITRY STEPANOVICH

25 10 1917   08 10 2001

HE WAS AWARDED FOUR ORDERS OF LENIN. A SOVIET RUSSIAN STATESMAN HE WAS THE CHAIRMAN OF THE COUNCIL OF MINISTERS OF THE RUSSIAN SFSR FROM 1958 TO 1962 AND FIRST DEPUTY CHAIRMAN OF THE COUNCIL OF MINISTERS OF THE SOVIET UNION FROM 1965 TO 1973.

https://en.wikipedia.org/wiki/Dmitry-Polyansky

POWER   GENERAL THOMAS SARSFIELD

18 06 1905   06 12 1970

AFTER A CAREER IN THE AIR FORCE HE BECAME VICE COMMANDER OF THE STRATEGIC AIR COMMAND IN 1948 AND IN 1954 WAS APPOINTED COMMANDER OF THE AIR RESEARCH AND DEVELOPMENT COMMAND. IN 1957 BECAME COMMANDER THE S.A.C. RECOGNISED AS A 'HARDLINER'.

https://en.wikipedia.org/wiki/Thomas-S.-Power

POWER   TYRONE EDMUND JNR.

05 05 1914   15 11 1958

AMERICAN FILM AND STAGE ACTOR.

https://en.wikipedia.org/wiki/Tyrone-Power

POWERS   FRANCIS GARY

17 08 1929   01 08 1977

WAS AN AMERICAN PILOT WHOSE C.I.A. U-2 SPY PLANE WAS
SHOT DOWN BY A SOVIET SA 2 SURFACE TO AIR MISSILE OVER
SVERDLOVSK CAUSING THE 1960 U- 2 INCIDENT.

https://en.wikipedia.org/wiki/Francis-Gary-Powers

PRIESTLEY   JOHN BOYNTON 'J.B.'

13 09 1894   14 08 1984

HE WAS AN ENGLISH NOVELIST, PLAYWRIGHT, BROADCASTER
AND SOCIALIST, INDEED IN 1949 HIS FELLOW NOVELIST
GEORGE ORWELL PREPARED FOR THE INFORMATION
RESEARCH DEPARTMENT A LIST INCLUDING PRIESTLEY
CONSIDERING HIM TO HAVE PRO COMMUNIST LEANINGS.

HE SERVED IN THE FIRST WORLD WAR BEING WOUNDED
TWICE AND AFTER DEMOBILISATION WENT TO TRINITY HALL,
CAMBRIDGE. HE HAD A DEEP LOVE OF CLASSICAL MUSIC,
WRITING THE LIBRETTO FOR THE 1949 OPERA, "THE
OLYMPIANS",BY ARTHUR BLISS (Q.V.) AND IN 1958 WAS A
FOUNDING MEMBER OF C.N.D.

https://en.wikipedia.org/wiki/J.-B.-Priestley

PROFUMO   JOHN "JACK" DENNIS

30 01 1915   09 03 2006

BRITISH CONSERVATIVE POLITICIAN INVOLVED IN A
NOTORIOUS SEX SCANDAL.

https://en.wikipedia.org/wiki/John-Profumo

RAKOVSKY   CHRISTIAN

13 08 1873   11 09 1941

BORN KRASTYO GEORGIEV STANCHEV IN WHAT IS NOW
BULGARIA HE WAS FIRST CHAIRMAN OF THE COUNCIL OF
PEOPLE`S COMMISSARS OF THE UKRANIAN SSR FROM 1919 TO
1923, AMBASSADOR TO FRANCE FROM 1925 TO 1927 AND A
FOUNDING MEMBER OF THE COMINTERN. HE WAS A
BULGARIAN SOCIALIST REVOLUTIONARY AND A LIFELONG
COLLABORATOR OF LEON TROTSKY (Q.V.) OPPOSED TO
STALIN (Q.V.).CONVICTED IN THE TRIAL OF THE TWENTY ONE
HE WAS IMPRISONED AND LATER EXECUTED.

HE WAS ULTIMATELY REHABILITATED IN 1988.

https://en.wikipedia.org/wiki/Christian-Rakovsky

RAMSEY   ARTHUR MICHAEL,

   BARON RAMSEY OF CANTERBURY

14 11 1904   23 04 1988

HE WAS THE 100TH ARCHBISHOP OF CANTERBURY SERVING
FROM 1961TO 1974

https://en.wikipedia.org/wiki/Michael-Ramsey

RANKIN   JOHN

01 02 1890   08 10 1973

LABOUR POLITICIAN AND PREVIOUSLY A SCHOOLTEACHER. HE
WAS AN M.P. FROM 1945 TO HIS DEATH.

https://en.wikipedia.org/wiki/John-Rankin-(politician)

RASHIDOV   SHAROF RASHIDOVICH

06 11 1917   31 10 1983

FULL MEMBER OF THE 22ND TO 26TH CENTRAL COMMITTEE
UNTIL HE COMMITTED SUICIDE. HE WAS FIRST SECRETARY OF
THE COMMUNIST PARTY OF UZBEKISTAN FROM 1959 TO HIS
DEATH.

HE HAD ORIGINALLY BEEN A TEACHER, JOURNALIST AND EDITOR OF A SAMARKAND NEWSPAPER AND WAS WOUNDED IN 1942 ON THE GERMAN FRONT.

HIS NAME IS SYNONYMOUS WITH CORRUPTION AND THE GREAT COTTON SCANDAL OF THE LATE BREZHNEV (Q.V.) PERIOD.

https://en.wikipedia.org/wiki/Sharof-Rashidov

RICHARDS   IVOR ARMSTRONG

26 02 1893   07 09 1979

INFLUENTIAL ENGLISH LITERARY CRITIC WHO IS REGULARLY CONSIDERED ONE OF THE FOUNDERS OF THE CONTEMPORARY STUDY OF LITERATURE IN ENGLISH.EDUCATED AT MAGDALENE COLLEGE, CAMBRIDGE WHERE HE TAUGHT IN LATER LIFE.

https://en.wikipedia.org/wiki/I.A.Richards

RICHARDSON ELLIOT LEE

20 07 1920   31 12 1999

LAWYER, TWENTY–SECOND AMBASSADOR TO THE COURT OF ST. JAMES AND REPUBLICAN POLITICIAN WHO WON A BRONZE STAR MEDAL AND THEN A PURPLE HEART WITH OAK LEAF CLUSTER IN LIEU OF A SECOND AWARD DURING THE SECOND WORLD WAR. HE IS ONLY THE SECOND PERSON TO HAVE HELD FOUR CABINET POSITIONS WITHIN THE UNITED STATES GOVERNMENT. AS THE ATTORNEY GENERAL,DURING THE WATERGATE SCANDAL, HE RESIGNED RATHER THAN OBEY PRESIDENT NIXON`S (Q.V.)ORDER TO DISMISS THE SPECIAL PROSECUTOR.

https://en.wikipedia.org/wiki/Elliot-Richardson

RIEFENSTAHL HELENE BERTHA AMALIE 'LENI'

22 08 1902   08 09 2003

GERMAN FILM DIRECTOR, PRODUCER, SCREENWRITER, EDITOR, PHOTOGRAPHER AND ACTRESS. HER MOST FAMOUS FILMS WERE THE NAZI PROPAGANDA FILM, TRIUMPH OF THE WILL AND THE OFFICIAL FILM OF THE 1936 OLYMPIC GAMES,

OLYMPIA. HER PROMINENCE IN THE THIRD REICH AND HER
PERSONAL ASSOCIATION WITH ADOLF HITLER (Q.V.)
DESTROYED HER FILM CAREER AFTER THE WAR WHEN SHE
WAS ARRESTED BUT RELEASED WITHOUT ANY CHARGES.

https://en.wikipedia.org/wiki/Leni-Riefenstahl

ROBESON   PAUL LEROY

09 04 1898   23 01 1976

AMERICAN SINGER AND ACTOR WHO BECAME INVOLVED WITH
THE CIVIL RIGHTS MOVEMENT. AT RUTGERS COLLEGE HE WAS
AN OUTSTANDING FOOTBALL PLAYER AND RECEIVED HIS LL.B.
FROM COLUMBIA LAW SCHOOL. HE HAD AN INTERNATIONAL
CAREER AS A SINGER AND LATER AS A FILM STAR IN MOVIES
SUCH AS SHOW BOAT. HIS POLITICAL INVOLVEMENT BEGAN
WITH SUPPORT FOR THE REPUBLICAN CAUSE IN THE SPANISH
CIVIL WAR.

https://en.wikipedia.org/wiki/Paul-Robeson

ROSENBERG ALFRED ERNEST

12 01 1893   16 10 1946

PHILOSOPHER AND INFLUENTIAL IDEOLOGUE OF THE NAZI
PARTY AND CONSIDERED ONE OF THE MAIN AUTHORS OF KEY
NAZI IDEOLOGICAL CREEDS, INCLUDING RACIAL THERORY,
PERSECUTION OF THE JEWS, LEBENSRAUM, ABROGATION OF
THE TREATY OF VERSAILLES AND OPPOSITION TO
'DEGENERATE' MODERN ART. AT NUREMBERG HE WAS
SENTENCED TO DEATH AND EXECUTED BY HANGING AS A WAR
CRIMINAL AND FOR CRIMES AGAINST HUMANITY.

https://en.wikipedia.org/wiki/Alfred-Rosenberg

ROOSEVELT   FRANKLIN DELANO

30 01 1882   12 04 1945

COMMONLY KNOWN BY HIS INITIALS FDR, AMERICAN
DEMOCRATIC POLITICIAN AND THIRTY-SECOND PRESIDENT
WHO WON A RECORD FOUR ELECTIONS AND SERVED FROM
MARCH 1933 TO HIS DEATH IN APRIL 1945. DURING THE
WORLDWIDE ECONOMIC DEPRESSION HIS PROGRAMME FOR

RELIEF, RECOVERY AND REFORM, KNOWN AS THE NEW DEAL, INVOLVED THE GREAT EXPANSION OF THE ROLE OF THE FEDERAL GOVERNMENT IN THE ECONOMY.THE REPEAL OF PROHIBITION ADDED TO HIS POPULARITY.

UNTIL THE UNITED STATES ENTERED THE WAR IN DECEMBER 1941 HE SUPPORTED THE BRITISH AND CHINESE SUPPLYING THEM WITH MILITARY AID UNDER A PROGRAMME OF 'LEND-LEASE'.

https://en.wikipedia.org/wiki/Franklin-D.-Roosevelt

ROSENGOLTS

ARKADY PAVLOVICH

04 11 1889   15 03 1938

HE WAS A BOLSHEVIK POLITICIAN,ADMINISTRATOR AND A DEFENDANT IN THE MOSCOW TRIAL OF THE TWENTY-ONE IN 1938, CONVICTED AND EXECUTED, HE WAS REHABILITATED IN 1988.

HE JOINED THE BOLSHEVIK FACTIONOF THE RUSSIAN SOCIAL-DEMOCRATIC WORKERS' PARTY IN 1905, PLAYED AN ACTIVE ROLE IN THE REVOLUTION OF 1917 BECOMING A LEADING OFFICER IN THE RED ARMY AND DURING THE CIVIL WAR WORKED CLOSELY WITH LEON TROTSKY (Q.V.). HE THEN HELD A NUMBER OF ADMINISTRATIVE POSITIONS AND BECAME AMBASSADOR TO THE COURT OF ST. JAMES FROM 1925 -27 AFTER WHICH HE BECAME A MEMBER OF THE CENTRAL COMMITTEE OF THE COMMUNIST PARTY OF THE SOVIET UNION AND FROM 1930-37 HE WAS PEOPLE'S COMMISSAR FOR FOREIGN TRADE AND SHORTLY AFTER BEING DISMISSED HE WAS ARRESTED.

https://en.wikipedia.org/wiki/Arkady-Rosengolts

RUSK DAVID DEAN

09 02 1909 20 12 1994

FIFTY-FOURTH UNITED STATES SECRETARY OF STATE UNDER KENNEDY AND JOHNSON (Q.V.) WAS A RHODES SCHOLAR AT ST. JOHN`S COLLEGE, OXFORD.

https://en.wikipedia.org/wiki/Dean-Rusk

RUSSELL JOHN, FIRST EARL

18 08 1792 28 05 1878

A LEADING WHIG AND LIBERAL POLITICIAN WHO SERVED AS PRIME MINISTER ON TWO OCCASIONS AND WAS THE PRINCIPAL ARCHITECT OF THE 1832 REFORM ACT.

https://en.wikipedia.org/wiki/John-Russell,-1st-Earl-Russell

RYAN GENERAL JOHN DALE

10 12 1915 27 10 1983

NICKNAMED, SOMETIMES DERISIVELY, AS 'THREE–FINGERED JACK', HE LOST A FINGER TO ENEMY ANTI AIRCRAFT FIRE IN THE SECOND WORLD WAR. HE WAS THE SEVENTH CHIEF OF STAFF OF THE UNITED STATES AIR FORCEAND MEMBER OF THE JOINT CHIEFS OF STAFF.

https://en.wikipedia.org/wiki/John -Dale-Ryan

RYKOV ALEXEI IVANOVICH

25 02 1881 15 03 1938

A RUSSIAN BOLSHEVIK REVOLUTIONARY AND SOVIET POLITICIAN. FULL MEMBER OF THE 11TH TO 16TH POLITBUROS AND MEMBER OF THE 10TH TO 12TH ORGBURO FROM 1921 TO 1924. CHAIRMAN OF THE COUNCIL OF PEOPLE`S COMMISSARS OF THE SOVIET UNION FROM 1924 TO 1930 AND CHAIRMAN OF THE COUNCIL OF PEOPLE`S COMMISSARS OF THE RUSSIAN SFSR FROM 1924 TO 1929. A CONTEMPORARY OF LENIN (Q.V.) HE HELD MANY POSITIONS IN THE NASCENT STATE BUT BY THE EARLY 1930S WAS EASED OUT OF HIS POSITIONS OF POWER AND INFLUENCE BY STALIN (Q.V.).

ON THE SEVENTEENTH OF FEBRUARY 1937-AT A MEETING OF
THE CENTRAL COMMITTEEE - HE WAS ARRESTED ALONG WITH
NIKOLAI BUKHARIN (Q.V.) AND IN MARCH 1938 THEY WERE
BOTH FOUND GUILTY OF TREASON AND EXECUTED.

https://en.wikipedia.org/wiki/Alexei-Rykov

SALAZAR   ANTONIO DE OLIVEIRA

28 04 1889   27 07 1970

PORTUGUESE PROFESSOR AND (RIGHT WING) POLITICIAN
WHO SERVED AS PRIME MINISTER FROM 1932 TO 1968. HE
FOUNDED AND LED THE ESTADO NOVO (NEW STATE) AND HIS
RULE WAS CORPORATIST, CONSERVATIVE, NATIONALIST IN
NATURE AND HE DEFENDED CATHOLICISM.

https://en.wikipedia.org/wiki/Antonio-de-Oliveira-Salazar

SCHRADER   GERHARD

25 02 1903   10 04 1990

A GERMAN CHEMIST EMPLOYED BY BAYER AG (A DIVISION OF
IG FARBEN), WHO ORIGINALLY SPECIALISED IN THE
DISCOVERY OF NEW INSECTICIDES. IN 1936 DURING THE
COURSE OF HIS WORK HE ACCIDENTALLY DISCOVERED THE
NERVE AGENT TABUN. LATER HE DISCOVERED SARIN (1938),
SOMAN (1944) AND CYCLOSARIN (1949).

https://en.wikipedia.org/wiki/Gerhard-Schrader

SEMICHASTNY

              VLADIMIR YEFIMOVICH

15 01 1924   12 01 2001

THIRD CHAIRMAN OF THE COMMITTEE FOR STATE SECURITY (K
G B) 1961 TO 1967.

https://en.wikipedia.org/wiki/Vladimir-Semichastny

SHAKESPEARE   WILLIAM

BAPTISED 26 04 1564   23 04 1616

AN ENGLISH POET, PLAYWRIGHT AND ACTOR, WIDELY REGARDED AS THE GREATEST WRITER IN THE ENGLISH LANGUAGE AND THE WORLD'S PRE-EMINENT DRAMATIST

https://en.wikipedia.org/wiki/William-Shakespeare

SHARANGOVICH   VASILY FOMICH

BO RN 1897   EX EC 1938

A FIRST SECRETARY OF THE BYELORUSSIAN SSR HE WAS EXECUTED AFTER THE LAST OF THE MOSCOW SHOW TRIALS BUT WAS REHABILITATED IN 1958.

https://en.wikipedia.org/wiki/Vasily-Sharangovich

SHELEST   PETRO YUKHYMOVYCH

14 02 1908   22 01 1996

FIRST SECRETARY OF THE COMMUNIST PARTY OF THE UKRAINE 1963 TO 1972 AND DEPUTY CHAIRMAN OF THE COUNCIL OF MINISTERS OF THE SOVIET UNION FROM 1972 TO 1973. FULL MEMBER OF THE 22ND TO 24TH POLITBUROS FROM 1964 TO 1973 WHEN BREZHNEV (Q.V.) FORCED HIM INTO RETIREMENT.

HE JOINED THE COMMUNIST PARTY IN 1928 AND IN 1935 GRADUATED FROM THE MARIUPOL METALLURGICAL INSTITUTE.HE WAS MAYOR OF KIEV BETWEEN 1954 AND 1962.

https://en.wikipedia.org/wiki/Petro-Shelest

SHEPILOV   DMITRI TROFIMOVICH

05 11 1905   08 08 1995

SOVIET POLITICIAN WHO JOINED AN ABORTIVE PLOT TO OUST NIKITA KHRUSHCHEV (Q.V.) FROM POWER IN 1957.

HEAD OF THE PROPAGANDA DEPARTMENT OF THE CENTRAL COMMITTEE 1949-1952, EDITOR-IN–CHIEF, *PRAVDA*,1952-56 AND MINISTER OF FOREIGN AFFAIRS 1956-57.

CANDIDATE MEMBER OF THE 19TH PRESIDIUM1956-57 AND MEMBER OF THE 19TH AND 20TH SECRETARIAT FEB–JUNE 1957.

https://en.wikipedia.org/wiki/Dmitri-Shepilov

SHERRIN   EDWARD GEORGE 'NED'

18 02 1931   01 10 2007

HE QUALIFIED AS A BARRISTER BUT BECAME A BROADCASTER, AUTHOR AND T.V. AND STAGE PRODUCER. HE WAS RESPONSIBLE FOR A NUMBER OF TELEVISION PROGRAMMES INCLUDING 'THAT WAS THE WEEK THAT WAS' AND 'UP POMPEII!' AND THE STAGE PRODUCTION OF JEFFREY BERNARD IS UNWELL.

https://en.wikipedia.org/wiki/Ned-Sherrin

SHVERNIK   NIKOLAY MIKHAILOVICH

19 05 1888   24 12 1970

SOVIET POLITICIAN, WHO JOINED THE BOLSHEVIKS IN 1905, FULL MEMBER OF THE 20TH AND 22ND PRESIDIUMS AND CANDIDATE MEMBER OF THE 18TH AND 19TH PRESIDIUMS. DURING THE GREAT PATRIOTIC WAR HE WAS RESPONSIBLE FOR EVACUATING SOVIET INDUSTRY FROM THE ADVANCING GERMAN ARMY. IN 1956, AFTER HIS WORK ON THE POSPELOV COMMISSION, WHICH WAS THE BASIS OF KHRUSHCHEV`S (Q.V.) 'SECRET SPEECH' DENOUNCING STALINISM WAS THEN PUT IN CHARGE OF REHABILITATING VICTIMS OF THE PURGE.

https://en.wikipedia.org/wiki/Nikolay-Shvernik

SIRHAN   SIRHAN BISHARA

19 03 44

PALESTINIAN OF JORDANIAN CITIZENSHIP WHO ASSASSINATED U.S. SENATOR ROBERT F. KENNEDY (Q.V.) IN 1968. KENNEDY WAS HIT BY THREE BULLETS DYING NEARLY 26 HOURS LATER. HE IS CURRENTLY SERVING LIFE IMPRISONMENT IN CALIFORNIA.

https://en.wikipedia.org/wiki/Sirhan-Sirhan

SLANSKY   RUDOLF

31 07 1901   03 12 1952

JEWISH ,CZECH, COMMUNIST POLITICIAN. AS THE PARTY`S
GENERAL SECRETARY AFTER WORLD WAR TWO HE WAS ONE
OF THE LEADING CREATORS AND ORGANISERS OF
COMMUNIST RULE IN 1948. FOLOWING A COUP IN 1951, ON THE
INSTIGATION OF STALIN (Q.V.), WHO WANTED TO CONTROL
THE NATIONAL COMMUNIST PARTIES, HE WAS ONE OF
FOURTEEN LEADERS ARRESTED AND CHARGED WITH HIGH
TREASON AND WAS ONE OF ELEVEN SENTENCED TO DEATH.

https://en.wikipedia.org/wiki/Rudolf-Slansky

SOBLE   JACK

15 05 1903   ?? ?? 1967

BORN IN LITHUANIA AS ABROMAS **SOBOLE VICIUS,** WAS A
SOVIET SPY ALONG WITH HIS WIFE MYRA. DURING HIS
CAREER, TO GATHER INTELLIGENCE, HE MET LEON TROTSKY
(Q.V.) IN TURKEY (1931) AND IN COPENHAGEN IN 1932. IN 1957
HE WAS CONVICTED OF SPYING AND SERVED SEVEN YEARS IN
A UNITED STATES PRISON.

https://en.wikipedia.org/wiki/Jack-Soble

STALIN   JOSEPH

18 12 1878   05 03 1953

BORN IOSEB BESARIONIS DZE **JUGASHVILI.** HE TOOK PART IN
THE RUSSIAN REVOLUTION OF 1917 AND IN 1922 WAS
APPOINTED GENERAL SECRETARY OF THE COMMUNIST
PARTY`S CENTRAL COMMITTEE. FOLLOWING LENIN`S (Q.V.)
DEATH AND SUPPRESSING LENIN`S CRITICISM OF HIM HE
CONSOLIDATED POWER, ELIMINATING OPPOSITION AND
EXPANDING THE FUNCTIONS OF HIS ROLE. HE REPLACED
LENIN`S NEW ECONOMIC POLICY WITH A HIGHLY CENTRALISED
COMMAND ECONOMY, LAUNCHING A PERIOD OF RAPID
TRANSFORMATION OF THE SOVIET UNION FROM AN AGRARIAN
SOCIETY INTO AN INDUSTRIAL POWER.

FROM 1934 ONWARDS AND UNTIL 1939 HE INAUGURATED A
RUTHLESS POLICY TO PURGE THE NATION OF HIS POLITICAL

OPPONENTS AND PERCEIVED ENEMIES DISPOSING OF THE ORIGINAL BOLSHEVIK REVOLUTIONARIES, HIS SUPREME POLITICAL OPPONENT, LEON TROTSKY (Q.V.) AND LEADING MEMBERS OF THE RED ARMY.

BETWEEN 1917 AND HIS DEATH IN 1953 HE WAS A FULL MEMBER OF THE 6TH TO THE 19TH PRESIDIUMS/ POLITBUROS. HE WAS ULTIMATELY RESPONSIBLE FOR ALL DOMESTIC, FOREIGN AND MILITARY POLICIES.

https://en.wikipedia.org/wiki/Joseph-Stalin

STEINBECK   JOHN ERNST JNR.

27 02 1902   20 12 1968

AMERICAN AUTHOR AND WINNER OF THE 1962 NOBEL PRIZE FOR LITERATURE. HE ATTENDED STANFORD UNIVERSITY WHERE HE STUDIED ENGLISH LITERATURE BUT LEFT IN 1925 WITHOUT A DEGREE. HIS BEST KNOWN WORKS WERE OF MICE AND MEN, THE GRAPES OF WRATH AND EAST OF EDEN.

https://en.wikipedia.org/wiki/John-Steinbeck

STREICHER   JULIUS

12 02 1885   16 10 1946

NOTORIOUS ANTISEMITE AND FOUNDER AND PUBLISHER OF THE NEWSPAPER DER STURMER IN 1923. HIS FIRM PUBLISHED THREE ANTISEMITIC BOOKS FOR CHILDREN INCLUDING DER GIFTPILZ. AFTER THE WAR HE WAS CONVICTED OF CRIMES AGAINST HUMANITY AND EXECUTED.

https://en.wikipedia.org/wiki/Julius-Streicher

STRONG   SIR KENNETH WILLIAM DOBSON

09 09 1900   11 01 1982

BRITISH ARMY OFFICER WHO SERVED IN THE SECOND WORLD WAR AND BECAME DIRECTOR GENERAL OF INTELLIGENCE. A GRADUATE OF THE ROYAL MILITARY ACADEMY, BETWEEN THE TWO WORLD WARS HE HELD A NUMBER OF POSITIONS IN GERMANY AND IN AUGUST 1939 BECAME HEAD OF THE GERMAN SECTION OF MI 14.BETWEEN 1943 AND THE END OF

THE WAR HE SERVED WITH THE COMMAND OF GENERAL DWIGHT EISENHOWER (Q.V.)

AFTER THE WAR HE WAS INVOLVED IN INTELLIGENCE, ULTIMATELY BECOMING THE FIRST DIRECTOR OF THE JOINT INTELLIGENCE BUREAU AT THE MINISTRY OF DEFENCE (FROM 1948 TO 1964) AND BEFORE RETIRING BECAME FIRST DIRECTOR GENERAL OF INTELLIGENCE AT THE MINISTRY OF DEFENCE .

https://en.wikipedia.org/wiki/Kenneth-Strong

SUSLOV   MIKHAIL ANDREYEVICH

21 11 1902   25 01 1982

FULL MEMBER OF THE 19TH TO 26TH POLITBUROS, HIS HARDLINE ATTITUDE TOWARDS CHANGE MADE HIM ONE OF THE FOREMOST ANTI-REFORMIST SOVIET LEADERS. HE JOINED THE COMMUNIST PARTY IN 1921 AND DURING THE GREAT PATRIOTIC WAR HEADED THE LOCAL STAVROPOL GUERRILLA MOVEMENT.

https://en.wikipedia.org/wiki/Mikhail-Suslov

TAL   MIKHAIL

09 11 1936   28 06 1992

LATVIAN SOVIET CHESS GRANDMASTER AND EIGHTH WORLD CHESS CHAMPION 1960 TO 1961.

https://en.wikipedia.org/wikl/Mikhail-Tal

TAYLOR   ALAN JOHN PERCIVALE

25 03 1906   07 09 1990

KNOWN AS 'A.J.P.'HE WAS A HIGHLY RESPECTED AND POPULAR HISTORIAN WHO SPECIALISED IN 19TH AND 20TH CENTURY EUROPEAN DIPLOMACY. THROUGH HIS TELEVISION LECTURES HE BECAME WIDELY KNOWN TO THE GENERAL PUBLIC. HE WAS A MEMBER OF THE LABOUR PARTY FOR OVER SIXTY YEARS, HOWEVER WHILST AT ORIEL COLLEGE,OXFORD, WHERE HE STUDIED MODERN HISTORY FROM 1924 TO 1927 , HE JOINED THE COMMUNIST PARTY OF GREAT BRITAIN BUT BROKE WITH THEM IN 1926 FOLLOWING WHAT HE CONSIDERED

TO BE THEIR INEFFECTIVE STAND DURING THE 1926 GENERAL STRIKE.

https://en.wikipedia.org/wiki/A.-J.-P.-Taylor

THATCHER   MARGARET HILDA (NEE ROBERTS),BARONESS

13 10 1925   08 04 2013

KNOWN AS THE 'IRON LADY' SHE WAS ORIGINALLY A RESEARCH CHEMIST, LATER BECOMING A BARRISTER WHO ENTERED PARLIAMENT IN 1959. SHE WAS LEADER OF THE CONSERVATIVE PARTY AND THEN PRIME MINISTER FROM MAY 1979 TO NOVEMBER 1990 WHEN SHE RESIGNED FOLLOWING A LEADERSHIP CHALLENGE. HER POLICIES REINVIGORATED THE BRITISH ECONOMY AND NATIONAL SELF CONFIDENCE.

https://en.wikipedia.org/wiki/Margaret-Thatcher

THOMAS   THOMAS GEORGE,

FIRST VISCOUNT TONYPANDY

29 01 1909   22 09 1997

LABOUR PARTY POLITICIAN WHO BEGAN HIS CAREER AS A SCHOOLTEACHER. HE WAS AN M.P. FROM 1945 TO 1983 AND HELD VARIOUS OFFICES IN HAROLD WILSON`S (Q.V.) ADMINISTRATIONS OF 1964 TO 1970. HE SERVED, WITH GREAT DISTINCTION AS THE SPEAKER OF THE HOUSE OF COMMONS FROM 1976 TO 1983.

https://en.wikipedia.org/wiki/George-Thomas,-1st-Viscount - Tonypandy

THOMSON   GEORGE MORGAN,

BARON THOMSON OF MONIFIETH

16 01 1921   03 10 2008

ORIGINALLY A LABOUR PARTY MEMBER, IN THE 1980S HE JOINED THE SOCIAL DEMOCRATIC PARTY AND FOLLOWING THEIR MERGER WITH THE LIBERAL PARTY, HE BECAME A LIBERAL DEMOCRAT AND SAT IN THE HOUSE OF LORDS AS A LIBERAL DEMOCRAT.

AS A MEMBER OF THE LABOUR PARTY UNDER HAROLD WILSON (Q.V.) HE HELD VARIOUS OFFICES NOTABLY SHADOW SECRETARY OF STATE FOR DEFENCE(1970-1972), TWICE CHANCELLOR OF THE DUCHY OF LANCASTER(1966-1967 AND 1969-1970) ,MINISTER WITHOUT PORTFOLIO(1968-1969) AND SECRETARY OF STATE FOR COMMONWEALTH AFFAIRS(1967-1968).

https://en.wikipedia.org/wiki/George-Thomson,-Baron-Thomson-of-Monifieth

TITO   JOSIP BROZ

07 05 1892   04 05 1980

BORN JOSIP BROZ, HE WAS A YUGOSLAV REVOLUTIONARY AND STATESMAN. FROM 1953 TO HIS DEATH HE WAS THE FIRST PRESIDENT OF YUGOSLAVIA AND FROM 1944 TO 1963 THE TWENTY-THIRD PRIME MINISTER.

DURING THE FIRST WORLD WAR, WHILST SERVING AS A SERGEANT MAJOR IN THE AUSTRO-HUNGARIAN ARMY, HE WAS SERIOUSLY INJURED, CAPTURED BY THE IMPERIAL RUSSIANS AND SENT TO A WORK CAMP IN THE URAL MOUNTAINS.LATER HE PARTICIPATED IN THE 1917 OCTOBER REVOLUTION BEFORE JOINING A RED GUARD UNIT.

HE LATER JOINED THE KPJ (COMMUNIST PARTY OF YUGOSLAVIA).

HIS PERIOD OF POWER IN MODERN YUGOSLAVIA WAS MARKED BY HIS INDEPENDENCE OF, AND DEFIANCE OF, SOVIET HEGEMONY.

https://en.wikipedia.org/wiki/Josip-Broz-Tito

TITOV   GHERMAN STEPANOVICH

11 09 1935   20 09 2000

PILOT AND SOVIET COSMONAUT WHO,ON AUGUST SIXTH NINETEEN SIXTY-ONE, BECAME THE SECOND MAN TO ORBIT THE EARTH, ABOARD VOSTOK 2, SPENDING TWENTY-FIVE HOURS AND EIGHTEEN MINUTES IN SPACE DURING HIS SEVENTEEN ORBITS. HIS JOURNEY INCLUDED A NUMBER OF

'FIRSTS' INCLUDING THE FIRST PERSON TO VOMIT IN SPACE AND TO PILOT A SPACESHIP.

https://en.wikipedia.org/wiki/Gherman-Titov

TOLLER   ERNST

01 12 1893   22 05 1939

GERMAN LEFT WING PLAYWRIGHT WHO SERVED ON THE WESTERN FRONT BUT SUFFERED A COMPLETE PHYSICAL AND PSYCHOLOGICAL COLLAPSE. HE SERVED AS PRESIDENT IN THE SHORT LIVED BAVARIAN SOVIET REPUBLIC CONSEQUENTLY SERVING FIVE YEARS IN PRISON DURING WHICH TIME HE WROTE A NUMBER OF SUCCESSFUL WORKS. IN 1933 HE WAS EXILED BY THE NAZIS BECAUSE OF HIS WORKS, FINALLY LIVING IN THE UNITED STATES WHERE HE COMMITTED SUICIDE ON LEARNING THAT HIS BROTHER AND SISTER HAD BEEN SENT TO A CONCENTRATION CAMP.

https://en.wikipedia.org/wiki/Ernst-Toller

TROTSKY   LEON

07 11 1879   21 08 1940

BORN LEV DAVIDOVICH **BRONSHTEIN** TO JEWISH FARMERS HE WAS A MARXIST REVOLUTIONARY AND THEORIST, SOVIET POLITICIAN, AND THE FOUNDER AND FIRST HEAD OF THE RED ARMY. HE WAS A FULL MEMBER OF THE 6TH TO THE 14TH POLITBUROS.

HE JOINED THE BOLSHEVIK FACTION OF THE RUSSIAN SOCIAL DEMOCRATIC LABOUR PARTY FROM THE MENSHEVIK FACTION IMMEDIATELY PRIOR TO THE 1917 OCTOBER REVOLUTION AND SERVED FIRST AS PEOPLE`S COMMISSAR FOR FOREIGN AFFAIRS AND LATER FOUNDED AND WAS COMMANDER OF THE RED ARMY AND A MAJOR FIGURE IN THE BOLSHEVIK VICTORY IN THE CIVIL WAR.

THE 1920S WAS A PERIOD OF STRUGGLE AGAINST THE RISE AND POLICIES OF JOSEPH STALIN (Q.V.) AND IN OCTOBER 1927 HE WAS REMOVED FROM POWER, EXPELLED FROM THE COMMUNIST PARTY THE NEXT MONTH AND IN 1929 EXILED FROM THE SOVIET UNION. HE OPPOSED STALIN`S NON AGGRESSION PACT WITH ADOLF HITLER (Q.V.) AND IN 1940,

INCITED BY THE JEW, JOEL BEN YITZHAK, STALIN ORDERED HIS ASSASSINATION IN MEXICO.

https://en.wikipedia.org/wiki/Leon-Trotsky

TRUMAN   HARRY S.

08 05 1884   26 12 1972

UNITED STATES SENATOR FROM MISSOURI 1935-45, 34TH VICE PRESIDENT OF THE UNITED STATES, JANUARY 1945 TO APRIL OF THE SAME YEAR WHEN HE BECAME THE 33RD PRESIDENT (UNTIL JANUARY 1953) WHEN HE SUCCEEDED FRANKLIN ROOSEVELT (Q.V.) ON THE LATTER'S DEATH.

WITHIN WEEKS OF BECOMING PRESIDENT THE WAR IN EUROPE WAS WON, HOWEVER THE WAR IN THE FAR EAST CONTINUED AND HE MADE THE MOMENTOUS AND LATER CONTROVERSIAL DECISION TO APPROVE THE USE OF THE NEWLY CREATED ATOMIC BOMB TO END THE WAR AND AVOID THE NECESSITY, WITH POSSIBLY HORRENDOUS CONSEQUENCES, OF INVADING THE JAPANESE MAINLAND. FOLLOWING THE USE OF TWO BOMBS, JAPAN SURRENDERED UNCONDITIONALLY.

POST WAR, HE ISSUED THE TRUMAN DOCTRINE TO CONTAIN COMMUNISM AND PASSED THE MARSHALL PLAN TO REBUILD EUROPE.IN THE FAR EAST HE SUPPORTED SOUTH KOREA WHO HAD BEEN INVADED BY THE COMMUNIST NORTH.

DOMESTICALLY HE BEGAN THE PROCESSTO RACIALLY INTEGRATE THE MILITARY AND FEDERAL AGENCIES.

https://en.wikipedia.org/wiki/ Harry-S.-Truman

TUKHACHEVSKY

MIKHAIL NIKOLAYEVICH

16 02 1893   12 06 1937

MARSHALL OF THE SOVIET UNION AND COMMANDER IN CHIEF OF THE RED ARMY (1925 TO 1928), HOWEVER HE WAS PURGED AND EXECUTED IN THE GREAT TERROR. AN ANTI- SEMITE, WHILST A PRISONER OF THE GERMANS` IN THE FIRST WORLD WAR HE SHARED A CELL WITH THE FUTURE FRENCH

PRESIDENT, CHARLES DE GAULLE (Q.V.), WHO REPORTED THAT HE SPOKE AGAINST JEWS WHOM HE CALLED DOGS WHO... 'SPREAD THEIR FLEAS THROUGHOUT THE WORLD'.

https://en.wikipedia.org/wiki/Mikhail-Tukhachevsky

TURNER   SIR COLIN WILLIAM CARSTAIRS

04 01 1922   21 03 2014

BUSINESSMAN AND CONSERVATIVE M.P. FOR ONE TERM (1959-1964). HE SERVED IN THE R.A.F. DURING THE WAR.

https://en.wikipedia.org/wiki/Colin-Turner

TURNER   LANA

08 02 1921   29 06 1995

BORN JULIA JEAN TURNER SHE WAS A SUCCESSFUL AMERICAN FILM AND TELEVISION ACTRESS

https://en.wikipedia.org/wiki/Lana-Turner

TYNDALL   JOHN HUTCHYNS

14 07 1934   19 07 2005

HE JOINED THE LEAGUE OF EMPIRE LOYALISTS IN THE MID NINETEEN FIFTIES BEFORE LEAVING TO FOUND OR CO FOUND VARIOUS RIGHT WING ORGANISATIONS INCLUDING THE BRITISH NATIONAL PARTY AND THEN, WITH COLIN JORDAN (Q.V.) ,THE NATIONAL SOCIALIST MOVEMENT. IN 1962 THEY, WITH OTHERS, WERE IMPRISONED HAVING BEEN FOUND GUILTY UNDER THE 1936 PUBLIC ORDER ACT FOR ORGANISING A PARAMILITARY FORCE. JORDAN `S EARLIER RELEASE FROM PRISON PERMITTED HIM TO HASTILY MARRY TYNDALL`S FORMER FIANCEE, FRANCOISE DIOR (Q.V.), SO SHE COULD AVOID BEING DEPORTED AS AN UNDESIRABLE ALIEN. HE OWNED THE COPYRIGHT OF THE TITLE 'SPEARHEAD'WHICH WAS A RIGHT WING MAGAZINE.

https://en.wikipedia.org/wiki/John-Tyndall-(politician)

ULYANOV   VLADIMIR ILYICH

22 04 1870   21 01 1924

ALSO KNOWN AS **LENIN**. RUSSIAN COMMUNIST
REVOLUTIONARY AND POLITICIAN. FULL MEMBER OF THE 6TH
TO 12TH POLITBUROS AND CHAIRMAN OF THE COUNCIL OF
PEOPLE`S COMMISSARS OF THE SOVIET UNION 1922 TO
1924.ALONG WITH LEON TROTSKY LED THE OCTOBER
REVOLUTION IN 1917 AND UNDER HIS LEADERSHIP THE NEW
GOVERNMENT LEGALIZED HOMOSEXUALITY AND NO FAULT
DIVORCE ALSO BRINGING IN UNIVERSAL FREE HEALTH CARE
AND EDUCATION.IN 1921 HE PROPOSED THE NEW ECONOMIC
POLICY TO CREATE AN INDUSTRIALISED STATE.

https://en.wikipedia.org/wiki/Vladimir-Lenin

URVALEK   JOSEF

?? ?? 1910   ?? ?? 1979

A PROSECUTING COUNSEL AND LATER A JUDGE OF THE
CZECHOSLOVAK STATE COURT HE WAS INVOLVED IN A
NUMBER OF 'SHOW TRIALS', THE MOST IMFAMOUS BEING OF
FOURTEEN COMMUNIST FUNCTIONARIES INCLUDING RUDOLF
SLANSKY (Q.V.) ON TRUMPED UP TREASON CHARGES.
IGNORING NATURAL JUSTICE, WHEN CROSS EXAMINING THE
ACCUSED, HE WOULD FREQUENTLY INTERRUPT THEM, MAKE
INTOLERANT REMARKS AND COMPARE THEM TO HUMAN
WASTE.

https://en.wikipedia.org/wiki/Josef-Urvalek

VON RIBBENTROP

                    ULRICH FRIEDRICH WILHELM JOACHIM

30 04 1893   16 10 1946

FOREIGN MINISTER OF NAZI GERMANY FROM 1938 TO 1945.
PREVIOUSLY HE HAD BEEN THE AMBASSADOR TO THE COURT
OF ST. JAMES `S FROM 1936 TO 1938.HE PLAYED A KEY ROLE IN
BROKERING THE PACT OF STEEL WITH FASCIST ITALY AND
THEN THE SOVIET- GERMAN NON-AGGRESSION PACT, KNOWN
AS THE MOLOTOV-RIBBENTROP PACT SHORTLY BEFORE THE

OUTBREAK OF THE SECOND WORLD WAR. TRIED, CONVICTED AND EXECUTED FOR HIS ROLE IN STARTING THE WAR.

https://en.wikipedia.org/wiki/Joachim-von-Ribbentrop

VORONOV   GENNADY IVANOVICH

31 08 1910   01 04 1994

RUSSIAN POLITICIAN, FULL MEMBER OF THE 22ND TO 24TH POLITBUROS AND PREVIOUSLY CANDIDATE MEMBER OF THE 22ND POLITBURO. CHAIRMAN OF THE COUNCIL OF MINISTERS OF THE RUSSIAN SFSR. 1962 TO 1971.

https://en.wikipedia.org/wiki/Gennady-Voronov

VYSHINSKY   ANDREY YANUAREVICH

10 12 1883   22 11 1954

SOVIET POLITICIAN, JURIST AND DIPLOMAT WHO WAS A CANDIDATE MEMBER OF THE NINETEENTH PRESIDIUM, PROCURATOR GENERAL OF THE RUSSIAN SFSR FROM 1931 TO 1934, PROCURATOR GENERAL OF THE SOVIET UNION FROM 1935 TO 1939 AND MINISTER OF FOREIGN AFFAIRS FROM 1949 TO 1953.

HE ATTENDED KIEV UNIVERSITY BUT WAS EXPELLED FOR PARTICIPATING IN REVOLUTIONARY ACTIVITIES AND LATER TOOK PART IN THE 1905 RUSSIAN REVOLUTION. AS A RESULT IN 1908 HE WAS SENTENCED TO PRISON WHERE HE MET STALIN (Q.V.). HE RESUMED HIS STUDIES AND BECAME A SUCCESSFUL LAWYER IN MOSCOW.

MUCH LATER HE WAS A STATE PROSECUTOR DURING THE PURGES AND TRIALS AND AFTER THE WAR PROSECUTED AT THE 1946 NUREMBERG TRIAL.

https://en.wikipedia.org/wiki/Andrey-Vyshinsky

WADE   DONALD, BARON

16 06 1904   06 11 1988

LIBERAL POLITICIAN AND M.P.

https://en.wikipedia.org/wiki/Donald -Wade,-Baron –Wade

GORDON-WALKER   PATRICK CHRESTIEN, BARON

07 04 1907   02 12 1980

LABOUR POLITICIAN AND AN M.P. FOR NEARLY THIRTY YEARS. AS ASSISTANT DIRECTOR OF THE B.B.C.`s GERMAN SERVICE HE BROADCAST ABOUT THE LIBERATION OF THE GERMAN CONCENTRATION CAMP AT BERGEN-BELSEN.

https://en.wikipedia.org/wiki/Patrick-Gordon-Walker

WALLACE   ALFRED RUSSEL O M, F R S

08 01 1823   07 11 1913

HE WAS A BRITISH NATURALIST, EXPLORER,GEOGRAPHER, ANTHROPOLOGIST AND BIOLOGIST. HE IS BEST KNOWN FOR **INDEPENDENTLY** CONCEIVING THE THEORY OF EVOLUTION THROUGH NATURAL SELECTION AND HIS PAPER ON THE SUBJECT WAS JOINTLY PUBLISHED WITH SOME OF CHARLES DARWIN'S WRITINGS IN 1858.

https://en.wikipedia.org/wiki/Alfred-Russel-Wallace

WALSINGHAM   SIR FRANCIS

CIRCA 1532   06 04 1590

PRINCIPAL SECRETARY TO QUEEN ELIZABETH I OF ENGLAND FROM DECEMBER 20TH 1573 TO HIS DEATH AND FAMOUS FOR HIS REPUTATION AS HER 'SPYMASTER'.HE ROSE FROM RELATIVE OBSCURITY TO BE PART OF AN INNER GROUP WHO DIRECTED THE ELIZABETHAN STATE, OVERSEEING FOREIGN , DOMESTIC AND RELIGIOUS POLICY. A COMMITTED PROTESTANT, WHILST SERVING AS THE ENGLISH AMBASSADOR TO FRANCE, HE WITNESSED THE ST. BARTHOLOMEW`S DAY MASSACRE.

HE OVERSAW OPERATIONS THAT PENETRATED SPANISH MILITARY PREPARATIONS, GATHERED INTELLIGENCE FROM ACROSS EUROPE AND SECURED THE EXECUTION OF MARY, QUEEN OF SCOTS.

https://en.wikipedia.org/wiki/Francis-Walsingham

WALTON   SIR WILLIAM TURNER

29 03 1902   08 03 1983

ENGLISH COMPOSER DESCRIBED AS A SLOW WORKER AND A PERFECTIONIST.

https://en.wikipedia.org/wiki/William-Walton

WARREN   (JUSTICE) EARL

19 03 1891   09 07 1974

MOST FAMOUS FOR CHAIRING THE 'WARREN COMMISSION' WHICH WAS FORMED TO INVESTIGATE THE ASSASSINATION OF PRESIDENT KENNEDY. HE HAD PREVIOUSLY A STELLAR CAREER BEING ELECTED THREE CONSECUTIVE TIMES AS (REPUBLICAN) GOVERNOR OF CALIFORNIA AS WELL AS MAKING LEGAL DECISIONS WHICH ADVANCED SOCIAL EQUALITY AND ESPECIALLY THE RIGHTS OF THE ACCUSED.

https://en.wikipedia.org/wiki/Earl -Warren

WASHINGTON GEORGE

22 02 1732   14 12 1799

FIRST PRESIDENT OF THE UNITED STATES OF AMERICA (1789-1797), THE COMMANDER IN CHIEF OF THE CONTINENTAL ARMY DURING THE AMERICAN REVOLUTIONARY WAR AND ONE OF THE FOUNDING FATHERS OF THE UNITED STATES. HE PRESIDED OVER THE CONVENTION THAT DRAFTED THE UNITED STATES CONSTITUTION. HIS FAREWELL ADDRESS AS PRESIDENT WAS A STATEMENT OF REPUBLICAN VIRTUES AND A WARNING AGAINST PARTISANSHIP,SECTIONALISM AND INVOLVEMENT IN FOREIGN WARS.

https://en.wikipedia.org/wiki/George-Washington

WAYNE   JOHN

26 05 1907   11 06 1979

BORN MARION ROBERT **MORRISON** (LATER MARION MITCHELL MORRISON) BUT KNOWN BY HIS STAGE NAME. HE WAS AN AMERICAN FILM ACTOR,DIRECTOR AND PRODUCER. AN

ACADEMY AWARD WINNER HE HAD A SUCCESSFUL CAREER FOR OVER THIRTY YEARS.

A PROMINENT REPUBLICAN IN HOLLYWOOD HE ADOPTED AN ANTI COMMUNIST POSITION.

https://en.wikipedia.org/wiki/John-Wayne

WEDGWOOD   COL. JOSIAH CLEMENT, 1ST BARON WEDGWOOD

16 03 1872   26 07 1943

HE WAS A BRITISH LIBERAL AND LABOUR POLITICIAN AND DURING 1924 WAS CHANCELLOR OF THE DUCHY OF LANCASTER. A DESCENDANT OF THE FAMOUS POTTER JOSIAH WEDGWOOD, HE SUPPORTED THE SUFFRAGETTES AND EARLIER HAD DEVELOPED A BELIEF IN A TAX ON PROPERTY TO REPLACE TAXES ON INCOME. IN 1918 HE WAS SENT TO SIBERIA WHERE HIS MISSION WAS TO ENCOURAGE CONTINUED RUSSIAN PARTICIPATION IN THE WAR AND TO GATHER INTELLIGENCE ON BOLSHEVIK CONTROL IN SIBERIA.

https://en.wikipedia.org/wiki/Josiah-Wedgwood,-1st-Baron-Wedgwood

WEIGHELL   SIDNEY

31 03 1922   13 02 2002

GENERAL SECRETARY OF THE NATIONAL UNION OF RAILWAYMEN FROM 1975 TO 1983 AND A PROFESSIONAL FOOTBALLER FOR SUNDERLAND FOR TWO SEASONS (1945 TO 1947).

https://en.wikipedia.org/wiki/Sidney-Weighell

WELLES   GEORGE ORSON

06 05 1915   10 10 1985

AMERICAN ACTOR,FILM AND THEATRE DIRECTOR,SCREENWRITER, PLAYWRIGHT, FILM PRODUCER AND ACCOMPLISHED MAGICIAN.

HE FOUND NATIONAL AND INTERNATIONAL FAME AS THE DIRECTOR AND NARRATOR OF A 1938 RADIO ADAPTATION OF H. G. WELLS'(Q.V.) NOVEL *'THE WAR OF THE WORLDS'*

PERFORMED BY HIS MERCURY THEATRE GROUP WHICH HE CO- FOUNDED. SUCH WAS ITS' CREDIBILITY THAT IT REPORTEDLY CAUSED WIDESPREAD PANIC.

HIS FIRST FILM WHICH HE CO-WROTE,PRODUCED, DIRECTED AND STARRED IN WAS THE EPIC *CITIZEN KANE* HAILED AS ONE OF THE GREATEST FILMS OF ALL TIME.

https://en.wikipedia.org/wiki/Orson-Welles

WELLS   HERBERT GEORGE

21 09 1866   13 08 1946

BRITISH SOCIALIST AND AUTHOR FAMOUS FOR HIS SCIENCE FICTION AND SOCIAL WORKS INCLUDING, RESPECTIVELY, THE TIME MACHINE AND THE HISTORY OF MR.POLLY.

https://en.wikipedia.org/wiki/H.-G.-Wells

WEST   MARY JANE "MAE"

17 08 1893   22 11 1980

AMERICAN ACTRESS, SINGER, PLAYWRIGHT, SCREENWRITER, COMEDIENNE AND SEX SYMBOL KNOWN FOR HER BAWDY DOUBLE ENTENDRES, WHO ORIGINALLY MADE HER NAME IN VAUDEVILLE AND ON THE STAGE IN NEW YORK BEFORE MOVING TO HOLLYWOOD.

HER FIRST STARRING ROLE ON BROADWAY WAS IN A 1926 PLAY ENTITLED *SEX* WHICH SHE WROTE, PRODUCED AND DIRECTED; THE THEATRE WAS RAIDED AND SHE, ALONG WITH THE CAST, WERE ARRESTED AND SHE WAS PROSECUTED AND CONVICTED FOR 'CORRUPTING THE MORALS OF YOUTH'. SHE SERVED EIGHT DAYS OF HER SENTENCE, BEING RELEASED TWO DAYS EARLY OF HER TEN DAY CONVICTION, FOR GOOD BEHAVIOUR.

HER NEXT PLAY WAS *'THE DRAG'* WHICH DEALT WITH HOMOSEXUALITY AND WHICH NEVER APPEARED ON BROADWAY DUE TO THE SUCCESSFUL EFFORTS BY THE SOCIETY FOR THE PREVENTION OF VICE.

https://en.wikipedia.org/wiki/Mae-West

WILSON   JAMES HAROLD, BARON WILSON OF RIEVAULX

11 03 1916 24 05 1995

BRITISH LABOUR PARTY POLITICIAN WHO SERVED AS PRIME MINISTER FROM 1964 TO 1970 AND 1974 TO 1976.

HE ENTERED PARLIAMENT IN 1945 AND WAS IMMEDIATELY APPOINTED THE PARLIAMENTARY SECRETARY TO THE MINISTRY OF WORKS, RISING THROUGH THE MINISTERIAL RANKS, BECOMING THE SECRETARY FOR OVERSEAS TRADE IN 1947 AND LATER HE WAS APPOINTED TO THE CABINET AS PRESIDENT OF THE BOARD OF TRADE.

https://en.wikipedia.org/wiki/Harold-Wilson

WOLF MARKUS 'MISCHA' JOHANNES

19 01 1923 09 11 2006

HEAD OF THE (EAST GERMAN) GENERAL INTELLIGENCE ADMINISTRATION, 1953 TO 1986.

https://en.wikipedia.org/wiki/Markus-Wolf

WOODCOCK GEORGE

20 10 1904 30 10 1979

ASSISTANT GENERAL SECRETARY OF THE TRADES UNION CONGRESS 1947 TO 1960 AND GENERAL SECRETARY FROM 1960 TO 1969.AT THE AGE OF TWELVE HE STARTED WORK IN A COTTON MILL AND IN 1924 BECAME A UNION OFFICIAL BEFORE WINNING, IN 1929, A T.U.C. SCHOLARSHIP TO RUSKIN COLLEGE, OXFORD.

https://en.wikipedia.org/wiki/George-Woodcock-(trade-unionist)

WOODWARD ROBERT UPSHUR 'BOB'

26 03 1943

AMERICAN INVESTIGATIVE JOURNALIST AND NON FICTION AUTHOR. AS A YOUNG REPORTER FOR THE WASHINGTON POST IN 1972 HE TEAMED UP WITH CARL BERNSTEIN (Q.V.) AND UNCOVERED GOVERNMENT IMPROPRIETY KNOWN AS THE

'WATERGATE SCANDAL' ULTIMATELY LEADING TO THE
RESIGNATION OF PRESIDENT NIXON (Q.V.).

https://en.wikipedia.org/wiki/Bob-Woodward

(THE) WRIGHT (BROTHERS)

WILBUR

16 04 1867   30 05 1912

ORVILLE

19 08 1871   30 01 1948

WERE TWO AMERICAN BROTHERS, INVENTORS AND AVIATION
PIONEERS WHO ARE CREDITED WITH INVENTING AND
BUILDING THE WORLD`S FIRST AIRPLANE AND MAKING THE
FIRST SUCCESSFUL POWERED AND SUSTAINED HEAVIER THAN
AIR HUMAN FLIGHT ON DECEMBER THE 17TH 1903 AT KITTY
HAWK , NORTH CAROLINA, U.S.A.

THEIR FUNDAMENTAL BREAKTHROUGH WAS THEIR INVENTION
OF A THREE AXIS CONTROL, WHICH ENABLED THE PILOT TO
STEER THE AIRCRAFT EFFECTIVELY AND TO MAINTAIN
ITS`EQUILIBRIUM.

https://en.wikipedia.org/wiki/Wright-brothers

YAGODA   GENRIKH

07 11 1891 15 03 1938

BORN GERSHEVICH IYEGUDA **YENOKH** AND WAS PEOPLE`S
COMMISSAR FOR INTERNAL AFFAIRS (THE N K V D) FROM 1934
TO 1936 WHEN HE WAS REPLACED BY NIKOLAI YEZHOV (Q.V.),
FINALLY BEING PURGED AND THEN CONVICTED IN THE LAST
OF THE MAJOR SHOW TRIALS AND EXECUTED.

https://en.wikipedia.org/wiki/Genrikh-Yagoda

YAKIR   IONA EMMANUILOVICH

03 08 1896 11 06 1937

RED ARMY COMMANDER AND ONE OF HIS COUNTRY`S MAJOR MILITARY REFORMERS DURING THE INTER-WAR PERIOD HOWEVER HE WAS PURGED AND EXECUTED.

https://en.wikipedia.org/wiki/Iona-Yakir

YAKUBOVSKY IVAN IGNATYEVICH

07 01 1912   30 11 1976

MARSHALL OF THE SOVIET UNION, TWICE A HERO OF THE SOVIET UNION, HE SERVED AS COMMANDER IN CHIEF OF THE WARSAW PACT FROM 1967 TO 1976.

IN THE 1939-1940 WINTER WAR AND THEN IN THE GREAT PATRIOTIC WAR HE SPECIALISED IN TANK WARFARE AND FOUGHT IN THE GREAT TANK BATTLE OF KURSK.

https://en.wikipedia.org/wiki/Ivan-Yakubovsky

YANGEL   MIKHAIL KUZMICH

25 10 1911   25 10 1971

A LEADING MISSILE DESIGNER IN THE SOVIET UNION. IN 1954 HE FORMED THE OKB 586 DESIGN BUREAU WHICH WAS RESPONSIBLE FOR THE R-12, R16 AND R-36 MISSILES.

https://en.wikipedia.org/wiki/Mikhail-Yangel

YEZHOV   NIKOLAI IVANOVICH

01 05 1895   04 02 1940

HEAD OF THE N K V D FROM 1936 TO1938 DURING THE MOST SEVERE PERIOD OF THE GREAT TERROR BUT WAS HIMSELF A VICTIM AND UNDER TORTURE CONFESSED TO ANTI SOVIET ACTIVITY AND WAS CONVICTED AND LATER EXECUTED.

https://en.wikipedia.org/wiki/Nikolai-Yezhov

ZHUKOV   GEORGY KONSTANTINOVICH

01 12 1896   18 06 1974

SOVIET CAREER OFFICER IN THE RED ARMY WHO JOINED THE BOLSHEVIK PARTY AFTER THE OCTOBER REVOLUTION IN 1917. HE PLAYED A PIVOTAL ROLE IN THE SECOND WORLD WAR LEADING THE RED ARMY IN THEIR DRIVE FIRST TO LIBERATE THE OCCUPIED AREAS OF THE SOVIET UNION AND THEN THROUGH EASTERN EUROPE TO GERMANY AND BERLIN.

HE FOUGHT IN THE RUSSIAN CIVIL WAR.

HIS EXPERIENCE COMMANDING THE FIRST SOVIET MONGOLIAN ARMY GROUP AGAINST THE JAPANESE KWANTUNG ARMY ON THE BORDER BETWEEN MONGOLIA AND THE JAPANESE CONTROLLED STATE OF MANCHUKUO CULMINATING IN THE STRATEGICALLY DECISIVE BATTLE OF KHALKHIN GOL WAS PERHAPS INSTRUMENTAL IN HIS LATER USE OF TANKS SUPPORTED BY FIGHTERS AND BOMBERS IN THE SECOND WORLD WAR.

https://en.wikipedia.org/wiki/Georgy-Zhukov

ZILLIACUS   KONNI

13 09 1894   06 07 1967

BORN IN JAPAN TO AN EXILED FINNISH NATIONALIST AND AN AMERICAN BORN MOTHER HE WENT TO YALE UNIVERSITY, GRADUATING FIRST IN HIS CLASS IN 1915. DURING A PERIOD IN THE GREAT WAR HE WORKED AS AN ORDERLY FOR A FRENCH MEDICAL UNIT NEAR THE FRONT LINES.

MULTILINGUAL AND SYMPATHETIC TO SOVIET POLICIES HE WAS THE BRITISH ENVOY TO THE LEAGUE OF NATIONS BUT RESIGNED FROM THE SECRETARIAT WHEN GERMANY INVADED CZECHOSLOVAKIA.

HE WAS A LABOUR M.P. FROM 1945 TO 1950 AND FROM 1955 TO HIS DEATH DURING WHICH PERIODS HIS LEFT WING VIEWS (HE WAS A FOUNDER OF C.N.D.) AND PACIFISM BROUGHT HIM INTO CONFLICT WITH THE PARTY.

https://en.wikipedia.org/wiki/Konni-Zilliacus

ZINOVIEV   GRIGORY YEVSEEVICH

23 09 1883   25 08 1936

BORN OVSEI GERSHON ARONOVICH **RADOMYSLSKY** AND KNOWN ALSO UNDER THE NAME HIRSCH **APFELBAUM.** HE WAS A BOLSHEVIK REVOLUTIONARY AND A SOVIET COMMUNIST POLITICIAN.

HE WAS A FULL MEMBER OF THE 6TH AND 10TH TO THE 14TH POLITBUROS AND A CANDIDATE MEMBER OF THE 8TH AND 9TH POLITBUROS.

FOR SOME YEARS HE WAS THE HEAD OF THE COMMUNIST INTERNATIONAL.

A LEADING BOLSHEVIK AND ONE OF LENIN`S (Q.V.)CLOSEST ASSOCIATES HE RETURNED WITH LENIN FROM SWITZERLAND IN THE SPRING OF 1917, HOWEVER THEY FELL OUT WHEN HE AND LEV KAMENEV (Q.V.) WERE THE ONLY TWO CENTRAL COMMITTEE MEMBERS WHO VOTED AGAINST AN ARMED REVOLT AGAINST THE SOCIALIST PROVISIONAL GOVERNMENT.THE TWO POLITICIANS SOON RECONCILED AND ZINOVIEV`S CAREER FLOURISHED .

JUST BEFORE AND AFTER THE DEATH OF LENIN A RULING TRIUMVIRATE OF STALIN (Q.V.), KAMENEV AND ZINOVIEV MARGINALIZED TROTSKY(Q.V.).

YEARS LATER STALIN, HAVING EXILED TROTSKY, BROUGHT DOWN ZINOVIEV WHO WAS THE CHIEF DEFENDANT IN A 1936 SHOW TRIAL THAT BEGUN THE GREAT TERROR.

https://en.wikipedia.org/wiki/Grigory-Zinoviev

CHARACTER BIOGRAPHIES
(SECOND SECTION)

PLEASE NOTE THAT THE FOLLOWING BIOGRAPHIES HAVE
BEEN DRAWN FROM VARIOUS SOURCES INCLUDING
'WIKIPEDIA' AND ARE IDENTIFIED WHERE EVER POSSIBLE AT
THE END OF EACH STATEMENT. IN CERTAIN CASES THEY ARE
INCOMPLETE AND THE AUTHOR WOULD APPRECIATE FURTHER
AND BETTER INFORMATION SUPPORTED WITH REFERENCES
AND DOCUMENTATION.

ATTLEE   CLEMENT RICHARD, 1ST EARL ATTLEE OF
WALTHAMSTOW, VISCOUNT PRESTWOOD

03 01 1883 08 10 1967

BRITISH LABOUR PARTY LEADER (1935-55) AND PRIME
MINISTER (1945-51). UNDER CHURCHILL'S WARTIME
GOVERNMENT HE WAS LORD PRIVY SEAL (FROM 1940-42) AND
FROM 1942, THE DEPUTY PRIME MINISTER. AS PRIME
MINISTER HE ESTABLISHED THE WELFARE STATE AND THE
GRANTING OF INDEPENDENCE TO INDIA. (SOURCE:
ENCYCLOPAEDIA BRITANNICA)

BOYNE   SIR HENRY BRIAN 'HARRY'

29 07 1910 18 09 1997

HE JOINED THE RANKS OF THE BLACK WATCH ON THE
OUTBREAK OF THE SECOND WORLD WAR, RISING TO THE
RANK OF MAJOR AND WAS SERIOUSLY WOUNDED IN THE
ADVANCE THAT FOLLOWED THE NORMANDY LANDINGS.
A JOURNALIST, HE BECAME THE POLITICAL CORRESPONDENT
OF THE DAILY TELEGRAPH FROM 1956 TO 1976 AND WAS
CHAIRMAN OF THE PARLIAMENTARY LOBBY JOURNALISTS
1958TO 1959 AND HON. SECRETARY FROM 1968 TO 1971
(SOURCE: THE INDEPENDENT)

BROWN   HENRY ARMITT

?? ?? 1844   ?? ?? 1878

LAWYER AND ORATOR. ON THE 19TH JUNE 1878, SHORTLY
BEFORE HIS DEATH, HE DELIVERED HIS LAST AND BEST
KNOWN ADDRESS, THE ORATION AT VALLEY FORGE.
(SOURCE:WHATSOPROUDLYWEHAIL.ORG)

CHERNOV   VIKTOR MIKHAYLOVICH

01 12 1873   15 04 1952

ALSO KNOWN AS BORIS OLENIN. FOUNDER OF THE RUSSIAN
SOCIAL REVOLUTIONARY PARTY IN 1902. HE RETURNED FROM
EXILE FOLLOWING THE FEBRUARY 1917 REVOLUTION AND
BECAME MINISTER OF AGRICULTURE BUT WAS OUSTED BY
THE BOLSHEVIKS LATER THE SAME YEAR. HE LEFT FOR
FRANCE IN 1920 AND EMIGRATED TO THE UNITED STATES IN
1939. (SOURCE: ENCYCLOPAEDIA BRITANNICA)

EVERITT   GROUP CAPTAIN GORDON HUGH

29 12 1917   31 07 2012

HE WAS DECORATED THREE TIMES DURING THE SECOND
WORLD WAR AS A BOMBER PILOT AND HE COMPLETED A
DISTINGUISHED CAREER BY BECOMING, IN 1960, THE
COMMANDER OF THE V BOMBER BASE AT
GAYDON. (SOURCE: THE DAILY TELEGRAPH)

HAYES   ROBERT LEE "BULLET BOB"

20 12 1942   18 09 2002

AT THE 1964 OLYMPIC GAMES IN TOKYO HE EQUALLED THE
EXISTING WORLD RECORD OF 10 SECONDS WHEN WINNING
THE 100 METRES AND WAS THE "ANCHOR" LEG IN THE 4X 100
METRE U.S. RELAY TEAM THAT WON WITH A NEW WORLD
RECORD. WHILST AT FLORIDA A & M UNIVERSITY HE HAD
BROKEN THE WORLD'S 100 YARDS RECORD IN 1963 WITH 9.1
SECONDS. AFTER THE OLYMPICS HE BECAME A
PROFESSIONAL FOOTBALLER WITH THE DALLAS COWBOYS.
(SOURCES:WIKIPEDIA AND THE 1965 EDITION OF THE
INTERNATIONAL ATHLETICS ANNUAL)

JEFFERY   JOHN

12 01 1944   27 10 2004

FORMER METROPOLITAN POLICE OFFICER, ATHLETE,
ADMINISTRATOR, TEAM MANAGER ,COACH AND PRESIDENT OF
BELGRAVE HARRIERS.BEST TIME 400 METRES, 49.6.(SOURCES:
THE AUTHOR AND ALAN MEAD/BELGRAVE HARRIERS)

QUESTAD   LAWRENCE RONALD "LARRY"

10 07 1943

GRADUATE OF STANFORD UNIVERSITY AND U.S.C. IN THE MID
1960S HE WAS A LEADING SPRINTER IN THE UNITED STATES
AND AT THE 1968 OLYMPICS FINISHED SIXTH IN THE 200
METRES. HE WORKED FOR I.B.M. AND AFTER RETIRING
PURCHASED SUPERIOR STEEL, A SUPPLIER OF BULK STORAGE
AND TRANSPORTATION TANKS. (SOURCES: THE AUTHOR, MRS.
ELIZABETH QUESTAD AND WIKIPEDIA)

SINFIELD   GEORGE

22 01 1899   ?? ?? 1973

ORIGINALLY A CRAFTSMAN IN A PIANO MANUFACTURERS, HE
JOINED THE COMMUNIST PARTY IN 1927. HE BECAME A
JOURNALIST ON THE DAILY WORKER, FIRST AS A SPORTS
REPORTER AND LATER AS A HIGHLY RESPECTED INDUSTRIAL
CORRESPONDENT. (SOURCE:UNATTRIBUTED INTERNET
BIOGRAPHY)

SWINDAL   JAMES BARNEY

18 08 1917   25 04 2006

PILOT AND COMMANDER OF AIR FORCE ONE WHO FLEW THE
BODY OF THE SLAIN PRESIDENT KENNEDY BACK TO
WASHINGTON. (SOURCES:ARLINGTON CEMETERY.NET,
NYTIMES.COM AND AERO-NEWS.NET)

WRIGHTON   MR.JOHN DEREK

10 03 1933
1958 EUROPEAN CHAMPION 400 METRES AND 1600 METRES
RELAY. CAPTAIN ,BRITISH TEAM 1960 OLYMPIC GAMES. A
SURGEON, HE IS NOW RETIRED, LIVING IN CORNWALL
(SOURCES: THE AUTHOR AND WIKIPEDIA)

ZINKIN   PETER

17 07 1904   11 07 1983

FORMERLY A MEMBER OF THE INDEPENDENT LABOUR PARTY,
HE JOINED THE COMMUNIST PARTY DURING THE NATIONAL
STRIKE ON MAY 9TH 1926. BY 1929 HE WAS THE ORGANISER OF
THE ST. PANCRAS COMMUNIST PARTY AND IN SEPTEMBER
1931 HE WENT TO MOSCOW TO WORK IN THE COMINTERN FOR
NEARLY A YEAR. A TRADE UNION OFFICIAL, HE BECAME THE
POLITICAL CORRESPONDENT OF THE DAILY WORKER IN 1945,
RETIRING IN 1974. (SOURCE: AS GEORGE SINFIELD[Q.V.] UN
ATTRIBUTED INTERNET BIOGRAPHY)

SOURCES

DEDICATIONS
Stephen John Edmondson, FRCP FRCS

INTRODUCTION
Emergency Powers Act 1964
David Burrowes M.P. and the Houses of Parliament-Parliamentary Archives

PROLOGUE

CH. ONE
Map reference
http://www.google.co.uk/maps

CH. FOUR
Semipalatinsk
https://en.wikipedia.org/wiki/semipalatinsk-Test-Site
Polaris and Nassau
http://www.ena.lu/europe/success-crisis/IndexEN.html
http://www.ena.lu/europe/success-crisis/harold-macmillan-john-kennedy-
nassau-1962.htm
TSR2
https://en.wikipedia.org/wiki/BAC-TSR-2

CH.FIVE
Gulag
https://en.wikipedia.org/wiki/Gulag
Typhus
http://en.wikipedia.org/wiki/Typhus

THE END OF DEMOCRACY
THE DECEPTION

CH. TWO
Sir Kenneth Strong King's College London, Strand, WC2R 2LS
President Eisenhower
https://en.wikipedia.org/wiki/Dwight-D-Eisenhower

CH. FOUR
Partial Nuclear Test Ban Treaty
http://en.wikipedia.org/wiki/Partial-Nuclear-Test-Ban-Treaty
Sir Ivone Kirkpatrick
http://en. wikipedia.org/wiki/Ivone-Kirkpatrick

CH. SIX
The Long March
https://en.wikipedia.org/wiki/Long-March
Chinese Nuclear Weapon
http://www.fas.org/nuke/guide/china/nuke/

CH. ELEVEN
Yamantau
http://www.globalsecurity.org/wmd/world/russia/yamantau.htm
http://www.viewzone.com/yamantau.html
(Xerox) Photocopying machine
www.digipro.co.uk/history-photocopier.html

CH. THIRTEEN
Ptchia
https://en.wikipedia.org/wiki/P%27tcha

CH. FOURTEEN
Ussuri river
https://en.wikipedia.org/wiki/Sino-Soviet-border-conflict
Chou En Lai
https://en.wikipedia.org/wiki/Zhou-Enlai
Markus Wolf
http://en.wikipedia.org/wiki/Markus-Wolf

Reinhard Gehlen
http://en.wikipedia.org/wiki/Reinhard-Gehlen

CH.FIFTEEN
Hot Line
http://en.wikipedia.org/wiki/Moscow-Washington-hotline

CH. TWENTY
Messerschmitt Me 163 Komet
https://en.wikipedia.org/wiki/Messerschmitt-ME-163- Komet
Arado Ar 234 Blitz
https://en.wikipedia.org/wiki/Arado-Ar-234

CH. TWENTY-ONE
Gettysburg Address
Lincoln goes to Gettysburg, Carl Sandburg, first published in 'The
Reader's Digest' in 1936. The Reader's Digest Omnibus, first
published 1953. The Reader's Digest Association Ltd., 27 Albemarle
Street, London, W.1.
Calendar, 1863
http://luirig.altervista.org/calendar/img.php?year=1863
Gettysburg Address
https://en.wikipedia.org/wiki/Gettysburg-Address
Mannlicher-Carcano
http://www.google.co.uk/search?hl=en&q=mannlicher-carcano&meta=
http://www.apfn.org/apfn/mann.htm
"Drawa"
Guildhall Library,Aldermanbury,London,EC2V 7HH
Spetsnaz GRU
http://en.wikipedia.org/wiki/Spetsnaz-GRU

CH. TWENTY-SIX
Interstate 35
http://mq-mapgend.websys.aol.cm

CH. TWENTY-SEVEN
U.S.Presidents
http://www.heptune.com/preslist.html

CH.TWENTY-EIGHT
"Hansard"
Cllr.John Dean and Grant Shapps MP

CH. THIRTY-ONE
St. Stephen's Entrance
Mr. Matthew Ball
Mrs.Margaret Thatcher
The Times GUIDE TO THE HOUSE OF COMMONS 1959

CH. THIRTY-SEVEN
Robert Kennedy assassination
http://en.wikipedia.org/wiki/Robert -F-Kennedy-assassination
Bob Woodward (and Carl Bernstein)
http://www.hrc.utexas.edu/exhibitions/web/woodstein
Richard Nixon
http://en.wikipedia.org/wiki/Richard-Nixon
Edward Kennedy
http://en.wikipedia.org/wiki/Ted -Kennedy

CH. THIRTY-EIGHT
Munich Agreement
https://en.wikipedia.org/wiki/Munich-Agreement
Air Force One
http://en.Wikipedia.org/wiki/Air-Force-One
Franco
http://en.wikipedia.org/wiki/Francisco-Franco
David Bruce
https://en.wikipedia.org/wiki/David-K.-E.- Bruce
Andrews AFB,MD
http://www.andrews.af.mil...military.com/misc/.../Base-Contents.js
Robert S.McNamara
http://www.spartacus.schoolnet.co.uk/JFKmcnamara.htm
http://www.nytimes.com/2009/07/07/us/07mcnamara.html

CH.FORTY
Armageddon
"On Thermonuclear War"- Kahn

CH.FORTY-ONE

Fifth Column(ist)
https://en.wikipedia.org/wiki/Fifth-column

CH.FORTY-TWO

Alexander Borodin
https://en.wikipedia.org/wiki/Alexander- Borodin
Boeing Works
http://www.boeing.com/history/index.html
http://boeing.co.uk/ViewContent.do
http://www.boeing.com/commercial/707family/index.html
http://www.flightlevel350.com/Boeing-707-aircraft-facts.html
Boeing An Aircraft Album Kenneth Munson Gordon Swanborough
London Ian Allan 1972 SBN 7110 0192 8

CH. FORTY-THREE

Leadership of the Communist Party of the Soviet Union
Malcolm Polfreman, Deputy Librarian, Marx Memorial Library
www.marx-memorial-library.org
http://www.terra.es/personal2/monolith/ussr2.htm
http://en.wikipedia.org/wiki/Politburo-of-the-Central-Committee
http://en.wikipedia.org/wiki/List-of- members-of-the- Politburo-of-the-
Communist-Party-of-the-Soviet-Union-in-the-1960s
Vasil Mzhavanadze
http://en.wikipedia.org/wiki/Vasil Mzhavanadze
Agence France-Presse(AFP)
https://en.wikipedia.org/wiki/Agence-France-Presse
(Film)Triumph of the Will
https://en.wikipedia.org/wiki/Triumph-of-the-Will

CH. FORTY-FOUR

Salazar
http://en. wikipedia.org/wiki/Ant%C3%B3%nio-de-Oliveira-Salazar

CH. FORTY-SIX

Pan American
http://en.wikipedia.org/wiki/Pan -American-World-Airways
Monroe Doctrine
http://en.wikipedia.org/wiki/Monroe Doctrine#Background
National Security Council
http://en.wikipedia.org/wiki/United-States-National-Security
Council#Membership

CH. FORTY-SEVEN
Campaign for Nuclear Disarmament(CND)
https://en. Wikipedia.org/wiki/Campaign-for-Nuclear-Disarmament

CH.FORTY-NINE
Sir Hendrie Oakshott
https://en.wikipedia.org/wiki/Hendrie-Oakshott-Baron-Oakshott
Clement Attlee
www.bbc.co.uk/history/historic-figures/attlee-clement.shtml
Suez Crisis
http://en.wikipedia.org/wiki/Suez-Crisis#Post-war-years

CH. FIFTY
C I A
wikipedia.org/.../Director-of-Central-...

CH. FIFTY-TWO
Frank Cousins
https://en.wikipedia.org/wiki/Frank-Cousins

CH. FIFTY-THREE
25th Amendment
https://simple.wikipedia.org/wiki/Twenty-fifth-Amendment-to-the-United
States-Constitution
http://www.usconstitution.net/const.html#Am25

CH.FIFTY-FOUR
Cultural Revolution
https://en.wikipedia.org/wiki/Cultural-Revolution

CH. FIFTY-FIVE
Rudolf Slansky Cold War
Julius Streicher
http://en.wikipedia.org/wiki/Julius-Streicher

CH. FIFTY-SEVEN
Valley Forge
ushistory.org

CH. FIFTY-NINE
Slansky Trial Cold War

THE ORIGINS OF THE CONSPIRACY

CH. ONE
The NKVD
https://en.wikipedia.org/wiki/NKVD

CH. TWO
US citizens in the USSR
Sunday Times book review:The Forsaken, Tim Tzouliadis

CH.THREE
H.G.Wells
https://en.wikipedia.org/wiki/H.-G.-Wells

CH. SIX
Film - Things To Come
https://en.wikipedia.org/wiki/Things-to-Come

CH. SEVEN
Lincoln Daily Star
journalstar.com/online/newspaper-services/the-lincoln-journal-star-a
history

CH.NINE
"Bentley"
Motor Sport October 1951 Vol.XXVII No. 10

CH.TEN
Magdalene College
The Alumni and Development Office, Magdalene College, Cambridge,
CB3 0AG; Mr. Sandy White.
Ivor Richards
As Above, Dr. John Constable &
http://www.litencyc.com/php/speople.php?rec=
true&UID=5183

Tommy Henn Magdalene College. However further and better particulars can possibly be obtained from St. Catherines

CH. TWELVE
The Grapes of Wrath
http://www.steinbeck.org/Grapes.html

CH.THIRTEEN
Anthony Eden
www.bbc.co.uk/history/historic-figures/eden-anthony.shtml

CH.FOURTEEN
Averell Harriman
https://en.wikipedia.org/wiki/W.-Averell-Harriman
Archibald Clark Kerr
https://en.wikipedia.org/wiki/Archibald-Clark-Kerr,1st-Baron-Inverchapel

CH. TWENTY
US Social Security Numbers
http://en.wikipedia.org/wiki/Social-Security-number
http://genrootsblog.blogspot.com/2007/05/gregory-peck-in-social-security death.html

CH. TWENTY-FIVE
Katyn Forest Massacre
https://en.wikipedia.org/wiki/Katyn-massacre
Babi Yar Massacre
https://en.wikipedia.org/wiki/Babi-Yar

CH. TWENTY-EIGHT
Turkey, geography
http://www.world-maps.co.uk/maps/600-middle-east.jpg

CH. THIRTY-TWO
"Diamonds"
the DiamondBuyingGuide.com

CH. THIRTY-EIGHT

The Tehran Conference
https://en.wikipedia.org/wiki/Tehran-Conference
J.Lyons & Co.
https://en.wikipedia.org/wiki/J.-Lyons-and Co.

THE ORIGINS AND BIRTH OF THE NEW ORDER

CH.TWO

Gerald B. Kaufman
politics.co.uk

CH. SIX

Train service Liverpool Lime Street to London
Mr. Barry Kendler – Davis &Charles 1969 reprint of the July 1938
Bradshaw guide
Devaluation
www.the guardian.com/century/1940-49/Story/0,,105127,00.html
Freshfield , Formby, Merseyside, L 37
Google Maps
Hungarian Uprising,1956 Cold War

CH. TEN

Porvoo
Graphic Maps.com
Pyhasalmi
Finland Google Satellite Maps

CH. ELEVEN

Finnair
http://www.timetableimages.com/ttimages/complete/ay58/ay58-01
Hotel Kamp
Google www.cosmopolis.ch
Helsinki Central railway station
https://en.wikipedia.org/wiki/Helsinki-Central-railway-station

CH.TWELVE

Ilyushin (11)-14
http://en.wikipedia.org/wiki/Ilyushin-11-14

CH. SIXTEEN

Gannex
https://en.wikipedia.org/wiki/Gannex
Sir John MacLeod
https://en.wikipedia.org/John- MacLeod-(politician)
John Rankin
https://en.wikipedia.org/wiki/John-Rankin-(politician)
Konni Zilliacus
https://en.wikipedia.org/wiki/Konni-Zilliacus

CH. SEVENTEEN

Baikonur Cosmodrome
https://en.wikipedia.org/wiki/Baikonur -Cosmodrome
Mityushikha Bay
https://en.wikipedia.org/wiki/Novaya-Zemlya
Yuri Gagarin
https://en.wikipedia.org/wiki/Yuri-Gagarin
Gherman Titov
https://en.wikipedia.org/wiki/Gherman-Tito

CH. NINETEEN

Richard Baker
https://en. wikipedia.org/wiki/Richard-Baker-(broadcaster)
Kenneth Kendall
https://en.wikipedia.org/wiki/Kenneth-Kendall

CH. TWENTY

Film-Went the Day Well?
http://www.britmovie.co.uk/2012/01/09/went-the-day-well-1942/

CH. TWENTY-ONE

That Was the Week That Was
https://en.wikipedia.org/ wiki/That-Was-the-Week-That-Was
David Frost
https://en. wikipedia.org/wiki/David –Frost
Ned Sherrin
https://en.wikipedia.org/wiki/Ned-Sherrin

CH.TWENTY-TWO

Aerodrome Road
War Plan UK
Rookes *V* Barnard
https://en.wikipedia.org/wiki/Rookes-V-Barnard

CH. TWENTY-THREE

Willie Gallacher
https://en. wikipedia.org/wiki/Willie-Gallacher-(politician)

CH. TWENTY-SEVEN

D Notice
http://en.wikipedia .org/wiki/DA-Notice
Konni Zilliacus
https://en.wikipedia.org/wiki/Konni-Zilliacus

CH.THIRTY-TWO

Miners' Strike - Martin Brandon-Bravo
Sidney Greene
http://en.wikipedia.org/wiki/Sidney-Greene.-Baron Greene-of-Harrow
Weald
www.guardian.co.uk/news/2004/jul/28/guardianobituaries.politics
Sidney Weighell
http://en.wikipedia.org/wiki/Sidney-Weighell

CH.THIRTY-FOUR

Rosa Luxemburg
www.historylearningsite.couk/rosa-luxemburg.htm
http://en.wikipedia.org/wiki/Rosa-Luxemburg
Vice-President Hubert Humphrey
www.lbjlib.utexas.edu/johnson/archives.hom/faqs/humphrey/hhhhhom
Eureka,Montana
www.visitnwmontana.com/eureka/

CH.THIRTY-FIVE

Bristol Olympus
102homepage.ntlworld.com/s.bulman2/assignment1/specs.html
Operation Cauldron
https://en.wikipedia.org/wiki/Operation-Cauldron.

CH.THIRTY-NINE
Michael Ramsey, Archbishop of Canterbury
https://en.wikipedia.org/wiki/Michael -Ramsey

CH.FORTY
Chelmsford
maps.google.co.uk/maps?q=map+of+chelmsford+essex&ie=UTF8&hq
=&hnear=Chelmsford,+Essex,
Tomorrow Belongs To Me/Cabaret
http://en.wikipedia.org/wiki/Cabaret-(musical)

CH.FORTY-TWO
"Blood libel"/Tiszaeszlar Affair
http://en.wikipedia.org/wiki/Tiszaeszlar-Affair
Menasseh Ben Israel
http://cf.uba.uva.nl/en/collections/rosenthalaliana/menasseh/biography.
html
Great Plague of London
http://en.wikipedia.org/wiki/Great-Plague-of-London
Great Fire of London
http://en.wikipedia.org/wiki/Great-Fire-of-London

CH.FORTY-THREE
The Greater Britain Movement
https://en.wikipedia.org/wiki/Greater-Britain-Movement

CH. FORTY-SIX
Kent and Canterbury Hospital
www.nhs. uk/Services/Hospitals/Overview/DefaultView.aspx?id=1967
Keith Wagstaffe
The late Phillip Knightley who was introduced to me by Richard
Davenport Hines

CH.FORTY-NINE
Registration of a Political Party
Jack Louis Posner

CH. FIFTY
Keystone Cops
http://en.wikipedia.org/wiki/Keystone-Cops

CH.FIFTY-THREE
West End Central Police Station
content.met.police.uk/PoliceStation/westendcentral
Protest March
content.met.police.uk/Article/Organising-a-protest-march-or-static
demonstration/1400002380711

CH.FIFTY-FIVE
Sir Joseph Simpson
http://en.wikipedia.org/wiki/Joseph-Simpson

CH. FIFTY-SIX
George Thomson
https://en.wikipedia.org/wiki/George-Thomson,-Baron-Thomson-
Monifieth
Justo Lopez I would appreciate further and better particulars
supported by documentary evidence (author)

CH.FIFTY-NINE
PeterZinkin
www.grahamstevenson.me.uk/index.php?option=comcontent&view=art
icle&id=650:peter-
zinkin&catid=26:z&itemid=129
George Sinfield
www.grahamstevenson.me.uk/index.php?option=com
content&view=article&id=800:george-
sinfield&catid=19:s&itemid=120
Harry Boyne
www.independent.co.uk/news/obituaries/obituary-sir-harry-boyne-
1240639.html

CH.SIXTY-TWO
Rugen
http://en.wikipedia.org/wiki/Rugen
F-4 Phantom11
http://en.wikipedia.org/wiki/McDonnell-Douglas-F-4-Phantom-
11#United States-Air-Force

CH. SIXTY-THREE
Arthur Horner
http://en.wikipedia.org/wiki/Arthur-Horner-(trade-unionist)

CH.SIXTY-FOUR
Bell Helicopter and Bell 204
http://en.wikipedia.org/wiki/Bell-Helicopter
http://en.wikipedia.org/wiki/Bell-204/205

CH.SIXTY-FIVE
Rygge
http://en.wikipedia.org/wiki/Moss-Airport,-RyggeTorp
http://en.wikipedia/wiki/Sandefjord-Airport,-Torp

CH.SIXTY-SEVEN
Robert Dougall
http://en.wikipedia.org/wiki/Robert-Dougall
Gordon Honeycombe
http://en.wikipedia.org/wiki/Gordon-Honeycombe

CH.SIXTY-NINE
Film-Dr. Strangelove
https://en.wikipedia.org/wiki/Dr.-Strangelove

CH. SEVENTY
Ballpoint pens
http://en.wikipedia.org/wiki/Ballpoint-pen

CH. SEVENTY-FOUR
Kovbasa
http://en.wikipedia.org/wiki/Kolbasa

CH.SEVENTY-NINE
Armand Hammer
http://en.wikipedia.org/wiki/Armand-Hammer
G.U.M. Department Store
www.moscow.info/red-square/gum.aspx
http://en.wikipedia.org/wiki/GUM-(department-store)
Chagan
http://en.wikipedia.org/wiki/Chagan-(nuclear-test)

CH. EIGHTY-ONE
"Fear itself"
http://en.wikipedia.org/wiki/First-inauguration-of- Franklin-D-Roosevelt

CH.EIGHTY-SIX

Yuri Andropov
https://en.wikipedia.org/wiki/ Yuri-Andropov
The Apocalypse
The New Testament

CH. EIGHTY-EIGHT

Fylingdales Moor
https://en.wikipedia.org/wiki/RAF-Fylingdales
Distance between Buckingham Palace and the Imperial War Museum
www.freemaptools.com/distance-between-uk-postcodes.htm

CH.NINETY-ONE

Weimar Republic
https://en.wikipedia.org/wiki/Weimar-Republic

CH.NINETY-TWO

Typhoid fever
http://en.wikipedia.org/wiki/Typhoid-fever
Film-The Way Ahead
https://en.wikipedia.org/wiki/The-Way-Ahead
Film-The Dam Busters
https://en.wikipedia.org/wiki/The-Dam-Busters-(film)

CH.NINETY-THREE

Armstrong Siddeley
http://en.wikipedia.org/wiki/Armstrong-Siddeley
Hieronymus Bosch
http://en.wikipedia.org/wiki/Hieronymus -Bosch

CH.NINETY-FOUR

Walter Cronkite
https://en.wikipedia.org/wiki/Walter -Cronkite
Radio broadcast-War of the Worlds
https://en.wikipedia.org/wiki/The-War-of-the-Worlds-(radio-drama)

CH.NINETY-FIVE

The "Rocking Horse" plan
The Mail on Sunday

CH.NINETY-SIX
Music- In the Steppes of Central Asia
https://en.wikipedia.org/wiki/In-the-Steppes-of-Central-Asia
CH.NINETY-EIGHT
Inuvik
http://en.wikipedia.org/wiki/Inuvik#History
www.worldatlas.com/webimage/countrys/namerica/lgcolor/cacolor.htm
Wrangel Island
http://en.wikipedia.org/wiki/Wrangel-Island
http://en.wikipedia.org/wiki/File:Chukchi-Sea.png
Pevek
http://en.wikipedia.org/wiki/Pevek

CH. NINETY-NINE
Tage Erlander
http://en.wikipedia.org/wiki/List-of-Prime-Ministers-of-Sweden

CH. ONE HUNDRED AND SIX
John Maxwell Edmonds
http//en.wikipedia.org/wiki/John-Maxwell -Edmonds
Trent Park Cemetery
http://www.islington.gov.uk/services/birthsdeathsmarriages/deaths/cem
etries/Pages/trent-park-cemetery.aspx

VICTORY OF FAITH

CH.ONE
"The *Slansky Trial*" Cold War-page 118
Lester B. Pearson
http://en.wikipedia.org/wiki/Lester-B.-Pearson
CH.TWO
The Domesday Book
https://en.wikipedia.org/wiki/Domesday-Book
Leprosy
http://en.wikipedia.org/wiki/Leprosy

CH.FOUR
Coppetts Wood Hospital
http://www.ezitis.myzen.co.uk/coppettswood.html

CH.SIX
L'Impartial
http://en.wikipedia.org/wiki/L%27Impartial

CH.EIGHT
Saddleworth Moor
http://en.wikipedia.org/wiki/Saddleworth-Moor

CH.FIFTEEN
Revolution in Munich (Bavaria) 1919
www.ww1-propaganda-cards.com/Munich1919.html

CH.SIXTEEN
Bernard Law Montgomery
http://en.wikipedia.org/wiki/Bernard-Montgomery,-1st-Viscount
Montgomery-of-Alamein

CH.TWENTY
Wrotham Park Estate
https://en.wikipedia.org/wiki/Wrotham-Park

CH.TWENTY-ONE
 Bell 47
https://en.wikipedia.org/wiki/Bell-47

CH.TWENTY-TWO
W53 Thermonuclear Device
https://en.wikipedia.org/wiki/B53-nuclear-bomb

CH.TWENTY-FIVE
(Chinese) Hydrogen Bomb
China Culture.org

CH.TWENTY-SIX
Film-The Third Man
https://en.wikipedia.org/wiki/The-Third-Man

CH.TWENTY-SEVEN
Senna
Drugs.com Copyright 1996-2014 Cerner Multum , Inc. Version:1.08.
Revision Date 2012- 06-12,2:07:14PM.

Golda Meir
https://en.wikipedia.org/wiki/Golda-Meir

CH.TWENTY-EIGHT
1950 Petrus Pomerol Grand Vin
Vintage wine gifts.co.uk 2014 (30 11 14)

CH.TWENTY-NINE
1811 Chateau de Fontainbleau 'Cave de L'Empereur'
Vintage wine gifts.co.uk 2014 (07 12 14)

CH. THIRTY-ONE
Defence Regulation 18B
https://en.wikipedia.org/wiki/Defence-Regulation-18B
CH. THIRTY-TWO
American Forces Network
https://en.wikipedia.org/wiki/American-Forces-Network

EPILOGUE

CH. ONE
Watergate Building
https://en.wikipedia.org/wiki/Watergate-complex
Ben Bradlee
https://en.wikipedia.org/wiki/Ben-Bradlee
CH.TWO
5712 Kenwood Ave
70 GOLDEN YEARS IAAF 1912-1982, Page 34

POLITICAL CONTROL
BY THE TOTALITARIAN STATE

An Essay On The Principle Of Population
Bibliography

AUTHOR'S COMMENTS

The Duomo
https:/en.wikipedia.org/wiki/Florence-Cathedral
Film-Z
http://en.wikipedia.org/wiki/Z-(1969-film)

ACKNOWLEDGEMENTS AND APPRECIATIONS

I could not begin this section without specially mentioning the contribution of my two sons-in-law and eldest grandson, Toby. First, my younger son-in-law Peter, who was a tower of strength when it came to the more sophisticated uses and techniques of a lap top and who, on more than one occasion, recovered 'lost data' from the ether that my lap top had voraciously swallowed and refused to regurgitate!

My elder son-in-law William, believed that he would **NEVER** see this investigation completed in **HIS** lifetime and his comments were consistently delivered with an overtone of incredulity and an undertone of cynicism and sarcasm, a habit which "infected" my eldest grandson, Toby. But the work was completed and the truth revealed.

Many people have knowingly or unwittingly given me assistance preparing background information in order that this work could be written. I would like to especially thank the following for their witting and unwitting assistance:

Rupert ALLASON (former M.P., who writes under the pen name Nigel West)

Martin BRANDON-BRAVO (former Conservative M.P. for Nottingham South and former President of the Amateur Rowing Association)

David BURROWES M.P.

John DEAN (Council Leader , Welwyn-Hatfield, Hertfordshire)

Michael FABRICANT M.P.

The late Sir GERALD KAUFMAN M.P.

Barry KENDLER (Councillor, London Borough of Harrow) for his knowledge and research of various matters concerning British railways, his enquiries of the speeches of Harold Macmillan and his research into the operation of the United States Social Security system

P.James McCANNAH (former councillor, London Borough of Enfield)

Grant SHAPPS M. P.

Mr. Edward HEATHCOAT-AMORY, Journalist

Matt (hew) BALL Political lobbyist

Rabbi Yoni BIRNBAUM

Dr. John W. "Ossie" BONE M.B., Ch.B., D.C.H., D. Obst. R.C.O.G. and M.R.C.G.P.

Mr. David E.BRANDER for access to his comprehensive collection of Motor Sport incorporating Speed

Tony BRISCOE (First Secretary) and **Ms. Dawn PORTER** (Administration Officer) The Morning Star

Mr. Kevin BROWNLOW Film producer, specifically for his permission to use the title of his nineteen sixty-four film as part of the title of my work

Mr. R. Paul BRUCK former International athlete and academic

Duncan CAMPBELL, Investigative journalist(with genuine SINCERE appreciation)

Daniel COHEN formerly of Trinity College, Cambridge

Dr. Neville COHEN J.P. MRCS, LRCP, D. Obst. R.C.O.G., T.H.F.C. (West Stand) Rtd. for his advices in respect of certain medical conditions and pharmacological matters.

Mr. Stephen DORRIL, Author (and especially for his patience)

Ms. Nancy DUIN for her wise words of wisdom

My dearest friend, the late **Mr. Stuart FOUX,** for his knowledge of certain arcane East European card games.

Mrs. Doreen MANDEL-GAINSFORD (of London and Tel-Aviv) for background details of the life of her uncle, Phil Piratin, who changed his family name from Piriatinsky. The family, who were part of the Grand Lubavicher dynasty, came originally from the shtetl of Piriatinsk in the Heim of Russia.

Mr. Peter J. GASSNER for his special knowledge of the topography of the Soviet Union, West of the Urals.

Mr. Richard DAVENPORT-HINES, Author

Ms. Margaret IRISH, Stars and Stripes

(Councillor) Barry KENDLER and **Ms. Elena TEPLOVA** of the Russian Embassy, London for their separate assistance locating transcriptions of the Cyrillic and English versions of Nikita Khrushchev's "secret" speech on February 24-25th 1956 to the 20th Congress of the Soviet Communist Party.

Mr. Simon KENDLER for his research of the East German railway system

The late Mr. Phillip KNIGHTLEY, Investigative journalist

Prof. Dr. Joachim KRAUSE

Mr. Jeffrey and **Mrs. Linda LINDSAY** for their research

Mr. Brian MANDEL for his esoteric knowledge of Yiddish etymology

Mr. Tom MANGOLD, Journalist

Mr. Jonathan MAURER, Gemmologist, for his advices on diamonds and diamond dealing

Mr. Rory C. Mc CARTHY for his knowledge of civilian helicopters

Mr. Peter Ewert OTTERY for his knowledge of nineteen sixties and seventies military and civil aviation.

Mr. Michael T. PINKER for his knowledge of Italian and German rifles and pistols.

Mr. Jack Louis POSNER for certain information requiring extensive research into various financial matters.

Mr. Michael RANDLE

Mr. Ben STEVENSON National Secretary of the Communist Party Of Britain

The late **Dr. Maurice SUSMAN** for his knowledge of biological and chemical weapons.

Mr. Colin WHARTON

Mr. Charles "Sandy" WHITE

...and finally **Sir Winston CHURCHILL**, the torchbearer of freedom and democracy, whose inspirational speeches I have shamelessly plagiarised and abused.

BIBLIOGRAPHY

PART ONE-NEWSPAPERS AND JOURNALS

I have mainly drawn upon back issues of The Daily Worker, The Daily Telegraph, The Times, The Sunday Times, The Daily Mail, The Mail on Sunday, the Daily Mirror, The Sunday Mirror, Sunday Citizen, The News Of The World, The Guardian, The Observer, The Sunday Express, The Jewish Chronicle, the Liverpool Echo, Soho Clarion and Lloyd`s List, together with extensive research into various academic works in the U.K. and U.S. including other newspapers.

PART TWO-FROM MY OWN LIBRARY

THE CONCISE OXFORD DICTIONARY OF CURRENT ENGLISH (FOURTH EDITION?)
OXFORD UNIVERSITY PRESS (1950?) PURCHASED 1955/6

THE COMPLETE WORKS OF WILLIAM SHAKESPEARE
OXFORD UNIVERSITY PRESS REPRINTED 1955

HOMAGE TO CATALONIA
GEORGE ORWELL FIRST PUBLISHED 1938.THIS EDITION PENGUIN CLASSICS 2000. ISBN 978-0-141-18305-3

THE LIFE AND TIMES OF NIKITA KRUSCHEV
ROY MACGREGOR HASTIE FIRST PUBLISHED NOVEMBER 1959 PANTHER BOOK, HAMILTON & CO (STAFFORD) LTD, LONDON,SW3

THE ASCENT OF MAN
JACOB BRONOWSKI FIRST PUBLISHED 1973. THIS EDITION BRITISH BROADCASTING CORPORATION 1975 ISBN0 563 10498 8

LONDON AFTER THE BOMB
OWEN GREENE,BARRY RUBIN,NEIL TUROK,PHILIP WEBBER, GRAEME WILKINSON FIRST PUBLISHED 1982 OXFORD UNIVERSITY PRESS ISBN 0-19-285123-3

WAR PLAN UK
DUNCAN CAMPBELL FIRST PUBLISHED 1982. THIS EDITION

PALADIN BOOKS, GRANADA PUBLISHING LTD 1983 ISBN0-586-08479-7

COLD WAR
JEREMY ISAACS & TAYLOR DOWNING FIRST PUBLISHED 1998 BANTAM PRESS TRANSWORLD PUBLISHERS LTD ISBN 0-593-04309-X

VENONA
JOHN EARL HAYNES& HARVEY KLEHR FIRST PUBLISHED 1999 YALE UNIVERSITY ISBN 0-300 07771-8

OOOOOOOOOOOO

THE KING OF SCHNORRERS ISRAEL ZANGWILL H.PORDES LONDON 1972

OOOOOOOOOOOO

INTERNATIONAL ATHLETICS ANNUALS 1959, 1960, 1962 ,1963 and 1965
GENERAL EDITOR R(OBERTO) L(UIGI) QUERCETANI- **MY HERO-** A WORLD SPORTS PUBLICATION EC4

THE SECRET WAR
BRIAN JOHNSON BRITISH BROADCASTING CORPORATION W1M 4AA PUBLISHED 1978

THE NEW JEWISH CUISINE
EVELYN ROSE FIRST PUBLISHED 1985.(ACTUALLY MY WIFE'S BOOK) THIS EDITION PUBLISHED BY PAPERMAC 1988 WC2R 3LF IN 1988 ISBN0-333-46409-5

TRACK & FIELD PERFORMANCES THROUGH THE YEARS VOLUME 2 1937-1944
PUBLISHED BY THE A.T.F.S. IN COOPERATION WITH THE I.A.(A?) F. COMPILED BY ROONEY MAGNUSSON,D.H. POTTS and R.L. QUERCETANI

70 GOLDEN YEARS IAAF 1912-1982
PUBLISHED BY THE INTERNATIONAL AMATEUR ATHLETIC FEDERATION 1982 EDITOR/CO-ORDINATOR JON V. WIGLEY

OOOOOOOOOOOO

PART THREE

(20) ALL QUIET ON THE WESTERN FRONT
ERICH MARIA REMARQUE FIRST PUBLISHED 1929 THIS EDITION
PUBLISHED IN 1996 VINTAGE, RANDOM HOUSE SW1V 2SA ISBN0
09 953281 6

(40) THE ARK BEFORE NOAH
IRVING FINKEL FIRST PUBLISHED IN GREAT BRITAIN IN 2014 BY
HODDER& STOUGHTON www.hodder.co.uk ISBN 978 1 444 75705
7(And PERSONALLY signed by the author in CUNEIFORM)

(44) AS FAR AS MY FEET WILL CARRY ME
JOSEF M. BAUER ORIGINALLY COPYRIGHTED (IN WEST
GERMANY) IN 1955 AND FIRST PUBLISHED IN THE UK IN 1957.
THIS EDITION PUBLISHED IN 2003 BY CONSTABLE& ROBINSON
Ltd. W6 9ER ISBN978-1-84119-726-5

(26) THE AUTHORITARIAN STATE
JOHN TYNDALL (FIRST) PUBLISHED APRIL 1962 THE NATIONAL
SOCIALIST MOVEMENT W11

(35) BEYOND THE BLUE HORIZON
BRIAN FAGAN FIRST PUBLISHED IN GREAT BRITAIN 2012
BLOOMSBURY PUBLISHING Plc WC1B 3DP ISBN 97814088 25068

(32) BHAGAVAD-GITA AS IT IS
HIS DIVINE GRACE A.C. BHAKTIVEDANTA SWAMI PRABHUPADA
THE BHAKTIVEDANTA BOOK TRUST PUBLISHED NO EARLIER
THAN 2003 ISBN 91-7149-467-7

(39) DER BOLSCHERVISMUS VON MOSES BIS LENIN("BOLSHEVISM FROM MOSES TO LENIN:DIALOGUES BETWEEN HITLER AND ME")
DIETRICH ECKART. TRANSLATION BY THE LATE DR. WILLIAM
L.PIERCE COPYRIGHT 1966 HOHENEICHEN VERLAG MUNCHEN
HANAISTRASSE8 PUBLISHED POSTHUMOUSLY
1925.http://www.archive.org/stream /BolshevismFromMosesToLenin-dj
vu.txt

(8) BRAINWASH
DOMINIC STREATFEILD HODDER & STOUGHTON LTD NW1 3BH
2006 ISBN 0 340 92103 X

(9) CHEMICAL WEAPONS IN SOVIET MILITARY DOCTRINE
JOACHIM KRAUSE & CHARLES K. MALLORY PUBLISHED IN 1992
IN THE UNITED STATES OF AMERICA BY WESTVIEW
PRESS,INC., COLORADO 80301-2877 ISBN 0-8133-8406-0

(31) THE **COLD WAR** DAVID MILLER FIRST PUBLISHED 1998 THIS
EDITION PUBLISHED IN 2001 BY PIMLICO SW1V 2SA ISBN 0-7126-
6477-7

(37) COLOSSUS BLETCHLEY PARK'S GREATEST SECRET
PAUL GANNON FIRST PUBLISHED BY ATLANTIC BOOKS WC1N
3JZ IN 2006 ISBN I-84354-330-3

(41) COMMAND AND CONTROL
ERIC SCHLOSSER FIRST PUBLISHED IN THE UNITED STATES
OF AMERICA BY THE PENGUIN PRESS IN 2013 AND IN GREAT
BRITAIN IN THE SAME YEAR BY ALLEN LANE WC2R 0BL ISBN
978-1-846-14148-5

(7) THE **COMMISSAR VANISHES**
DAVID KING FIRST PUBLISHED 1997 THIS EDITION FIRST
PUBLISHED IN THE UK BY CANONGATE BOOKS EH1 1TE IN 1997
ISBN 0 86241 724 4(**HIGHLY RECOMMENDED!)**

(19) AN **ESSAY ON THE PRINCIPLE OF POPULATION**
THOMAS ROBERT MALTHUS THE FIRST **FULL** VERSION
PUBLISHED IN 1803 THIS EDITION PUBLISHED BY J.M. DENT &
SONS LTD W1M 8LX IN 1982 ISBN 0 460 01692 X

(14) FASCISM A HISTORY
ROGER EATWELL FIRST PUBLISHED 1995 THIS EDITION
PUBLISHED BY VINTAGE SW1V 2SA IN 1996 ISBN 0 09 944191 8

(43) THE **FASCISTS IN BRITAIN**
COLIN CROSS FIRST PUBLISHED 1961 BY BARRIE AND
ROCKLIFF (BARRIE BOOKS LTD) WC2

(38) DER **GIFTPILZ(THE POISONED MUSHROOM)**
ERNST HIEMER VERLAG DER STURMER NURNBERG 1938

(23) THE **GRADUATE**
CHARLES WEBB FIRST PUBLISHED 1963 THIS EDITION
PUBLISHED IN 1972 BY CONSTABLE AND COMPANY LTD WC2
ISBN 0 09 452240 5

(5) THE **GREAT TERROR**
ROBERT CONQUEST FIRST PUBLISHED 1968 THIS EDITION
REPRINTED 1969 MACMILLAN AND CO LTD WC2**(VERY HIGHLY
RECOMMENDED)**

(45) GROWTH AND STRUCTURE OF THE ENGLISH LANGUAGE
OTTO JESPERSEN FIRST PUBLISHED IN LEIPZIG BY B.G.
TEUBNER ON SEPTEMBER 30 **1905** AND REPRINTED **2015** ISBN 9
781177 766593

(18) I AM LEGEND
RICHARD MATHESON FIRST PUBLISHED (?) 1954 THIS EDITION
PUBLISHED IN OCTOBER 1997 AS ORB TRADE PAPERBACK,TOM
DOHERTY ASSOCIATES NY10010 ISBN 0-312-86504-X

(36) INSIDE HITLER'S BUNKER
JOACHIM FEST FIRST PUBLISHED (IN GERMAN) IN 2002 THIS
EDITION PUBLISHED 2012 BY PAN BOOKS N1 9RR ISBN 978-1-
4472-1860-9

(16) KNOW YOUR ENEMY
PERCY CRADDOCK FIRST PUBLISHED IN 2002 BY JOHN
MURRAY (PUBLISHERS)LTD. W1S 4BD ISBN 0-7195-6048 9

(10) MAKING THE RUSSIAN BOMB FROM STALIN TO YELTSIN
THOMAS B. COCHRAN, ROBERT S. NORRIS and OLEG A.
BUKHARIN PUBLISHED IN 1995 IN THE UNITED STATES OF
AMERICA BY WESTVIEW PRESS INC.,COLORADO 80301-2877
ISBN 0-8133-2328-2 (HC)

(34) THE **MAN IN THE HIGH CASTLE**
PHILIP K. DICK FIRST PUBLISHED 1962 THIS EDITION
PUBLISHED IN 1965 (?) BY PENGUIN BOOKS WC2R 0RL ISBN 978-
0-14-028562-8

(29) THE **MILITARY BALANCE 1964-65**
PUBLISHED (?) NOVEMBER 1964 THE INSTITUTE FOR
STRATEGIC STUDIES WC2 (R 3DX)

(30) THE **MILITARY BALANCE 1965-66** REPRINTED,WITH MINOR
CORRECTIONS, DECEMBER 1965 THE INSTITUTE FOR
STRATEGIC STUDIES WC2

(50) THE **MURDER OF WILLIAM OF NORWICH**
E.M. ROSE FIRST PUBLISHED 2015 OXFORD UNIVERSITY
PRESS 198 MADISON AVENUE,NEW YORK, N.Y. 10016 ISBN 978-
0-19-021962-8

(6) MY STRUGGLE
ADOLF HITLER THIS EDITION APRIL 1937 THE PATERNOSTER
LIBRARY(HURST & BLACKETT, LTD.) EC4

**(22) NUCLEAR WEAPONS DATABOOK VOLUME 1 U.S.NUCLEAR
FORCES AND CAPABILITIES**
THOMAS B. COCHRAN, WILLIAM M. ARKIN and MILTON M.
HOENIG BALLINGER PUBLISHING COMPANY, CAMBRIDGE
MASS.(FIRST) PUBLISHED 1984 ISBN 0-88410-172-X(C)

**(25) NUCLEAR WEAPONS DATABOOK VOLUME IV SOVIET
NUCLEAR WEAPONS**
THOMAS B. COCHRAN, WILLIAM M. ARKIN, ROBERT S. NORRIS
and JEFFREY I. SANDS BALLINGER DIVISION, HARPER & ROW,
NEW YORK.(FIRST) PUBLISHED 1989? ISBN 0-88730-048-0

(21) THE **PARALLAX VIEW**
LOREN SINGER FIRST PUBLISHED 1970 THIS EDITION
PUBLISHED IN1981 BY JAY LANDESMAN LIMITED,LONDON 0-
905150-28-7

(47) PASTRAMI ON RYE
TED MERWIN NEW YORK UNIVERSITY PRESS NY 10003
PUBLISHED 2015 ISBN978 -0-8147-6031-4**(IF YOU ARE JEWISH
AND LIKE HEIMISCHE FOOD-RECOMMENDED)**

 (3) THE **PROTOCOLS OF THE MEETINGS OF THE LEARNED
ELDERS OF ZION**
SERGIUS NILUS UNIVERSITY PRESS OF THE PACIFIC
HONOLULU,HAWAII 2003 ISBN 1-4102-1021-9

(46) QUICK SOLUTIONS TO COMMON ERRORS IN ENGLISH
ANGELA BURT FIRST PUBLISHED 2000 THIS, FOURTH EDITION,
PUBLISHED 2009 BY HOW TO BOOKS Ltd., OX5 1RX ISBN 978 1
84528 361 2

(12) DER **RING DES NIBELUNGEN:GOTTERDAMMERUNG**
RICHARD WAGNER. VOLLSTANDIGER KLAVIERAUSZUG KARL
KLINDWORTH. SCHOTT &Co. Ltd. LONDON W

(1) THE **RUBA'IYAT OF OMAR KHAYYAM** TRANSLATED BY
PETER AVERY and JOHN HEATH-STUBBS THIS EDITION
PENGUIN BOOKS 1981

(24)RUBAIYAT OF OMAR KHAYYAM PUBLISHER UNNOWN

(2) THE **RUBAIYYAT OF OMAR KHAYAAM** TRANSLATED BY
ROBERT GRAVES &OMAR ALI-SHAH THIS SECOND EDITION
CASSELL&COMPANY LTD,WC1 NOVEMBER 1967

(4) RUSSIAN STRATEGIC NUCLEAR FORCES
OLEG BUKHARIN, TIMUR KADYSHEV, EUGENE MIASNIKOV,
PAVEL PODVIG, IGOR SUTYAGIN, MAXIM TARASENKO, and
BORIS ZHELEZOV. EDITED BY PAVEL PODVIG. THE CENTER
FOR ARMS CONTROL, ENERGY AND ENVIRONMENTAL STUDIES
AT THE MOSCOW INSTITUTE OF PHYSICS AND TECHNOLOGY.
THE M.I.T. PRESS, CAMBRIDGE MASS.,U.S.A.FIRST PUBLISHED
2001.ISBN 0-262-16202-4

**(27) SECRETS AND STORIES OF THE WAR VOLUME ONE-HOW
BRITAIN'S WEALTH WENT WEST**
LELAND STOWE THE READER'S DIGEST ASSOCIATION LIMITED
LONDON W1 1963

(15) THE **SECRET STATE**
PETER HENNESSY FIRST PUBLISHED BY ALLEN LANE WC2R
0RL 2002 ISBN 0-713-99626-9

(11) SMEAR!
STEPHEN DORRIL & ROBIN RAMSAY FIRST PUBLISHED IN
GREAT BRITAIN IN 1991 BY FOURTH ESTATE LIMITED W11 2QA
ISBN 1-872180-68-X

(33) THE **SONG OF GOD:BHAGAVAD-GITA**
TRANSLATED BY SWAMI PRABHAVANANDA and CHRISTOPHER
ISHERWOOD WITH AN INTRODUCTION BY ALDOUS HUXLEY A
MENTOR BOOK NEW AMERICAN LIBRARY. PUBLISHED IN
ENGLANDBY PHOENIX HOUSE LTD.NO EARLIER THAN 1972

(28) SOVIET AIR POWER
BILL SWEETMAN, BILL GUNSTON PUBLISHED IN 1978 BY
SALAMANDER BOOKS LTD, WC1N 3AF ISBN 0 86101 015 9

**(13) SOVIET TANKS AND COMBAT VEHICLES 1946 TO THE
PRESENT**
STEVEN J. ZALOGA and JAMES W. LOOP FIRST PUBLISHED IN

GREAT BRITAIN IN 1987 BY ARMS AND ARMOUR PRESS LIMITED
BH15 1LL ISBN 0-85368-743-9

(17) ON **THERMONUCLEAR WAR**
HERMAN KAHN FIRST PUBLISHED BY PRINCETON UNIVERSITY
PRESS 1960 THIS EDITION A REPRINT OF THE 2D ED1961
PRINTED IN 1978 BY GREENWOOD PRESS INC. CT 06880
(ORIGINAL?) ISBN 0-313-20060-2

(42) WARRANT FOR GENOCIDE
NORMAN COHN FIRST PUBLISHED IN 1967 THIS EDITION A
REPRINTOF1969 HARPER TORCHBOOK EDITION SCHOLARS
PRESS CA95926 ISBN0-89130-423-1

PART FOUR

Ask.Com

(The) British Library NW1 2DB

Geographers' A-Z Map Company Ltd.

Guildhall Library Aldermanbury,EC2V 7HH

Magdalene College Cambridge, Ms Rachelle Stretch, Bye – Fellow, Dr. John Constable, Emma Tunbridge

Mapquest

The Metropolitan Police, Public Order Branch, New Scotland Yard

The Tank Museum

House of Commons Information Office

House of Lords Record Office

Houses of Parliament, Parliamentary Archives, London ,SW1A 0PW.

Office of the Parliamentary Counsel

The International Institute for Strategic Studies Library, London,WC2 3DX

Royal United Services Institute for Defence and Security Studies. London, SW 1A 2ET

Embassy of the Federal Republic of Germany, London

Office of the Defence and Air Attache, SW1X 8PZ

Bundesarchiv-Militararchiv

Wiesentalstrabe 10

79115 Freiburg

GERMANY

Marx Memorial Library, EC1R 0DU

The Wiener Library, 29 Russell Square, London, WC1B 5DP

Royal Norwegian Embassy,SW1X 8QD.

Defence Attache`s Office,

Ms. Siv Eide.

Norwegian Defence Museum and (Norwegian) Royal Air Force Museum, Bodoe.

Rabbinical Council of the United Synagogue.

Electoral Services, London Borough of Enfield

Dr. Khayke Beruriah Wiegand, Woolf Corob Lector in Yiddish,

Oxford Centre for Hebrew and Jewish Studies, Clarendon Institute Building, Oxford.

... And finally (the LAST finally!) special thanks

to WIKIMEDIA UK AND especially Richard Nevell

www.ingramcontent.com/pod-product-compliance
Lightning Source LLC
Chambersburg PA
CBHW072058020726
47501CB00003B/629